BAREFOOT
ON A
Starlit Night

**Also available from
Jo McNally
and HQN**

Slow Dancing at Sunrise
Stealing Kisses in the Snow
Sweet Nothings by Moonlight (ebook novella)

For a complete list of titles available from Jo McNally,
please visit jomcnallyromance.com.

JO McNALLY

BAREFOOT
ON A
Starlit Night

HQN

ISBN-13: 978-1-335-13695-4

Barefoot on a Starlit Night

Recycling programs
for this product may
not exist in your area.

This edition published by arrangement with Harlequin Books S.A.

For questions and comments about the quality of this book,
please contact us at CustomerService@Harlequin.com.

HQN
22 Adelaide St. West, 40th Floor
Toronto, Ontario M5H 4E3, Canada
www.Harlequin.com

Printed in U.S.A.

Dedicated to the laughing Irishman who gave me
the real life happily-ever-after I never dreamed possible.
To himself, with all my love.

Acknowledgments

Anyone who knows me knew that someday I'd have to write a romance with a genuine Irish hero. Set in an Irish pub. With green beer. I married my own Boston Irish hero twenty-four years ago, and he introduced me to all things Irish, including his relatives in the Emerald Isle. This book is set in a fictional Irish pub in the Finger Lakes area of New York. While I've frequented a number of Irish pubs both here and in Ireland, I'd like to give a special shout-out to our favorite—Kitty Hoynes Irish Pub & Restaurant in Syracuse, New York. The proprietor, David Hoyne, has made us feel welcome there for more than twenty years, with the best-poured pints, delicious food, great music and brilliant Irish coffee.

I'm thankful for the helpful information on work visas and green cards I received from Nicole Allaoui.

One of the characters is dealing with breast cancer in this story. Unfortunately, I know a number of friends and family members who have had or are dealing with this disease. Survival rates for breast cancer continue to improve year after year, but the disease still takes far too many lives. A portion of the proceeds from this book will be donated to the Susan G. Komen 3-Day Walk, a fundraiser supported by my lovely friend and survivor, Donna B. If you are dealing with breast cancer, please seek out some of the wonderful support groups out there, either in person or online. I sat in on a few of the online groups and am in awe of these women and the way they lift each other up.

And ladies—don't put off getting that mammogram!

CHAPTER ONE

THIS McKINNON FAMILY meeting she'd called was going about as well as Bridget McKinnon expected—a complete circus. She glared at her cousins as they sat around the kitchen table, but her grandmother was the only person who noticed the optical daggers Bridget was tossing. Nana's eyes were bright with suppressed laughter. Not helping.

Kelly was doodling something in her notebook. Michael was staring at his phone with a sly, secretive grin, ignoring all the actual humans sharing the room with him. His twin, Mary, was trying to placate her two-year-old son, Nathan, who was clamoring to get up onto her lap. There wasn't much room there, since Mary was seven months pregnant with Number Three. Little Nathan sat down hard on the floor at Mary's side, folding his arms tightly and giving his mother his fiercest look. The kid's last name might be Trask, but his temper was pure McKinnon.

Nathan's big sister, Katie, came running in, clutching Mary's phone. "Mommy! I did it! I crushed level fifteen!"

Everyone stopped what they were doing to look

at the game on the screen in the five-year-old's hand. That they'd stop for, but not to listen to Bridget. Typical. She looked at the list of business items in front of her and flipped it over with a sigh of surrender. She'd spent most of her life trying to wrangle her extended family into some sort of order. Looked like today wasn't going to be the day it happened, either.

Mary gave her daughter a sideways hug. "Great job, baby! Do Mommy a favor and take Nathan in the living room with you, okay?"

Nathan let out a piercing howl of disapproval, quickly followed by Katie's protest.

"Mommy, no! He grabs the phone and messes up my game! Why do I always have to be in the same room with him? He's so—"

Mary tugged Nathan to his feet, wiping tears from his chubby cheeks with her fingers as she spoke to Katie. "I'm sure you were about to say he's so adorable and you love your brother so much, right? Don't be a drama queen. We'll be done soon. Just take your brother's hand and go."

For one brief moment, Bridget saw an opportunity to bring this "meeting" under control. But before she could speak, the kitchen door flew open with a bang. Timothy McKinnon rushed in, apologizing with every step. "Sorry, sorry, sorry! Did I miss the meeting? I swear, Zaniya's first trimester hormones have made her flippin' insatiable. I had to sneak out of bed— Oh…sorry, Nana. Didn't see you there." He pushed a shock of dark auburn hair off his forehead and plopped down on the chair next to Bridget. "So what's this big meeting about today? Does our Bridget want to convert the family pub to a nautical theme? Or are we going with the wine bar idea again? Or is it brick oven pizza time?"

Bridget laughed, giving up all hope of controlling this group. She scrunched her napkin into a tight ball in her hand and tossed it at Tim. Every family had a class clown, and Tim was theirs. He caught the napkin and tossed it right back at her. She tried to be annoyed, but all she could think was what a great father he'd be in seven months, with his quick wit and giant heart.

"The idea of a nautical restaurant in a waterfront town is not that crazy." She looked at each of them, although all she saw of Mike was the top of his head as he continued tapping on his phone. She tossed the napkin at him this time, and he dropped the phone on the table after flipping her his middle finger. "I wanted to meet so we could finalize the 'Turn the Page' party details. And figure out who's going to check on zoning for the outdoor patio I want to add this spring."

Mary shook her head, cringing at the sound of an argument between her son and daughter in the next room. "It's January, Bridget. Why are we talking about the patio now? And aren't beer gardens German? Is that your next idea for reinventing the place? The Purple Lederhosen?"

Michael glanced up, stealthily sliding his phone

off the table. "That could be fun. Look, I'm sorry, Bridg, but can we wrap this up? I've got a crap-ton of work to do at the office."

Bridget suspected that little smile of his as he snuck another glance at his phone had nothing to do with his law office. Was her oldest cousin finally getting a love life after losing Becca two years ago?

Tim grabbed one of Nana's famous scones from the table. Floury crumbs flew when he spoke. "I second that. I'm swamped, too. Why don't you save the money you're going to spend on the patio and use it to buy us out while we're still breathing? Besides, can't you just email us a party schedule? We've got a week yet…"

"Oh my God." Bridget threw her hands up. "Do you guys hate all change—anywhere, anytime? Or is it only when it's a change that I suggest?"

Michael arched one brow, humor bright in his eyes.

"Really, Bridg? You got us all together just so you could have a pity party? Do you need our approval for that, too?"

"I give up." She said, holding up her hand and extending her middle finger at Michael. "I guess I'm the only one in this family with the planning and organization gene. My dad wanted the Purple Shamrock to be a family pub. That's why he left everyone a piece of it. So yes, I want to include you…"

Mike moved as if to stand. "We never asked your dad to do that. You're majority owner, so do what you

want. I love you, kid, but you don't need our blessing for every little thing." He nodded at Tim. "And
he may be right about the patio. Buy us out before
you start spending."

"I swear, trying to get you guys to work with me
is like herding feral cats." She slumped back in her
seat. "Do what I want? What I want is for the bar to
start making money again. I want the loans paid off.
And yes, I want to be able to buy you out."

She also wanted to own a house that wasn't draining her physically and financially. She wanted her
grandmother to be healthy. She wanted a good night's
sleep for once, without worrying about all these
things she wanted. Her eyes started to burn with
tears. That had been happening a lot lately. It was
Nana who came to the rescue. All the woman had to
do was raise her hand, and everyone sat straighter,
kept quiet and paid attention. Michael sat back down.

Maura McKinnon had turned seventy-two three
weeks before Christmas. Which was one week
after she'd learned she'd be starting chemotherapy
for breast cancer. She was just as intimidating as
ever, though—all five-foot-four-inches of her. Nana
insisted to everyone that she "refused" to lose her
shimmering dark auburn hair, but Bridget noticed it
had been thinning rapidly over the past week. Nana's
dark eyes were sharp, and her lips pressed tight. And
yet…Bridget saw the slightest of twitches at the corner of her mouth. With all this chaos and arguing
around the woman's dining room table—when she

had to be exhausted and distracted—Nana was trying not to laugh. She seemed to thrive on all the energy of her grandchildren.

"You all rely to some extent on the Purple Shamrock," she said. "My husband didn't build that business to have you fritter it all away. Lord knows, Bridget's father came close enough before he died." She pointed at each of them as she spoke. "Michael and Timothy, I know you two have your own careers now, but your names are still on the deed to that pub. Mary, with a third babe on the way, you should want to see as much profit from the place as possible. And Kelly, for God's sake girl, stop scribbling and pay attention. The Shamrock is the only job you have, and it's paying for your college classes." Bridget didn't escape Nana's wagging finger. "And girlie, like it or not, your father left you in charge. So act like it. Stop dillydallying and do whatever you think is best. We'll all support you." She looked around the table. "Won't we?"

Between Bridget's outburst and Nana's scolding, her cousins finally began to look a little chagrined. To be fair, none of them had asked to be in her father's will. Everyone wanted Bridget to buy their shares out. But until she could afford to do that—if she could ever afford to do that—they were all stuck working together. Which meant navigating their way through meetings like this. She wanted them to be a part of the business. She blew out a long breath, reminding herself that she loved each and every one of them. Most of the time, anyway.

"Thank you, Nana." She reached out to take her grandmother's hand. "I'm trying so hard to turn things around, but Dad really let the place slide. I know you all want out, but I can't afford to buy your shares yet. Hell, I can barely afford the mortgage on the place with the income I'm pulling." That's why she was looking for a new tenant in her downstairs apartment. Desperate times and all that. "It might go against logic, but sometimes you have to spend money to make money. Like adding an expanded serving area this summer by building that patio. The space behind the building isn't being used for anything, and it has a great view of Seneca Lake. We're wasting an opportunity by not using it. I need your support on this, guys."

There were a pair of outraged screeches from the next room, and Mary got to her feet as quickly as a very pregnant woman could. She nodded toward Bridget before leaving the table.

"Simon knows a guy who does landscape design on the side. He might be able to help with figuring out the patio build. I'll ask him about it tonight. For now, I need to get my two monsters home and get off my feet." She glanced at their matriarch. "And you should do the same thing, Nana. Go lie down for a bit, and I'll check on you later."

"I'll come up with a work schedule for the party," Kelly said. "I'll text it to everyone."

Mike and Tim stood, both offering to help at the party. Tim gave Bridget a quick hug, whispering in her ear.

"Chin up, cuz. I'll stop by the house tonight and help you get the apartment ready to show again, okay?"

And just like that, her cousins went from being the bane of her existence to being her beloved and irreplaceable family.

FINN O'HEARN STARED in horror at the glass of green beer in front of him. He'd heard Americans did stuff like this, but Jaysus, Mary and Joseph, who would desecrate a good pint of beer like that? He took a cautious sip. Ah, that explained it. 'Twasn't a good beer at all.

His expression must have given away his disgust, because his drinking partner started to laugh. Rick Thomas was a good twenty years older than Finn, but he was the first guy Finn met on campus when he arrived a month ago. Rick taught English lit. Finn taught medieval history. They were both bookish bachelors who liked old things and sarcasm. Rick raised his glass of neon-green beer and clapped Finn on the back.

"Happy St. Paddy's Day, Finn!"

"It's January, mate. What kind of lunacy is this?"

The Purple Shamrock was packed with people. Music from Riverdance was blaring from the speakers. He caught sight of two young women toasting each other with…was that green wine? He was trapped in a nightmare of green booze.

Rick followed his eyes and laughed again. "It's a tradition that's been going on for decades, my friend. The Shamrock celebrates the end of the holiday season with a January 17 'Turn the Page' party. Christmas is over, and it's two months until St. Pat's." Rick nodded toward the boisterous crowd. "You said you missed your Irish pubs. This is as good as it gets in Rendezvous Falls."

There were a few Irish touches in the place, with the snug wooden booths lining the paneled walls and lots of cardboard shamrocks taped to the walls. Even the bar itself had a flavor of Ireland, with the dark wood and mirrored back. But this was what Finn liked to call American-Irish. Lots o' green but not much genuine Irish charm.

Rick took a sip of his beer. "So tell me about this housing problem you're having."

"It's all gone arseways. I made the rental arrangements online—even talked to the guy by phone—then arrived to find he'd sold the feckin' place." Finn couldn't help thinking he'd been placed under some curse that his life would forever be filled with liars and cheats. Or maybe that was just the way the world truly was, and he'd never realized it before now. "Old Man Greer is giving me a hard time about living in a hotel, but what am I supposed to do?"

Rick chuckled. "Don't let Iris Taggart hear you

calling the Taggart Inn a hotel. She'll have you out on the street."

Finn took a drink of the foul beer. "Wouldn't be the first time a woman kicked me to the curb."

"Wow. So the rumors are true, then."

He tensed, wondering how much Rick knew about his last teaching position. "What rumors?"

"That the Irish are a dark and gloomy bunch."

Finn's shoulders eased. He looked around the bar, which was noisy with so-called Irish celebrants drinking green alcohol and wearing silly green beads around their necks. He grunted.

"You've learned our deep, dark secret, Rick. The true Irish are not happy step-dancing leprechauns chasing rainbows." Finn had given up chasing rainbows a long time ago.

Rick gave him a sarcastic dose of side-eye before draining his glass. "Dude, I'm an English lit professor. I've read Beckett and Joyce. I know how dark the Irish can get. I just didn't know you were one of them."

"Our dark roots run deep, my friend." Finn shrugged. The shock of having nowhere to live when he'd arrived in town in late October had left him scrambling and on edge. People tended to assume all Irishmen were full of wit and charm, with a beer in one hand and a fiddle in the other. Those expectations could be exhausting for an introverted bookworm like him. "I'll mind what you said about Iris Taggart, though. I like the woman, and her inn.

Great place to visit. I just can't live there. Greer is all over me about not having any 'true ties to the community.'"

"Yeah, I've heard Greer is all about appearances." The college president was in his midseventies and had been teaching at Brady College for almost fifty years. A bit of an eccentric, Dr. Howard Greer had very strong opinions on how his staff should behave. He'd agreed to bring Finn on board despite Finn's recently checkered past, but Greer made it clear from the start that he'd be keeping him on a very short leash. If that leash snapped, Finn's job—and his work visa—would be in dire jeopardy.

"It's not like I intended to be homeless, but here I am. I've been busy getting ready for classes to start next week, but I have to find something fast." He slumped back in the bar stool and held his glass up to the light. "As soon as I finish this nasty-ass beer. What is wrong with this place?"

Rick slapped him on the shoulder with a laugh. "Are you talking about the town or the bar? Rendezvous Falls is a good place, and nowhere near as provincial as it might look." Finn reserved comment, because his first thought when he drove into town was that he'd been transported back to the 1800s, with all the wildly painted Victorian homes. Apparently, the town was famous for the houses with their colorful paint schemes and fanciful trim work.

But he'd wanted a quiet little college where he could rebuild his life and reputation, and he couldn't get much smaller than Rendezvous Falls. Rick continued. "If you're talking about the bar...well, it's in the midst of some changes. The previous owner passed away, and his daughter came home from California to run it." Rick gestured to their green beers. "But you can't blame her for this tradition. Like I said, it's been going on for ages. Rumor has it she's looking to give the place a makeover, though, and she might ditch the Irish feel."

Finn barked out a laugh. "My man, there is no Irish feel in here, other than a few shamrocks." He finished his beer and firmly refused the bartender's offer of another. He'd have to recuse his Irish citizenship if he had another feckin' green beer. Rather than being insulted, the guy behind the bar grinned and nodded at Rick.

"Shot of Jameson to wash down that swill?"

"Make it two. My Irish friend here is appalled at our customs." Rick nodded between the two men. "Finn, this is Luke Rutledge, winemaker extraordinaire and part-time bartender—although I thought he quit this gig. Luke, meet Finn O'Hearn, straight from the Emerald Isle, here to teach medieval European history to our fine young minds at the college."

Luke reached over to shake Finn's hand. "Welcome to Rendezvous Falls. Sorry about all the green booze. Tradition—what can you do?" His eyes slid to Rick. "I did give up my regular hours here, but I'm on call for emergencies. Hal Gentry retired, and the boss has a reputation that makes it tough to hire

someone new. With the party and all, tonight qualified as an emergency."

"Christ, that woman can't hang on to employ-
ees, can she?" Rick asked. "Is she really that tough
to work—"

Rick was interrupted by a crash of dishes coming
from behind what Finn assumed were the kitchen
doors, followed by a loud string of very colorful
curse words in a female voice.

Luke poured two shots of whiskey, then tossed his
bar towel over his shoulder and headed toward the
kitchen. "Did I mention the cook quit, too? She's on
her own in there. I'd better make sure she's okay."

Finn and Rick clinked their shot glasses together
and drained them, both letting out long sighs of satisfaction as the heat of the whiskey burned its way
down. Rick had introduced himself on Finn's first
official day on the campus of Brady College, when
Finn unintentionally parked in Rick's spot. The snow
had been coming down so heavy that late Novem-
ber afternoon that Finn didn't see the sign. Rick had
been a good sport about it, teasing him about trying to get a reputation as a "troublemaker" right out
of the gate. Rick had no idea that Finn had already
been-there/done-that at a much larger and more prestigious university.

Luke was back in just a few minutes, shaking his
head as he refilled their shot glasses. Rick pushed
his glass Finn's way, reminding him that Rick was
driving. Good thing it was a Friday night, or Finn

would be worried about getting himself out of bed in the morning after three shots and a beer.

"She's on a roll tonight." Luke glanced back at the kitchen. "All that swearing? She was yelling at herself for knocking over a tray of dirty dishes. That woman's just gotta yell, even if there's no other person there to yell at."

The two men started sharing stories of the apparently fearsome woman running the place. Finn excused himself and headed into the back where the restrooms were located. Didn't take long for that green pisswater they called beer to run through him. On his way back, he noticed a bulletin board in the hallway. In the center was a bright orange sheet of paper that read,

Apartment for Rent
1st Floor—Furnished—No Pets
$600 per month
See Bridget

No phone number. Just "See Bridget." A flat wasn't ideal, but the price was lower than what he'd been seeing for rental houses, and he was running out of options. Furnished was a bonus, since he hadn't salvaged much furniture from his failed marriage. A young guy with dreadlocks and shoulders like a pro wrestler walked by. Finn stopped him, pointing to the sign.

"Hey, mate. Where do I find this Bridget?"

"Kitchen usually."

Finn frowned, but thanked him. The kitchen was where the cranky, sweary lady worked. He looked at the price again. Furnished. It was worth taking the chance. He went to the kitchen and peeked through the small, square window in the door, but he didn't see anyone. He pushed his way in and looked around.

A woman was working near the sink, loading a small commercial dishwasher on the countertop. The scary, screaming owner must have stepped out, leaving this one to deal with the mess left behind. She was average height, and on the slender side. She wore dark capris, sturdy black sneakers, and a grease-stained— or was it sweaty?—green cotton shirt. Her copper-red hair was twisted into a tight knot under a hairnet, although a few long tendrils had broken free. He cleared his throat.

"Excuse me, are you Bridget?"

She rounded on him in the blink of an eye, gripping a suds-covered chopping knife in her hand.

"Holy… You scared the shit out of me!" She pointed at the door with the knife. Her eyes were deep mahogany brown. They were also red-rimmed. He wasn't sure if it was from the steamy water or if she'd been crying. Maybe her cranky boss had gotten on her case over something. She had a rich, whiskey voice that was strong and confident, despite her puffy eyes. "You can't be here. Go back to your beer buddies at the bar." She waggled the knife back and forth. "Out!"

"Please…put the knife down." He held his hands up in front of him. "I'm just here about the apartment. Are you Bridget? Is it still available?"

She gave him a sweeping look from his scalp to his feet and back again.

"Maybe."

"Maybe you're Bridget, or maybe the apartment's still open?"

The corner of her mouth lifted, and he realized with a bit of a jolt that she was attractive. Not that he'd thought her ugly before, but his first impression was that she was pretty basic. Now that he had a chance to really see her, she was anything but basic. Her features were bold. Angular. High cheekbones and a chiseled, narrow jaw. Whiskey-colored eyes. That copper hair. And the hint of a soft smile, which had vanished as quickly as it had appeared.

"Both. I'm Bridget. And the apartment's open. But I usually rent to wom…I mean…students. Or profs."

"Well, I'm not a woman." He splayed his hands. "But I am a professor."

Her eyebrows furrowed. "That accent. Where are you from?"

Ah—the accent. He gave her his standard response to the question he heard almost daily here in the States. "Originally? My mother."

Her mouth opened, then snapped closed, but he saw the spark of laughter in her eyes. "Very funny. Irish, right? Came in for the green beer?"

He grimaced. "No self-respecting Irishman would go anywhere for green beer."

Her eyebrow rose. "Well, excuse me, Mr. Fancy Pants." She looked at the pile of dishes and cooking pans in the sink. "Look, I'm swamped. Stop by tomorrow if you want to see the apartment."

"But…"

She pointed to the doors. "Tomorrow. The house is next door. Blue-and-white Victorian." She turned her back to him. "And make it early—I have to be here for the lunch shift tomorrow, and I've got a delivery coming. If you knock on the door after nine, you'll be outta luck."

With those encouraging words, he knew he'd been dismissed. She was probably afraid her boss would come back and catch her with a customer in the kitchen. He headed back to the bar, where Rick and Luke were still chatting, in between Luke serving people.

"Hey, there you are!" Rick said as Finn sat down. "Thought maybe you got lucky or something."

Finn looked around at the youthful, drunken crowd. "Not that I'm lookin', but if I were, I don't think I'd find my type here."

Luke refilled Rick's cola. "What's your type, Finn?"

Faithful.

"No one's my type right now. I'm lickin' my wounds and stayin' single."

Rick's laughter faded. "Coming off a bad one, huh?"

"The worst." Just thinking of Dori made him tighten up in anger. Time to change the subject. "But on the bright side, I got a line on a flat."

Luke wiped down the surface of the bar. "In the time you were gone? How'd you manage that?"

"Flyer on the board back there. I talked to Bridget…"

Both men froze, staring at him with wide eyes.

Rick spoke first. "You talked to Bridget? Bridget McKinnon?"

"The redhead in the kitchen? Yeah."

Luke coughed out a sharp laugh. "You…you went into Bridget's kitchen? And lived?"

Finn sat back. "Wait, are you sayin' this Bridget is the same woman you were talkin' about earlier? Who can't keep an employ…" Ah, no wonder she was alone in the kitchen. But she'd smiled at him. Sort of. And she'd been crying—he was sure of it.

Luke handed some change to two young guys who'd just ordered—Finn checked—yup, green beer. "She's showing you her place, huh?"

"Why? Is it a house of horrors or something?"

"Nope," Luke said. "But it's in her house."

"As opposed to her renting a place in someone else's house?"

Luke scratched the back of his neck. "It's in her house. She lives upstairs in her dad's old place, and there's a small apartment below it. Almost a studio. You have to go in her house to get to it."

Finn considered that for a moment. Living under the same roof as angry, sweary, teary-eyed Bridget

McKinnon? He came here to get away from drama, not live with more of it. But then again, she was an interesting woman, with all that…bristle…to her demeanor.

Rick sighed and rose to his feet. "Here's the thing, Luke. This guy—" he patted Finn's shoulder "—needs an actual place to live, with an actual address instead of a room number. And he needs it now, or he might get his ass shipped back to Ireland. I never imagined Bridget would be the one to save the day, but if that apartment's available, I'm guessing Finn's taking it."

And that was the rub. He did need a place, and—thanks to Dori—his funds were on the limited side. If he could get through the semester and secure his spot on the tenure track, he could always look for a small house this summer. So, if Miss McKinnon deemed him acceptable, it would only be temporary. He could make that work.

CHAPTER TWO

BRIDGET WOKE THE next morning hoping the guy from the bar was just a figment of her imagination. She'd spent yesterday arguing with her grandmother over whether or not her hair was falling out (it was), so it made sense she'd dream up some Irish hunk looking to move in downstairs. It would be just her grandmother's style to put some Celtic hex on Bridget's life.

Two mugs of scalding coffee and a bagel later, there still hadn't been a knock on the door. Maybe she really had dreamed him up. She propped her hip against the gold-and-white laminated countertop and watched the snow come down outside. Did he ever say his name? Did she ever give him the chance? Probably not. She'd been on her feet for hours and was so tired. Even worse, she'd been on the verge of tears with all her worries spinning through her head.

Would Nana be okay? Would the bar cover expenses this week? Was there ever going to be a day that didn't end with her back aching and her brain begging for sleep? Add in her worry over getting a tenant so she could cover her mortgage, and yes, a few traitorous tears had managed to escape.

She knew she had a reputation as a bit of an angry harpy since her return to Rendezvous Falls. People cut her slack at first because of her father's sudden death, but lately she'd caught the looks and heard the whispers. She was a shrew. She swore too much. She was "impossible" to work for, whatever the hell that meant. She hadn't done much to refute that reputation last night. Her cook, Jimmy, had a temper tantrum and quit. Again. At one of their largest events of the year.

All because Bridget had changed the age-old menu for the annual party and added more appetizers instead of just corned beef sandwiches and shepherd's pie. It's not like she'd asked Jimmy to cook the appetizers—she took care of that herself. It was just the idea of change.

She swore there was something in the water in this town that made people, especially those related to her or connected to the pub, absolutely allergic to new ideas. Not only had Jimmy walked out in a huff, but he'd taken his wife, Marta, with him. Marta did the dishwashing, so Bridget had called Timothy in to help with the cooking, and then she did the cleaning up on her own. Which, to be honest, was just how she liked it. Alone. Where she could control what happened.

Jimmy and Marta had worked for her dad for years. They'd adored him. The problem was, Jimmy thought he was the kitchen boss. Even though Bridget had a culinary degree and, you know, owned the place. Neither of them had handled the power struggle well. One snarky comment too many from her had led to Jimmy and Marta walking. Leaving Bridget with plenty of alone time, doing all the work. With so much control. Winning.

That's when the tall, dark-haired stranger with the delicious Irish accent showed up, asking about the apartment. And somehow, as brief as their encounter had been, she could tell he…knew. He knew she'd been crying. There'd been just a glimmer of something when his eyes had met hers. Oh, God… what if it had been pity? She shuddered. No way would she let that man move in. She had enough on her plate without some softhearted Professor Mc-Dreamy living downstairs, thinking she was some fragile flower. If he didn't hate the apartment, she'd come up with some reason why he couldn't have it that wasn't discriminatory.

She glanced at the clock. Eight thirty. Looked like he wasn't going to show anyway. Probably just some drunk guy who didn't even remember their conversation. Just as well.

A knock at the door made her jump, sending her coal-black coffee—her third—swishing in her mug. Fine. He was here. She'd show him the apartment, then show him the door. He'd probably hate the apartment anyway. It was tiny. It was also furnished and decorated for a female, with soft pastels and overstuffed chintz. She set her coffee down, then grabbed it again as she left the kitchen. She needed all the fortification she could get.

She headed down the wide center staircase to the foyer. This would be such a pretty house if it wasn't so boxed in with walls and doors that didn't belong. The furnished apartment on one side. An unfinished library-slash-studio apartment was on the other.

Her dad had the idea to chop up this poor old house into apartments for college kids. Bridget never imagined herself as a landlord, but along with the house, she'd inherited the mortgage Dad had taken out on it. He'd taken that mortgage to add the new kitchen to the Purple Shamrock. If she ever got herself out of debt, she hoped to slowly convert this back to a single-family home. It was a big "if" and an even bigger "hope," since she had no idea how to go about remodeling a house.

She opened the door, and the Irishman stood there, bundled against the cold wind in a leather jacket that matched his black hair. That hair was short, but had a definite curl to it. Her first random thought was that he must have been an adorable child, with those black curls and intense green eyes. He was tall and lean, and had a way of standing— legs apart, hands in his pockets, head tipped to the side—that suggested he was confident. And, judging from the slanted smile, easily amused. A gust of wind blew a cloud of snowflakes through the door, and Bridget realized she'd been staring at him while he got covered in snow. She stepped aside.

"Come on in, Mr....?"

The slant of his smile increased, causing his cheek to crinkle and a dimple to appear. Yikes. This guy was seriously good-looking. Women probably fell all over him. Another reason to deny him the apartment. She didn't want it to be some playboy bachelor's pad, especially with the bedroom directly under hers. Ew.

He straightened and extended his hand. "Finn O'Hearn. My apologies for not introducing myself last night. I think that blade you were swinging around scared my manners outta' me."

She thought back...oh, yeah—she'd had her favorite chopping knife in her hand when he'd come in. And tears in her eyes. Great. She'd probably looked like a psycho.

"Bridget McKinnon." She shook his hand and nodded toward the mahogany staircase. "My apartment is upstairs. Yours..." Damn it. "I mean...the available apartment is here." She gave him her scariest glare. "If you take it, there will never be a reason for you to set foot on those stairs." She unlocked the door, still clutching her coffee mug, then stepped back to let him walk ahead. His brows rose in surprise at her.

"Ladies first."

"Not a chance. I have a cousin in real estate, and she told me to never turn my back on a stranger." Why was she telling him about that? To his credit, he didn't laugh at her, or take offense. He simply considered her words, then nodded and walked by her and into the apartment. "Is that why you only rent to women?"

"Umm…I don't know how rentals work in Ireland, but here in New York, I can't admit to discriminating based on gender."

Finn's eyes shone even brighter. "Cleverly put, Miss McKinnon. You can't admit it, but you didn't deny it." He looked around the space that served as living room, dining room and kitchen. "More modern than I would have thought."

No surprise there. The house was built in the late 1800s, and the original lacy gingerbread trim still lined the roof edges and crowned the porch posts. But the interior had been updated back in the 1980s. It was almost jarring compared to the exterior, and that was another thing on her someday list—redecorate. It was way down low on a very long list, though.

"Probably more frilly than you'd like." But if she hoped the curtains and ruffled pillows would chase him off, she was clearly mistaken.

"'Tis fine. Reminds me of my ma and da's house in Sallins. Not a lot of room for my books, but I can deal with it."

They walked back toward the small kitchen tucked behind a laminated peninsula. She pointed to two doors on the left. "Bathroom. Bedroom. Nothing fancy."

Finn inspected the rooms. She thought maybe the peach-colored walls in the bedroom would put him off, but he didn't even blink.

"I'll take it."

"Uh…I haven't said I want you to take it."

She had no reason not to rent to him. Lord knew, she needed the money. Yes, he was a man, but he didn't give off any obvious alphahole vibes. And he sure was easy on the eyes. But having him living downstairs felt risky somehow. There was something about him. In what little interaction they'd had, he had a way of looking at her that made her feel… seen. And she'd worked really hard to build defensive walls to protect herself. She had too much to do to be vulnerable to anyone.

He turned and gave her a long look. There was less humor in his eyes now. He looked more guarded than before. She cleared her throat and started a very firm lecture.

"I don't allow any parties or nonsense down here. I don't want people coming in and out, especially at night. No one gets a key other than the tenant. That front door to the house stays locked all the time. And I mean all. The. Time. The walls aren't exactly paper-thin, but there's not a lot of soundproofing, either. I expect quiet after ten. If you're using the laundry area in the basement instead of a laundromat, it's an extra twenty per month. And it's my laundry area, too, so you can't leave stuff around. There's absolutely no smoking. I get the driveway parking, since it's only one car wide. You can park in the bar lot and walk over." She scrunched her eyes tightly shut. Why did she keep using *you* like it was some kind of done deal?

She knew why—she needed a tenant and fast. Finn had walked back out to the kitchen, and was now opening and closing the refrigerator and stove. He looked over his shoulder.

"Like I said, I'll take it." Her mouth opened, and he held up his hand to stop her. "No parties. Quiet. Can't park here. No smoking. Lock the door. Don't leave my laundry in the dryer. I got it. I want the place." He slid his hands into his jean pockets. "Look, I need a place. I'm livin' at the Taggart Inn right now, and the college thinks I'm some kind of flight risk because of it. I'll lay low and stay out of your way. My credit…" He hesitated, and Bridget tensed. She should have known he was too good to be true.

"And there it is. Your credit sucks, right? Let me guess—you need a little time to scrape together the security deposit? But I should trust you for it and let you move in anyway? Thank you—next." More than one student had suckered her in with their tale of woe. She waved her hands toward the door. "Bye."

"Easy there, Quick-Draw." He chuckled as he straightened. "I've got the money. I'll give you cash today if that'll do it. It's just that my…uh… divorce…" His voice trailed off as quickly as his smile did. "Stuff happened. My credit took a hit.

But I've got enough cash to handle this. And steady income from the college."

She studied him through narrowed eyes. She knew how hard it was when a relationship ended unexpectedly. Clark was out in California enjoying the furniture, rugs and lamps that she'd paid for. But she relied on the income from this place to cover most of her mortgage. Her previous tenant, Cyndi, had been a student. A junior, so Bridget had figured she was pretty stable when she moved in last August. But Cyndi had transferred in from a school in Texas. After raving all through the fall months about how excited she was to see snow, she went home to Houston for the holidays, and never came back. A couple early winter snowstorms were all she'd needed to see.

Bridget had to find a new tenant. Finn wanted to be one. It would be weird to have a man living down here, but it's not like she'd ever seen much of her previous tenants—just the occasional pass in the foyer or bumping into them doing laundry. But if this guy had credit issues… She brushed past him and went to the front window, pushing the curtains aside. Her dad used to insist she could learn a lot about a person from their vehicle.

"What do you drive?"

"What?" His footsteps came closer, but stopped a few feet away. She had to give him credit—he was careful not to invade her space. "A Forester. Why?"

She saw the Subaru SUV behind hers in the driveway. It was newer, but was so covered with salt from the roads that she couldn't tell if it was blue or black. The same was true of any other vehicle in Upstate New York this time of year. Not the type of vehicle some broke loser would be driving. Or some flashy playboy. It was…practical.

"Owned or leased?"

"Um…owned. And paid for."

She turned, surprised to find him closer than she'd thought. His hands were back in his pockets again. Did he do that on purpose, just to look super-cool and unruffled? One hand slid out, and he ran it through his hair, leaving wavy curls standing up in its wake. She had a sudden and nonsensical urge to see what those curls felt like.

"I can go to the bank, get two month's rent in cash, and be back here in half an hour."

She glanced at her watch. "Should have thought of that before you showed up so late. I have to get to work."

He huffed out a soft laugh. "The bank doesn't open 'til nine. I wasn't gonna stand at an ATM after midnight last night to get that kind of cash. You've got a tenant standing here ready to sign on the dotted line or whatever it is you Yanks call it. I'm basically a hermit, which translates to a perfect tenant."

He was making good points, but instead of agreeing, she grabbed for the tiny red flag she'd just heard.

"A hermit? You mean the kind of guy everyone always describes as 'quiet and keeps to himself' after he goes on some murdering spree?"

The slanted smile returned, along with the spark of laughter in his eye. "No. The kind of hermit who teaches history and finds curling up with an eight-hundred-page book on the subject of hygiene in the Middle Ages to be a fun Friday night."

"You're not the type of professor who hoards piles of books and papers and stuff, are you? I expect this apartment to be kept clean…"

Finn's head tipped to the side in that way he had. She barely knew the man, but she could already tell this was another trait of his. "Do you ask your female tenants if they're hoarders, Bridget?"

Oh, touché.

"It's a brand-new question on my tenant application."

He released a long sigh. "With the way you're waiting to pounce on my answers, I think I'll confine myself to a simple *yes* or *no* from now on. As in no—I'm not a hoarder. But yes, I own a lot of books. Any more questions?"

She did her damnedest to come up with one, but couldn't. He gave a quick nod.

"Right. I'll go to the bank and be right back. Will you be here or at the pub?" He started to turn, as if wanting to escape before she could object. But he caught himself and stopped. "Any chance I can get in before the first? Like…next week? I'll pay a pro-rated amount, of course."

She'd kept Cyndi's security deposit, which covered the surprise loss of January's rent. But still, a little extra wouldn't hurt. "I guess it's okay. I'll give you the key when you come back with the cash. And I'll have a lease ready for you to sign."

He thanked her and walked out the door, leaving the flat feeling suddenly lifeless. It was as if Finn O'Hearn had lit the place up, then extinguished the flame on his way out. She had a hunch he was going to bring more than just energy to the house.

She headed upstairs to print out a lease agreement and finish getting ready for the longest day of her week. Although being wintertime, it should be a moderately slow Saturday, especially after the big Turn the Page party last night.

She thought of Finn's face when he was in her kitchen at the Shamrock, grimacing at the mention of green beer. She agreed completely, of course—the stuff was gross. But it was a McKinnon tradition. Even she wasn't brave enough to ask their regulars to give that up.

Bridget texted her cousin Mary, to see how Nana was doing today. The response was slow in coming, and did nothing to reassure her.

Chemo's kicking her ass this week. No appetite. Freaking out about her hair.

She took a deep breath, blinking rapidly. Her grandmother had basically raised Bridget after her mom died. Bridget had been ten at the time, mad at the world and everyone in it. It was Nana who'd diverted all that anger into cooking. For Bridget, there was great comfort in precise measuring and planning. That little bit of control had given her peace. Nana knew what she'd needed back then. It was up to her to return the favor now. She typed her reply.

Tell her I'll make a shepherd's pie for her with no spices.

Spice was one of several things Maura McKinnon couldn't handle since she'd started chemo. She used to love hot wings and Bridget's Irish tacos with jalapeño peppers. But now any spice at all set off her nausea. The woman was barely eating as it was, and couldn't afford to lose more weight. Bridget slipped her jacket on, figuring Mary wasn't going to reply. She was on her way across the parking lot when the phone vibrated in her pocket.

She'll love that. She's finally agreed to let me cut her hair short this week. Even her eyelashes are shedding.

Bridget unlocked the back door to the pub kitchen, then locked it behind her. She hung her coat and started flipping light switches to get the place ready for whatever lunch crowd they might get in this snow. Once she had the lights on and the ovens, steamers and fryers warming up, she pulled her phone back out and stared at it. Nana was so proud of her gleaming auburn hair. They'd all known hair loss was likely, but Nana kept finding posts on the in-

ternet from people who didn't lose their hair, and
she'd read them out loud to Bridget and her cousins.

"See?" she'd say. "Not everyone goes bald!"

If anyone could will themselves not to lose their
hair during chemo, it was Maura McKinnon. Bridget
looked at the phone again, as if she could find an
answer to the dilemma there. When Kelly showed
Nana a catalog of human hair wigs a few weeks ago,
their grandmother had thrown it into the corner in
an uncharacteristic show of anger. Temper tantrums
were more Bridget's thing than Nana's. But she knew
Nana wouldn't want to walk around bald, either. And
it was wintertime. She tapped on her phone screen.

Want me to bring her a new hat or scarf to try?

She could picture Mary, probably sitting at her
desk and designing a website for someone, in spite
of her children creating chaos all around her. She
was almost as driven as Bridget was. But without
the quick temper. A few wavy lines appeared on her
screen as Mary typed.

Can't hurt. Something bright. Not pink! She hates
that color more every day.

Bridget stared out the window for a minute,
watching big soft snowflakes drift down from a gray
sky. Across the lot she could see her house, a narrow blue-gray shadow in the snow. Her father had

left her the house along with the bar, but neither were exactly a prize.

Daddy had always said the Purple Shamrock would be hers someday, even in the days when she'd lived in California and insisted she didn't want it. Maybe that's why he'd included her cousins in the will, with Bridget holding a controlling share. When Dad died, she'd had no choice but to move back home to Rendezvous Falls. It had all been for the best with Nana getting sick and needing her. And it allowed her to find out just how little Clark had actually cared about her, since he let her go with barely a wave goodbye. He'd moved another woman in within weeks. She tapped her fingers against her thigh. So much for being soul mates.

Finn's SUV pulled up to the side door and he hopped out, fixing a testy look at the sky that wouldn't stop snowing. Letting him have the apartment felt like a colossally bad idea.

But she couldn't help thinking that her grandmother would love this handsome Irish guy with the crooked grin and the lilting brogue.

MAURA PUT HER right hand into the hands of her best friend, Victoria Pendergast, and sighed as Vickie started massaging her fingers. Having breast cancer was bad enough at her age, but when she got the news, she figured she was up for the fight. After all, she'd given birth to her first of three children at eighteen. She'd buried her husband at thirty. She'd

helped her son Patrick run the family pub for decades, and did her best to keep him from running it
into the ground completely. Then she'd discovered
him there one morning, dead of a heart attack at only
fifty-two. Maura had dealt with all of that, damn it.
She could surely take on cancer.

But no one told her it wasn't just the cancer she'd
be fighting. Despite her brave talk, she knew she'd
probably lose her hair, but never considered that
meant losing her eyebrows. And now her eyelashes
were falling out, too. Somehow, that made it so much
worse. Even after she gave in last week and conceded to wearing a pretty scarf, her face looked like a
chalky mask, with no sign of her there anymore when
she looked in the mirror. There were days when she
couldn't feel her own hands or feet. It felt like she
was losing her body, and it scared the hell out of her.

She expected chemotherapy to make her sick, but
she didn't know she'd end up with this awful neuropathy. Vickie gently rubbed Maura's fingers and
up across the back of her hand to her wrist. The
chemo caused a numbness that made her feel clumsy
and awkward. Sometimes the tingling was more
like sharp needles stabbing into her flesh, but today
was "just" a tingling day. The massaging helped,
although some articles said that was all in her head.
Whatever—it made her feel better and that's all that
mattered. The doctor said the neuropathy wasn't in
her head, though. It was her nerves sending off hay-
wire signals because the chemicals killed good cells

as well as bad ones, especially nerves. That was just great.

Her eyes fell closed as Vickie started working on her wrists, rubbing her skin gently, but pressing just enough to make the tingling stop.

"Hey," Vickie's voice was soft and low. "If you're too tired and want me to come back later, I…"

Maura blinked, then felt her face flush when she realized she'd almost nodded off. That happened a lot these days. She shook her head with a smile.

"No, Vick, don't stop. This is by far the best part of my week."

Vickie snorted. "You really need to get a life."

"I'm trying to."

Vickie arched a brow at Maura's dark humor, then smirked. "You couldn't pick a life with hair?"

Maura barked out a laugh. This was what friends gave her that family could not. The ability to be… her. To laugh. To be snarky. To be normal. Her family loved her, but they couldn't hide their fear for her. They wanted to make things soft and easy and quiet and relaxing. That was sweet. But none of those words had ever described Maura before cancer, and she'd be damned if she'd let them describe her now. She ran her hand across the blue silk scarf covering her scalp.

"Well, I heard that post-chemo hair grows in thick and curly, and I have always wanted thick and curly hair. I figured flooding my body with poison and being sick for months was a small price to pay."

Vickie's fingers hesitated just a fraction, recognizing the slight bitter edge to Maura's voice. But her friend pursed her lips and played along. "Doesn't surprise me. I've known you all my life, and you've always taken the most pigheaded path possible to anything you've ever wanted." Vickie looked up. "Speaking of pigheaded, how's Bridget doing with her plans to bring the Purple Shamrock into the twenty-first century?"

"Oh, she's determined, that's for sure. She wants to add a beer garden behind the pub this summer. I guess it's the 'in' thing now. Her cousins aren't convinced, but of course they will be. Bridget's a force of nature."

"Gee, I wonder where she got that from?" Vickie was putting lotion on Maura's hands now, rubbing them together between hers. She held one hand up and examined it. "You ready for a manicure? I brought hot pink…" Vickie winked, knowing Maura had a slightly irrational dislike for the way everyone wanted her to wear pink all the time. As if she was supposed to suddenly love a color she'd never liked before just because she had breast cancer. Vickie held up another bottle of polish. "Or we could use this pretty coral?"

"I'll take the coral. It's like a slice of summer in January."

Maura enjoyed having Vickie do her nails. There was something touching—and amusing—about the wealthy thrice-married divorcée dressed in head-to-toe Ralph Lauren and sporting her own expensive acrylics, doing someone else's nails. People thought Vickie was a snob, and she could be, but Maura had learned long ago that it was her friend's defense mechanism. If people couldn't be bothered to get to know the real person behind the carefully coiffed facade, then Victoria Pendergast couldn't be bothered with them.

Vickie grabbed a dish towel from the oven door and folded it on the kitchen table for Maura to rest her hands on. She started filing Maura's nails lightly, then looked up.

"Oh, I forgot to ask—how did the Turn the Page party go last week?"

"From all reports, a rollicking good time was had by all." Maura grinned. "Except Bridget, of course, but she wouldn't admit she had fun even if it was the truth."

Her granddaughter had more defense mechanisms than three Vickies. No matter how much Maura had worked to make sure Bridget found her place in the McKinnon family, Bridget still seemed to be struggling. She was a go-it-alone person in a family full of opinions. Noisy, squabbling opinions, but loving ones. Her desire to have things—and people—under control didn't always go over well with her cousins. They didn't realize it was her coping mechanism. Even as a child, she'd seemed overwhelmed by her rowdy family. But Maura gave her a cookbook when she was twelve, and Bridget put her energy into cooking, carrying that preciseness into her life.

Bridget's father Patrick, God rest his soul, had done his best, but he left most of the child-rearing to Maura while he worked at the pub. The Purple Shamrock was his home, and Bridget had been so desperate for his attention that it became her home, too. She'd started working the kitchen as a teen, and then perfected her skills at culinary school in New York. She'd had her sights set on opening her own restaurant somewhere as far from the Finger Lakes as possible. Maura understood. Bridget wanted to make her own mark, free from the rest of the McKinnons and the town that knew her too well. But when her father died, she'd given up that dream, and the man she said she'd loved, to take over the Purple Shamrock. Because that's what Patrick had stipulated in his will.

Vickie started applying the nail polish, which was a shade or two brighter than Maura thought it would be. "I don't get it." Vickie was frowning at the nail she was painting. "Why is Bridget always so testy? She has a reputation as the crankiest business owner in town, and that's saying something when our friend Iris is in the mix!"

"That's probably why she and Iris get along so well." Maura smiled. Iris owned the Taggart Inn, and, and at eighty, refused to admit she no longer controlled it now that her grandson and his fiancée were running the place. "Two tough women determined to have everything their way. But Bridget isn't…testy…all the time. She's more…tasky. She has a lot on her shoulders, and she gets through it by being very focused on checking off each little task."

"Is tasky another word for short-tempered?" Vickie examined her work, then started on the other hand. "Unfriendly? Because some people say…"

Maura stiffened. "Victoria Pendergast, if I'd believed half of what people said about you, we'd never have become friends. Stuck up. Bitchy. Husband-stealer."

"I never stole anyone's husband, and you know it." Vickie smirked, not bothering to deny the other labels. "He walked away from Beatrice of his own volition, and it was before we ever dated. I didn't steal him. I…found him."

"Yeah, you found him on your doorstep, because you already knew each other."

"That may be, but it wasn't my fault." Vickie looked up from her work, her violet eyes shining with humor. "I didn't ask men to fall at my feet back then. They just…did." She lifted her shoulder. "But those days are long gone, my friend. And so are all the men. And fair or not, you're right—those labels stuck, all these years later. So Bridget should do something to change things. All work and no play makes your granddaughter seem cranky and unapproachable. She needs a hobby." Vickie winked. "Or a man."

Maura nodded as Vickie brushed on the quick-dry

top coat to protect the manicure. "Maybe. But she's so busy these days. I loved my son, but he wasn't exactly a visionary when it came to the Shamrock. He was convinced there was nothing wrong with the old place or the old ways and old decor. Business has been sliding for years, and Bridget's trying to turn it around. But there's only so much she can do with limited funds."

"How is she going to buy out her cousins if she doesn't have the money?"

"That's a very good question. Her father's house has always been a money pit. Then he took a second mortgage on it to pay for the kitchen at the pub a few years back. She's using all her income to cover the mortgage. That's why she's been taking in tenants in the downstairs apartment, even though she hates having strangers in her house." Maura glanced out the window. She could just see the pointed tower roof of the blue house through the trees, only three lots away from her own house.

Bridget's dad bought it ages ago because it was next door to the pub. All he had to do was walk—or stumble—across the parking lot to get home. But he'd never done a thing to make the big Victorian feel like a home. He'd divided it into apartments after his wife, Monica, died, figuring the upstairs was big enough for him and Bridget. He rented the downstairs apartment to whoever came along. Usually college students, but Patrick had never been all that careful about who he had living under the same roof as his daughter. She'd never asked Bridget why she was so careful to rent to only female tenants, but Maura had a hunch something must have happened.

"I heard she lost her last tenant over the holidays," Vickie said. "It'll be tough to find someone in the middle of the school year."

"Mike told me she had it leased already, so she must have gotten lucky." Maura wondered why she'd heard that from Mike, and not from Bridget. She'd visited Maura twice since the Turn the Page party and never mentioned it.

Vickie touched Maura's nails lightly, and smiled when she saw the polish had set. "Have you made a decision about the book club meeting next week? It's not that big a group in the winter, so we could gather right here if it would be easier, or I can drive you up to the winery. We've missed you."

The book club often met up at Helen Russo's Falls Legend Winery. The tasting room made a great meeting place for local groups, and Helen made the best cookies and snacks.

"I can't next week—I have a treatment, remember? Besides, I haven't been part of the book club for five years. I'm not sure this is the time…"

"I forgot about your appointment—and I think I'm taking you, right? On Tuesday?" Vickie checked her phone. "Yes, I have it in my calendar. Okay, forget next week, but we're flexible with our meetings. We could put it off a week, so we'd catch you on the rebound." Maura usually felt strongest the week after treatment, but never strong enough to think of it as a rebound. The upcoming treatments and the crushing exhaustion that followed were always hanging over her head. And she had a few more months of this. Vickie was still rattling on. "And not coming for five years is nothing. Helen was out for a couple years after Tony died, and Iris hardly ever comes anymore unless we have it right there at the inn. It's not like we take attendance or collect dues." Vickie put her manicure supplies away. "You need to do something other going to chemo and thinking about cancer and that stupid bar."

Maura chuckled and nodded in agreement, as Vickie expected her to do. But inside, Maura was biting back tears. She adored her dear friend and knew Vickie would walk through flames for her, but Vickie couldn't possibly understand that Maura had thought of little else but cancer since she found it was trying to stake a claim on her body. It wasn't like she chose to focus on it. It was the other way around—this cancer chose her, and wouldn't be ignored.

CHAPTER THREE

FINN HUNG UP the last of his clothes in the cramped closet and closed the door. Rick and Luke were laughing in the kitchen—more like a kitchenette— and he went to see what was so hilarious about his new home.

"…don't let him see that. He might panic, and my back can't take lugging all those books again…" Rick looked up in surprise. "Oh, hi, Finn. I think we're done in here, although it'll probably feel like a scavenger hunt when you start cooking and need to find anything. Do you cook, by the way?"

Luke slid something off the countertop and behind his back as Rick talked. Finn walked over and held out his hand. "I cook enough to survive. Give it up, mate. What'd ya' find, a cockroach or something? It'll take more than that to scare me off…"

Luke dropped a narrow, unopened box in Finn's hand, stopping his words cold. Finn looked at the pregnancy test, then burst out laughing. His friends joined in, and Rick clapped him on the back.

"It was under the kitchen sink, which seems an

odd place, but what do I know about these things? I'm guessing you won't need it?"

Finn shook his head. "I'm pretty sure no matter how many times I pee on that wee stick, it will never show positive. Feel free to take it home with you."

"Me?" Rick put his hand over his heart in dramatic fashion. "Trust me, the men I sleep with never worry about getting pregnant. Maybe Luke can take it home to Whitney?"

Luke's cheeks went ruddy, and he looked everywhere but at the box. The corners of his mouth twitched repeatedly, until he finally gave in and smiled. There was a glint of pride in Luke's eyes.

"We have no need for it. Not anymore."

"Not anymore? What…" Rick stepped back, his mouth falling open. "Are you saying you and Whitney…? Oh, wow—congratulations!"

Luke held up his hand to slow Rick down, but his smile didn't fade. "It's not public knowledge yet, so keep it between us. Whitney and her aunt are adamant that we can't tell people until after this week, when it will officially be three months. I guess that's some magical threshold. I think she's being paranoid, but whatever. The doctor said everything looks and sounds perfect."

Finn congratulated Luke and shook his hand. "Oi, good luck to you, lad." He tossed the box into a drawer. "I'll get rid of that later. Lord knows, I won't be needing it." He looked around the tiny apartment. There were many boxes of textbooks and research material to be unpacked and sorted. He'd take care of that tonight, after he grabbed something to eat. He opened the refrigerator and handed out bottles of Guinness. "Thanks, guys. I really appreciate all your help today. Maybe I can finally get the college president off my back about not putting down roots here."

Rick shook his head. "Old Man Greer is a stickler on some of the most ridiculous things."

Luke raised a brow. "Old Man Greer is only a few years older than you, isn't he?"

"Kiss my ass, Rutledge. He's fifteen years older in age, and a century older in attitude. But Finn having an apartment with an actual lease should make Greer feel a little better."

Luke's forehead furrowed. "Finn, why is he so convinced you're a runner?"

Finn grimaced, eager to steer the conversation away from his work history. "I screwed up in Durham. There were…complications. Not my finest moment."

"You mean when you punched your colleague in the face?" Rick said it as matter-of-factly as if he were speaking of the weather, then put the bottle to his lips, winking as he drank. Finn chewed the inside of his cheek to maintain his composure. He shouldn't be surprised—the video went briefly viral the previous spring. It wasn't every day people saw a professor knock another prof out cold during commencement.

Luke looked back and forth between them. "I'm

confused, but also impressed. Did the guy deserve the beat down?"

"Oi, he did." And then some. Vince had been his best friend. Until he'd stolen Finn's wife.

"Then well done." Luke drained his beer and set the bottle on the counter. He turned to Rick, who was still staring at Finn. Did the older man know more than he was letting on? Luke filled the silence. "We gotta get going, Rick. One thing I've already learned about pregnant women is you do not want to piss them off. Whitney's feisty on a good day. And now that she's loaded with hormones? I don't need to be setting off that kind of dynamite, trust me."

Rick nodded, then drained his beer. "Sounds good. I've got an early lecture to give on Beowulf tomorrow. Not that I don't know every word I'm going to say, but I like to make sure I appear energetic so they don't tune me out completely." He looked around, then tipped his head toward the chintz sofa. "Not sure this is exactly your style, Finn, but at least it's an address for your paychecks. And speaking of feisty women? Tread carefully around your landlady—I've heard she can be a firecracker."

Luke laughed as he grabbed his jacket and tossed Rick's at him. "I've worked for Bridget since her dad passed, and she's got an edge, for sure. Her bark is worse than her bite, though. She blows hot, but she's always fair about things in the end."

Finn spent an hour or so unpacking, then rearranged the kitchen a bit so he could find stuff. He was starving but was too tired to cook, so he ordered up a pizza. What he didn't eat tonight would be dinner—or maybe breakfast—tomorrow. He'd just started pulling books from boxes when he heard a sharp rap on the door.

"Come in!" he hollered, his arms loaded with books on Celtic history. Should he stack them on the floor by time period or by subject matter? Either way, the living room was going to be buried in books. The door opened behind him, and he didn't even glance back. "Thanks, mate. You can put it on the counter there. Hang on just a sec." Finn dropped the stack of books and reached for his wallet. "Let me get your tip for ya…" He turned with the cash in his hand, then froze. This was no ordinary pizza delivery.

Bridget McKinnon stood just inside the door, holding what he assumed was his pizza. She was looking none too pleased.

"Oh, hey, Bridget." He glanced down at all the boxes, half empty, half not, scattered around the room. "Sorry for the mess, but I'm just getting settled." Her expression didn't soften one bit, and he rushed on. "We did agree on today for the move-in, right? I gave you the prorated amount with the deposit…" Why was he blathering on to this woman? He was a grown man—a college professor—and had nothing to apologize for. At least…he didn't think he did. But her eyes were hard and angry. And she was still holding his dinner. He didn't realize how hungry he was until he smelled the sausage and mush-rooms. He splayed his hands. "What have I done?"

"Did I not give you a lengthy lecture about se-curity when you paid your deposit and signed the lease?" She was easily eight or ten years younger than he was, but her voice held all the gravelly strength of a woman who'd been around the world a few times and was in no mood for nonsense. "Did I not point out the specific paragraph about privacy?"

Finn was stumped. "I haven't been upstairs. I haven't been in the laundry room yet. Did I park my car in the wrong spot or something?" He stepped forward, his stomach grumbling. "Here, let me get that. Wait…did you pay the delivery guy? Do I owe you—"

She tossed the pizza box at him, but he managed to catch it and keep it right side up. "What you owe me is the understanding that you don't ever leave that front door unlocked. And you sure as hell don't leave a stone propping it open!"

Finn did have a vague memory of reading that in the lease. "Oh…uh…yeah. We did that while we were carrying boxes. But I was right here, and I knew it would only be the pizza delivery and I wanted to get the books…I mean…who else would just walk in…" As he said the words out loud, he realized he sounded like an inconsiderate ass. "Well, I guess… anyone could have walked in. And this is your house. Your home. I'm sorry. Truly."

He let the apology hang there between them. Her

shoulders eased, and her eyes softened just enough to let him know she'd heard him. Luke said she was fair. She finally nodded sharply and turned on her heel.

"It's your first night, so I'll give you a pass. But I want that door kept locked, okay?" She stopped at the door, then glanced back at him. "I need to know who's in this house, or at least know that anyone here has been let in by you or me. It's important."

"I get that." He wondered if there'd been some kind of trouble with a previous tenant. "Did something happen in the past?"

She pulled the dark wooden door open, then turned back to face him again. "That doesn't matter…" She frowned, then blew out a sigh. "A college student had some of her friends over and they were drinking. One of the guys thought it would be fun to trespass into my apartment. It was not fun."

"Damn. Did he…do anything? Hurt you?"

Her lips pressed together tightly, as if she was trying to stop talking, but couldn't.

"No. He didn't even know I was home. Waking up to a man in my bedroom was…not fun." Her words were clipped. "I screamed. He ran. I gave the tenant her notice. End of story."

Bridget seemed to have a continual air of tightly wound self-control. Not as much strong as…brittle. Fragile. Her gaze fell to the floor. He wondered if she had anyone to talk to, then remembered Rick and Luke talking about her big Irish family. And yet she seemed very alone standing there, and something tapped at his chest, making him want to comfort her.

"I'm sorry. That must have been terrifying. I promise you I'll never leave that door unlocked again. And if there's anything else I can do to make you feel safer while I'm here…"

She looked up in surprise. "I'm fine." She let out a soft sigh and shook her head. "This hasn't been the nicest welcome, has it? Sorry about the pizza, I just…"

He waved her off. "Don't. I deserved it."

"Are you done moving in? Any problems? Any questions?"

"Yes. No. And yes." He smirked at her look of confusion as she tried to apply the answers to her questions. Her eyebrows rose.

"You have a question? What is it?"

"Wanna join me for pizza?" After she'd tossed it at him, he'd noticed the exhaustion in the lines around her eyes, and the invitation came out without thinking.

Her mouth fell open. "Me?"

"Uh…yeah." He wasn't much of a social butterfly these days, but it couldn't hurt to make peace with his landlady. To reassure her that she was safe with him. "I assume you eat meals like a normal person, and this is a meal…not a fancy one, but still…"

She shook her head sharply, her lips pressed tight together. "I don't think that's a great idea. We're not roommates. We don't need to be friends." Her voice softened. "I mean…thank you. But…no. Besides, I'm working tonight. I just came over to change."

He knew she ran the pub, but Rick said her whole family was involved. "Do you work every night?"

"Not quite, but I may as well. We're closed on Mondays, and have a limited kitchen menu Tuesday through Thursday, so sometimes I can let one of my cousins step in." Her face twisted. "On a really good week, I might even have a cook on staff, but…"

Finn had heard her reputation for not keeping staff. "But good help is hard to find?"

She hesitated, then nodded with a soft smile. "Something like that."

"Well, I worked in a chipper as a lad in Dublin, so if you ever…" Her forehead wrinkled and he realized she had no idea what he was talking about. "I worked at a fry shop…we did fish and chips…or fish and fries, whatever you want to call it. It's the Irish equivalent of a fast food joint, but everything cooks in a vat o' bubblin' grease." He shrugged. "If you're in a bind, just ask."

She gave him a head-to-foot scan as if she wasn't sure he was real. There was a glint of offense in her eyes. "I do not need anyone's help. I either hire someone to do a job or I do it myself." She gestured toward him with her hand. "I don't even know you. And you think I'm just going to say, 'Oh, Finn, I need your help with the fryer!' Why? Because you're a man? Uh, no." She glared at all the boxes on the floor. "I don't know what you thought was going to happen once you moved in, but we are not pals and I don't need any of your favors." He opened his mouth to speak but she shut him down. "Seriously. Don't be charming. Don't be friendly. Just be quiet, don't set the place on fire and keep the door locked, okay?"

And she was gone, leaving Finn holding a cooling pizza and wearing a wide grin. Getting Bridget McKinnon fired up was just too easy to resist—she reminded him of his wee sis, Sally, at home. He used to bet his friends on how fast he could get Sally to throw something at him in anger. His smile faded. Pissing off his landlady was a bad idea. She could throw him to the curb. He needed to keep this place. He looked around at the cardboard boxes and ruffled curtains. Home Sweet Home.

"He offered to cook, Nana! Or fry, or…something." A week later, Bridget was still fuming. "Like I'm some damsel in distress who needs my tenant—a total stranger!—to come rescue me." She knew she was making too big a deal of Finn's offer, but he'd thrown her off kilter by getting her to talk about that awful night when that kid showed up in her bedroom. Hell, her own family didn't even know that. Her friend, Kareema, was the only person she'd told. Then he'd asked her to eat with him and offered to help. Was he trying to be her white knight? Because she definitely didn't want one.

Besides, she was a trained chef, and didn't need some dashing Irishman to come fry her freaking food. Her eyes closed. She really needed to stop thinking of how good Finn would look sweating over the commercial fryer in her kitchen, dark hair curling around his face and his sleeves rolled up to expose arms she now knew were rock solid.

Last night she'd watched from her apartment as he carried yet another box of books into the house. It was one of those rare almost-warm February days and he'd pushed up the sleeves of his rugby shirt, exposing a surprising Celtic tattoo wrapping around his forearm. The professor had a tat. Interesting.

He was actually an ideal tenant so far. She barely heard him downstairs. No loud music. Not even the murmur of a television most nights. And ever since she'd lambasted him about leaving the door unlocked, he'd been meticulous about that. He'd even swept out the entry hall and had taken the trash to the curb last week. He was the type of tenant landlords dreamed of. And that was the problem. She couldn't stop dreaming about him.

"Bridget! Are you listening?" Nana's voice cut into her daydreaming.

"What? I'm sorry, Nana."

"So this tenant of yours offered to help, and that annoyed you because…?"

Why indeed? Lord knew she needed help at the Shamrock these days. Jimmy and Marta had "quit" before, but they always came back. Until now. Bridget was determined not to beg, but handling the kitchen alone was wearing her down. She might have to swallow her pride and call Jimmy this week. She gave her Nana a half-hearted smile.

"I don't know. I'm just…tired."

Nana's mouth slid into a grin. "That look in your eye when you were complaining about this Finn guy had nothing to do with being tired, girlie. Tell me more about this annoying tenant of yours. He's actually from Ireland, right? Is his brogue delicious?"

"Yes." Bridget's eyes went wide in horror. "I mean, yes, he has a brogue." *And it's delicious.* "But he's just a tenant. We have a contractual agreement and nothing more."

"Nothing more, eh? Is that why you're still talking about the man today?"

Her grandmother laughed with more energy than Bridget had seen since the chemo started. She had one of Kelly's thin ski caps on. She said it was for warmth, but Bridget knew it was to hide her newly shaved scalp. They were sitting at Nana's kitchen table in the rambling Victorian she shared with only Kelly these days. But this house had seen several generations of McKinnons grow up, including Bridget after her mom died. It hadn't changed much. The kitchen was a sunny yellow, with a greenhouse window over the deep porcelain sink. The old wooden cabinets had been painted a creamy white about ten years ago, which brightened the room even more.

"I'm talking about him to keep you happy, you nosy ninny." Bridget shook her head. "You ask about him every time I see you, and today I finally had a story for you. You're just obsessed with his Irishness, admit it."

"Maybe. I'd like to meet this Irish tenant of yours. When is he usually home?" Nana took a sip of her tea, doing her best to look innocent, and failing. Badly.

Bridget's laughed. "Why? What are you planning? Just to knock on his door and introduce yourself?"

"Why not? That used to be my son's home, and the last I knew I was welcome to use my key to gain entrance." Nana's brow, hairless as it was, rose high enough to make her point. Bridget held up a hand in surrender. Her grandmother didn't have Bridget's quick temper, but the woman sure had a way of getting what she wanted.

"You know you can use that key anytime. But it won't get you into his apartment."

"I would hope not. I'm not looking to rifle through his things. Your hot Irish boy needs his privacy."

Bridget sat very still, juggling those words in her head and trying to decide which to tackle first. "He's definitely Irish, but he is not mine, and he's no boy."

He'd put his birthdate on his rental agreement, so she knew he would turn forty in the fall.

Her grandmother leaned forward with a sharp twinkle in her eye. "Ah-ha! You don't deny he's hot! He's a looker, eh?"

Bridget let her head fall back and stared up at the ceiling in defeat. "You are relentless. I don't know if I'd call him hot…" She totally would, but not to her grandmother. "But he's not ugly, either. An interested woman would definitely be…interested. But I'm not. Interested."

Nana's smile softened. "And why is that, honey?"

"Seriously? I don't have the time or energy for anything like that."

"And why is that, honey?" Nana's repeated question had a bit of an edge to it now.

Wasn't it obvious?

"Nana, you know why. I'm barely keeping up with the bills. I've been doing all the cooking since Jimmy and Marta quit. The house needs work. And with you being…"

There was a beat of silence.

"With me being sick? Don't you think you're taking care of enough without trying to control my illness, too?" Nana sighed, her fingers tapping on the table as if she was playing an invisible piano. "If you keep taking on all the worries of this family, you'll never have time to take care of yourself, Bridget. You don't have to manage the McKinnons."

But…didn't she, though?

"Who else is going to step up? Your children have scattered across the country and have their own careers, and your grandchildren still in town have their own lives, and aren't interested. Mary's ready to pop. Kelly is in school and working at the pub. Timothy's getting ready to be a dad. And Michael thinks if he ignores things long enough at the pub that they'll take care of themselves." She paused for a breath.

"I'm the one with the organization skills and the time to do it, because I don't have…"

"A life?" There went Nana's naked brow again. It wasn't a lie, but Bridget wasn't ready to admit it.

"Because I don't have some man to worry about. That's what we were talking about, remember? I have the pub and…the family at large. Including you." She patted her grandmother's hand. "And that's a good thing. I'm the best at managing, so let me manage things and don't worry about my personal life. I'll have time for that when you're better and I've got the pub making money again so I can relax." She had no idea when that magical moment would arrive, but surely it would…someday.

Her grandmother stared at her for so long that Bridget had to fight the urge to squirm in her chair. She'd often wondered if her grandmother had some of those mysterious Celtic powers, as her father had often claimed. Dad swore his mother could see the future and spot a lie faster than any machine ever could.

The woman nodded slowly and grasped Bridget's fingers.

"Okay, hon. You've always had a need to be in charge, and I can't deny you're good at it. Maybe too good, but that's a talk for another day." She took a deep breath, and Bridget noticed a grayish pallor to her face.

The chemo was taking its toll. Nana was exhausted most of the time. She was having a hard time maintaining her appetite, so she'd lost some weight. That made her look even more frail. Some days she was in pain. Other days, she seemed disoriented. Bridget blinked and looked away for a moment, collecting her emotions and getting them under control. She wanted to make things better. She needed to. She'd lost her mom way too early, and the thought of losing Nana filled her with a bottomless sorrow, as well as a fierce determination to fix things.

Nana's gaze sharpened. "Girl, you can't put off livin' your own life until the timing is perfect. You might just wake up some morning to discover time's up. I know you never planned on coming home to run the Shamrock. It wasn't your dream. You gave up California. You gave up what's-his-name." Bridget smiled. Clark had never once come back to Rendezvous Falls to meet her family. That should have told her something, but she'd missed the warnings. Nana leaned forward and continued. "Don't make yourself a martyr for the McKinnons. We're tougher stock than you give us credit for. Remember that, okay?"

She started to speak, then thought better of it. There was a lot of wisdom in what her grandmother had just said. She knew that. But she couldn't help thinking the wild McKinnons would have spun out of control if Bridget hadn't worked so hard to keep them on track. She ran the business. She organized the family events. She'd established a schedule when Nana was diagnosed. She kept the family focused on priorities. Maybe Bridget had put some of her own dreams aside, but that was her choice. She had plenty of time to look for love. She just didn't have time to do it right now. And she definitely didn't need to do it with the Hot Irishman—thanks, Nana, for that name—living in her house. Or with the Hot Irishman, period.

There was a sharp rap on the kitchen door, and it opened at almost the same instant. Nana's best friend, Victoria Pendergast, walked in. She seemed surprised to see Bridget there, but recovered quickly. The woman was all about the fast recoveries and social niceties. A society maven—as much society as there was in Rendezvous Falls—Vickie was Nana's opposite in so many ways. Vickie was all about appearances. In the middle of a weekday afternoon, she was clad head-to-toe in designer clothes, probably from her last shopping trip to Manhattan. While Nana had been married once and still pined for her late husband, gone forty years now, Vickie had been married at least three times that Bridget knew of, and always seemed on the cougar-like prowl for another.

"Hi, Bridget." Vickie smiled, then turned to Nana. "Maura, I was driving by and wondered if you might reconsider the book club meeting tomorrow night. It's up at the winery, and Helen said she'd love to see you. We all would." Vickie pulled out a chair and made herself comfortable, tugging off her leather gloves. "I could pick you up around six thirty?"

Bridget spoke up before Nana could answer, eager

to protect her. "I'm sure she'll be too tired by that hour, Vickie. She needs to conserve her strength."

Her grandmother bristled, sitting ramrod-straight in her chair and giving Bridget a look that could freeze burning oil.

"Just because I said you're good at being in control doesn't mean I want you trying to control me." Her words were clipped and sharp. "I'm perfectly capable of making my own decisions."

She felt her cheeks flame. It wasn't like Nana to scold her like that in front of someone else. Bridget had gone a step—or three—too far. But she did it out of love and concern. Why couldn't anyone see that she was just trying to take care of things?

Vickie cast a quick, sympathetic glance at Bridget, then chuckled at Nana. "Well, you haven't lost your salt, old girl. Does that mean I'll be picking you up?"

Nana's eyes narrowed. "Having cancer doesn't make me incapable of driving, you know."

"Maybe not technically." Vickie stared down her friend, not in the least intimidated. "But you know you shouldn't drive with the meds you're on, and I'll be driving right by here. Six thirty?"

Now it was Bridget's turn to bristle. It felt like Vickie was pressuring Nana. She started to object, but then she saw a warmth in Vickie's eyes that stopped her. She reminded herself that Nana and Vickie had been friends for decades, and they knew how to deal with each other without her help. Nana thought for a moment, then nodded.

"I'm tentatively saying yes." Her glance slid to Bridget, who was smart enough to keep her mouth shut. "I'll text you if I don't think I'm up to it, but you were right about me needing to get out of this house for a bit."

Bridget lowered her head to keep her emotions to herself. She didn't approve, but Nana was right—she didn't need Bridget's approval. There were only so many things Bridget could control, and her grandmother's friendships weren't on that list.

CHAPTER FOUR

"Professor O'Hearn!"

Finn was walking across the frigid campus quad
when Christina Moore called his name. He'd just
left Howard Greer's office, where he'd let his boss
know his move was completed and his long-term
commitment to staying in Rendezvous Falls was secure. Hopefully that meant his job—and his visa
application—were secure, too. He turned and greeted
the sophomore who'd called his name, wondering
again if students were getting younger every year.
Christina was out of breath when she caught up with
him, but it didn't slow her words any. Her long blond
hair blew across her face, and she swept it back with
a laugh.

"There you are! I went to your office but it was
locked and I was afraid I'd missed you completely
since it's Friday and you don't have any classes this
afternoon and oh my God it's so freakin' cold! Is it
this cold in Ireland? I swear I'm going to transfer to
a Florida school as soon as I can convince my parents to let me go somewhere warm…"

She finally paused for a breath. Finn had no idea what her point was.

"Christina, I'm on my way home for the day. And yes, it gets this cold in parts of Ireland." The winter winds howling off the Irish sea could freeze a man to the bone. "Do you have any other pressing questions to ask?"

Her smile brightened exponentially. Christina was one of those students who were just as clever as any other classmate, but didn't want to overexert themselves too much. She'd probably perfected this winning smile as a lass in public school. It was full of charm, but her eyes had a glint of desperation every teacher recognized. She wanted something.

"Professor, I need my history credits for pre-law, but this medieval stuff is killing me. You rejected my idea for my final paper, so now I don't know what to do. I thought my idea of showing the historical accuracy of *Highlander* would be really interesting. Maybe let me do a paper on something that isn't so… you know…medieval?" Her voice went up another octave to sell her suggestion. "I'm a visual learner, so I'm better watching movies than listening to lectures." Yeah, he found that easy to believe. "Can you recommend a show I could write about? No offense or anything, but this class is such ancient history."

Finn had been teaching at university level for ten years now, and he'd heard variations on the same theme a hundred times. He still had to concentrate to avoid rolling his eyes at the young woman, so clearly looking for an easy way out.

"There are tutors for most subjects posted on the college website. I haven't been here long enough to recommend anyone, but most are seniors who could probably help you. As for your other thoughts…" He tried to smile but knew it was a thin one. "Since the class is called Medieval History 101, options for your paper can not be 'less medieval.' And while I don't necessarily object to analyzing history against contemporary media, *Highlander* is not even set in the medieval period. Which, by the way, is not 'ancient history.' That's another class entirely."

"Well, it's ancient to me." Her face fell. "There has to be something I can do for extra credit, Professor O'Hearn."

"Seriously? It's only February. You have plenty of time to find an acceptable topic, research it and write a paper. It's way too early to worry about extra credit projects, which I rarely dole out anyway."

A quick flash of anger went across her face, but she managed to hide it quickly behind her smile. Finn knew he sounded like a pompous old grump of a professor, but sometimes he grew weary of explaining historical significance to students like Christina, who were only in his class for the credits. He sighed. She wasn't going to give up, so he may as well offer her something.

"You're looking to be an attorney someday, right?" She half shrugged and half nodded. Not exactly an inspiring endorsement of her dedication to pre-law, but that wasn't his problem. "Why not do a paper on medieval law? Did you know the practice of using precedent for rulings came to England after the Norman invasion? In fact, Henry II…" Finn stopped at her blank expression, then shook his head. "Look, Christina, there's no shortcut to passing my class. No movie or TV series will ever substitute for actual research. But if you focus on the medieval law angle now, it might give you an advantage in law school a few years down the road when you impress an instructor with your knowledge." Somehow, he had a hard time imagining that ever happening. "It might save you from having to ask for special favors in law school, where they'll be less frequent than here at Brady College. That's the best I can offer. I'll put a list together of some texts in the library you may find helpful."

Her smile vanished so fast it was almost laughable. "But can't I—"

"Miss Moore, I'm sorry if Medieval History is too medieval for you, but I have to get to—"

"Professor O'Hearn! Just the man I was looking for!" Rick Thomas walked up behind Finn. "I have an urgent question about a historical reference in an Old English poem I found… Oh, hi, Christina." Rick gave the young woman a pointed look, resting his hand on Finn's shoulder and giving a quick squeeze to silence him. "Have you started my assignment from American lit yet? I look forward to your thoughts on Nathaniel Hawthorne."

A particularly icy blast came in off the lake, making all three of them gasp and brace their feet. Christina grabbed at her scarf to keep it from flying away, glaring at both men.

"I hate this place!" She stomped off, not even pretending to be charming anymore.

Rick chuckled once she was out of earshot. "Was it something I said?"

"Thanks for the save, man. She was…"

Rick held up his gloved hand. "Let me guess. She wanted an extra credit project that has nothing to do with your course syllabus?"

Finn laughed. "Good guess."

"She pulls the same game with everyone." Rick held his hands over his heart dramatically, pantomiming her pleading. "Oh, please, Mr. Professor! This class is hard and I didn't have to do hard things in high school! I just smiled and people helped me because my daddy is important and I'm pretty. Did you notice I'm pretty?" Rick pretended to flip his make-believe hair, but he dropped the routine after that. "Dude, I've seen some spoiled princes and princesses in my life, but she's one of the…well, best isn't the right word…most impressive, maybe? Some kids really have a culture shock when they get to college and actually have to do the work to get the grades."

"I'm glad students like her are the exception." Finn tugged his jacket tighter. "Where you headed?"

"Home, thank God." They walked toward the parking lot, both lowering their heads against the wind. "Hard to believe a week ago it was in the fifties, and now the wind chill is headed below zero tonight." The older man tipped his head to look Finn's way. "Are you unpacked and feeling at home yet?"

"Hopefully I'll finish up this weekend. I'm running out of room for books. I may have to make end tables out of the stacks." The apartment was tinier than his first flat in Dublin years ago. One open space for the kitchen and living area, and one fair-sized bedroom and a small bath with a shower. The tall Victorian windows let in a lot of sunlight, which was nice. And the original crown moldings and hardwood floors gave it character. But it was…compact.

"Was Greer happy to see you had a real mailing address?"

"As happy as the codger can be, I guess. The ax is off my neck for now."

"And from your visa?"

"As far as I know. It's not the visa as much as trying to get that green card. My record needs to be spotless." Changing jobs while on a visa was frowned on, but Greer had agreed to pick up his sponsorship, so he should be safe. It was just unsettling to have his future in someone else's hands. The guy wouldn't make any commitments on tenure, but that was reasonable considering Finn had only been teaching a few weeks, even if he'd arrived in town late last fall.

"And you and Bridget McKinnon?" Rick asked.

Finn came to an abrupt halt. "What about her?"

"How are you getting along?"

"Oi, she's just my landlord. That's it. In fact, she literally told me we weren't to be friends or roomies. I honestly haven't seen her much."

He was hoping to catch her later that week, though, and ask about the empty room across from his apartment. The door had been open one day last week, and he saw the walls were lined with empty bookshelves. There was a big old mahogany desk in there, covered with dust and a few old magazines. If he could convince Bridget to let him use it as his home office, he'd have room for his reference books and a dedicated area to finish up the paper on Brian Boru and Irish history he hoped to get published. Greer had been pushing publication almost as hard as he'd pushed Finn to get an address. Finn just had to convince Bridget to lease him that extra room, which, judging from the dust and unused shelves, she didn't seem to be using.

The school had received a substantial endowment that was to be specifically used to build a new history school on campus. The building currently housing history lectures was also home to the growing art and design school, and quarters were getting cramped. Greer had come right out and said an Irish-born history professor…looked good. Or sounded good. Or something like that.

It felt like Dr. Greer wanted to pimp Finn out to

the alumni as the charming Irish guy—a role he'd always been loath to play, even before his marriage and career had imploded. But, what the hell. He was here, and if he wanted to salvage his career and stay in the States, he'd have to play along.

He and Rick parted ways quickly as the wind picked up again, waving to each other as they leaped into their vehicles and shut out the icy weather. When Finn got back to the house, he spotted an older woman crossing the parking lot from the Purple Shamrock. She was moving slowly, and a bit unsteadily in the wind. Her head and face were covered with a thick wool scarf and hat. Finn was getting out of his car when she hesitated at the corner of the house, reaching out to steady herself on the wall. He rushed toward her.

"Oi! Are you alright, ma'am? Can I help you?"

She looked up in surprise, her dark eyes sharp and bright as she took him in. She reached for his extended arm.

"Oh, you must be Mr. O'Hearn! That brogue…you remind me of my dad with that accent. I'm Maura McKinnon, Bridget's grandmother."

He helped her up the front steps and brought her inside to the warm foyer. He hadn't seen Bridget's car in the driveway.

"Please call me Finn, Mrs. McKinnon. 'Tis a pleasure to meet you. But I don't think Bridget is at home…" The woman had a firm grip on his arm, but he sensed a frailty about her that didn't match her strong voice. He didn't want her going up the grand staircase alone, especially if she couldn't get into Bridget's flat.

She waved her other hand in dismissal. "Oh, I know. She and her cousins are over at the pub, getting ready for the Friday night crowd. I snuck out while she was in the kitchen."

Finn hesitated. Did she wander away often? If they missed her, would they know to look over here? Should he call Bridget? She'd given him her cell phone for emergencies, but had warned him of dire consequences if he used it for anything less than the house being in flames. But this was her grandmother...

"No, Finn, I'm not a doddering old fool who wandered off into the winter cold without a clue." Finn's brows rose. How had she known what he was thinking? She smiled. She was attractive now, but she must have been a knockout as a younger woman. She tugged at the scarf around her neck. "And I told Bridget's cousin, Kelly, where I was going, so you don't need to tattle on me."

Again, she'd read his mind. The hairs on the back of his neck rose. He'd had a great-aunt who could do that sort of thing—she could read people and situations as if she'd seen it already. As if she was looking back on what was everyone else's present moment.

"But why..."

"Why come here when I knew she wasn't home?" She finished his question, then answered it. "I came to meet you, of course. You're sleeping under my granddaughter's roof, so I think it's only fair that someone in her family knows who you are."

Maura's look sharpened again, and he realized with a jolt that he was looking at an older version of Bridget. Shorter, but with Bridget's quick mind. He hadn't seen a full smile on his landlord's face yet, but he had a hunch it would look just like Maura's. Bright, but with a saucy slant.

Apparently, she didn't know he'd already met some of Bridget's family over the past few weeks. Luke Rutledge introduced him to Bridget's younger cousin Kelly, who waited tables at the Purple Shamrock. And he'd met Timothy McKinnon, too. Tim was a high-spirited lad with a penchant for laughter and Irish whiskey. Both Kelly and Tim seemed far more easygoing than their uptight cousin Bridget.

You're sleeping under my granddaughter's roof…

Rick had described Bridget as prickly, and that was as accurate a description as he'd heard so far. Bridget was like a cactus, stiff and full of needles. But even a cactus bloomed occasionally. Bridget would have to slow down before that could happen. He'd never seen a woman who was so constantly in motion. She didn't walk up and down the stairs outside his flat—she ran. Every time. And at the pub, she was always on the go. Carrying boxes, cleaning tables, taking inventory. Dashing in and out of the kitchen. She always had spots of color high on her cheeks and a determined set to her jaw, as if she was heading into battle. More than once he'd been tempted to reach out and urge her to sit at his side and just…breathe.

But he had a feeling that wouldn't go over all that well.

"So, are you going to invite me in, Finn?"

"Yes, do come in, although I confess it's a bit of a wee mess…" He opened the door and ushered her in. She looked around, not missing a single corner or stack of books. She shook her head with a smile.

"You know this place is too small for you, right?"

"To be honest, I didn't have a lot of options. Dr. Greer at the college insisted I have a real address, and this was available, so…"

She rolled her eyes, and Finn realized she didn't seem to have eyebrows. Or even eyelashes. She'd loosened her scarf, but hadn't touched the soft hat on her head. There was no hair peeking out at the edges of that hat. He swallowed hard, thinking of when his Aunt Catherine had gone through the same fight back home. Maura McKinnon had cancer. His mind was still wrapping around that when she walked to the kitchen, nodding in approval, then faced him again.

"You're neat and organized, for a man. You take care of things. You take care of people, too, I imagine."

It was an oddly personal observation, but she wasn't far off. He liked order. He used to take care of people. Before Dori and Vince betrayed him. He was a lot more cautious these days. But Maura didn't need to know that.

"I try to keep things in their place." And people, too. "Would you like to sit? I have some Irish tea if you need a warm-up…"

"Well, aren't you sweet?" She tilted her head to the side. Damn it, now that he'd realized she had no hair, he couldn't stop looking at the hat. She smiled again, but the corners of her mouth didn't lift as high as before. "But no, thank you. I just wanted to set eyes on the hot Irishman sharing my granddaughter's house."

Hot Irishman? Was that how Bridget had described him? The thought set off a rush of adrenaline, unexpected and unwanted. He liked the woman, but he didn't need her liking him back. A relationship was the last thing he wanted right now. After all her protests of "we're not friends," it didn't make sense. Maura walked closer, waving her finger under his nose and making him lean away from her.

"Hot is as hot does, though, so don't think you can flash a smile and use that accent of yours to get away with anything. Bridget's a bright girl who won't be fooled."

Finn felt adrift. What the hell was happening? First Greer wanted him to use his accent to charm more money from alumni, and now Maura was accusing him of using it to charm Bridget. Maybe his brogue was more of a superpower than he'd ever realized.

"I…had no intention…" He took a step back and collected his thoughts. He heard a sound in the hall and hoped he'd remembered to lock the front door when they came in. "Maura, I'm just a tenant. And your granddaughter is a grown woman, not a girl. She runs her own business, and I don't think she's the type to fall for anyone's charm—or accent—against her will. I don't know what you're thinking, but…no."

She stared up at him, then nodded again. Did he just pass a test of some sort? Before she could speak, there was a sharp rap on his apartment door. Along with the rattle of a key. What the effing hell? The door swung open. Bridget stood in the doorway, one hand on the doorknob—where her key dangled—and the other on her hip. She was clearly not happy.

"Nana, what the fu… What are you doing? I about had a heart attack when I couldn't find you at the pub, and then Kelly told me you were over here. In some stranger's apartment."

Maura stiffened, but Finn rested his hand on the older woman's shoulder.

"You need to slow down, McKinnon. Your grandmother is fine, and was just headed out."

For a moment, he thought actual flames might shoot from Bridget's eyes.

"First, don't ever tell me to slow down. Second, if you were about to let my sick grandmother walk across the lot alone in this weather…"

"I had no intention of letting her leave alone—"

Finn's voice rose "—and as far as her being in my place goes, at least your grandmother was invited."

Maura ended the debate by yanking off her hat to expose her pale, hairless scalp. She pulled away from his touch, but her fury was aimed straight at Bridget. She was practically vibrating with it.

"So that's what I am to you now? Your 'sick grandmother'?" Bridget's mouth dropped open, but Maura didn't wait for her to answer. "I'm not the woman who raised you. I'm not Nana anymore? I'm sick Nana who can't be trusted to walk a few hundred feet in the same weather I've lived through for seventy-one years. Is that how you all see me? Some helpless old woman?" She rounded on Finn, who leaned back again. Damn, this tiny woman was scary when she wanted to be. Now he knew where Bridget got her fire. "Yes, I have breast cancer, but that is not…" She glanced back at Bridget, whose face had gone pale. "Cancer is not who I am. I am Maura McKinnon. Not sick Maura McKinnon." She jammed the hat back on her head and pushed her way past Bridget and out of the apartment. "Now if you'll excuse me, I have a book club meeting to get ready for tonight. With my friends. The ones who don't see my cancer before they see me." She paused and took a shaky breath at Bridget's side, her voice softening. "I know you love me, Bridget, but you don't see me anymore."

Bridget looked like she'd been stabbed in the

heart. "That's not true. It's because I love you that I…" Bridget struggled. "I don't mean to…"

"That's just it, honey." Maura put her hand on Bridget's arm. "It hurts whether you mean to or not. Yes, I'm sick, but I need to be me. If you want something to control, then try controlling how you and your cousins look at me. I'm not cancer. I'm Maura McKinnon." Her voice broke as she put her hand on her chest, and Finn winced at her raw pain. "Don't let me get lost."

And she was gone, leaving Finn staring at Bridget, and Bridget staring at the floor.

IT WASN'T OFTEN that Bridget was left speechless, but she had zero words after her grandmother dressed her down in front of Finn. After Finn dressed her down in front of her grandmother. All because she cared about Nana and wanted her safe. A quick surge of righteous anger rose up. This was the thanks she got for trying to take care of her grandmother, herd all her cousins in the right direction, and keep the business above water. Fucking perfect.

But if she was being honest with herself… Nana was right about Bridget seeing the specter of cancer every time she looked at her. She couldn't help it. And Finn was right about her having a ton of nerve to just burst into his apartment. What had she been thinking?

Bridget did not like it when everyone else was right but her. She raised her chin in defiance…of herself?…

and narrowed her eyes at the nearest target. Finn. She did her best to ignore the tears burning in her eyes. She was so damned tired.

"Look," she said, working to steady her voice. "I don't know you, and my family is none of your business. So the next time my grandmother comes calling…"

Turns out Finn's anger hadn't cooled one little bit.

"The next time your grandmother, or your cousin, or your friends, or the goddamn pizza guy comes knocking on my door—" he stepped toward her, and she fought the urge to step back from the coldness in his eyes "—I will decide who comes in and who doesn't. This may be your house, but I'm paying rent here, and if you think you can just unlock that door and stroll in here anytime you want to…" He pointed to the open door behind her. She felt herself deflate inside. He was right. Again. She swallowed hard, willing herself to hold strong.

"I'm sorry about that." She met his eyes. "I was just so upset when I found out Nana had walked over here in that cold…"

His brows gathered. "Why? She had a coat, and the woman seems in full control of her faculties."

"Oh, she is definitely just as sharp as she ever was." Bridget sighed, still stinging from Nana's dress down. "But she really is sick, and I worry about her. Hell, I worry about everything these days."

"Why is that?" His voice lowered. He wasn't radiating anger anymore.

How could she explain?

"I've always been the…the one who sees three steps ahead and tries to avoid trouble before it happens. But lately…" She stared at the corner of the room, not really focusing on anything. "Lately I'm running three steps behind and losing ground. And no matter how hard I run, I can't catch up. I can't get there." Wherever there was. "And I have no idea why I'm telling you this."

What was it about this man and his damnable green eyes that made her spill her guts?

"Your grandmother would blame my Irish accent and charm. She warned me not t' use it on you."

She stared at him in shock, then started laughing. "Did she really? I think she's the one with a weakness for Irish blarney."

Although Bridget was wondering if maybe she'd inherited that weakness, because right now she wanted to just walk into this man's arms and forget the world for a little while. He had a way of getting her to talk. And talking relieved some of her pressure.

Finn put both hands on his chest in fake offense, giving her a wide grin. "Blarney? Dinna' throw that word at me, lass, or I'll have to turn my full leprechaun charms on you."

Yes, please. She blinked. No, she didn't want any leprechaun charms. She was afraid she might not be strong enough to resist them. She shook her head, and noticed the still-open door behind her.

"Unlocking your door was…so wrong."

"Agreed." He ran his fingers through his thick black hair. "Look, the last thing I want—like literally the very last thing—is drama. I've had enough to last a lifetime, and I don't need anyone else's. Maura seems like a lovely woman, but…" He glanced around the apartment, which was overcrowded with books, furniture and papers. How did he relax with so much…stuff? "I have my own nutty family back in Ireland, and I truly have no interest in taking on you or yours."

Was he calling her nutty? She closed her eyes. Of course he was. She'd just caused a scene in the apartment he paid rent for.

"Fair enough. Like I said, I'm sorry, Finn." She shook off her strange urge to ask for a hug. As if. "I'll leave you alone."

She turned to the door, but his voice, suddenly as warm as an Irish coffee on a cold day, stopped her.

"I'm sorry, too. I'm not saying you were right to barge in, but…I get it. You were worried about Maura. That's not a bad thing." She bit back a grin. She liked the way that word always sounded like ting when he said it. He surprised her by extending his hand. "I was a bit of an arse, too. I don't handle confrontation well." A troubling shadow crossed his deep green eyes. She wondered just how ugly his recent divorce had been. She took his hand, and immediately felt an odd surge of…something. Energy? Attraction? Agitation? He released her quickly, as if perhaps he'd felt the same thing. Ting. She had no idea why her brain went there, but she couldn't hold back the smile this time.

His head tipped to the side. "What?"

She couldn't tell him she was laughing at his accent. Rude.

"Uh…nothing…just…" Her eyes went to the clutter behind him. "Why do you have all these books?"

Finn chuckled, rubbing his neck as he scanned the room. "Oi, I ask myself the same question most days. I cherish the feel of a real book in my hands, especially a history book. There's some sort of disconnect for me when I'm reading about the Battle of Clontarf while staring at a cold blue electronic screen." He picked up a nearby reference book that had to be three inches thick. "The good news is most people don't feel the same, so I can get great deals on these big old volumes. The bad news is I can't resist a great deal."

"So…is there a special store for these? Maybe Giant Dusty Books R Us?"

His laughter was full. Damn, this man had one fine laugh.

"Sadly, no. I have to troll the internet for out-of-print textbooks and the like. Technology is an evil necessity, and I know how to use it to my advantage."

"You're such a nerd." She clapped her hand over her mouth in shock at both her laughter and her words, but Finn didn't seem to be offended at all. In fact, he flashed a devastating grin at her. Maybe

Nana was right in warning him to harness that charm of his.

"I teach history, much of it medieval or pre-medieval, so I think nerd comes with the territory. I've been known to wear glasses, but I've managed to avoid the tweed jacket with elbow patches." He set the book back on a stack of other thick volumes. "So far, at least."

"Are you saying you're more of an Indiana Jones type?"

"Only in my dreams." Was he blushing right now? "But Indy was an inspiration when I was a lad."

She tried to imagine Finn as a teen, with a tousle of black hair and such a sharp mind. She couldn't help thinking he probably had to beat the girls off with a stick. But apparently his ex-wife hadn't been the staying kind. Or maybe Finn hadn't. She took him in for a moment without saying anything. She didn't know him, but she could already tell he was serious. Thoughtful. Kind with her grandmother. He didn't seem the type to step out on his wife.

Was that why she was having all these weird… feelings…about Finn? Maybe because he was the first man in the apartment, and thus this close to her life, since she'd found out Clark had been the kind of guy to cheat?

"Uh-oh." He smiled. "I nerded out and lost you with the Indiana Jones confession, didn't I?"

"No. My dad and I watched those movies together all the time. All except *Temple of Doom*—that was

a little too graphic for me with the monkey brains…
Ew." She shuddered. She and her dad had had their
issues, but there were fun memories, too. Like popping a movie into the DVD player and watching it
on a Sunday afternoon. She glanced at her watch.
"Oh, damn. I need to get back to the pub and finish
setting up for tonight." She pulled her key from his
door, shaking her head at herself. "I promise not to
use this again unless I think you're dying in here.
Other than that, I'll knock and wait for you to invite me in."

He dipped his head. "I appreciate that. And I'll
do my best not to disturb your life any further. But
I do have one favor to ask."

She had to give him credit for good timing. She
owed him one. "What is it?"

"That office across the hall…do you use it?"

She hadn't expected that. Dad had tried to convert the small library into a studio apartment, but it
was too tiny to be practical. There was a sofa bed in
there, but you'd have to slide the heavy antique desk
aside to open it. The so-called kitchenette was just a
mini-fridge Dad kept his beer in, and a microwave
sitting on a wheeled cart. With the original mahogany bookcases lining two walls, and deep window
seats Bridget had always adored, it felt even smaller
than it was. So it had sat empty for years, used as
basically a storage room. Every house needed a junk
room, right? She couldn't imagine why Finn would
be interested in it.

"Why do you ask?"

He lifted one shoulder. That was another tell of his. He did that little shoulder twitch—it wasn't quite a shrug—when he wasn't sure of himself.

Why do I know this stuff about him?

"As you can see, I have a few books." That was an understatement. The apartment had mountains of books on every surface and covering much of the floor. "I'm working on a paper to be published... Part of the whole professor thing, ya know?" She didn't, but she nodded for him to continue. "The door across the way was sitting open last week, and I saw the desk and the bookcases, and wondered if I could rent the space to use as an office."

"Doesn't the college give you an office?"

His jaw worked back and forth. Then he blew out a breath.

"The truth is, I'm a bit of a night owl. I'll wake up with an idea and run with it, even if it's two in the morning. I like to keep my school office for class resources and meeting with students. When I'm researching a paper to publish, I tend to...spread out." He gestured widely with his arms, as if spreading papers across the desk. "Having a room where I can close the door to the mess, but go back to right where I left off whenever I get the urge...well, 'twould be helpful. If the room's available, that is."

She thought about it for a moment. "I store some seasonal stuff in there, like Christmas decorations from the pub, but if you can work around that..."

"No worries. I only need the desk and book-shelves."

She nodded. "We can work something out. I'll get you the key."

"What do you want for rent?"

"Nothing. You're already paying rent, and the room is just sitting there. Consider it a gesture of goodwill after all the stuff I've had to apologize for."

"There has to be something I can do." His hands slid into his pockets again, and he studied the floor again with a frown. Then he looked up with a glint of humor in his eyes. "You said you didn't want my help in the kitchen, but maybe I could help. Luke Rutledge said there was some debate about the direction of the Purple Shamrock. Remodeling? Rebranding?"

Bridget narrowed her eyes. Where was he going with this? Finn splayed his hands in front of him.

"If you want to make it a true Irish pub, who better to advise than an Irishman?"

She was annoyed that Luke had been talking about her business, but she knew he, Rick and Finn had shared a few beers together. It's not like Luke had broadcast it far and wide. She was skeptical of Finn's offer, but was that because she doubted his knowledge, or because she didn't like anyone advising—telling—her what to do?

"You're saying that just because you come from Ireland, that you—a college professor—can advise me—a pub owner with a culinary degree—on how to run my business? As if I don't already have a whole bunch of relatives doing that? Am I supposed to think that's some kind of gift?" She crossed her arms with a laugh. "Full of yourself much?"

"Your pub is American-Irish, like you. I can help you make it Irish-Irish." He held his hands up. "Or not. Just an idea. But one thing I can do is tend bar for you if you need it. One of my many jobs to pay my way through university as a lad. Luke said he'd be getting busy at the vineyard once spring arrived."

She did need a bartender. She'd interviewed a few, but none of them felt right, and most wanted more money than she could afford.

"That might work. If you can give me one night a week at the bar—assuming you know what you're doing—that can be your rent for the office. And you can keep the tips, of course."

"That's a deal then." He nodded once. "And I'll do my best not to interfere with your life too much."

Her life. She struggled to picture exactly what that was anymore. Lately it felt like a mindless scramble to stay ahead of the bills, her family, the pub and the house.

I'm really tired...

She didn't realize she'd said it out loud until his eyebrows rose.

"Maybe you need a vacation. Or a few days off."

Bridget straightened, her hand grasping the doorknob tightly.

"I don't have the luxury of taking days off, Finn.

I'm majority owner of the pub, and I'm the chef, so I have to be there. I'm trying to single-handedly drag both my family and the business kicking and screaming into the twenty-first century."

"Why single-handedly? No one's on your side?"

It was a good question, veering this conversation quickly into uncomfortable territory. And leading her to a deeply personal confession.

"I guess I don't play well with others." She shrugged. "That's why I stay back in the kitchen and let everyone else man the front of the pub."

He digested that for a moment. This was something she'd rarely, if ever, discussed with anyone. Much less examined in depth herself. She was startled when his mouth slid into a crooked smile.

"We're not that different, you and I."

Her shocked laughter bubbled up. "Excuse me? We are nothing alike, Finn O'Hearn. You're a nerdy Irish recluse, and I'm a…" Her voice trailed off. What was she exactly? Finn answered for her.

"And you're a cranky Irish-American recluse?"

"I…" She stopped, unable to come up with one damn objection. Her eyes narrowed. "Like I said, I have work to do."

He was still grinning when she slammed the door.

Bastard.

CHAPTER FIVE

"WE'RE SO GLAD you're back, Maura!" Cecile raised her glass in Maura's direction across the table in the tasting room at Falls Legend Winery. "I'm sorry you and your granddaughter argued today, but good for you for standing your ground." Vickie raised her glass, too. Their host, Helen Russo, stared at the table as if lost in thought after Maura told them about her argument with Bridget. Then she smiled and joined the toast.

"It's good that you let them know you're still you," Helen said. "I got lost after my Tony died, and after a while, people just saw 'Sad Helen' and started tip-toeing around me and talking in hushed voices. It didn't help. If anything, it made me more convinced I'd never be myself again. Too many people let me fade away."

That was exactly what Maura feared. It was bad enough she'd always have the specter of cancer in her own mind. She hated the idea that everyone else in her life would see her disease before they saw her.

Rick Thomas, tall and lanky, scoffed as he drank his wine instead of pretending to toast. "For the record, I didn't let you fade away, Helen. And neither did Vickie. Or Iris." He looked at Maura. "And we won't let you fade away, either. My sister is a survivor and she's been active in the prevention charities. She wanted to control her own narrative and she has. You'll figure out your narrative, too. But don't expect it to be the one you had before cancer."

"But I don't want to be different." She raised her hand to stop any comments. "I know, I know. Tough luck, right?"

Vickie patted her hand. "Everything changes us, sweetie. Illness. Divorce." She nodded toward Helen with a gentle smile. "Death. But Rick, as much as I hate to admit it, might just have a point." He rolled his eyes and Vickie stuck her tongue out at him before turning back to Maura. "You need to control how it changes things."

She thought about that. "Right now, all I can focus on is getting through this damn chemo with my dignity intact." She brightened. "And nights like this help. You guys help me keep it real, so thanks for taking me back."

Rick waved her off. "We never considered you gone. And speaking of gone, where's Iris tonight?"

Cecile giggled, making her bottle-blond curls bounce. "Believe it or not, she's babysitting! Logan and Piper went up to Syracuse for the night to see a show, and Iris is watching Ethan and Lily."

Rick's forehead wrinkled. "Isn't Ethan a teenager?"

Lena Fox sat down after pouring herself a drink, shaking the gold bracelets circling her wrist so they settled near her hand. Lena had joked earlier that her hairstyle was closest to Maura's, with a tightly clipped Afro hugging her head. Her dark eyes shone with amusement. "It's the teenagers that need watching, Rick. Ethan's a thirteen-year-old boy. My guess is Ethan is watching Lily, and Iris is making sure Ethan stays put." She turned to Maura. "I missed some of your story earlier. What did Bridget say after you told her off?"

She thought of the devastated look on her granddaughter's face in Finn's apartment. "I didn't really give her a chance to say anything. I went back to the pub and left her and Finn to fume at each other. Kelly took me home to get ready for tonight. And here I am, back with the infamous book club again." She didn't want to discuss her blowup with Bridget anymore. "Vickie tells me you helped Logan and Piper get together?"

Lena picked up her paperback and ruffled through the pages to her bookmark. Her long brown fingers were tipped with bright red nails. Lena was an artist, and more recently, a fashion model for a designer in Manhattan trying to appeal to mature women. She'd entered the contest last fall to appease her friends, but she'd kept insisting a black woman would never make the cut. She'd not only made the cut—she'd won, and signed a contract.

"I think we nudged more than anything," Lena

said. "And we got Piper's former mother-in-law out of their way."

Maura laughed. She'd met Susan Montgomery a few times, and the woman was formidable. "That sounds ominous."

"Not like that!" Lena waggled her eyebrows. "Although I think Iris would have considered it." Heads bobbed in agreement around the table. "Susan just needed to see she wasn't doing her grandchildren any favors by making their mother unhappy. That Iris's grandson, Logan, wasn't replacing their father's memory. He's a good man, and we…um… urged Susan to recognize that."

"And what an adorable couple they are," Vickie added. "Tall, dark and rugged Logan with sweet little blonde, blue-eyed Piper. Although there's nothing sweet about the looks she gives him sometimes. Yowza! I think they're keeping each other very happy, if you know what I mean."

Rick leaned forward. "Our track record is pretty good, Maura. Don't you still have some single grandchildren? Like Bridget? We might be able to help…"

"Pretty good?" Helen scoffed. "Vickie tried to hook my Whitney up with Mark Hudson and you tried to fix her up with some old fart professor! We didn't see she was falling for Luke until they were already head-over-heels."

Cecile lifted her hand. "But we did help them patch things up when Luke got cold feet." She grinned. "Maybe we're not perfect at the matchmaking part, but we're two-for-two with the keep-them-together business."

"Whatever happened to being a book club?" Maura laughed. "You all got bored and started being busybodies instead?"

"No…" Rick paused. "Well, sort of. We got into a book rut and decided to…diversify. So, about your grandchildren…?"

"Forget it." Maura's voice was firm. Her family had enough turmoil. "Mary and Timothy are happily married. Michael's not recovered from losing his wife. And Bridget is…well…Bridget. She's married to the Purple Shamrock."

Vickie ran her finger slowly around the top of her wineglass. "And to running the McKinnon family?"

Maura sighed. It was true—Bridget was the heir apparent to Maura's role of family matriarch.

"What about the young girl who waits tables?" Cecile asked. "Kelly? She's single, right? We could find her a nice guy…"

Rick spoke before Maura could. "That would be a waste of time. Kelly plays on my team, and she's in a relationship."

"On your team? Like…your billiards team?" Cecile seemed perplexed. Maura smiled. The woman had a heart of gold, but sometimes she wondered if all that hair bleach had affected Cecile's brain. Rick lowered his head and stared at Cecile from beneath his heavy eyebrows.

"She's on the rainbow team, honey. She has a girlfriend."

Cecile frowned, then her mouth fell open as the message got through.

"Oh! She's gay. Well…" She looked at Maura. "That's…wonderful, right?"

"I don't know if it's any more wonderful than being straight. It's just who Kelly is. She's known since ninth grade, and it didn't change anything for the people who love her the most." Sadly, it changed something for her parents, especially her mother, who still hadn't accepted it as anything other than a phase Kelly must be going through.

Cecile's face reddened. "I didn't mean anything… you know I believe love is love, right?"

Rick put his large hand over Cecile's on the table. "That's a fact, hon. That's a fact." He glanced at his watch. "And speaking of love, did everyone else figure out the wife was the killer in the first twenty pages of this book, or was it just me?"

"I don't think it took me that long," Lena answered. "Sorry, guys. This was my pick, but it's becoming more and more obvious this writer is relying on his team to write the books. He's become a business instead of an author."

"And seriously—" Vickie tapped her e-reader "—did you read those sex scenes? Why the hell can't men write about women without sounding like idiots?" She slid her reading glasses onto her nose and scowled at the screen. "'Her breasts pulsed with need'? Any of you ladies ever had a breast pulse with…" Her voice trailed off when she saw everyone was looking around the room and trying to avoid looking at Maura. "Oh, crap, Maura. I'm an idiot…"

But Maura laughed, waving her hand for Vickie to continue. "I just reamed my granddaughter for only seeing me as her sick Nana. If my best friend starts seeing me that way, too, I'll be really upset. There are no off-limit words around me. So do tell me more about these pulsing boobs, because I didn't have time to read the book. What else did the magic boobs do? Tell time?"

Vickie snorted. "No, but apparently they can see things, because it was his…um…member…that made them start pulsing in the first place. Because you know when men write sex scenes, it's all about how the hero affects the woman. They make us pulse and gasp and quiver."

Lena flipped through more pages. "And don't forget those boobs can point, too! The hero notices several times that her nipples are always pointing at him."

Rick nodded. "Didn't he refer to them as being like heat-seeking missiles taking aim or something stupid like that?"

"Yup!" Cecile pushed her bosom out and tried to aim her ample breasts in Rick's direction. "See? My boobs want you!"

At that point, everyone dissolved into hysterical laughter, including Maura. Good God, she'd needed this. Vickie had been a champ since the diagnosis, but Maura had spent most of her time with her family. She understood their fears, but it was nice to be with people who could forget the illness and treat her like Maura. Not Maura-who-has-cancer.

Rick wiped tears from his eyes, gasping as he replied to Cecile. "Go home and point those things at Charlie, woman. Your missiles are wasted on me."

Cecile cupped her hands lightly under her breasts. "Trust me, my husband conquers these mountains on a regular basis."

There was more laughter as the meeting broke up and everyone headed out, after helping Helen clear the table and reset the room for wine tasting tomorrow. Even in the dead of winter, dedicated wine lovers would be driving the Seneca Lake wine trail over the weekend to sample the region's award-winning wines.

Vickie pulled into the driveway of Maura's green-and-yellow Victorian home. She set her hand on Maura's arm before she could open the door.

"Are you and Bridget going to be okay after your little blowup today?"

Maura sat back, soaking up the feel of the heated seat through her heavy coat.

"Oh, I think so. Bridget's a good girl…" She thought of the way Finn had come to her granddaughter's defense. "I mean, a good woman. She's just so on edge all the time. Like she's trying to prove something to someone, but I'll be damned if I know who or what. She's always been a control freak, but the gir…woman knows what she wants and how she wants it. She honestly is right a lot of the time, but her communication…"

"Sucks?" Vickie asked with a short laugh. Maura chuckled. It was always funny when prim and proper Victoria Pendergast spoke so directly. She wasn't the woman a lot of people thought she was. And neither was Bridget.

"I know Bridget has a reputation for being difficult, but people forget the fighting spirit she has is the reason that pub is still in business." Maura straightened. "And who do you think planned my treatment schedule and coordinated with the doctors and treatment centers after I was diagnosed? She's passionate because she cares."

"Hey, you don't have to sell it to me, girlfriend. I know Bridget and I butt heads once in a while, but that's because we're both so sure of ourselves. I like that in her, even if she hasn't figured out if she likes me yet."

"Sure of herself." Maura nodded. "That's a good way to put it. Although I think my illness has her feeling a lot less sure of herself. It's something she can't control, and she's not handling it well." She opened the car door. "But that's something she has to figure out for herself. I'm navigating my own journey. I can't navigate hers for her."

"Maybe that hot Irishman will help her navigate a path or two."

Finn O'Hearn was a charmer, but despite his defense of Bridget, he'd been none too pleased at the way she'd barged into his place and thrown a hissy fit. Poor guy. She got out of the car, but leaned over to respond to Vickie.

"The only path that man will be navigating is one that's nowhere near his grumpy landlord."

"I CAN'T BELIEVE you're actually sitting here." Kareema Justice took a bite of her powdered donut and laughed out a cloud of powdered sugar in Bridget's direction. They were sitting at the Spot Diner in downtown Rendezvous Falls.

Bridget sipped her coffee. "I don't know why you're surprised, since you physically dragged me here." She'd badgered Bridget until she finally agreed to an early morning coffee and bagel at the diner.

She and Kareema had been best friends since grade school. Bridget had told the little black girl that Kareema Justice sounded like a superhero name and asked what her superpower was. Kareema answered that she could eat two double scoop ice cream cones in one sitting. Bridget told her to prove it. That afternoon she did, and a friendship was born. People called them the Odd Couple, with Bridget's freckled pale face and red hair, and Kareema's dark skin and poofy pigtails. They'd bonded in the back corner of the library over Harry Potter books. These days Kareema was the school librarian with a full and bouncy head of natural hair, and Bridget was trying to keep her head above water at the pub.

"I didn't have any choice but to drag you here after you started ignoring my calls and texts." Kareema shrugged, dabbing her lips with her napkin. "You know I don't put up with that for long. I couldn't physically grab you when you ghosted me when you lived in California, but now that you're back here, you're mine, girl." She leveled a firm gaze at her. It was a gaze Bridget called The Librarian Look, and Kareema had perfected it.

"What are you talking about? I didn't ghost you. I've just been busy…"

Kareema made a talking motion with her hand. "Wah wah wah. You were born busy. Too busy. Now spill it. What's going on?"

"Nothing!" Her face heated. Kareema was impossible to lie to. "Okay, there's a lot going on. You know Nana's going through chemo…"

"How's she doing?"

Bridget shook her head. "Not great, but she's a trooper. Enough of a trooper to bite my head off the other day."

She told Kareema about the scene at Finn's apartment when she'd made such a fool of herself. When she'd hurt her grandmother's feelings. When Finn had been nice to her. Again.

"So tell me about this Irishman."

She sat back. "Seriously? I tell you about an argument with my grandmother, who has cancer, and you want to know about the Irish guy who just happened to be there?"

"Uh…yeah. He happened to be there because you let yourself into his apartment. You never rent to men, especially after that kid…" She was referring to the guy who was standing next to Bridget's bed one night. He'd scared her nearly to death. To be fair, her scream had scared him half to death. She didn't sleep well for weeks after that, and still had the occasional nightmare about it. Kareema cupped her chin in her hand. "And he's Irish? Accent and all?"

"Accent and all."

"And you hired him to bartend at the Shamrock? Just like that?"

Bridget rolled her eyes. "I didn't hire him. He offered to trade his services in exchange for using Dad's old office. Until I can actually hire someone, it will give Luke and Timothy a break. It made sense."

Kareema's mouth twisted as she tried not to laugh. "Uh-huh. Perfect sense. When's he going to be there, because I need to see this guy who got you to trust him just like that." She snapped her fingers. "It's not like you, so he must be something special."

He kinda was, but she wasn't ready to admit that yet. Not to her best friend or to herself. Finn was settled. Steady. At peace with himself somehow. And that seemed to rub off on her when she was with him. When she wasn't trying to fight it, he settled her, too. He got her to talk about stuff that she normally kept bottled inside. It was like flipping a release valve, and it felt good.

"Ooh, girl, he is special!" Kareema laughed and

playfully swatted Bridget's hand. "He's got you going all dreamy-eyed. Are you two—" she winked "—getting it on or something? 'Cuz God knows you need some."

"Need some what?" Bridget waved to Evelyn Rosario behind the counter for her tab. Evelyn and her daughter Evie ran the Spot, but Evie was traveling with her husband, Mark, that week. "And no, I'm not getting it on with Finn O'Hearn. Get real. Like I need that kind of complication in my life."

Her friend watched her over the rim of her coffee cup. "If you ask me, that's exactly the kind of complication you need." They paid up and walked outside together. It was a little warmer today, and the sun was bright, making downtown Rendezvous Falls look like a sparkly Christmas card. Kareema gave her a hug. "Make things right with your grandmother, hon. I don't like the idea of you two fighting. And stop ignoring my calls. If you aren't gonna get it on with McIrish, then you need to spend time with your friends. You know what they say about all work and no play."

Bridget nodded, ignoring the suggestion that she should pursue some…adventure…with Finn. Not a chance. Totally bad idea. She made the short drive back home, trying to remember exactly why it was such a bad idea. He was her tenant…awkward. He was older…but not by that much. She had too much happening in her life…but a diversion might be fun. And he was tempting… She slammed her car door.

She was really bad at coming up with reasons not to think about being with Finn.

I like the feel of a real book in my hands…

She wondered what else he liked in his hands. She shook off that fantasy as she went upstairs. Focus, Bridget. She had stuff to do. Vacuum and dust. Put together a liquor order for the bar. Do laundry. Avoid Finn.

She started sorting her clothes to wash. She couldn't believe she'd used her key to go into his apartment. She'd knocked first…but barely. She came in hot, and Finn had rightly been angry about it. Then she'd hurt Nana's feelings. She could see it in the way Nana had physically recoiled, then come in for the attack before storming out. Bridget had been an idiot. It seemed to be her new fallback position. She was a bundle of rage these days, and she'd crossed a line. A whole bunch of lines.

Including baring a bit of her soul to Finn O'Hearn after Nana left. Of course, he'd shared a bit of himself, too, with all his talk of Indiana Jones and his books.

She looked around her home as she sorted her laundry. The upstairs apartment was spacious and bright, painted a sunny yellow that Nana had picked out. She'd told Bridget she spent so much time in a dark, noisy pub that she needed her home to be the opposite. Light, peaceful, open. And she was right. It was easier to breathe here, away from the pressures of her life.

She'd pulled her long hair into a braided knot that morning. She was always threatening to cut it short, but she never quite got there. The dark red hair was a reminder of her father. Flawed though he may have been, she'd loved him. And he'd left far too soon. It hardly seemed fair that he'd worked so hard to beat his alcoholism, then died just a few years later. She got his red hair. And the bar.

She changed into a pair of leopard-print leggings— a joke gift from Kelly last Christmas—and a bright orange T-shirt before slipping her feet into an old pair of canvas flats by the door. Nice, comfortable house-work attire.

Dad made more than a few decisions in this old house that really could have used a woman's input. Like…leaving the laundry hookups in the base-ment. And not adding a light switch at the top of the stairs. To his credit, he'd cleaned up that corner by the cellar stairs and painted the floor a silver-gray. The walls, though, were the dark, rounded stones of the hundred-and-some-year-old foundation. Despite her father's efforts, the basement always felt a little creepy to her.

She got to the bottom of the cellar stairs, then bal-anced the clothes basket on one hip while reaching up for the string to turn on the light. That's when her fingers came in contact with a warm hand that did not belong to her already on the light string.

She let out a scream, throwing the basket to fend

off whoever, or whatever, was hiding down there waiting for her. Then she started swinging her fists.

Through her panic, it started to register that a male voice was speaking.

"Sorry. Shit. Sorry. Ow! Sorry. Bridget, it's me… it's Finn!"

She stopped hitting him, her chest rising and falling as she fought for breath.

"Finn?"

The light came on, making her blink. She hardly recognized him in his basketball shorts and ragged T-shirt, hair tousled and on end. And oh good Lord, he was wearing glasses. Dark-rimmed, studious, sexy glasses. He'd grabbed one of her hands and was holding it just inches from his face. His eyes were dark with regret.

"Oi, I'm so sorry, Bridget. I swear I wasn't trying t' spook you."

She pulled her hand back and placed it over her heart, which was threatening to leap out of her chest.

"I'd hate to see what you could do if you were actually trying. What the hell are you doing down here in the pitch dark?"

"It's not that dark once your eyes adjust. I'd forgotten to get my last load of laundry out of the dryer last night, so I just ran down to grab it. I heard you on the stairs and reached for the light. Maybe I should have spoken first, but I thought a voice from the dark would scare you."

It probably would have terrified her. The guy had

been in a no-win situation. Her heart rate began to settle.

"Okay, yeah…that probably would have been worse." There was a pile of socks and…men's underwear…on the dryer. He ran his fingers through his dark hair, and she realized he was sweaty. Not nervous sweaty. Workout sweaty. His arms were sinewed and lean, with that Celtic knot tattoo she'd spied before, as well as another tat peeking out from under the sleeve of his tee. Was that a dragon tail? If only she could push up that sleeve and see… Bridget took a step back. Whoa. It must be the adrenaline from her scare making her think so crazy.

"Okay…" She tried to rein in her scattered thoughts. "Okay. No harm, no foul. I'm sorry if I hit you…" Her shoulders fell. "It seems all I do is apologize to you. It's been a tough month. Winter. Year. Or two." Saying that out loud deflated her.

Finn paused, and his voice went soft. "Have you cleared things up with Maura?"

"Not yet. But I will. I'm just…tired, like I said. I'm worn out, and I took that out on you."

They both bent to pick up her laundry from the floor, nearly bumping heads in the process.

Bridget pulled back. "I'm sorry…"

"You really need to stop sayin' that." Finn's voice was firm, but not angry. More like…insistent. Concerned.

"I know. I'm…" She caught herself with a short laugh. "Oh my God, you're right. I don't know what… Oh, no! Give me that!" She snatched a silky pink bra with molded cups out of his hand. Good Lord, the man was picking up her dirty underwear! Her cheeks went hot. "Look, I promise to never say the s-word again if you'll please stop handling my underwear!"

His right brow rose at that sentence, which came across more suggestive than intended.

"I mean," she stammered, "I'll pick this up. I don't want you—or any man, for that matter—touching my dirty undies."

Nonplussed, he kept tossing items back into the basket. "I grew up with a wee sis who left her dainties hanging over the shower bar every damn day. It's just cloth, Bridget." He picked up a fistful of panties in a rainbow of bright colors, rendering her speechless. The corner of his mouth twitched, but he seemed to think better of whatever he'd been going to say, and put them in the basket. That was the last of it, and they both stood.

He'd piqued her curiosity. "Do you miss your family? Are they all in Ireland?"

He leaned back against the dryer, hands in his pockets. She'd figured out that was something he did when he was thinking through what to say next. It was a tell of his. The fact that she'd picked up on it meant she'd been paying a little too much attention to the man.

"My mum and dad are in Sallins, outside o' Dublin. My sis and her fam are in Kildare. I have aunties and uncles and cousins all over—Spain, London, Australia. But somehow I'm the only one who landed in the States." He hesitated. "And yeah, I miss them. I'm heading home this fall for my parents' fiftieth anniversary, but that'll be my first trip in two years."

"Why?"

"Eh, the divorce, mostly." He stared at his feet, his voice low. "Money was tight. And I wasn't the best company for a while. I shut out a lot of people, the good along with the bad." He straightened, pulling his hands from his pockets and clearing his throat. "And most important was goin' back coulda' messed up my visa application. Especially while I was…between jobs."

She stuffed her laundry into the washing machine so it wasn't out on display.

"You want to become a citizen?"

He shrugged. "Maybe. But I just want some stability for now. I…I made a mess at my last job, and your government frowns on switching visa sponsors when you're going for a green card. I wanted to avoid any hassles."

"A green card? Can't you just marry someone for that?"

He grinned. "Why? Are you offering?"

Her laughter sounded high-pitched and nervous in her own ears.

"Hey, you already got an office out of me. Don't go asking for marriage, too." She tipped her head to the side. "Even needing a green card couldn't keep your marriage together?"

His green eyes cooled. "For one thing, marrying your way to a green card is a lot more complicated than it looks in the movies. And I didna' marry Dori for a green card. I loved her."

Bridget's voice dropped to a near whisper. "What happened?"

"There are a lot of things I can forgive, but shaggin' another man and throwing it in my face isn't one of them."

She sucked in a sharp breath. "Oh...ouch. I know from experience that a cheating partner can really mess you up." He gave her a curious look, and—as always around this guy—she spilled the story. "I didn't find out until after he dumped me that my so-called fiancé had been sleeping around. With pretty much everyone on the West Coast."

"What an arse."

"No argument here." The washing machine was gently tossing her lingerie back and forth across the glass door. "Well...I've got stuff to do." She turned for the stairs and went back up to the main floor, with Finn following. Instead of going to her place, she stopped by the big staircase, not eager to leave his company. He seemed to feel the same, because he stood there beside her.

"Is that why you came back here from California then? You found out he was playin' you?"

She sat on the steps and looked up at Finn. "No.

My dad died unexpectedly and left me the bar. And the house. And his debts. Yay, me."

He looked around the hallway. It was clean, but outdated and tired. Just like her.

"If you need any work done, I'm fairly handy," he said, still looking around. "I could help around here if you'd like. Seems you're under a bit of stress…"

That was the understatement of the century.

"Not necessary, but thanks. I'll get to it eventually. I can handle it."

He sat on the step below hers, resting his arm on his knee. "It's not a matter of what you can do, it's a matter of letting someone else share the load. Your fiancé didn't come back to help when your dad died?"

"Nope. Turned out my commitment to the relationship was very different than his. He acted like I suggested he move into a cave somewhere when I told him I had to come back and asked him to come with me. Dropped me like a hot rock, and I never saw it coming. I guess he actually left the relationship a year before, and just forgot to tell me. You know what they say—love is blind."

He huffed a soft laugh. Seated above him, she could see the swirling curls in his dark hair. She closed her hands into fists to keep from reaching out and touching them. Then he looked up. "I missed the signs, too. Late-night classes and meetings. The furtive looks and touches between them. I didn't see any of it until all of a sudden I saw all of it. I felt like a dunce."

She nodded, knowing just how he felt. They sat there in silence, and it was…nice. Comfortable. As if she was finally still, letting the rest of the world spin without her for once. Finn cleared his throat.

"Have you thought any more about taking my help with updating the pub with a more Irish feel?"

He'd jumped the tracks on their conversation topic, but she went with it. Things had been getting a little too intimate. "Right now, I'm just trying to get ready for our busiest month. March has St. Patrick's Day, and things get crazy. Besides, I told you before that just because you're from Ireland, that doesn't make you a bar expert."

"Have you been t' Ireland?" Finn's right brow arched, telling her he'd guessed the answer.

"No, but…"

"Then yes, just because I'm actually Irish, I know enough to help at least a little on things Irish. Oh, and did I mention my sis and her husband own a pub in County Kildare?"

"Uh…no. You might have led with that, you know."

"Just to be clear, I'm not looking t' tell you what to do. I'm just saying I can answer questions on decor and food and such." His face screwed up. "For example, unicorns aren't Irish."

She cringed. Nana loved unicorns, and they were scattered around the pub—posters, figurines, and there was even a Unicorn Cocktail on the menu, with edible glitter on top.

"But that song…an Irish group sang it, about how the unicorns were playing around and missed Noah's ark. It's one of Nana's favorite Irish songs!"

Finn scrubbed his hands down his face, then gave her a pointed look. "You see? This is what I'm talking about. You Yanks think that song's Irish. Sure, it was written by the famous Irishman, Shel Silverstein."

She laughed. Damn, it had been a while since she'd belly-laughed like that. "Really? I mean, I knew it wasn't an ancient traditional song or anything, but I thought it was at least Irish."

Something shifted in his expression as he watched her laughing. Did she see a flare of heat there? And why did something flutter inside of her at the same time? She blinked and looked away. Her laughter faded, but not her smile.

"You're saying if I want to make the place more sincerely Irish in food and decor, that I should come to you for guidance?"

He nodded. "I'm happy to help, Bridget. By the way, did you know you were named for an Irish saint from County Kildare?"

She nodded. "I'm glad to hear you confirm that at least that story is true. St. Bridget is the patron saint of beer, right?"

Finn chuckled. "Yeah. She turned a whole lake

into the stuff, according to legend. Did you know she was named for a pagan goddess, Brigid?"

"No way! A goddess? Nana never told me that." Which made sense. Nana wasn't one to talk about pagans of any sort. Father Brennan would never approve.

His smile deepened, and so did the heat in his gaze. Had he moved closer? Or was it her leaning toward him? Her leg was almost brushing his arm. He reached up and tucked a strand of her hair behind her ear. Such a sweet, intimate gesture. Her heart skipped a beat. Or three. His voice lowered.

"Aye, makes sense, really. Brigid was the Goddess of Fire and Hearth. Appropriate for a chef and pub owner, right? And someone who acts just a bit like a goddess herself?" His fingertips lingered on the soft skin behind her ear, and she didn't mind it at all. His touch was warm. Comforting. Inviting. And then it was gone.

He seemed surprised to realize how close they were, clearing his throat and standing abruptly. She stood too, refusing to acknowledge her irrational disappointment at his move. She was one step above him, leaving them eye to eye.

"Just to be clear," she said, "I do not act like a goddess…I'm just…"

"Wanting everyone to do what you say without question?" His crooked smile told her he was teasing. She gave a playful shrug. Things had grown weird there for a moment, but she'd regrouped.

"I can't help it if I'm just...right...most of the time. It's a lot easier for all concerned when people don't test me."

Now it was his turn to laugh out loud.

"Well said, goddess." He turned and picked up his laundry from where he'd set it on the steps. "I'll leave you to your busy day ruling the world."

She sat there a long time after he left, wondering at how his touch made her feel. How he'd made her laugh. Their relationship, for lack of a better word, had gone from adversarial to...friendly? With a hint of chemistry? She scoffed at herself. She had to be imagining that part.

But when he called her a goddess, there was something in his voice. His gaze. Something that almost made her believe she was one.

CHAPTER SIX

"So, ARE YOU getting settled in at your new place? It must feel good to have an actual address again." Howard Greer glanced up over the rim of his glasses at Finn. Greer was going over the draft of Finn's article for the European Historical Review publication. Finn knew the research was solid, but Greer had a reputation for micromanaging everyone, and it seemed especially true with Finn. The man's suspicious nature was starting to grate on Finn's nerves, but he also had half a hunch that's exactly what the old man wanted—to test Finn to see if he'd lose his cool.

It was Finn's own damn fault. He'd created a reputation for himself that was the polar opposite of how he'd lived his life right up until the moment he discovered his wife was sleeping with his best friend and coworker. That sort of thing tended to push any man to act out, right? Eh…maybe punching Vince in the face at commencement was a step too far. Or at least too public.

"Finn? Your apartment? You're not having trouble there, are you?"

Finn straightened. "No, sir. Not at all. The apartment is perfect, and my landlord is…" He almost said a delight, but that might sound a bit much. But Bridget had brought a lightness into his life over the past few weeks, especially after their conversation in the basement. She was smart and funny under that sharp exterior, and he was starting to look forward to their almost chats in the neutral territory of the office he'd taken over across the hall. He liked working late at night. She'd made a habit of stopping by after the pub closed. "My landlord is kind and fair. We're getting along great."

Greer's bushy gray eyebrows shot upward. "Bridget McKinnon? Don't get me wrong, she's respected and thought of fondly because of her family, but I don't think I've heard the word *kind* used to describe her. More like tough and maybe even difficult." The man sat back in his chair and stared hard at Finn. "Is there anything going on you want to tell me about, O'Hearn?"

"What? No! Bridget's allowed me to make use of some vacant space downstairs to accommodate my books. She's a grand girl, really. I mean…"

Greer huffed, and then his mouth flattened into a hard line. "I thought for a minute there you might be making some actual connections in Rendezvous Falls, Finn. Some friends. A social life. You know, like you were someone who really wanted to stay. I took a chance when I sponsored that work visa for you." Finn willed his face to stay expressionless until he knew where Greer was going, but his back straightened just a little. Greer pointed at him. "The other candidate for your job may not have been as qualified, but he was more stable, with a wife and a family. He reached out to me last week to see how things were going."

Yeah, Finn could just bet he did. His jaw tightened. "Are you threatening to give my job to someone else?"

"No. But I am reminding you that I have options. I like you, O'Hearn, but eventually the bigger schools will forget about your little…situation…in North Carolina. You'll get offers. I'm just skeptical that you'll want to stay at Brady College if you get a call from Yale or something."

Finn started to relax. Greer didn't have a grudge against Finn. He was just afraid Finn was going to bail on him.

"Okay. That's fair. But right now I need you a hell of a lot more than you need me, so you don't have to worry about me going anywhere. There is no way I want to switch schools again until I have a green card securely in my hand, and that takes time. Even then, I don't know that I'll want to go anywhere. I'm very appreciative of the chance you took on me, and I owe you. Truly."

Greer stared at him, then nodded. "I'm glad you feel that way. I told you about that endowment we got for a new history building. We have to match those funds in order for the project to move forward, and I still think you're just the guy to do it."

"Me?" Finn put his hand on his chest. "I just got here. No one knows me." The one thing he didn't miss after teaching at a major university was all the glad-handing he'd been expected to do with donors and alumni. "I'm more of a desk guy."

"Not anymore, you're not. Look, people love that accent of yours. Chat up the locals, attend some receptions I'm putting together so you can meet the movers and shakers. But the local folks are going to want to see you somewhere other than just receptions. They want to see you in the community. Make some friends. Find a girl. Or a guy if that's your thing. I don't care. Just get out there and pour on some Irish charm for people. Let them get to know you."

"I've only been here since before the holiday break." Finn gestured toward the papers on Greer's desk. "And I've been busy working on this article, working on class plans, finding a place to live. Besides, I have friends. Rick Thomas. Uh…Bridget, of course. And Luke Rutledge. Give me more than a minute living here, and I'll have a whole circle of pals." Agitation simmered under Finn's skin. Would he always be dancing so hard to manage other people's expectations of him? "To be honest, sir, I scheduled this time to discuss my paper and my possible tenure. Not my personal life. I'm a private man."

"Before I can talk tenure, you're going to have

to step up. Like I said, I did you a favor bringing you here."

Finn threw his hands up. "I get that you took a chance, and I'm grateful. But let's not forget that your college landed a tenured professor from a major university. Why can't I get tenure here?"

He saw the chill settle over Greer. He knew better than to snap at the old guy. His boss stared down at his desk, brows gathered together, not saying a word. The tall clock in the corner was tick-tick-ticking in the silence. Finn waited.

"I know you want more, but like you said, you haven't been here long. Finish the semester. Secure us some funds for that building. After that, we'll talk tenure."

Greer hesitated, his gray eyes fixed on Finn. "I know you think I'm being a pain in your ass just for the pure hell of it." The language made Finn sit straighter. Who knew Old Man Greer could swear? "And yes, you've told me your side of things, but that doesn't change the fact that you used a colleague down in North Carolina as a punching bag on stage. During graduation. Whether you like to admit it or not, you're just going to have to tolerate my suspicions, even when they involve your so-called personal life." Greer removed his glasses and started cleaning the lenses with a tissue. He seemed to be settling into this little lecture of his.

"Because it seems to me it's your personal life that keeps interfering with your professional one.

You're not the first man to be cuckolded by his wife, O'Hearn. But you need to decide if you're going to let someone else's actions define who you are, or if you're going to start living your own life again. You know what they say about all work and no play, my boy. Closing yourself up in that apartment with a pile of books isn't doing a thing to inspire my confidence in your commitment to this town or this college."

Finn jammed his fingers into his hair, grinding his words through clenched teeth. "Christ, man, I'm just trying to keep my head down and do my job. I know my personal life destroyed the career I had, but I'm trying to rebuild something here. I've learned from my mistakes, and I'm making an intentional effort to keep my job and my life separate." He closed his eyes tight, swallowing his frustration before opening them again. "You want to see a commitment from me to the school and the town and all, but I need to see some commitment, too. This paper should be enough to get me tenure. You said I needed to have something published quickly, which isn't easy, but there it is."

Greer flipped through the outline, his mouth twisting. Maybe Finn was being paranoid, but he got the distinct impression the man was irritated that he couldn't find anything wrong with it. He slid the papers back across the desk toward Finn and shook his head.

"It looks good, but we need to see if Brady College is really a good fit. For you. For us. You've not taught at a small college like this before. It's not everyone's cup of tea. The college is an integral part of…"

"Let me guess—the community, right?" Finn's annoyance flared. "You've made that abundantly clear."

"I'm a little concerned that the request seems to have you chafing already. I know Rendezvous Falls is no Raleigh or Dublin, but…"

Finn leaned forward. "I grew up in a town in County Kildare that was less than a quarter the size of Rendezvous Falls. Small towns don't chafe at me or frighten me or bore me or anything else. I'm highly adaptable. But I'm more than a little concerned that you're so thoroughly convinced I'm not going to stay. What do you want me to say? That I'm marrying a nice local girl and we're going to have a houseful o' wee bairn so there's no way I'll ever leave?"

Greer's eyes lit up. "Are you?"

Finn's brain stuttered to a halt. "Am I what?"

"Marrying a local girl?"

Finn started to laugh. Had Greer been drinking? He thought of the red-haired woman who'd jokingly suggested he marry for his green card.

"Yeah sure, haven't you heard the news? Bridget McKinnon and I are getting married. I'm head over heels with the lass." Greer's brows went ever higher, until his eyes were wide and round. The Irish were known for their storytelling, and Finn was just getting warmed up. May as well carry this farce to its conclusion. He leaned forward in his chair. "Oi, the whole renting the apartment thing was just a ruse. We've been secretly in love all this time and couldn't bear to be apart. But we wanted to keep it on the down low, you know? By renting her apartment, she and I can be…you know…together." He winked. "With no one being the wiser. Except you, of course. We couldn't fool you."

The older man puffed out his chest and raised his chin, preening under Finn's praise. And he wasn't laughing. Wait a minute… Greer wasn't buying this nonsense, was he? Was he so eager for Finn to show he was putting down roots that he fell for the wild story? Nah, he had to know it was a joke. Greer's smile grew wider.

"Well, I'll be damned. That's great news, Finn. I'm thrilled to hear it!"

Oh, shit. He really did believe it. Now what?

"Oh…uh…no…I mean…thanks, but…"

Jaysus! His mother had warned him about his flippant responses to serious questions. She always said he was too clever for his own good. His response to her scoldings was usually to laugh and thank Ma for calling him clever, which often resulted in her boxing his ears. And now his stupid mouth had walked him right into a corner and trapped him. If he told Greer he was joking, his boss might laugh at being fooled. Or he might just sack Finn on the spot for lying to him. His visa application would never survive another firing.

Greer was standing now, extending his hand. Like an idiot, Finn stood and took it.

Don't wait another minute or you'll be in too deep!

But his visa...

"Congratulations, Finn!" Greer was pumping his hand up and down. "Now I know why you've been so coy about your personal life—you were keeping secrets, but the happy kind!"

"Uh...well, no...actually..."

"The McKinnons are a wonderful family, and well respected in Rendezvous Falls." Greer was practically gushing. "Bridget's always been a bit of an outlier, of course, and she can be bristly, but she owns a local business and cares about this community. With you marrying a McKinnon, raising that money will be lot easier. Well done, O'Hearn. Well done."

Finn had to clear this up.

Right this minute.

Instead, he let his mind wander to what it would be like to have flame-haired Bridget as a girlfriend. A lover. A fiancée. Would it soften her hard edges? Would he want it to? Would it be too cute for the Irishman to date the owner of an Irish pub? The future of the pub was one of the things they'd debated in the downstairs office. Bridget would stop by at the end of her shift, and they'd start discussing the menu or the setup or the decor, and soon they'd be arguing and laughing about the best way to update the place. He shuddered at the thought of the debate they'd have if she ever learned of this conversation. There'd be no laughing then.

"I haven't exactly… I mean, we're not really…" Finn had to tell Greer the truth. He had to. But he also needed to get tenure and secure that visa. If he got fired, he might have to start the process all over. He might not even be able to have an application accepted again. And what school would want to sponsor him with such a checkered record? He needed some semblance of stability in his life, and if a harmless little fib could do it…?

He analyzed the data in his head. It's not like he and Greer—or Greer and Bridget, for that matter—hung out in the same social circles. He didn't need to extend a wedding invitation to the guy or anything. He started to shake his head in disbelief at what he was thinking. This was crazy. Crazy enough to work? Finn put a big, bright smile on his face. "What I mean to say is, she hasn't told her family yet, so we need to keep it on the down low, if you know what I mean. With her grandmother being ill, she doesn't want to freak them all out with a wedding. We're… uh…taking it slow." That would at least buy Finn some time to come up with a plan.

Greer barked out a sharp laugh. "Taking it slow? You're engaged to the woman just a few months after you moved here! But I get it. I'll keep it between us until you've made your announcement." He leaned in and winked. "I'll admit, the Purple Shamrock isn't a place I frequent very often. I prefer to enjoy my cocktails in a quieter sort of place, like the marina restaurant. But I know Maura McKinnon pretty well. With everything she's dealing with, a happy occasion like this might be exactly what she needs, you know. Don't wait too long."

Finn ran his tongue along his lower lip. This was a supremely bad idea. But he was in it now. Admitting the ruse would mean losing Greer's respect for good…at the very least. Once Finn got tenure and put in his green card application, he could tell Greer he and Bridget broke up. It happened all the time. Just another sad story. It was a victimless crime.

He blew out a long breath. There was no doubt who'd be the victim if Bridget ever found out about this. She'd skin him alive. Kick him out of her house. And make sure he was run out of Rendezvous Falls… and straight to Immigration.

MARY WALKED INTO the Purple Shamrock early Tuesday afternoon and sat at the bar without saying a word. Bridget and Kelly looked at each other uneasily. It wasn't all that unusual for their cousin to crave silence once in a while, with two little ones at home and one in her belly. She sometimes stopped by before the place was open to chat, but this seemed… different. Kelly lifted her hands in a shrug. Bridget watched for another minute before walking down to where Mary sat.

She set a tall, frosty glass of lemonade with a

twist of lime in front of her cousin. "You look like you need something stronger, but…you know…" She gestured at Mary's rounded stomach. "What's going on?"

Mary blinked a few times, and Bridget realized two things with a thud of her heart. Mary was fighting tears, and today had been Mary's morning to take Nana to a doctor's appointment.

"Nana…? The doctor…?"

Mary's shoulders slumped. "The doctor's appointment went fine, but she's just so…tired, Bridg. She's really down, and kind of out of it. Dr. Blakefield said it was probably what they call 'chemo brain.'"

"That doesn't sound good," Kelly blurted out, walking up behind Bridget. "Why is chemo in her brain? Is the cancer…"

"No, no. Not that. The tumor is shrinking, and the doctor was actually pretty pleased." Mary reached out and took Bridget's hand and nodded toward Kelly. "I'm sorry, I must have scared you two to death. My hormones are crazy right now. I cry at everything, I swear." She wiped her cheek with the back of her hand. "Nana was just…really upset. I mean, it's one thing for me to cry—that's a daily occurrence right now—but you guys, Nana cried."

Kelly and Bridget both sucked in their breath at the same time. Nana cried? Nana never cried. Not where anyone could see her, at least. The idea of her tough grandmother weeping was enough to shake the foundation of Bridget's impression of who

Maura McKinnon was. There was nothing wrong with tears, of course. But still…when someone who never cried broke down, it was…troubling. It would be like someone discovering Bridget in tears, which would never happen. Although Finn O'Hearn had come close to seeing it that first night he walked into the kitchen.

Bridget frowned. Her mind seemed determined to circle back to Finn, no matter what subject was at hand. Kelly rested her hand on top of Mary's, which was covering Bridget's on the bar.

"I've never seen Nana cry," Kelly said, "other than a drop or two when Uncle Patrick passed. What's this chemo brain thing the doctor mentioned?"

"He told me it varies, but the chemo can cause some people to get foggy and forgetful, or easily confused. And some people get unusually emotional." Mary frowned. "And before you ask, there's not much we can do. It should go away eventually, after chemo, but it might take a while. He said it can come in waves, and we should avoid stressing or confusing her when she gets like that. We need to be as positive as possible around her, and give her happy, stress-free things to focus on."

Kelly gave Bridget a quick side glance. "You mean like having a big St. Patrick's Day bash at the Shamrock?"

She groaned. They'd talked about this, and agreed that things were too complicated this year to go too crazy with a party. Nana's favorite thing to do was decorate for the annual event, but with her being sick, they'd decided it a good idea to skip it this year. Just serve some green beer and call it a day. But Nana had not been happy with the decision. And Nana's mental health was more important than keeping things "easy." Bridget finally raised both hands in surrender.

"Fine! We'll have a St. Patrick's Day party. We'll make it the biggest and best ever." She thought of Finn's complaints about the green beer. "But let's do it right. We'll make it genuinely Irish, not just a bunch of green alcohol. But we'll have to make sure Nana doesn't do any work. Are you sure a big party won't just stress her more?"

Mary had perked back up at the news of a party. "We can keep her away from the big crowd—maybe use that back corner booth. Oh, she'll be thrilled! Especially if you do a real Irish thing. Think Finn would help you? After all, the guy's been pestering you about it for weeks."

Kelly clapped her hands together. "Yay! The party's back!"

Her enthusiasm made Bridget suspicious. "You two didn't plan this just to get the party back, did you? Is Nana really…?"

Mary raised her hand to her chest in dramatically feigned offense.

"Are you suggesting I'd use Nana's health to coerce you into having the bash? It's pretty brilliant, as Finn would say, but I would never." She lifted her hand in a pledge. "I swear."

"I would," Kelly giggled, "but I didn't think of it. There's no evil plot here, Bridg. Just a party to make Nana happy."

Bridget looked between her two cousins through narrowed eyes, then nodded slowly in satisfaction. "Okay. We'll do it up big this year. For Nana's sake."

Mary scoffed. "As if you're working with Finn just for Nana."

"What does that mean?"

"It means I think you like this guy. And I approve."

"Me, too!" Kelly grinned. "He's been doing a great job at the bar. I wish we could get him more than one night a week. And even I think he's hot."

"You guys know I am not looking for a man. I've got enough…"

Mary shook her head. "Do not tell me again that you're too busy to have a relationship. That's an excuse and you know it."

"An excuse?" Bridget laughed. "Have you seen my life?"

"Stop." Mary gave her a hard look. "I'm a website designer who's about to have three children with a husband who spends more time in Albany than he does Rendezvous Falls." Simon Trask was a state legislator for their area. "Kelly's juggling her classes as well as working the pub and she found time to fall in love. So why can't you?"

"But Nana…"

Kelly laughed. "You really aren't going to use the woman who's grandmother to all three of us as your excuse?"

She shrugged. "I guess not. But honestly, the pub can be all-consuming…"

Mary stood to go. "Only if you let it be. And dating doesn't get much easier than having a gorgeous guy living right downstairs."

Bridget turned back to the kitchen with a wave. Easy wasn't exactly how she'd describe having Finn live under the same roof as her.

"You two are crazy."

But as she walked away, she wondered. Were they?

CHAPTER SEVEN

FINN WALKED ACROSS the lot to the pub Thursday
night, pulling his coat snug around him. Ireland had
its share of gray, raw weather, so American winters
hadn't caused him much worry when he came here
ten years ago. But his years in North Carolina had
spoiled him. He wasn't ready for the icy, snowy blast
of an Upstate New York winter. Temperatures were
headed below zero overnight, for the fourth night in
a row. With this wind it would feel downright arctic.

People here had laughed at his wool coat, insisting he'd need to get a down jacket or some sort of
high-tech insulation. But they didn't understand the
insulating factor of the hand-knit Irish sweater he
wore under the Irish wool coat. His grandmother
had made this sweater for him for Christmas, sending it to him in Raleigh eight years ago. He'd worn
it exactly once before moving to New York, but he
was sure glad to have it now.

The Shamrock was pretty busy for a Thursday
night. Looked like Bridget's cousin, Michael, had
a good idea with Trivia Night. Finn shrugged off
his coat and put it on a hook near the door. There

were some new faces in the crowd. Bridget would be happy to see that, since she was convinced they'd never bring new customers in unless they changed the restaurant's image completely. Michael was behind the bar, along with Kelly. Luke Rutledge walked out of the back, carrying two cases of beer. He saw Finn and nodded his way. Finn raised his hand in greeting, then froze.

Oh, shit. Howard Greer was standing at the bar. What the bloody hell was his stuffed-shirt boss doing in the Purple Shamrock? Hadn't he just told Finn he didn't come here? Why the ever-loving hell wasn't he sipping cocktails at the marina bar? Finn's pulse jumped. But wait, he'd told Greer that the so-called engagement was a secret, so there was no reason to think the guy would mention it here at the Shamrock…right?

Should Finn join him? Avoid him? Dash back out the door? Kick his own ass forever letting that little "joke" get so far out of hand? His dilemma was solved for him when Bridget peeked out from the kitchen and saw him standing there. Her face lit up, and all thoughts of leaving evaporated. Why had he never noticed that her smile extended up to put a light in her eyes? That it eased the corners of her mouth, leaving her lips full and soft?

She stepped out of the kitchen, and he headed toward her as if drawn by a magnet. Instead of wondering how to keep his phony engagement a secret, he wondered again what it would be like to be engaged to Bridget McKinnon. To make her smile the way she was smiling… Her eyes sharpened as she looked around the pub. Her lips moved just enough that he could tell she was counting heads.

When he reached her, she held up her hand to silence him as her survey continued. She shrugged, pinching her lips together as if impressed, but not wanting to be.

"Damn," she muttered. "Not bad for a weeknight."

Mike walking past them with a smirk. "Trivia Night was an awesome idea, and it's killing you that I was right." He practically sang the words. She flipped him a hand gesture, and he shook his head. "Nice. Don't you have cooking to do? I've got this under control out here."

She watched him walk away through narrowed eyes. Nearby, four older couples had pulled two tables together, and they simultaneously burst into laughter about something, raising their glasses of wine and beer and clinking them together. Bridget watched them for a moment, then lowered her shoulders with a half smile. "Ah, screw it. I don't care if it was Mike's idea or Santa Claus's. I'm just happy to see more than ten people here on a weeknight. Hey, have you eaten? I've got some of Nana's favorite chili back there."

"Wait. Your very Irish grandmother eats chili?"

Before Bridget could speak, Kelly rushed by with a tray of drinks and answered for her. "Nana may be Irish, but she's also an Upstate New Yorker. In February, chili is our go-to warm-up comfort food, and Bridget makes the best."

Bridget's mouth opened, then closed, as if Kelly's praise had left her speechless. Her cheeks went pink, and she blinked a few times, then looked up at Finn. "Wow. Is there some special alignment of the stars tonight or something? Mike had an actual good idea, my grandmother is here and Kelly just gave me a compliment. I feel like I should buy a lottery ticket or something."

Finn looked around, scanning faces. "Your grandmother's here? I thought she was avoiding crowds?" He spotted Maura at a corner booth. She had a bright green scarf tied around her head. She had Bridget's sharp features, including the cheekbones. Her pallor was a little dull, but she was laughing softly at something Father Brennan was telling her.

Finn had met the good Father before Christmas. Rick was convinced they'd get along, since they were both Irish. Finn had learned since coming to America that people tended to lump groups together and think they had to be friends if they were both Irish, or black, or professors, or whatever identification people assigned to them. Therefore, from Ireland meant instant bond.

And damn if, with Father Joe, it hadn't happened just like that. A large part of the credit went to Joe, of course. The priest was impossible to dislike, with his quick laugh and deep wisdom both shared liberally. Finn had to admit it was nice to speak with someone knowledgeable of Irish hurling teams without the jokes about the American definition of the word hurling. In Ireland, it was a brutal sport similar to lacrosse in that wooden sticks were swung, trying to capture a small ball. But the sticks were more like hockey sticks. Finn had played in a county league for a year or two and had the scars to prove it. But gah, it was fun.

"When she makes up her mind to do something, there's no stopping her," Bridget said. "She was determined to support Michael's idea of Trivia Night. I tried to tell her she shouldn't come, but…" Her voice faded off.

"Is everything okay?"

Bridget blinked. "Yes, it's fine. Nana's just had a rough week or two. We're trying to put on our happiest faces for her. At least she agreed to sit in the back corner. Father Joe's making sure she stays there." She watched Michael come back out to the bar. He looked her way and nodded toward the back in a clear suggestion that that's where she needed to be. "I'd better get going. Are you staying for trivia?"

He'd had no intention of doing so, but he needed to keep an eye on Greer. "Um…yeah. Definitely. Promised Mikey and all that. Gotta do my part, right?"

"Do your part for who? You don't owe Michael anything, do you?"

"Well, Mike's a friend of mine." That was a stretch at this point, but he and Mike did share the same dark humor. "But I meant do my part for you, Bridget." Her eyes went wide and he realized that may not have come out right. "I mean…I know it's not my night to tend bar, but I want the place to succeed, so I came to support you." He gave her a wink, trying to lighten the awkward moment. "I'm not a monster."

Mike whistled sharply to get her attention again, and she headed back toward the kitchen. "Gotta go. And the jury's still out on the monster thing." She returned his wink before leaving, and his chest went tight. He really liked it when Bridget let her guard down and showed her playful side. He had no business liking her this much, though. A relationship, real or fake, was the last thing he needed. He glanced Greer's way.

If she ever caught wind of the ridiculous tale he'd let the man believe, she'd boot his ass to the curb, and he'd deserve it. He was glad to see her leave the bar area. With any luck, she'd be too busy to come back out here while Greer was around.

MAURA HAD BEEN blinking back tears all night. She didn't even know why this crying jag was prowling under the surface. She was sick of riding this emotional roller coaster she'd been on. She had cancer. That sucked. She was having caustic chemicals pumped into her body through a port in her chest. That sucked. Her hair was gone. She was always tired. In a few months, she'd be having surgery. That all sucked. But "chemo brain" was the final straw.

She'd been through tough times before. She'd buried a husband, a son, a daughter-in-law, her sister… Had she shed tears then? Of course. But almost always in private. Publicly, she'd been a proper matriarch—strong, confident, composed. She was the one who kept the family moving forward, who came up with the plans and set them in motion.

But now? Now she felt her emotions and reactions were either out of control like tonight, or buried in a thick cover of fog layered over quicksand. She was forgetful and fuzzy-brained. It was a constant struggle not to cry all the time. For no specific reason. Just…cry. She wanted it more than she'd ever wanted anything—to sob and throw things and curse the world and everyone in it.

"Maura, are you feelin' alright?" Father Joe Brennan leaned toward her. "You look a bit off."

She adored the Irish priest who'd come to town a few years ago and had quickly become everyone's favorite holy man, whether they were Catholic or not. There was something about his quick wit and sparkling eyes that never missed a trick. He'd been in the States a lot longer than Bridget's tenant, Finn, but he still had his gentle Irish brogue. He was of average height, but people described him as a leprechaun because of his accent and happy attitude. He was also a human lie detector, so there was no sense in trying to fool him.

"The doctors and nurses call it chemo brain. The meds are reacting with my emotions, and…" She fought back the tears that brimmed in her eyes. "I'm just a mess, Joseph. I'm sad all the time. And please don't tell me to count my blessings or whatever. I'm not in the mood. It's like being a darkened room and not being able to pull the curtains back to let the sun in. I know it's shining, but not for me. Not right now."

A few tears broke free, and she rushed to brush them from her cheeks. Father Joe patted her hand.

"Maura, love, it's part of my job description to see blessings everywhere. But it's not part of yours. It's perfectly okay to let yourself be sad and tired and even angry. I have it on good authority that the Guy Upstairs can take it." He smiled. "I'll keep track of the blessings when you cannot."

She did her best to smile, but felt it tremble on her lips. "Thank you, Father Joe. I just hate feeling as if my own thoughts and feelings are not under my control."

A round of cheers came from a table with four couples seated at it. Cal Watkins, from the college's art department, was emceeing the trivia contest, and apparently that table had all ten questions in the first category correct. Maura pulled her shoulders back and raised her chin in determination.

"I'll be fine. Tonight's just what I needed. Look how successful Michael's idea was! I know he didn't exactly invent bar trivia, but he'd pushed Bridget hard to bring it to the Purple Shamrock. And did I tell you the kids are going to have a St. Patrick's Day bash here next month? Just like old times, when my husband, and then my son, were still alive."

Joe's eyebrows rose. "Truly? I thought Bridget was determined to leave all the Irish stuff behind? What happened to all her plans of changing the place?"

Maura shrugged. She had a feeling Bridget's change of heart about keeping the pub Irish had to do with Maura's illness, and being appeased wasn't what Maura wanted. At least…it shouldn't be what Maura wanted. But if it kept the shamrocks in the Shamrock, she'd take it. Seeing the place reinvented as some modern wine bar or whatever would depress Maura more than she already was.

"I think she's only doing it to make me happy, bless her heart. And I have to admit I'm looking forward to the party. She's even managed to locate a band from Buffalo who was available to play Irish music." Maura saw a familiar face across the room. Victoria Pendergast was standing at a table near the door, laughing with an older man. It took Maura a moment to place his face—damn this chemo brain—but she figured it out eventually. It was Howard Greer from the college. He tended to be a bit of a stick-in-the-mud, and she'd hardly ever seen him at the Shamrock. But tonight, he was smiling so widely that Maura could see his gleaming teeth, even from this distance. Had he had those teeth whitened?

He reached out and took Vickie's hand. Oh, boy. Maura thought her friend had given up her man-hunting ways after her last husband left her for a much younger woman. But there was a gleam in Vickie's eye when she smiled at Howard that said she was very much back in the game. Greer pulled a chair up to the table and she sat at his side, scooching up nice and close. He physically preened at the attention, making Maura chuckle. Father Joe followed her gaze and nodded.

"I heard Vickie and Howard were gettin' on. They

were at the Spot Diner for breakfast together a few days ago." Of course he knew. The priest had the best gossip grapevine in town. "Howard has a spring in his step I haven't seen from him in a long time. D'ya think it's serious?"

"I'm not sure." Strange that Vickie hadn't mentioned this new relationship of hers. It made her wonder what else people weren't telling her. Did they think they were protecting her somehow? Of all people, Vickie should know better.

Vickie's eyes suddenly went wide and round at something Greer said. Maura could tell she was saying what? in shock. Had Howard gotten fresh? Nah—Vickie liked a flirtatious man, so she wouldn't be upset at that. Then Vickie looked over and met Maura's eyes, mouthing wow. Now Maura was really curious. Vickie grilled Howard for another few minutes. When the trivia contest moved into the third category, Vickie left his table with an affectionate pat of his shoulder, and headed straight for Maura.

She greeted Father Joe as she sat, then turned to Maura. "Have you been keeping secrets, my dear?"

Maura had a feeling it wasn't just the chemo that made the question so confusing. "Me? What about you and your new friend, Howard?"

Vickie waved off the question, but her cheeks went pink. Yup, she was falling for a new man. "We're just friends," Vickie lied. "It's not like we're engaged or anything." Vickie gave her a suggestive and expectant look, but Maura had no idea what she was fishing for. Vickie tried again. "I don't have a wedding to plan—not yet, anyway—but it appears you do."

"What the hell are you talking about?" She glanced at Joe. "Sorry, Father. But really, Vickie, who is it you think is getting married?" Even Joe seemed lost, and he knew everything.

Maura looked toward the bar, where Kelly was laughing with Michael. Kelly was with a lovely young woman named Cecily, but that wasn't news. Michael had barely dated since losing his wife. Mary and Timothy were happily married. And Lord knew it couldn't be...

"Bridget, you ninny!" Vickie crowed. "Finn told Howard all about it. They're engaged. They met when he got here last fall, and I guess it was love at first sight." Vickie was practically gushing. There was nothing she liked better than weddings—hers or anyone else's. "And now they're engaged!" Vickie was bouncing in her seat. "Of course, Finn told Howard to keep it quiet, but he knew he could trust me. And Howard can't keep a secret to save his life." Neither could Vickie, apparently.

Maura's mouth was open, but she had no words. Father Joe jumped in. "Perhaps Bridget's been waiting for the right moment to surprise you, Maura."

Vickie took in a sharp breath. "Oh my God—you didn't know?"

"It must be a mistake. Greer's not exactly a spring chicken, and he must have been confused..."

Vickie bristled in defense of her man. "Howard is a college president. There's nothing wrong with his cognitive skills. Finn told him the whole story—how he only took the apartment so they could be living together without anyone knowing…" She hesitated. "Oh, maybe she did want to keep it a secret from you. But why would she be afraid to tell you? Do you not like Finn O'Hearn?"

Maura looked around the bar. People were milling about as Cal compiled all the trivia scores from the various teams, but she thought she'd seen Finn earlier. Ah, there he was, leaning against the bar, talking quietly with Cecily, who laughed at something he said. Kelly walked over to join them. They all seemed familiar and friendly with Finn. Did everyone in the family know about this but her?

He seemed like a lovely man, and the fact that he spoke with that Irish accent was a bonus. But all Bridget did was complain about the guy! He had all sorts of opinions about the bar, and Lord knew Bridget didn't want any more of those. She complained about the way he "hogged" the laundry room, and how he'd taken over the vacant office…although it seemed she'd given him permission for that. She said he was "stodgy" and "bookish." But as Maura watched him now, hip against the bar, smiling at Bridget's cousins, all she saw was a man comfortable in his skin. Comfortable where he was, with the people he was with.

"I bet Father Joe is right," Vickie was saying. "They probably wanted to surprise you, and I just blew it." Vickie was watching Finn, too. "On the bright side, the man is a catch and a half, Maura.

Better than anyone the book club could have come up with. Oh, look—there's Bridget now! And Howard is talking to her. I'll bet he's congratulating her on the news…"

Maura watched and wondered. Her granddaughter did not look like a happy bride-to-be being congratulated. While a wisp of a steely smile remained on her face, those McKinnon eyes were full of murder. Was it Maura's fuzzy brain that was making everything seem…off? Or was something seriously off kilter with this engagement?

Father Joe apparently picked up on the same undercurrent Maura had as he watched Bridget and Howard across the pub. "Perhaps she's just angry the secret is out?"

There was a flurry of motion near the bar. Finn O'Hearn was practically sprinting toward Bridget and Greer. And again, Bridget's reaction was off. She didn't greet him as a lover would. She fixed him with a glare that could peel paint, her eyes dark and hard.

But wait…Finn slid his arm around her waist. He tugged her stiff body close, then lowered his head and whispered something in her ear that made her laugh sharply. She pushed on his chest. When he didn't budge, she looked up into his eyes and, after a brief moment, her expression softened, her mouth going slack. She mouthed the word *really?* at him, and he nodded, glancing at Greer before moving away from her with a slow shake of his head.

"Holy cats," Vickie muttered. "Now do you believe what Howard said? There's a whole romance novel's worth of chemistry going on between those two."

Maura couldn't disagree, although she wasn't sure if it was tension or heat between them. Maybe a bit of both. She couldn't hold back her smile. There was something about the look in Bridget's eyes as she gazed at Finn. They were having a silent exchange, the way lovers did. Damn. Maybe Bridget and Finn really were engaged.

A quick surge of excitement pulsed through her. Maura hadn't felt this vibrant in weeks. A wedding! Maybe in the fall? She'd be done with chemo and surgery by then, and hopefully well on the mend. But would she have her hair back? She touched her hand to her scarf. Maybe she could talk Bridget into waiting for a winter wedding.

Vickie leaned toward her. "I wonder what's going on over there? Howard looks so confused. I hope they aren't fighting… Oh, look at that…"

Finn had been moving away from Bridget, but she stopped him, reaching up to grab his shirt, sliding closer to his side before turning to Howard with a bright smile. Then she looked over at the corner booth where Maura was. Again, something was off with Bridget, but she regrouped and smiled up at Finn. And then…they kissed.

CHAPTER EIGHT

"Why yes, it is true, Dr. Greer. Finn and I were just trying to keep it a...surprise."

Bridget's brain was spinning. No, that wasn't right. It had screeched to a complete halt. Spit and sputtered. Spun around and flipped upside down. Then stopped abruptly. The changes in speed gave her whiplash. That's the only possible explanation for the fact that she'd just told Howard Greer, in front of a table full of people, that she and Finn O'Hearn were engaged.

To be married.

Her and Finn.

Surprise!

Greer was looking at her, his brows raised in anticipation of more words. Sure. Words. Words would be good. She glanced up at Finn, who looked a tender shade of green, and tucked a few very special words away for him later. She sucked in a sharp breath.

"Um...yeah...a surprise for my grandmother."

"For Maura?" Greer pursed his lips. "I told your fiancé you shouldn't waste any time. Your grandmother needs that good news now, not later."

Bridget looked across the room to where Nana was sitting with Father Joe. Vickie Pendergast had joined their table. All three of them were staring straight at her and Finn. Vickie looked positively diabolical in her glee, and Nana was smiling warmly. Tenderly. At Bridget. Like she knew. Oh, damn. She knew. Bridget tried to keep her voice level. Finn was no help at all, frozen at her side, arm stiff around her waist. A deer in the headlights. She flashed a dark look at him. A man on death row was more like it.

"You're probably right, Dr. Greer. I suspect our little secret is out. Has anyone else mentioned it to you?"

He'd reached back for his drink and he took a sip before nodding. "I spoke with Vickie Pendergast. She acted surprised at first, but I think she was just trying to keep up the game for you." He tipped his head and...twitched. Was that supposed to be a wink? He chuckled softly. "Vickie is clever like that. And if she knows, your grandmother knows. The two of them are joined at the hip."

Bridget glanced over at Nana. She was practically glowing with happiness. Over Bridget's fictional engagement to Finn? Suddenly murder felt too good for the man.

But the rush of words he'd whispered in her ear a few minutes ago, his arm tight—and trembling—around her waist, were still bouncing around in her head.

I'll explain later, but I'm ruined if you don't play along. My career. My visa. Please...I need you.

When she didn't respond to his begging, Finn had started to step away, defeat dulling his eyes. But she'd stopped him. She had no idea why. She'd thought Greer had been joking when he congratulated her and told her what a "great catch" Finn O'Hearn was. She'd laughed. And then Finn had rushed up. He'd put his arm around her as he greeted Greer with a strained smile. Then he'd leaned close as if to kiss her and whispered his urgent plea.

She should have slapped him in the face, right there in front of his boss and her customers. He'd lied about her. He'd humiliated her. She should have screamed obscenities at him and thrown him out of the pub. Out of town. That's what she should have done. What she would have done without hesitation if it was anyone else but Finn. She'd looked into his desperate eyes...it would have felt like kicking a puppy. Besides, Nana and Father Joe were watching. She couldn't make a scene in front of them. At the very least, she'd give Finn a chance to explain. To fix this. Whatever this was. There had to be an explanation.

I need you...

She lifted her chin and smiled at the older man. "You're right—if Vickie knows, so does Nana. And if Nana knows..." She gave Finn a twisting pinch through his sweater to snap him out of his stupor. The hiss of pain he gave was enough to make her smile sincere. If he thought that hurt, just wait until she got him in private. But with her grandmother watching so closely, payback would have to wait. She fluttered her eyelashes up at him like a playful coquette. "Well, if Nana knows…darling, then there's no sense hiding our love any longer, is there?" Finn's eyes widened. Warming to her role—and to making him squirm—she lifted her hand and waggled it near his face. "And now I can finally wear that big, beautiful ring you promised, sweetheart."

He finally found his voice. And the hint of a relieved smile. "'Tis true, dearest. But didn't we agree 'twas dangerous for you to be cooking with a great rock on your finger?"

She leaned into him. Tomorrow they could call it off. For tonight, she'd have fun letting him twist in the wind. "Oh, don't worry, baby. I'll be careful. I mean…you did say I deserve the best."

His smile deepened enough for a dimple to appear. "Oi, you're a minx, Bridget McKinnon." He tapped his finger under her chin. "Life will ne'er be dull engaged to you, will it?"

For an instant, she could imagine it, like a quick video playing out before her. Laughing with Finn. Marrying Finn, surrounded by her family. Raising a family… She blinked and looked away from his damnable eyes, which had darkened as if he was seeing the same ridiculous fantasy.

"You know, O'Hearn—" Greer cleared his throat. "—I'll admit I had some doubts when you told me

you two were engaged, but now that I see you together, there's no doubt at all. You may as well seal
the deal with a kiss."

Bridget recoiled. Kissing hadn't even occurred to
her—outside of her fantasies, that is.

A cheer went up around them. She assumed it was
for the end of the trivia competition, but to her horror, nearly everyone in the place was looking at her.
At her and Finn. Kelly ran up and threw her arms
around Bridget's neck.

"Oh, my God! This is amazing! A wedding! To
an Irishman!" She lowered her voice to a whisper.
"And he's a hot fuckin' Irishman! I can't wait to
hear this story."

No, no, no, no.

Kelly was already turning away, lifting a glass of
beer in the air. Everyone in the place lifted a glass of
something. Even Nana, on her feet now, was holding up a glass of sparkling water. Kelly shouted to
the crowd.

This is a nightmare...

"Cheers to the engaged couple, Finn and Bridget!
Welcome to the family, Finn!"

Everyone hooted and hollered and shouted for
them to kiss. What. Was. Happening? Finn turned
her slowly to face him, muttering an apology under
his breath before his lips touched hers. Her ears
registered the pandemonium going on in the Purple
Shamrock, but every other sense was strictly focused
on her mouth, now held captive by Finn O'Hearn.

He started by just pressing his lips against hers.

It was an act, just to make everyone happy. A quick press of lips together, and then they'd pull apart and figure out how to end this engagement farce without him losing his job or her breaking Nana's heart. Fine. Get it over with.

Except…Finn didn't pull away. His arm tightened around her back and drew her in. Her hands rested on his shoulders, but she didn't push at him. In fact, her fingers curled into his shirt and held on tight. His head turned slightly, and his lips moved ever so gently. There was a gentle sound of surrender, and she realized it came from her. Her mouth went soft and pliant, and she pressed against him. He gave a low growl and ran his tongue along the seam of her lips. And she let him in. God in heaven, she let the man kiss her senseless, right there in front of the whole world. She didn't want him to stop. Ever.

Someone whooped near them, and Finn drew back as if stung. He looked around, his face reddening.

"I…I'm sorry…" He mumbled the words, his face close enough to hers for the words to be private. "That's not what I expected…I mean…intended. It won't happen again." The corner of his mouth tipped up. "But damn, woman. You're good at this."

THERE WAS A storm of emotion in Bridget's eyes, and Finn got the distinct impression that when she finally picked one to go with, he was a dead man. For some bizarre reason, she'd gone along with him in front of Greer. And then the entire bar. But he had no doubt she was now ready to eviscerate him. Bright spots of pink rose on her cheeks as a few more people congratulated them. Then Michael started announcing the trivia winners and the crowd was blessedly distracted. Even Greer turned away to rejoin his table, oblivious to the fact that'd just blown up Finn's life. And Bridget's. Her smile was so brittle Finn thought it might crack. Her voice was even more so.

"Can you join me in the kitchen…honey?" Her tight grip left him no choice as she tugged him along. The kitchen was where the knives were. Not good.

"You're not going to serve me up for dinner, are you?"

She laughed, but there was no humor in it.

"Don't be scared, snookems." She glanced over her shoulder at him as her free hand punched the kitchen door open. "Although that's not a bad idea."

Marta Leveritt was washing dishes while Jimmy manned the grill. The couple had returned last week. Bridget said she had to do a lot of graveling—and offer a raise—to get them to come back. He'd met them briefly last week. Marta's thick, dark hair was pulled up in a knot on top of her head. Her husband's was tugged back into a tiny silver man bun. They barely glanced up when Bridget and Finn walked in.

Bridget looked around, then growled. Like…actually growled as if she were an angry, trapped animal. Finn gestured toward the back door. It was cold as hell outside, but at least they'd have privacy. Of course, there'd also be no witnesses if she opted for murder.

She headed out, grabbing a jacket from a hook

and sliding it over her shoulders. She stood with her back toward him, staring out across the area she'd told him would be a beer garden by summer. As soon as the door clicked shut, she spoke.

"I am so freaking angry with you right now that I can't…even…" She spun to face him, swinging her arm to point to the pub. The cold made little puffs of steam rise from her words. "What the ever-loving hell happened in there? Engaged? You're telling people we're engaged?" Her anger was just heating up, and he knew better than interrupt her explosion. "Are you some sick stalker, fixated with your landlady? What is it, Finn? Did I smile at you funny and you took that as hey-she-loves-me-let's-get-married? Is there a wall in your apartment covered with creepy photos of me?"

She stepped up so close that Finn could see the fire in her eyes. "You told your boss? And it never occurred to you to mention this little fantasy to me? I fucking live in this town, and you show up with all your Irish charm and everyone falls for you and they believe you so you figured you'd just spin a tale and see what happened? Is this that Irish blarney I keep hearing about? Is it some kind of green card con game?" She clasped her hands to the sides of her head, like she thought it might come apart. "My family believes it now. My grandmother…"

Bridget's voice broke, and the small sound sliced right through Finn's chest. He'd told himself the engagement story was a victimless crime, but he was staring at the victim right now. He'd done this to her.

"I'm an ass." It was time to start telling the truth. He reached for her.

"You think?" She swatted his hands away. "I played along in there to avoid a scene. But this little engagement of ours?" She gestured between the two of them. "It's over. Consider us officially broken up. You can tell your boss the tragic news in the morning. Blame it on me…whatever…I don't care. Just end it."

"Not yet…" He spoke his panicked thoughts out loud. "Look, we don't need any more PDAs, but can we just let the story ride a while longer? Until Greer takes the ax away from my neck? I'll do whatever you want. I'll tend bar every night. I'll wash dishes. I'll mop floors. Hell, I'll change the oil in your car and rotate your tires." He finally brought himself more under control. He knew he sounded terrified. "I not only like this job, I need it. I need the work visa. He just wants proof that I'm not a flight risk."

"Why does he think…?" Her voice softened for a moment, then hardened again. "You know what? I don't care. I just want to know why you thought dragging me into your problems was a good idea."

Finn stared up at the starlit sky. The night was cold and crisp, and the stars were sharp and bright against the pitch-black backdrop. He rubbed his neck, trying to come up with a logical explanation and knowing there wasn't one. He met her gaze and shrugged.

"It was supposed to be a joke. Greer was hassling me about not being a part of the community.

He kept threatening and pushing. I sarcastically said something about you and me. And hell if he didn't believe it!" Bridget huffed out a laugh of surprise, and he nodded. "I know, I know. It didn't occur to me that he was serious until I was too deep into it to retract..." He frowned. "No, that's not true. I could have stopped it, but for the first time since I got here, I didn't feel like he was looking for a reason to fire me. He acted like tenure was an actual possibility. I was basking in the feeling and before I knew what was happening, I was answering questions about us and..."

Why had he kept going? He thought of the doubt in Greer's eyes when they'd started their meeting. The mistrust. Finn just wanted people to respect him again.

Bridget's mouth had fallen open. "Answering questions? Tell the truth—you were just making shit up. There is no 'us,' Finn. You had to know I'd hear about it."

"I told him it was a secret..." His voice trailed off. The more Finn spoke, the more idiotic he felt. "Oi, I know it was a stupid thing to do, okay? I know that. But it was like I was in a trance or something. I kept talking and talking, and by the time I snapped out of it, I couldn't fix things without admitting I'd just lied to the man."

"You figured lying to me was okay, though." There was a hurt in her voice that bounced right back at him.

"I'm so sorry. I swear to God I didn't think... I

told him to keep quiet, damn it. He told me he didn't come to the Shamrock. I thought I'd wait until the semester is over and once I got tenure I'd just tell him we broke up."

Her right brow arched high. "So you weren't going to carry it all the way through and marry me, then?"

"Of course not. This isn't a green card thing. I mean, it is, but it's not a green card marriage proposal."

She huffed out a laugh. "There is no 'of course' with you, because you are clearly a loose cannon. But I can tell you one thing, the engagement is off. I've got too much on my plate to play green card princess for you."

Her phone had been chirping with incoming texts, and she snatched it out of her pocket. Her face went pale. He had a feeling things just went from very bad to much worse.

"What's wrong?"

"What have you done to my life, Finn?" Her voice was low and tense. "Kelly and Michael have been busy sharing our news with the family. My cousin Mary is asking if it's going to be a shotgun wedding. If I'm not pregnant, she's demanding we wait until after she has the baby so she can be my matron of honor. Timothy wants to host the engagement party. Oh, and look—Kelly talked to Nana, and says Nana is thrilled. Nana says we should have a Christmas wedding so…" She sucked in a breath, then looked up at him with tears in her eyes. "So her hair will be grown back."

Finn closed his eyes tight. The pain on her face was unbearable. Knowing that he'd put it there made his chest ache.

"You son of a bitch," she hissed. "Now I have to go tell my grandmother—my grandmother who has effing cancer—that ha-ha it's all a bad joke. Sorry, Nana. No wedding for you! You've been depressed, but too bad. Now you'll be even worse, all because Finn O'Hearn has no attachment to reality."

He reached out to her again, but she jumped back. "Don't touch me! I hate you, Finn. I am barely hanging on to this business, to my house, to my sanity. And as if that wasn't enough, you just threw a grenade right in the middle of it all. Get away from me. This joke of yours is over." She moved around him and grabbed the door. "And find another apartment. I want you out of my house."

Finn stood there in the frigid cold like a statue. His body was immobile, but his brain was racing straight for a cliff. He'd lose his job. He'd lose his visa. He'd never work in academia again. And this time he'd brought it all on himself. Maybe he could find a job teaching preteens in some small Irish village. Far away from the wreckage of his life, and the wreckage he'd left for Bridget. His shoulders fell. He had to fix things first. He had to explain and apologize to her family.

He couldn't just walk away and leave her to clean up his mess.

CHAPTER NINE

THE EMERGENCY FAMILY meeting the next morning was fully attended. Everyone wanted to gawk at the new bride-to-be in their midst. To hug her and exclaim how surprised and happy they were. And to make plans. So many plans.

She'd barely sat down before calendars were spread out on the table and dates were being tossed around for engagement parties and showers and dress shopping and the wedding. When would it be? Where would it be? Mary said it would naturally be at St. Vincent's church, but Kelly thought the waterfront might be nice and Timothy's wife said the Falls Legend Winery would be a perfect setting for a small fall wedding.

Mary scoffed at that idea. McKinnons didn't do anything small. They needed a venue for at least two hundred, which made Bridget wonder if she even knew two hundred people well enough to invite them to her wedding, which finally brought her back to her senses. She raised her hand, Nana-style, to stop—or at least slow—the conversation.

"Guys! Seriously…guys! Stop! There isn't going to be…"

Nana walked into the kitchen with little Katie holding her hand, and everyone turned to greet her. She was smiling ear to ear. It was the happiest Bridget had seen her grandmother since the cancer diagnosis.

"There's our beautiful bride!" Everyone cheered while Bridget groaned to herself. "And you're marrying an Irishman!" More cheers. Damn Finn O'Hearn to hell. If she had a voodoo doll, she'd be stabbing it into oblivion right now. "This was exactly the news I needed to hear." Nana moved toward her chair, and for the first time, Bridget noticed she wasn't very steady on her feet. She was shuffling, and reached out for the table's edge. Tim stood up to take her arm.

"Nana? You okay?"

She waved him away, her smile still beaming. "I'm fine, dear. Just a little tired from the excitement last night. But my gosh, I'm happy."

Kelly got up and started refilling everyone's coffee, as Tim started to sit again. "I know, right? And it happened under our noses without any of us seeing it! You're a better actress than I thought, Bridg."

Bridget swallowed hard. Now was the time to tell the truth. Right this minute. Before this farce went any further. "Look, everyone…the reason I called a meeting was because I have to tell you that Finn and I…"

"Look out!" Michael jumped to his feet with a yell

as Nana stumbled and dropped to one knee with a small cry. Timothy managed to catch her and ease the impact, but the room erupted into chaos.

"What happened?"

"Is she okay?"

"Should we call the doctor?"

"Did she trip on something?"

"Here, help her into this chair."

"Call the doctor!"

"Nana, did you faint?"

"Are you going to throw up?"

"Mommy, why did Great Nana fall down?"

"Someone grab a dishpan in case she throws up!"

"She's not going to throw up."

Nana finally slapped her hand on the table as Timothy eased her into her chair, bringing instant silence to the kitchen.

"That's enough. I fell because I can't feel my damn feet. The doctor said it's neuropathy. Some days they hurt, some days I can't even tell where they are. But I'm fine. It's just another side effect of the chemo. But forget about me. Let's get back to this wedding news."

Everyone other than Nana was looking around the room, asking a thousand silent questions and voicing a thousand worries with their eyes. Their matriarch was tired. Bald. Stumbling. Sick. And, even if she wouldn't admit it, afraid. They could see it in the way she stared at the table, blinking rapidly as she tried to move the conversation back to the wedding without making eye contact with anyone. If Nana sensed the tension swirling around the room, she didn't acknowledge it. She straightened and fixed her attention on Bridget.

"So, have you picked a date, dear?"

This was the moment of truth. This was her opportunity to say there was no date because there was no engagement. She swallowed and looked Nana straight in the eye, McKinnon-style. This family had never tolerated bullshit. Nana would expect nothing less than honesty, and that's what Bridget would give her. And yet, she hesitated. Which gave Mary a chance to jump in, telling Nana "they" were talking about a late fall wedding date.

Mary suggested the engagement party could be held during the St. Patrick's party at the pub. Nana was nodding in agreement, and the room filled with her family's voices again as they debated other options. But now, instead of the tension and dread that hung over the room when Nana stumbled a few minutes ago, the voices were full of laughter and excitement. This kitchen hadn't had this much joyful energy in it since Nana's diagnosis. And it was all because of Bridget's totally fake engagement to Finn. She had to tell them it was all a lie. Or that they broke up. Or…something. She had to stop this freight train that felt like it had already left the station without her.

But if she did that, the excitement would be gone. That sparkle in Nana's eyes, even after falling in front of everyone—something that would normally horrify the woman—would be gone. They'd all go back to arguing over the pub and debating who would take Nana to her next appointment. This new energy that had filled the room and lifted her family would vanish. She looked at Nana, and her grandmother winked back at her playfully.

Her phone buzzed with a text. It was from Finn.

Got a meeting with Greer at one. I'll come clean about everything.

She tapped the keyboard quickly.

Don't.

Bubbles floated there, then stopped, then floated again.

Don't what?

Now she knew what he'd meant when he said the story spun out of control with Greer. He said it got away from him. She thought that was nonsense, but she was watching it happen right here in front of her. Sure, she could tell her family the truth, but to what end? Would it be so bad to give her grandmother something joyful to think about while she was dealing with chemo and surgery and neuropathy and whatever else her disease and its treatments might bring?

Bridget closed her eyes and took a long, slow

breath. She couldn't believe what she was considering. But after the initial pandemonium wore off, and before any real money was spent or dates were set, she and Finn could announce a breakup. Finn would protect his visa. Maura McKinnon would have had something to look forward to during chemo. It was wrong to lie, of course. But who were they really hurting?

She looked back at her phone and typed her reply to Finn.

Don't say anything until we talk first.

His answer was swift.

Tonight? I'm working the bar with Luke and can help you close.

She typed a quick agreement, smiling in amazement at what they were doing.

"Oh my God, how cute is our little Bridget?" Kelly cried. "Are you texting Finn right now? Look at that smile. You are, aren't you? You and your fiancé are texting sweet nothings…"

Mary reached for the phone, but Bridget locked the screen before putting it in her pocket with a laugh.

"Yes, if you must know, I was texting Finn. And now you know why we kept it a secret. You guys are insufferable!"

There had to be a reason why it was so easy to

keep the lie going. It was almost as if she was having an out-of-body experience, looking down at some other Bridget spinning the story. Was she telling it only for her grandmother's sake? Or was she trying to fit in with her cousins, who were—or had been— married while she was alone? What it would it be like to be engaged to Finn, with his soft, serious eyes and all those books? Who knew a bookish professor could kiss a woman like he'd kissed her last night? Her lips tingled from the memory of it. But, good kisser or not, he was still the one who got them both into this complicated web of deceit.

FINN DID HIS best to avoid Bridget's family at the pub that night. But it wasn't easy when they, and practically everyone else, wanted to clap him on the back and congratulate him. His face hurt from forcing a smile on it for so many hours as he poured drafts and mixed the occasional cocktail. Fortunately, the Shamrock didn't have a complicated drink menu, and Luke had taught him all the basics.

Bridget had been in avoidance mode, too. She'd only come out into the pub a couple of times, and was quickly swamped with well-wishers each time. She'd been a good sport, but had escaped as quickly as possible without even looking his way. That didn't bode well for the talk she wanted to have later.

Her text just said don't. Was that don't tell him today or don't tell him ever? Her last spoken words to him were to move out, and her text hadn't retracted that order. He had no idea if he was home-less or engaged.

The Shamrock was noisy with a bunch of women in their thirties and forties, dancing to some Whitesnake cover band out of Rochester. Luke Rut-ledge came up beside him and started a Guinness pour.

"Are you sure you want to bartend here? Nights like tonight are nuts." He squinted at the pint glass, apparently satisfied with the domed head of creamy foam on it. He slid it in Finn's direction. "That one's for you, pal. There are a hell of a lot of single women around. And a few not-single ones." Luke nodded to-ward a table of women laughing in the corner. "The one drinking seltzer water is my pregnant wife, Whitney. The others are her pals—Piper, Chantese, Kareema, and Evie from the diner. I swear if I hear 'Here I Go Again' played one more time, I'm going to lose my mind. Wait—you're not a closet Whitesnake fan, are you?"

"You're safe, mate. I appreciate classic rock as much as anyone, but they're not at the top of my list." Finn took a sip of the dark brew. "And I'm not in the market for a woman." Luke's brows went high. "Oh, yeah, I heard something about you two. Whitney told me she heard you were getting married, but I told her there was no way…" He looked at Finn's carefully blank face. "Oh, shit. You're…really?"

"Ask me tomorrow. She wants to talk later, and you know that might not be good…"

If Bridget was ending everything, as he expected

she would, he didn't want to reinforce their ruse to anyone.

"Ouch." Luke grimaced. "Nothing strikes fear in a man's heart like his woman needing to talk about something. My advice? Apologize before she even gets to tell you what you did. Just say you're sorry and offer to take her to dinner. Apologize and deflect, man."

Finn chuckled, taking his beer with him as he headed to the kitchen. "I'll bear that in mind."

Luke had no idea how much Finn had to apologize for. Or how small his chances were to deflect her from what he'd done to their lives.

Bridget was scrubbing the grill. The surface was hot, and her face shone with sweat as she moved the scrubbing pad back and forth. The sleeves of her shirt were pushed up, and her hair was pulled back into a messy twist. She tossed the scrubber aside and picked up the metal scraper, removing the loosened grease and char from the grill and into the catch tray. The lean, hard muscles in her arms and shoulders flexed as she worked. She was in the zone, and hadn't even noticed him enter. The sink was piled with pans, so Finn headed over and started filling it with soapy water.

The sound of the faucet made her turn in surprise. "Oh...hi! I thought you were avoiding me." She blew a loose strand of hair from her face with a puff of breath. "I was going to do those...but yeah, go ahead and get started." She grinned. "After all, you did say you owed me, right?"

He gave her a quick salute, and a spray of soap bubbles flew off his fingers. She laughed, but now that she was facing him, he could see how tired she was. "Busy night, eh?"

"Long day and a busy night. I didn't realize how many women this band would draw. And they wanted to nibble on appetizers all night long, so I've been crazed. Jimmy and Marta were here for dinners, but they left around nine." She wiped her arm across her forehead. "I'm dead on my feet."

"Scrubbing a few pans is the least I can do."

She huffed out a laugh. "No argument here." She arched a brow at him and turned back to the grill. There were a few moments of silence between them as they settled into their tasks. It felt safer somehow when they had their backs to each other like this. But they had to talk. Finn started.

"Why did you text me to wait earlier?"

She hesitated. "You and I need to stay on the same page and keep our stories straight. I mean, we need to end this fiasco, but let's not spring any more surprises on each other."

They still weren't facing each other, so he spoke to the large commercial sink. "I know I've said this already, but I'm so sorry. Let's just tell folks we broke up, yeah?"

"But what will Greer say about your visa and stuff?"

He scrubbed hard at a bit of burnt on residue on a pan.

"I'll deal with it. Goin' home t' Ireland isn't the

worst thing that could happen to me. It's not like I hate it there." But going home felt like a huge step backward.

"Then why are you here?"

He shook his head. "I met my ex here, and she was American. And…I like the place. There's a lot of opportunity here. But I need to get you and me out of this mess I created before it gets any stickier."

She didn't answer. She just moved on to cleaning and organizing the refrigerators and freezers. He kept washing and drying. The band stopped playing…finally. Luke stepped into the kitchen to say good night. He looked back and forth at the distance between Finn and Bridget and his forehead wrinkled as he looked at Finn in question. Finn just shrugged in response. He had no clue where this was going.

Instead of finishing the conversation, Bridget started turning off lights and locking up the place in silence. He followed suit, putting the last of the utensils away and making sure the fryer was off. They went out the back and walked quietly to the house. As he locked the house door behind them, she watched with furrowed brows.

"I'm not saying I want to keep up this act, but…" She looked around the hall, twisting her hands together. "But let me tell my grandmother first, before you tell Greer, okay? She deserves that much." She shook her head. "She's pissed that she heard it from Vickie, and Vickie and Greer are a thing these days, and since Greer can't…"

Finn sighed. "Can't keep his mouth shut?"

"Apparently not." She finally met his gaze. "Let me get Nana settled. Maybe I'll tell her we broke up. No one to blame, we moved too fast, blah blah blah. Then you can tell Greer." She looked resigned to this, and Finn set his troubles aside. He had to support her. But there was one thing in her plan that surprised him.

"You said you couldn't lie to Maura. But you're going to tell her we broke up? Isn't that...?"

Anger flashed in her eyes now. "Yeah, I know what I said. But I've already lied to her, Finn. And I don't think she needs to know that, okay? I don't think she needs to be any more disappointed than she already will be." She crossed her arms tightly. "You've put me in an impossible situation. Maybe I'll break down and tell her the sordid truth, but I just don't know if I can do that. If not, the breakup story will work. That's why I want to do it before you tell Greer." She turned away and headed up the stairs. "I don't trust myself to tell the whole story, so let me figure that out before you make a move. Same page, remember?"

She didn't wait for an answer, climbing the stairs to her apartment in angry, hurt silence. Finn stood there at the base of the staircase for a while, berating himself for selfishly bringing pain to the McKinnons. And fighting the urge to go upstairs and comfort her. In his arms. As if she'd ever want to be there now.

CHAPTER TEN

EVIE ROSARIO HUDSON slid into a booth at the Spot Diner, squeezing Whitney Rutledge closer to the wall across from Bridget and Kareema. Evie stared hard at Bridget, and Bridget realized just how challenging this fake engagement would be to maintain long-term. As soon as she talked to Nana later that afternoon, it would be over, one way or the other. But until then, she needed to act her socks off.

"So let me get this straight," Evie said. "You met this guy a month or two ago—the timeline's a little fuzzy—and you…" Evie waved her hand up and down at Bridget. "The woman who hasn't been on a date that I know of since you moved back here two years ago, just…fell in love. And got engaged. Just like that. And didn't tell anyone."

Evie was just as much a straight-talker as Bridget was. She and her mom had owned The Spot, a popular breakfast and lunch place on Main Street, for years. Momma Rosario was wiping down the counter now and stacking clean coffee cups. Business had slowed now that lunch was winding down, and the diner would close in an hour.

Bridget looked from Evie to Whitney to Kareema at her side. Her three closest friends in Rendezvous Falls and, for now, she had no choice but to lie to them.

"That's right." She cleared her throat and pushed on. "When you know, you know. I mean, you and Mark didn't waste any time once he came home."

Evie and Mark Hudson had been high school sweethearts until he'd abruptly left town after graduation. Evie swore she hated the guy until he moved back and declared he wanted her back. She didn't exactly make it easy for him, but they'd become engaged in a matter of weeks. But Evie wasn't buying the comparison.

"Mark and I have known each other since grade school, Bridg. We weren't strangers. He wasn't from another damn country."

Bridget turned to Whitney. "What about you and Luke? That was fast, wasn't it?"

Whitney pursed her lips, probably evaluating dates and measuring them against Bridget's. The woman was a human calculator, and was now running a successful accounting business here. The Purple Shamrock had been one of her first clients. She finally looked up from her decaf coffee.

"We were strangers, but I don't know. I mean… we met in June and didn't officially get engaged until October." She took as sip of coffee. "This Finn guy still popped the question faster than Luke did. And let's not forget, none of us even knew you were seeing someone."

"To be fair," Evie laughed at Whitney, "you and Luke hated each other those first couple of months."

Whitney patted her barely swollen stomach. "Yeah, but we fixed that."

"Hey, how is Luke's brother doing?" Bridget asked. "I haven't seen Zayne in a while."

"He's doing great these days. I mean, he's still a bit of a hermit, but his businesses are doing well. He's like a new man. He and Luke have been seeing a lot more of each other these days." She tipped her head to the side. "You graduated with Zayne, right?"

"Yeah. We were good friends in school. After he had the accident, we stayed friends, but you know Zayne—he only shows up when he wants to."

Kareema leveled a pointed look at her. "That's something you two have in common, right?"

"Oh, ha-ha." Bridget knew Kareema was jabbing her again for not returning calls. Then Kareema grabbed Bridget's left hand.

"And why are you not wearing a ring?" Damn it, she and Finn needed to figure out a ring story. Then again, they were about to "break up," so it probably didn't matter. Kareema held Bridget's hand up high, shaking it at the other women. "Since when do people get engaged with no ring?"

"It was impulsive, okay?" She yanked her hand away. "He popped the question before he bought a ring. Ring or no ring, we're engaged."

Evie finished her root beer float, which was the drink the Spot was famous for. Evie always sported a bright streak of color in her dark hair, and this week it was fluorescent red, probably left over from Valentine's Day. She'd been staring at Bridget nonstop since she sat down.

"This makes zero sense, Bridget. I mean, I know you've been stressed with your grandmother and all, but engaged? And you didn't tell any of us. I had to hear it through gossip at the diner. Are you sure it's not some, I don't know, distraction mechanism or something? None of us even know the guy. Are you sure he's not taking advantage of you?"

And just like that, Bridget was annoyed. Why couldn't she have fallen in love overnight?

"Can you guys give me at least a little credit for knowing what I'm doing? And maybe a congratulations or two? Not one of you has even said you're happy for me yet!"

Evie's mom, Evelyn, called over from behind the counter. "She's right, you know. All three of you have been grillin' her and not one of you has asked about her fiancé!"

Her friends looked appropriately chagrined. Kareema gave her a gentle shoulder bump.

"Sorry, girl. We're just worried, you know? We care about you. And I don't get the secrecy, but whatever. If you say you're in love with this Irish dude, that's all we need to know. More than any of us, you protect your heart the hardest, so if some history professor has managed to win it, we already love him."

Whitney raised her empty cup. "And we admire him for bravery. He captured the fierce heart of our Bridget."

Evie chuckled, but doubt still clouded her eyes. "Of course, if you love him, we love him. I've actually seen him in here a few times, and he is hawt. He was nice, too, if a bit quiet. Always has a book with him."

Bridget smiled to herself. Her nerdy, bookish recluse. Well, not really hers, but hers for now. Make-believe hers.

"Wow," Evie said, smiling for real this time. "If I had any doubts, that smile just took care of them. You are in love!"

"What?" She started to protest, then realized she couldn't. Maybe she was a better actress than she'd thought, if she'd managed to convince her best friends that this thing with Finn was genuine. "Um...I mean...yeah, sure. Why else would I agree to marry the guy?" She swallowed hard, fixing her smile in place. "And just because we got engaged impulsively, that doesn't mean we're getting married tomorrow." Or ever. "We haven't even talked about a date or anything."

"That makes sense," Kareema nodded. "Sorry we hassled you, but honestly, if you'd told us instead of keeping this big dark secret..."

"I told you why we did that. We weren't sure how my grandmother would take it."

Whitney laughed. "You weren't sure how Irish-to-the-core Maura McKinnon would take you getting married to a real live Irishman?"

"Well, it wasn't as much that as wanting to keep her stress levels down. Too much excitement…"

Kareema finished her coffee. "Your cousin Tim said Maura is over-the-moon happy about it."

Yeah, that was the problem.

"It does explain why Bridget's been so hard to get together with lately." Whitney started to shrug on her heavy coat. "I thought you were mad at me or something. You haven't returned my calls for a month, but I forgive you now that I know you've been shacking up with Finn. Luke really likes the guy, by the way. Like Evie said, he's a hottie nerd." She grinned. "The pub owner and the professor. It's like you're hot for teacher, Bridg. And speaking of Luke, he's picking me up because he was all freaked out about me driving in the snow. This is going to be a long pregnancy if he keeps trying to wrap me in cotton balls to protect me."

The women headed their separate ways with hugs and laughter. Bridget was determined to talk to her grandmother today and tell her the truth. She'd finally made her mind up on that last night. She couldn't stand the idea of lying to Nana. Maybe Nana would even have some advice for her on how to get

out of this. Nana would probably laugh herself silly.
Or box Bridget's ears for being a complete idiot.

But as she drove to Nana's house later that afternoon, Bridget wasn't as worried about telling Nana
the truth as she was about her time with her friends
just now. She couldn't stop thinking about how they
all agreed so quickly that she'd been out of touch for
a while. Kareema had told her that a few weeks ago,
but she hadn't realized how many calls and texts
she'd missed since Nana got sick. She kept telling
herself she'd get back to her friends "later," but later
kept running longer than she'd planned. All the way
to never. She'd been so focused on managing everything that she'd forgotten to take time for her friends,
and that was her loss. Laughing with them, even
though she was fibbing about the engagement, had
felt good. Cathartic, even.

And all because of a "hawt" Irish professor and
his crazy scheme.

FINN STARED AT the images from the famous Book
of Kells on his forty-four inch curved HD computer
monitor. He'd been obsessed with the beautiful book
from the moment he saw it at Trinity College in Dublin as a lad. The illuminated manuscript was fasci-
nating. He'd always thought so. He had three pages
side by side on the screen, trying to determine exactly when each bit of art had been added. Hand-
painted over a thousand years ago, the artistry of
the tiny little decorations meticulously added to each

page was incredible, but some marks had been added as recently as the 1800s.

He was at the desk in his new office space, his own books lining the shelves previously used by Bridget's dad. He kept trying to focus on the images before him, but the manuscript just couldn't hold his attention tonight. All he could think about Bridget McKinnon. He stared blankly at the monitor, restless, but not sure what to do with himself. She'd told him this morning that she was telling her grandmother the truth today, no matter what. She refused to lie to the woman who'd basically raised her. Finn got it, but it probably meant this disaster he'd created was about to go nuclear. No way a woman with Maura's integrity would allow the ruse to continue, even if Bridget considered it. She'd shocked him when she told him not to say anything to Howard Greer yet, but she was just delaying the inevitable.

He couldn't blame Bridget for not wanting to go along with the made-up engagement story. Hell, he wouldn't have gone along with it, either, if anyone else had come up with it. The whole thing was a colossally stupid idea, but he was in it now. If Maura McKinnon insisted that Bridget spill the beans, as she definitely would, his career was over.

He pushed his chair back and rose to his feet to start pacing. He'd been doing that a lot today. But no matter how many steps he walked, he couldn't find a way out of this.

He'd never been an impulsive guy. It wasn't like

him to make up stories. Technically, he hadn't made up a story this time, either. It was Greer who got carried away with everything. Finn stopped to stare out the window at the drifting snow. Who was he kidding? Sure, the guy jumped to one conclusion after another, but Finn could've stopped it at any time. He just hadn't been paying enough attention to see what was going on.

That had been happening a lot. He hadn't been paying enough attention to notice that his wife was cheating on him with his best friend. You think he'd learn his lesson, but no. He'd probably end up going home—back to Dublin. Maybe it was what he deserved. He hadn't been able to hold on to his wife. He hadn't had very good taste in best friends. When everything fell apart, he hadn't handled it well. He still wasn't handling it well. Maybe home to the old sod would be the best thing for him. Maybe he should do it before the truth came out. He started pacing again, but more thoughtfully this time.

That wasn't a bad idea. He hated giving up, but going back to Ireland would save face for him and for Bridget. If he left now, she could tell everyone he was the asshole who dumped her and left. It wouldn't be fun for her. She'd get attention she probably wouldn't appreciate. There'd be some gossip. Some strange looks and questions. But it would be better if that happened rather than have the truth come out that the story was made up. He mentally kicked himself in the ass. It wasn't like he'd had a lot of honest peo-

ple in his life. And the one honest person he'd met…
he'd dragged into a lie.

He looked at his watch. Bridget should be getting
back anytime now. Maybe it was time to start packing. Rick would call this one of Finn's dark Irish
moods, and maybe it was. Finn might be three kinds
of an idiot, but he was smart enough to know when
he'd defeated himself. He'd just stepped into the hallway from the office when Bridget came in the front
door, brushing snow from her shoulders. She froze
when she saw him standing there, but her gaze was
unfocused. Her eyes were puffy and red. Looking
at her pale face, and knowing she'd been crying because of something he'd put in motion…

It gutted him.

He took a step toward her. "Ah, shite, I'm so
damn sorry. Do you want me to go talk to Maura
right now?" His chest ached. "I'll explain everything to her, Bridget. I'll apologize. I'll throw myself on my sword as many times as it takes. Damn
it, I should have been the one to tell her in the first
place." Bridget stared at him as if she didn't recognize him. Then her head dropped.

"I didn't tell her." Her voice was so soft, so…sad.
After all her anger earlier, he was having a hard time
reconciling what she'd said. He stepped toward her.

"It's okay. I should be the one to tell her. Look,
I'll go do it right now." He grabbed for his coat, but
Bridget's hand snaked out and grabbed his wrist like
a vise.

"No! You can't tell her. None of us can."

Finn tried to make sense of those words. Did she change her mind? Wasn't that a good thing? It didn't feel like a good thing. She looked more than upset. She looked...traumatized. He was missing something.

"Tell me what happened, love."

She blinked and looked away. But not fast enough to hide the tears gathering again. He reached behind her and opened the door to his apartment.

"Come on in. I'll make some tea for you."

She gave a hollow laugh. "That's what my grandmother just did. You're gonna need to up your game."

"O-kay. How about something stronger?"

It was the first sign of a smile he'd seen since she walked in. Just a little flutter at the corner of her mouth. Her head barely nodded, as if she didn't trust herself to speak. He held the door open and waited.

She looked up at him, and he knew she was thinking of the very first day. When she didn't trust him enough to let him walk through the door behind her. That corner of her mouth lifted even higher now. She walked past him into the apartment. The show of trust did something funny to his heart. He grabbed the Paddy's whiskey from the counter—he hadn't bothered putting it away last night—then pulled down two glasses and looked over at her.

She was curled at the end of the small sofa. Another show of trust?

"Ice?"

She frowned for a moment as if she didn't understand the question. Then she saw the bottle in his hand and recognition brightened in her eyes.

"I drink it straight, thanks."

Like a good Irish lass. He splashed a generous portion in both glasses.

He joined her on the sofa, sitting in the opposite corner, and handed her the glass. "Tell me what happened. How can I fix it?"

"I have no freaking idea how to fix it. All I know is—for the time being—you and I are engaged."

Again, he should be happy. The idea of the fake engagement was stupid, but if she was going to keep up this ruse, he'd get to keep his job. It didn't feel like something to be happy about, though. And he had a feeling there was more to the story, so he waited.

"I went there to tell her," she said. "That was the plan. But…" She looked up, her eyes sad and dark. "Nana had a really bad day. Bad night last night. She's been so sick this week…"

He wanted to reach for her, but he held back.

"The chemo?"

"Yes." Bridget wiped her nose with the back of her hand. "She's been okay. Well, not okay, but considering what she's going through. She's been tired but… okay. But it's really walloped her this week. She was sick to her stomach all night. Can't sleep. She said her whole body aches. Her joints hurt. She fell the other day. They gave her medication, but she's already on so much medication…" Bridget stared down at the glass she was holding in her lap. "She's the strong one, you know? She's the strongest one of us all."

Finn could believe that. Maura was a tough one.

"You're a strong one, too."

She looked up, surprised.

"I wasn't strong enough to tell her the truth."

"Not because you weren't strong. There had to be another reason. What was it?"

She rested her head back against the sofa, staring at the ceiling.

"Finn, she believes it! She not only believes it… she's in love with the idea of us."

"The idea of…us? You and me? She's in love with that?"

"Yeah, I can't figure it out either. But there it is." Her eyebrows lowered and she looked at him again. "She's freakin' thrilled, which makes no sense. She doesn't know you. Why would she be happy that I'm engaged to you? She should be telling me to run for the hills. Instead…instead she's throwing us an engagement party this weekend."

His glass had been just about to touch his lips when she said that last sentence. He looked at her over the rim of the glass. "Excuse me?"

"You heard me. An engagement party. For you and me."

He raised his hand. "I know I said I wanted to keep this going for a little while, but…"

Her voice went brittle. "What the hell did you think was going to happen? You thought we were just gonna tell the town—this town—hey we're getting married, and no one would care? I mean, I know you haven't been in Rendezvous Falls very long, but this is a town that likes weddings. That likes happy stories. This is a town…and the McKinnons are a family… Everyone knows who we are. And why are you upset? This whole thing was your idea."

"I know this was a stupid thing to do. I get it. I never meant to drag you into this. But I was picturing us more as a low-key sort of couple. No dates set. We got engaged in a hurry, so we can tell everyone we're gonna take our time. Right?"

"A long engagement is fine, but I still have to deal with my family. And a long engagement is still engaged. And Nana wants a party. Don't you Irish love parties?"

He chuckled. "You've seen my lifestyle, Bridget. My idea of a party is drinking a pint of Guinness while reading instead of a cup o' tea."

"Well, you'll have to suck it up and leave your books at home to come to a McKinnon party. Where people drink and sing and argue and all the normal party stuff."

"Arguing is normal party stuff?"

She shrugged. "It is for the McKinnons."

The web of this story was getting twisted more than he'd anticipated. "I hate to ask this, but seriously, if Maura's that sick, is she even up for a party? How will she handle learning the truth after we let her throw a freakin' party? I know you're worried about her health, but won't this thing make the truth hurt her all the more?"

"Finn…" Bridget chewed her top lip, looking more vulnerable that he'd ever seen her. She shifted to face him. "She looked at me and said our wedding gave her something to live for. That our engagement news made the treatments worth it."

Never saw that coming.

Finn set his glass down on the coffee table and scrubbed his hands up and down his face.

"I don't know what to say." He lowered his hands and looked at her. "I honestly have no clue. Sorry doesn't cut it…"

"Please just stop with the apologies, okay?" She drained her glass and glared at him. "There's no question you screwed up, big time. But I screwed up, too." She slapped her hand to her chest. "I could have told you to go screw yourself in the pub the other night. I could've laughed in your face in front of your boss. But I didn't. God knows why. So here we are. And honestly…"

She took in a shaky breath, raking her fingers through her long hair and pulling it back from her face so firmly it looked like it hurt. As if she needed to have her hair tight in order to think this through. He waited. She finally released it and looked at him with a shrug. "We both got ourselves here. My nana wants us engaged. And she wants a party. So guess what? You and I are engaged. And she's getting a party."

Finn groaned, looking away from her and staring at the wall. If he could turn back time, he'd undo all of this, but she was right. They were in it now.

"I'm not much of a party person." It was the only thing he could think to say.

Bridget laughed in earnest now. "Really? I'm not much of a let's-pretend-to-be-engaged person either. But Nana wants this." Her voice cracked. "We're giving her what she wants."

"Of course." He nodded. "Of course. If that's what you need from me, I'll do it. I'll do anything. For your grandmother. For you. And it doesn't hurt my career, either. If a party is what it takes to keep this game going? I'll be all the party animal you need. I just wonder…" She arched one eyebrow at him in question, and he pushed ahead. "What else are we getting ourselves into? If we're really doing this, what are people going to expect from us?"

Her face scrunched up as if finding the question distasteful. "Well…at the minimum, there will have to be a few PDAs. I suppose we have to be nice to each other in public. We live under the same roof, which actually helps." She smiled at his look of confusion. "People can imagine whatever they want as far as what happens in this house. There are no prying eyes, so they'll just assume we're…" She paused, a soft pink spreading on her cheeks. "Well…you know. It shouldn't be that difficult once we get past the party." She waved her left hand in the air. "I've already been asked why I don't have a ring, by the way. I mean, I'll give it back when this is over, but I should have something, right?"

He tensed, remembering the last time he bought an engagement ring. Dori had been at his side and they'd had nothing but dewy-eyed hope for the future. He'd been so naive then, with no idea how deep her betrayal would cut him one day. This plan was starting to poke at pieces of his heart that were already scarred and tender. He cleared his throat.

"Uh…yeah," he muttered. "A ring. Brilliant. I'll come up with something, but if I buy one you won't be giving it back."

"You want me to keep a fake engagement ring?"

She was laughing, and he shook his head, pushing Dori memories out of his mind. "I'll pay to have it made it into something else when things are… done. A necklace. Whatever you want. But…you're not giving it back. That feels like it would be bad juju or something."

"Um…okay. Nana always says the Irish are a superstitious lot. As far as what else…" She shrugged. "We'll have to figure that out as we go, I guess. Do we need to do anything specific to keep your boss happy?"

"I think Greer is happy just knowing I have my roots in the community."

Finn stood to get the bottle of whiskey, bringing it back to the sofa to refill their glasses.

"Are you really that much of a flight risk, O'Hearn?"

"Not anymore. Now I'm engaged to be married to a nice local girl."

She sipped her whiskey, tension easing from her shoulders as she snuggled into the corner of the sofa. She'd kicked off her boots, and her long jeans-clad legs were tucked under her body, her dark sweater hugging every curve. Her smile was softer and more relaxed now, either from the whiskey or the fact that they'd agreed on some sort of plan—crazy as it was. There was genuine amusement shining in her eyes.

"I don't know where you ever got the idea I was a nice girl."

Finn shifted, tearing his eyes away from her and draining his glass. After that kiss in the Shamrock the other night? Her not being a nice girl was exactly what he was afraid of.

"One Minute" Survey

You get up to **FOUR books** <u>and</u> Mystery Gifts...

ABSOLUTELY FREE!

Romance

Suspense

YOU pick your books – WE pay for everything!

See inside for details.

Dear Reader,

Your opinions are important to us. So if you'll participate in our fast and free "One Minute" Survey, **YOU** can pick up to four wonderful books that **WE** pay for!

As a leading publisher of women's fiction, we'd love to hear from you. That's why we promise to reward you for completing our survey.

IMPORTANT: Please complete the survey and return it. We'll send your Free Books and Free Mystery Gifts right away. **And we pay for shipping and handling too!** *We pay for EVERYTHING!*

Try **Essential Suspense** featuring spine-tingling suspense and psychological thrillers with many written by today's best-selling authors.

Try **Essential Romance** featuring compelling romance stories with many written by today's best-selling authors.

Or TRY BOTH!

Thank you again for participating in our "One Minute" Survey. It really takes just a minute (or less) to complete the survey… and your free books and gifts will be well worth it!

Sincerely,

Pam Powers

Pam Powers
for Reader Service

"One Minute" Survey

GET YOUR FREE BOOKS AND FREE GIFTS!

✓ Complete this Survey   ✓ Return this survey

1 Do you try to find time to read every day?
☐ YES   ☐ NO

2 Do you prefer stories with happy endings?
☐ YES   ☐ NO

3 Do you enjoy having books delivered to your home?
☐ YES   ☐ NO

4 Do you share your favorite books with friends?
☐ YES   ☐ NO

YES! I have completed the above "One Minute" Survey. Please send me my Free Books and Free Mystery Gifts (worth over $20 retail). I understand that I am under no obligation to buy anything, as explained on the back of this card.

☐ I prefer Essential Suspense 191/391 MDL GNT4

☐ I prefer Essential Romance 194/394 MDL GNT4

☐ I prefer BOTH 191/391 & 194/394 MDL GNUG

FIRST NAME

LAST NAME

ADDRESS

APT.#

CITY

STATE/PROV.

ZIP/POSTAL CODE

READER SERVICE—Here's how it works:

▲ If offer card is missing write to: Reader Service, P.O. Box 1341, Buffalo, NY 14240-8531 or visit www.ReaderService.com ▲

BUSINESS REPLY MAIL

FIRST-CLASS MAIL   PERMIT NO. 717   BUFFALO, NY

POSTAGE WILL BE PAID BY ADDRESSEE

READER SERVICE
PO BOX 1341
BUFFALO NY 14240-8571

NO POSTAGE
NECESSARY
IF MAILED
IN THE
UNITED STATES

CHAPTER ELEVEN

"IT'S NOT THAT I'm not happy for Bridget, but the whole thing is just...odd."

Maura nodded at Vickie's comment as she took a sip of the peppermint tea Iris Taggart had brought to the book club meeting. The feisty octogenarian had insisted that Maura have some right away, saying it would help settle her stomach. It was only a few days after her fourth chemo session, and the nausea was getting worse every time. Along with the aches in every joint, the needly tingles in her feet, and the fogginess in her head.

Cecile and Lena voiced their agreement, but Helen Russo frowned over her glass of wine. She'd brought a few bottles of the latest vintage of pinot noir from her winery to the meeting, which was at the Purple Shamrock. They were holding the meeting there to make it easier for Maura to get home if she couldn't last the whole time. It was three o'clock on a Tuesday, so the place was in the peaceful lull between lunch and dinner servings.

"I wondered about the suddenness of it all myself," Helen said, "but Whitney had lunch with

Bridget, and she said the woman seemed truly in love. Said she was talking about Finn and got all misty-eyed and everything."

Maura smiled in spite of her doubts. "Bridget stopped by the house a few nights ago, and she was adamant that it was basically love at first sight between her and Finn."

"Ooh!" Cecile squealed. "That can happen! Charlie and I fell in love in a week! We were engaged two months later and married in six. I'll tell you, when I saw that man, I was just…" She pretended to fan herself.

Cecile and Charlie were an interesting couple. They both seemed so average and nondescript, and had been all their lives. He was a plumber. She'd worked at the college as a receptionist for years until her retirement a few years ago. But boy, they'd been head over heels in love from the start. And very… passionate. Just last week, Maura saw Charlie dip Cecile low on the dance floor, and his hand had spent a lot of time on Cecile's derriere.

Helen joined in. "Tony and I were quick, too, although he fell first. He said he knew the minute he saw me in art class that he was going to marry me." She smiled. "I took a little convincing, but who could resist that gorgeous man for long?"

Iris reached out and patted Helen's hand. "We all miss Tony, sweetie. He was a heck of a catch. As for me, I fell in love fast, and out of love just as fast."

She took a sip of her tea. "Turns out I was the only one who'd actually fallen at all."

Maura listened to all of their stories. Maybe it was possible Finn and Bridget were really in love. She'd fallen for her Patrick on a more traditional trajectory, dating for almost a year before getting engaged, and waiting another year to be married. Bridget acted as if she had more to say about the engagement the other night, but she'd waved off Maura's questions. After Maura mentioned something about having the engagement party at her house, and how the wedding gave her something to look forward to, Bridget started talking about how much fun the party would be. It didn't send up any red flags at the time, but Bridget had never been one to like being the center of attention. And she always complained that she had more than enough of a party atmosphere at the pub, so she didn't like parties away from work. For birthdays or anything else. She took another sip of Iris's tea, which did seem to be settling her stomach.

Iris nodded at her in approval. "I do think it's odd that she didn't tell you. You two are so close."

"My granddaughter is a very…private…person. It's not that shocking that she'd keep a whirlwind love affair to herself instead of telling everyone." But it stung that she hadn't even hinted at it with Maura. That was hard to believe. Everything about it was hard to believe.

Vickie's mouth twisted in thought. "Maybe. But Iris is right. Wouldn't she normally tell you about it?"

Cecile fluffed her hair and shook her head to set the blond curls swirling. As usual, she was dressed practically head-to-toe in pink. It was Maura's least favorite color, but Cecile was always draped in it. She was like a loveable but overly enthusiastic puppy dog.

"To be fair," Cecile pointed out, "she may not have wanted Maura stressing about her dating someone." She looked at Maura over the top of her wineglass. "She has been very protective of you. Are you still planning to have their engagement party at your house?"

"Yes. It's the easiest place to have it, and Bridget agreed." And the family had gone along with the plan, knowing Maura could quietly escape upstairs if she felt tired, which was happening more and more these days.

Iris turned and narrowed her eyes at Rick, who'd yet to say a word. "What the hell is up with you today, Rick? You love gossip and speculation more than most women do. I'm not used to you being the silent one at the table."

All heads turned to Rick, and his cheeks reddened. Vickie pounced on that.

"Are you blushing right now? I've known you for decades, and I don't think I've ever seen you blush." She punched his arm. "What's going on? Are you hiding something? Do you know something we don't?"

Iris nodded. "Of course he does. He works with

this Finn guy. You're buddies. So why didn't you tell us they were dating?"

Rick stared hard at the book sitting in front of him. None of them had even mentioned the book yet. Seemed this book club had turned more into a social club these days. Maura didn't know Rick as well as the other women did, but she'd never thought of him as being bashful about…anything. But he was practically squirming in his chair right now. Then he straightened, pulling his shoulders back and smoothing his facial expression into one of careful disinterest.

"This may come as a shock to you ladies, but men don't sit around and gossip about their dating lives with each other. Especially when they're dating women and I'm…not." He gave Vickie a pointed look. "Finn and I talk about school and literature and history."

Iris gave a quick cough that sounded a lot like bullshit.

Rick held up his middle finger in her direction. "And when we're not talking about those things, we drink beer and bitch about the weather. He's becoming a true Upstate New Yorker." He shrugged, lifting his hands and dropping them flat to the table. "I'm sorry to disappoint you vultures, but they both kept their secret well. I had no idea anything was going on—not even when he moved into that apartment." He cleared his throat, taking a sip of wine. Was his hand shaking a little? But he looked her straight in the eye when he continued. "I was genuinely just as surprised as everyone else."

Vickie's brows lowered and she stared at him for a long time, even as everyone else finally started discussing the latest J.D. Robb mystery they were supposed to be reading. While they marveled at any author creating a fifty-book series, Vickie watched Rick. He'd jumped into the book conversation with a great deal of enthusiasm, as if eager to change the subject away from Finn and Bridget. He and Vickie were close friends, but right now Vickie looked very suspicious of Rick's behavior.

Before she could pull Vickie aside to ask about it, a wave of exhaustion and nausea washed over her. Maura pushed her chair away from the table, hoping the wave would pass before she had to rush to the restroom. The loud scraping sound stopped the conversation. It also caught the attention of Maura's granddaughter Kelly from behind the bar, who rushed over.

"Nana, are you okay? I should get you home."

Vickie reached out and took Maura's hand. "It'll get better, hon. This is just the chemo talking, not the cancer, and you only have two more treatments to go."

Her stomach rolled. She gave up on keeping a brave face. What was the point?

"Right now, the chemo is just hell, Vickie. It's hell." She blinked away her gathering tears. "I don't know if I can keep going…"

"Nana!" Kelly gasped. "Don't say that!"

Vickie smiled at Kelly. "Don't pay your grandmother any mind. Did you know she played Blanche
DuBois in the school play the year they did *A Street-
car Named Desire*?"

Kelly's eyes went wide with shock. "Are you saying she's acting? I can't believe you—you're supposed to be her friend." She urged Maura to her feet.
"Come on, Nana, you should get home."

Maura had no idea what Vickie was up to, but she
couldn't help but laugh. "For God's sake, Vickie. You
were Blanche in that play."

Vickie preened, squirming in her seat and smiling
proudly. "True. But you should have been. You knew
I wanted it, so you volunteered to be stage manager
instead and bossed us all around for weeks." Vickie
winked at Maura. "You took charge and found the
role of your life. Not as the diva..."

Rick huffed out a laugh. "Clearly you nabbed that
role."

"Screw you, Rick." The corner of Vickie's mouth
lifted. "But yes, that's true."

Everyone laughed at that, including Maura. These
friends had a way of making her laugh, and laughing
made her feel more like herself. Like her former self.

Vickie was enjoying having everyone's attention.
She stood next to Maura and Kelly. "My point is that
your grandmother was the best manager ever. And
she's gonna manage this cancer right the hell out of

here. And then she's going to walk her granddaughter down the aisle."

She turned back to Maura. "So suck it up, sweetheart. You're tough. You can outlast chemo and you can beat cancer."

Everyone applauded, including Maura. Thank God for friends like this. Kelly nudged her arm, reminding her that she really did need to go home and get some rest. But she'd do it with a smile now.

IF FINN EVER had any doubts about the Irish roots of the McKinnons, they were dispelled at the engagement part Monday night. His engagement party. It was an odd night for a party, but it was when the pub was closed. The McKinnon house was rocking. He'd expected a nice family dinner with a toast to the so-called happy couple or something, but clearly the McKinnons liked to think big.

There had to be at least fifty people crammed into the house. Every level surface was being used as either a table or a seat. It was a nice house—a Victorian, of course. That's what Rendezvous Falls was famous for, after all. This was a big one, with a huge foyer and winding mahogany staircase. By the staircase was a table loaded with food. Pocket wooden doors were open to allow traffic to flow from there into a dark paneled library, then through to the dining room, a butler's pantry, and the kitchen. From the kitchen, the flow moved across the center hall to the living room and smaller parlor at the front of the house. And traffic was definitely moving. And talking. And drinking. And laughing.

Rick Thomas nudged his elbow, his voice low so no one else would hear. "How's it feel knowing all this work was done just so you could keep your job?"

Finn shook his head sharply. At times he wished Rick wasn't in on the secret, but they'd been friends almost from the moment Finn had arrived in Rendezvous Falls. Rick knew damn well that Finn hadn't been seeing anyone, so there'd been no point in trying to lie to him. The upside to Rick knowing was that Finn had someone to talk to where he didn't have to be constantly on guard to avoid slipping up. It had only been a week, and he was exhausted already. "Keep your voice down and quit playin' about, Rick. I can't change it now without hurting more people than I already have." He lifted his chin toward the library. "Besides, this isn't just about my job anymore."

Maura was in an overstuffed leather recliner, with extra pillows behind and around her. The joint pain that had started after her last treatment wasn't responding to medication yet, but she wore a wide smile as she greeted guests. Her friend, Vickie Something—there was no way Finn was going to remember all these names—was in a wooden dining chair at Maura's side. Vickie was watching Maura like a worried mother hen. If anyone stayed and talked too long, Vickie stood and gently moved them along to give Maura a chance to rest.

Bridget said Maura had been getting more forgetful lately. It was something the nurses described to her as chemo brain. It made some people fuzzy-headed and easily confused. That was the other thing Vickie seemed to be doing for her friend—she'd lean over and murmur people's names as they approached, just in case Maura forgot.

Rick followed Finn's gaze and his mouth twisted. "You've put me in a hell of a spot, you bastard. You know that, right?" He turned his back to Maura and Vickie, probably to keep them from hearing or see-ing what he was talking about. His voice lowered again. "It's one thing lying to Maura, who I don't know all that well. But Vickie Pendergast? She's a good friend, Finn. She may look like an overaged Barbie doll, but she's smart as a whip and can sniff a lie from twenty yards away."

Finn tugged Rick farther from the library door-way. "You're not lying. You're just not telling what you know. And you can't tell anyone, Rick. You know what will happen—one person tells only one person in confidence and that person tells one other person in confidence and pretty soon the whole flip-pin' town knows."

Rick squinted his eyes, staring at some vague spot over Finn's left shoulder for a moment as he con-sidered his words. "Vickie will skin me alive if she ever learns the truth and realizes I knew and didn't tell her." He scrubbed the back of his neck with his hand and sighed. "But I guess that ship has already sailed. What difference will it make if I keep the secret for a few days or a few weeks? Skinned is skinned either way."

"There you are!" Iris Taggart interrupted them. The owner of the Taggart Inn was tough to ignore. She wasn't a large woman, nor a loud one, but she had a powerful presence. Finn had gotten to know her during his stay at the inn, and he liked her. She was a tough old bird, and reminded him of his granny back in Ireland. Everyone in Sallins feared the wrath of Molly O'Hearn, even as they sat beside the meek-looking woman in church every Sunday.

Rick rolled his eyes at Iris, but there was warmth under his sarcasm. "Can't two men have a conversation in peace? What do you want, old woman?"

Iris swatted Rick's arm. "You call me an old woman one more time, and you won't know a peaceful moment again, jackass. I need your partner here. The lucky groom-to-be." Her head tipped to the side. "I don't get fooled very often, but you sure fooled me, Finn. I had no idea you were seeing Bridget while staying at the Taggart." Her eyes bore into him, and it took all of his willpower to keep his innocent expression in place. Jaysus, it felt like she was drilling straight into his brain, looking for…something. Or maybe his guilt was making him paranoid. She patted his arm. "But then again, I was distracted with my grandson's romance over the holidays, so that probably explains how I missed you and Bridget becoming an item. There must have been something in the air last fall." She straightened, barely putting any weight on the carved mahogany cane she was using. "Maura wants a word with you, dear."

Finn put his hand on his chest. "Me? Why?" Damn, he had to stop acting like a lad with a pocket full of stolen candy. He cleared his throat. "I mean… of course. Should I find Bridget?"

Iris was already turning away. "Nope. Maura just wants you for now."

As he got closer, he could see Maura's skin had a grayish pallor. This party was probably a bad idea for her, but he could tell the set of her jaw that she was a woman who got her way. Just like Bridget. Vickie jumped to her feet and gestured toward the chair she'd been using. It looked as though it had been borrowed from the dining room.

"Sit down, Finn. I have to go get a plate for Maura anyway." He started to object, but she raised her hand to stop him. "Don't worry about being chivalrous, although it's sweet. This will be a private conversation, which will be easier without you having to bend over to hear her." She gave him a hard stare. Why did he get the feeling Maura's friends were skeptical of this whole thing? Vickie's face softened into a smile. "Congratulations, by the way. Life will never be dull with Bridget, that's for sure. She's a tough gal, but she's our tough gal. This town loves the McKinnon family."

The words were said with a smile and an airy tone, but Finn didn't miss the unspoken threat. The town loved the McKinnons and wouldn't want one of them hurt in any way. He'd have to discuss that with Bridget before they ended this sham engagement. It wouldn't do any good to keep his job if the whole town hated him for being the evil man who broke the heart of the sweetheart daughter of Rendezvous Falls. He didn't like the idea of being run out of town on a rail. Vickie headed for the food table, weaving between groups of talking people, and Maura patted the empty chair beside her.

"Have a seat, young man. I have something for you."

Curiosity piqued, he did as she asked.

"How are you feeling tonight, Maura?"

She straightened and gave him a bright, if slightly artificial, smile.

"I'm fine, dear. It's a lovely party, isn't it?"

If that's how she wanted to play it, he'd go along. He returned her smile, nodding at the festive scarf wrapped around her head.

"'Tis that. Quite lovely. Those shamrocks suit you."

She reached up and touched the soft green-and-white scarf.

"I thought it was appropriate for tonight." She leaned toward him. "And speaking of appropriate, there's still no ring on my granddaughter's finger."

His face went hot. He'd suggested ring shopping before the party, but Bridget kept pushing it off. He should have insisted. Hard to be pretend-engaged without a real ring.

"I know, and I'm sorry. It all happened so fast, and I want to make sure she likes the ring…"

"Of course you do. After all, she'll be wearing it for the rest of her life, right?"

Finn swallowed hard. Twice. The lies were really piling up now.

"That's the plan, yes." He was going straight to hell when he died. He wouldn't need to bother with St. Peter. Just walk straight into the flames.

Maura nodded. "Well, I think I have just the thing."

She reached out and placed something small and light in the palm of his hand. It was a ring. A dainty, lacy gold ring with two small diamonds framing a larger oval stone. It wasn't huge and flashy. But it was lovely and he had a feeling it would be just Bridget's style. Classic and understated.

"Where did you get this? It's beautiful."

"I thought so when my Patrick slid it onto my finger once upon a time."

The noise of the party receded into a soft blur of muted sound. Maura wanted him to give Bridget her ring? His brain started spinning out scenarios. Was this worse or better than him buying a ring? At least Bridget could give it back to her grandmother when they ended things. There wouldn't be a fight about Bridget keeping whatever he bought, and he knew she was going to fight him on that.

But using Maura's own wedding ring while lying to Maura felt very wrong. Like a whole new level of

wrong. Was there a place even worse than hell waiting for him if he took this ring?

"Finn, I know what you're thinking." Even without actual hair there, Maura's brow rose and he felt a
flush of panic. Did she know? "It pricks your manly
pride not to buy some fabulous ring that costs half
your salary, right?"

He blew out a sharp breath. "Not exactly…"

"Look, I practically raised that girl, and she will
love this ring more than any gaudy sparkler you buy."

"That's exactly what I thought when I saw it."

Maura was quiet for a moment. "You know her
better than I thought. I'm glad." She closed his fingers around the ring. "So take this and give it to her.
Tonight, while everyone's here."

"Tonight? Oh, I don't know…" It was so public.
A very public lie. But Maura had made up her mind.

"I know. You need to get a ring on that girl's finger, and this is the ring." She looked up and nodded
toward her friend Vickie, who was clearly in on this
plan. Vickie flashed a smile and disappeared into
the crowd. "You robbed me of the chance to see the
actual proposal with all your secrecy nonsense. So
give me this tonight. Bridget is special to me, Finn."

He nodded. "Because you two are so alike."

Her sharp laughter turned heads in the room.
"Wow—you really do know her." Her expression
went somber. "It would mean a lot to me to be able
to see this happen."

In that moment, he understood why Bridget hadn't

told Maura the truth about them last week. She'd wanted her grandmother to have some moments of joy, and this cooked-up engagement had brought her that. There was a brightness in Maura's eyes that he had no desire to extinguish.

Before he could answer, there was movement at the doorway. He looked up to find Bridget looking between him and Maura in concern. Vickie was right behind her. She'd clearly gone to find her once Maura gave her the signal. Bridget took a step forward. They'd promised to be on the same page, but there was no way to warn her what was coming. She'd understand. He hoped.

"Is everything okay?" Bridget asked. "Nana, are you…?"

Finn stood, shaking his head. "Everything's fine… honey."

Her eyes narrowed, but this was all part of the deal—public displays of affection to sell the act. He reached out and took her hands in his. There were storm clouds in her dark eyes, but she didn't pull away. Her mouth twitched as if resisting her command to smile, but it finally got there.

"Then what did you need…baby?"

He didn't like the way that word sizzled against his skin when she said it, even under duress. Dori used to call him "baby" all the time, and look how great that turned out. Even with the memories the word invoked, when Bridget said it in her husky voice, something started humming in Finn's veins.

Maura tapped her fingers sharply on the arm of her chair behind him. "There's no time like the present, Finn."

"Time for what?" Bridget asked. She pulled her hands away. "What's going on with you two?"

Oi, he'd already cut the brake lines on this runaway train, so he may as well enjoy the ride. He quickly whispered "sorry" as he dropped to one knee. There was a collective gasp from everyone in the room. Bridget's face went white, her eyes round.

Maura hissed out a quick "Yes!"

"Um…" Bridget stammered as he took her hand. "What are you doing…sweetheart?"

"I know we're already engaged, but I hadn't found the perfect ring yet. Until tonight." He held up the ring and ignored the whispered sighs going around the house. It felt like all fifty guests were crammed into the doorway. "Your grandmother offered me her ring, and I accepted. And now I'm offering it to you. Will you wear this ring, Bridget McKinnon? Will you agree—again—to marry me?"

Her mouth dropped open and stayed that way. Everyone was holding their breath, including Finn. Would this be the moment her conscience woke up and made her tell the truth to everyone? And told him to go to hell in the process? Her eyes began to shimmer with unspilled tears. She looked to Maura, and her voice cracked.

"Nana, you gave him your ring? For me? I…"

Someone from the back—one of her cousins, he suspected—called out.

"Say yes!"

Applause broke out, and Bridget's cheeks went from pale to bright pink. She laughed awkwardly and tugged gently at her hand, as if she wanted to flee. He didn't release her, though. She glanced around the room. The next move was all hers. Her eyes closed briefly, then she nodded.

"Um...yes. I'll...wear the ring."

The room went wild, but he only saw Bridget. She was frozen in place. They both were. Her cousin Kelly let out a catcall and yelled out, "Put a ring on it, Finn!"

He slid the ring onto her finger, then stood.

This time it was Michael calling out helpful advice.

"Kiss her, man!"

More cheers from the gathered crowd.

He hesitated. Bridget's eyes flickered to Maura, then back to his face. Her shoulder barely moved in a private shrug, and she stepped forward. Her next words were for him alone.

"All part of the show, right?"

Before he could examine the sting of what she'd said, she grabbed his shirt and pulled him roughly forward until her lips hit his. Once that happened, words weren't necessary.

His arm slid around her waist and he tugged her body against his. Her lips were soft and warm. And her eyes were wide open, staring into his so close he felt she should be able to see right into his soul. But her shutters were still down, making it impossible to read her thoughts. Her hand grabbed his ass, and then he had a pretty good idea what she was thinking. Their mouths moved against each other, and… for just a moment…hers parted enough to let his tongue trace against her teeth.

She took a sharp breath, then surrendered, allowing him to kiss her the way he'd been aching to—deep, long and hard. A moan vibrated in her throat, her head turning as if to give him better access. Yes, please. Her hands slid up his back. Her fingers started digging in. And he was drowning in her. Falling into this perfect vortex she'd created for just the two of them…

"Okay, you two." Maura's warm chuckle may as well have been ice water for the effect it had on them. "Save something for the wedding night!"

Bridget flinched at the very first word, and now she pulled away from him with a shattered mix of confusion, lust and anger in her eyes. He held on, whispering into her ear before she slapped him.

"Easy, lass. Part of the show, remember?"

That cooled off whatever was burning inside her. She pulled away from him, emotionally as well as physically. Apparently he wasn't the only one stung by those words. But this was a show. It wasn't real. He had to remember that. They both did.

The room erupted in yet more applause and cheering, and he forced himself to smile and nod to the high-spirited response to his proposal.

Call it whatever—fake, faux, not real, acting, a show. A very firm voice in his head told him what he already knew. That kiss was as real as it got. That kiss was smokin' hot and hypnotic. That kiss left him craving more.

And that was going to be one big damn problem, wasn't it?

BRIDGET FINISHED SWEEPING the floor and straightened with a groan. The bar looked like a leprechaun festival was about to begin. That wasn't far from the truth—the annual Purple Shamrock St. Patrick's Party was coming up the following day. Everything in the place was covered in green, orange and white bunting. There were sparkly green shamrocks hanging from the ceiling in the dining area, and by the time the party started, the dance floor ceiling would be wall-to-wall green balloons.

Per tradition, she and her cousins had worked that morning to pack away anything breakable or of sentimental or monetary value to the family or to the pub. The St. Patrick's party crowds could get rowdy. Nana always called it "amateur night" because people—most of whom didn't have a lick of Irish in them—used the day as an excuse to drink until they were falling-down drunk. Things got broken. Or stolen. The night was a moneymaker for the bar, but it was also a night where they had to stay vigilant. The whole family would be on hand to keep an eye on things tomorrow night.

But tonight it was just her, working in blissful silence. The Purple Shamrock was always closed the Friday before the party to give the family a chance to prepare. They'd all headed home for dinner an hour ago, leaving Bridget to do the last-minute details. She looked around the place and sighed.

Yes, the parties were a huge hassle, but they were also more fun than she wanted to admit. They brought the McKinnons together. They brought the community together. The Purple Shamrock would always be an Irish pub. Maybe Finn was right—instead of fighting the tradition, maybe she needed to embrace it and build on it. Figure out a menu that honored their Irish roots. Have a few genuine Irish entertainers once in a while. Maybe even have a traditional Irish music session a few weekends every month. In an artsy town like Rendezvous Falls, there were probably fiddlers and other musicians who'd love to get together.

If they could open the patio by summer, they could have live music out there. She grabbed the dustpan and bent over to scoop up her sweepings. She could see it in her mind—strings of lights over the decking, with an entertainer set up in the far corner and people dancing under the lights. Under the stars. The moon would be rising over the hills on the far side of Seneca Lake. A guitar strumming, and an Irish ballad being sung. Finn's arms around her...

Whoa!

Where did that very specific image come from? Their fake engagement would definitely be over by summer, so there'd be no reason for them to be dancing. Not on the patio. Not anywhere. Ever.

The front door clicked shut behind her, and she straightened and spun so fast that the dust from the dustpan flew up in a cloud, covering her black shirt and making her cough and sputter. Finn stood there, his hand on the door handle, with a wide grin on his face. He had such a nice smile…

Stop it!

This engagement was fake. Sure, they'd had a couple of smoking hot kisses, but she was just a means to an end for this guy, and she needed to remember that. She waved her hand in front of her face to clear the dust cloud away, then started brushing the dirt off her shirt, glowering at his laughter.

"I'm beginning to think you enjoy scaring the shit out of me, Finn O'Hearn. What are you doing here?" One of her cousins must have left the door unlocked. She'd deal with them later. His smile deepened.

"Right now I'm thinkin' I'd like to help w' that." His brogue was thicker than usual.

"With what?" She continued to brush her shirt, then realized what he meant. Her hands had been sweeping down across her chest, where most of the dust had landed. And he was staring at her hands. And her breasts. Oh.

She dropped one hand to her hip, gesturing to

her face with the other. "Very classy, professor. My face is up here. Do you always leer at the women you sneak up on?"

His gaze darkened. "Only the ones I'm engaged to, love."

Bridget's chest—the one he'd just been admiring—warmed a bit at his words. He didn't sound playful. Or remorseful. He sounded serious. And…interested. Was it possible he'd been thinking of those kisses as much as she had? What would she say if he wanted to kiss her again? Silly question—she'd say yes, please. After all, hadn't she just been daydreaming about dancing with the guy? Maybe another kiss was what she needed to get him out of her head. And if he wanted to get closer to the chest he'd just been caught ogling? Well, hell. It had been a long damn time since a man had touched her, and she'd have a hard time saying no to one who talked to her with that lilt to his voice and that heat in his eye.

He walked toward her, and weaved a little as he passed between the tables. Had he been drinking? Maybe that wasn't heat in his eye. Maybe it was just whiskey-passion. The kind that gave a man enough ego to think he should flirt with every female in his vicinity.

She should turn away. She should send him home. She should give him hell for thinking it was okay to openly stare at her chest. Maybe she should even slap his face. But she didn't do any of those things. She stood there and waited. If she'd had any illusions he

might sweep her off her feet and kiss her senseless—
a girl can dream, right?—they quickly vanished.

He reached out, but it wasn't for her. It was for
the broom.

"Why are you in here alone at this hour, with the
door unlocked?" He started sweeping up the mess
she'd made when she jumped. "For someone who
does na' like t' be frightened, you do take some risks,
lass."

Her spine stiffened. "If you're referring to the risk
of some drunk dude walking in and staring at my
boobs, you're right. I should have anticipated that."

He froze, head down, looking up at her through
his heavy brows. "I'm not drunk."

"But you don't deny staring at my boobs. Awesome."

He stood up straight, and a smile tugged at his
mouth. "I'm engaged to those boobs, so I should be
able to look at 'em once in a while."

"Seriously? You're engaged to me, not my boobs.
And you're not really even engaged to me. It's all a
sham, remember? Just a show." Lord knew, she kept
forgetting. Especially after that kiss last week at their
phony engagement party. That not-so-phony kiss she
kept dreaming about...

"You're right, o' course. Sorry." His smile faded.
He leaned on the broom. "I'm not drunk, but I am...
um...mellow. Rick was at my place to help with some
research, and we had a shot of whiskey before he

left." He shrugged. "And I had a couple more after that. I shouldna' been so forward."

Now it was her turn to have a smile tugging at her lips, begging to be set free. She finally surrendered.

"Whiskey brings out your accent, Finn." And she liked it.

"Does it?" His head tipped to the side, his green eyes shining with humor. "Musta' been the taste o' home and all that." He swept the dust into the pan, then straightened and looked around the pub, where only half the lights were lit. She had to save money every way she could these days. He gave her an exaggeratedly stern look, lowering one heavy brow. "You shouldn't be here alone."

"Michael was supposed to lock up on his way out, but he and Mary's husband were yukking it up about something when they left. Guess he forgot. What brought you over?"

The energy in the pub had shifted from the moment he'd first walked in. It felt amped up. More electric. Something was popping and sizzling under her skin. She looked at his lips that had done such a lovely job kissing her last week. They were moving, and she realized with a jolt that he was answering her.

"You did. I walked Rick out and saw the lights on and no cars here. Kelly told me yesterday that the place would be closed tonight. I thought I should check." He looked up at the shamrocks and leprechauns hanging everywhere. "'Tis very…green…in here. May not be the most authentic way to honor dear ol' Patrick. He came to Ireland to save souls, not pickle them in green beer."

She put her hand on her hip. "I'll have you know Father Joseph Brennan himself gave our party his blessing. In fact, he'll be doing the ribbon-cutting tomorrow at three o'clock to get things started."

Finn shrugged off his coat. He wore a dark Henley and jeans. Maybe it was the lighting, but it seemed his clothing was particularly...clingy...tonight. He'd kept the broom, and started sweeping around the bar area. He was moving away when he replied.

"I've seen the good Father drink, so I'm sure he blesses the event and everyone here and every glass served." He looked back over his shoulder and waggled his brows playfully, rendering her knees surprisingly weak. "Don't get me wrong—I love the man. But his blessing on the party still doesn't make it authentic."

"I can't tell if you're joking or being genuinely passionate about your heritage." She went with his playful mood and started to tease. "Or maybe you're just a snob."

Finn froze, his back to her. Then he started sweeping with a bit more energy. Angry energy.

"Oh, sure." Finn's voice chilled. "Pull the snob card. That's me. Big fuckin' snob."

"Whoa." Bridget put down the paper centerpiece she'd been arranging. "What just happened? I was kidding."

He kept pushing the broom, not answering her. She walked in front of him and forced him to stop. It took a moment for his gaze to meet hers. His eyes were guarded. He seemed…hurt. His fingers were holding the broom so tightly his knuckles were white. More than hurt. He was angry. Who had called him a snob before in his life? A parent? A friend? She let out a breath. Or his ex-wife.

She knew Finn's divorce had been ugly. Nana had heard about it from Rick in the book club. Something about his wife leaving him for a trusted friend. Did the woman try to blame her infidelity on Finn?

"Finn, you are not a snob. You're a sarcastic pain in my ass, but a snob? No. A snob wouldn't be pushing a broom in a tacky American-Irish pub for his faux fiancée."

His mouth opened, then snapped shut. He looked down at the broom, and his expression finally softened. So did his stance. His shoulders relaxed, and he gave her a brief nod.

"Sorry. Touchy subject."

"I can see that." She hesitated. Should she mention her hunch or leave it alone? "An ex-wife sort of subject?"

"Something like that, yeah." The corner of his mouth lifted, but his voice was firm. "A subject I don't want to discuss."

"Have you talked about it with anyone?"

All hints of a smile were gone. "There's nothing to talk about. I fell in love." He stared down at the floor.

"I thought we had a perfect, golden life. But she was bored. Boredom turned to anger, and we fought for a few years. That's when she threw the 'snob' thing at me. Then the fights stopped, and I thought we were okay." He looked up. "And they were. For her. She'd fallen in love with someone else."

His mouth pressed into a hard line. No wonder he didn't want to talk about it. She could sympathize.

"I'm with you on the don't-talk-about-exes thing. Been there. Done that. Got the bruises to show for it."

She hadn't talked about Clark much with anyone since coming home. Partly because she was embarrassed. Once she got to Rendezvous Falls, she got busy taking care of the pub and the house and her grandmother. No one had asked many questions about her life on the West Coast, and she'd pushed her former lover into the furthest back corner of her mind. Almost forgotten. But not quite.

She started fluffing the centerpiece on the table nearest her, knowing they'd probably end up being used as footballs by the end of the party. That's why they used paper flowers and shamrocks. And no candles. Finn's hand on her shoulder made her flinch—she thought he'd gone back to his broom duties.

"What do you mean about having bruises, lass?" There was a tender concern in his rough voice that turned her belly into a quivering mess. "Did he…?"

"What? Oh…no. I was referring to metaphorical bruises. You know, the kind you get when someone you trust rips the rug out from under your feet?" She told him how Clark had laughed when she asked him to come to Rendezvous Falls to help her. So much for her being his soul mate as he'd claimed so many times. He didn't even pretend to think about following her, after she'd bounced from city to city for his career. She huffed a soft laugh. "I was his treasured 'muse' right up to the moment I asked him to sacrifice something for me. He dropped me like a hot rock." She lifted her shoulder. "I'm better off, right?"

Finn set the broom against the bar and took both her hands, pulling her close. She didn't resist, basically hypnotized by the dark fire in his eyes. If the look wasn't enough to render her mute, his deep, gravelly voice finished her off.

"You are better off, I'm sure. Just as I am."

"Our stories aren't that different. Clark was bored. Then he was angry. Then he tuned out. If I hadn't left to come home, he would have found someone else." Finn stared at her, still holding her hands. She took a quick breath. "You told me once that you and I were a lot alike. I laughed then, but you may have been right."

"Because we both have lousy taste in mates?"

She laughed, and his body language eased, as if her laughter had released something inside of him. He moved a step closer. And that brought him really close. He smelled really good. What were they talking about again?

"Uh… Yes, we have lousy taste in mates." She thought about it. "I don't know about you, but I ended

up feeling pretty beat up in the heart department."
He nodded in understanding, and she kept thinking
out loud. "And I haven't had anyone in my life since
then. Have you?"

He shook his head. It was a bit of an epiphany.
She kept dismissing Clark as a mistake in her past
that was over and done. But maybe her friends were
right. Maybe she had been using her busy life as an
excuse not to see anyone. Maybe Clark's betrayal
was the real reason.

Finn smiled at her, holding her hands as she continued to psychoanalyze herself. As usual, his presence opened up something inside of her.

"So if I'm still mad about Clark and have trust
issues, and you're still mad about… What was her
name?"

"Bridget…"

"No way—her name was Bridget?"

He laughed. "No love, it wasn't. But I've got
things I'd much rather talk about right now. Don't
you?"

He squeezed her fingers before raising one hand
to cup the side of her face. What. The. Hell. Was.
Happening? His gaze held her captive. And made her
voice disappear. Finn O'Hearn was cupping her face
with his hand, saying sweet, understanding things in
that amazing accent, and her emotions welled up out
of nowhere. Along with a flood of words.

"I have no idea why I just dumped all of that
psychobabble on you. You unlock something in me,

and I don't know why. It's like I start talking and I start saying all this stuff that I didn't even know was inside of me. That I don't talk about with anyone. I…"

"Bridget." His voice was low and tender. "Stop talking."

The only sound in the pub was the hum of the furnace, interrupted by the occasional whir of the ice machine under the bar. She looked away from his face and found the power to step back, but his other hand was on her hip—she had no idea when that happened—and he wouldn't release her. Her face went hot. What more was there to say? She'd just spewed her whole failed relationship history at him. Who knew what would come out of her mouth next? She fixed her eyes on the back wall of the pub, ignoring the magic ninja of his eyes, and doing her best to ignore the heat of his fingers moving gently on her hip. Pulling her in. She sucked in a broken breath, knowing she wouldn't be able to resist him much longer if he kept touching her.

She stepped out of his reach. "Sorry. I don't know why we keep doing this little dance, but it's a bad idea. We should just stick to the fake stuff, and only when we have an audience to perform for. No more soul-baring, I promise."

Finn tipped his head to the side and stared hard at her with eyes that grew darker and more intense by the second. Her hands twisted together under his steady gaze, like a schoolgirl finally getting the attention of her high school crush. She didn't know what to do with herself. And the man wouldn't speak, so she felt compelled to fill the silence.

"So…uh…hey, thanks for stopping to check on me. Sorry things got weird. Let's not let that happen again, okay?" She reached for the broom. "I'm almost done here, so you can go…" As she reached past him, his arm wrapped around her waist.

"Finn…" She closed her eyes, knowing if she looked up she was a goner. His fingers touched her chin, lifting her head.

Nope. Not gonna look. Do not look at…

"Open your eyes, Bridget."

And she did. Just like that. He said the words and her eyes opened of their own accord. When did he get so close? Why was his face right above hers? Damn, another kiss from this man would undo her. He knew how to freakin' kiss a woman. His green eyes went soft and dark and tender. And she was lost, sagging into him in surrender, raising her hands to his shoulders because the floor felt like it was slipping away beneath her feet.

"I know all about bad relationships, love. I could win awards for the bad choices I've made when it comes to women." He hesitated, a distant look crossing his face. "And friends. And jobs." He smiled softly. "And lies to keep jobs."

She huffed out a laugh, about to say something sarcastic, but he wasn't finished.

"But this?" His arm tightened. "This…what did

you call it? This weird thing that happens between us? I think it needs a bit of our attention." He brushed her hair behind her ear, tracing his fingers down the sensitive skin on her neck. He smiled when she couldn't hold back a shudder. "Because I'm not sure why we're fightin' it so hard."

"Seriously?" She told her body to move away. Her body did not move. "You and I are an act. We're not really in love, remember?"

He was close enough that his warm, whiskey-scented breath moved across her face.

"D'you need love to have sex with someone, Bridget? Is that one o' your rules?"

Hearing Finn say the word sex while holding her made her insides turn to lava. Hot, liquid, danger-ous. Was he actually suggesting what she thought he was suggesting?

"No, not really…" She stumbled over her words, feeling way out of her depth. "But Jesus, Finn. You and I having sex? Isn't that the definition of bad choices? Not to mention being complicated as hell."

His arms were resting at her waist. Encircling her, without holding too tight. He was giving her room to run if she wanted it. She didn't move. His smile deepened.

"Think about it. We don't have to worry about get-ting caught or being careful, because people already think we're together. We plan to fake break up our fake engagement in May. We have an end date, so not messy. We're two adults who have something…

weird…going on, with no genuine reason not to explore it."

Her laughter was high-pitched and nervous in her own ears. "What exactly are we exploring, again?"

"Babe, am I really the only one feeling this chemistry between us? When we kiss…do you not feel that heat? Don't you want to see where that might take us?"

She couldn't argue there. "We kiss really well. I'm just trying to be…"

"What? Practical?" He brushed his lips against her hair. "Isn't it a bit late for that? You already accepted my wedding proposal, love."

"I accepted a fake proposal. You're talking about a very real night of getting naked together."

She closed her eyes, but that didn't help, because all she could see was her and Finn together. Naked. And that vision was very, very tempting. The warmth in her chest dropped lower and heavier. She swayed against him.

"Ah, Bridget…" She loved the way his accent rolled the *r* in her name just enough to make it unique—Brih-jit. He dropped his head, breathing the words across her ear. It was intimate. And sexy as hell. "Do you not want to get naked together? It doesn't have to happen if you don't want it to. If I misread…"

"I want to." His arm tightened around her when she said it. "I really want to. But I'm trying to be logical here…" She had no idea why. Who used logic when anticipating sex with a gorgeous, kind, funny man like Finn?

His voice was gentle. "We're just gonna explore the possibilities and see where they take us, love. Perhaps we won't get any farther than me kissing my way down your neck and my hands sliding under this sweatshirt, yeah?" His voice dropped even lower, starting a fire burning in her abdomen. "And then we'll deduce the next step together, yeah? Nothing happens unless we both want it to."

There were probably a hundred reasons to say no. But Bridget couldn't think of a single one as Finn's lips moved lightly across her ear and down her neck. His mouth was magical. That's the only explanation. That's why his kisses knocked her sideways—magic.

"It's not fair…" She whispered her thought aloud.

"What's not fair, love?" He spoke against her neck, kissing the base of her skin. Her head automatically dropped back to give him easier access.

"Your mouth…what it does to me…"

His laughter against her skin was her new favorite thing.

"As you Yanks like to say, you ain't seen nothin' yet…" His hand slid under her shirt as promised, his fingers hot and soft on her back, stroking her in a rhythm that matched the way his mouth moved against her.

She pulled back just enough that he raised his head to look at her, a shadow of concern in his expression. She needed to be looking him straight in the eye one last time.

"Just to be clear, we're exploring chemistry here. No obligation. No commitment. No messy emotion."

His smile slanted up on one side. "I agree on the first two. But no emotion? Not possible. We'll have pleasure and passion for sure." He gave her a brief, hard kiss as if to prove his point. "Desire is an emotion, yeah? 'Cuz I'm feeling a lot o' that one, too." His smile faded. "I'm not looking for a quick emotionless bang, Bridget. If we do this, it's gonna be more than just physical activity." His fingers started moving again, making her moan as her eyes fell closed. "I want you to feel something. Lots of things, actually."

She was feeling something, alright. She was feeling hot and bothered. Her hands gripped his butt, pulling herself tight against the erection pressing against his jeans. His emerald eyes went black and he hissed at the contact, growing even more rigid. Why was she trying to fight this?

"Make me feel something, Finn."

CHAPTER TWELVE

Finn was feeling all sorts of things. He was so hard it hurt, but that wasn't what he was focused on most. His top feeling was…wonder. Bridget had just consented to this crazy idea of his, and it felt like he'd just been given a precious gift. He wanted her. Lord knew, he wanted her. But even more, he wanted to give her pleasure. To make her moan like she had just a moment ago. To make her cry out his name. He went a little light-headed—so much so that he dropped his head to her shoulder to gather his thoughts.

Bridget's hands cupped the back of his head, fingers working through his hair. He moved his hands against her back, sliding up to unhook her bra. Then sliding forward to cup her breasts in the palms of his hands, where they fit perfectly. He kissed the tender skin beneath her ear, where her pulse raced beneath his lips. His fingers rubbed against her nipples, back and forth until she twisted and pushed against him, murmuring words he couldn't decipher. It didn't matter. She was telling him she was feeling the same thing he was. Hot, molten desire.

"I want you so fucking bad." His thoughts sounded crude out loud, but he'd never said anything more true. "I'm thinkin' we need to do that naked thing you mentioned earlier."

His fingers continued their work on her breasts, and she gave a little whimper before answering.

"Oh, hell yes!" Another gasp. "But where?"

Good damn question. Doing it on a bar table might make for a hot memory, but was that what either of them wanted for their first time? Bridget deserved candlelight and silk sheets. And had he ever locked the front door? Could someone else walk in? Bridget read his mind.

"Go lock the door. I'll hit the lights. We'll go out the back…but hurry."

He couldn't help thinking that if he stepped away from her right now, she'd have very visible evidence of his mental state. Then he remembered she'd already grabbed his ass and rubbed against him. There was no way she'd missed the ridge behind his zipper. He sucked in a breath and gave her breasts one more playful squeeze before turning to rush toward the door. He didn't want time apart to burst this bubble of desire. Bridget laughed that whiskey laugh of hers, deep and rough, then hurried toward the back hall to turn off the lights.

The only light when he rejoined her was coming through the window in the storage room from the parking lot light, casting the narrow hallway in a soft, gray glow. It made the space seem other worldly. As if all the colors had been turned down a few notches, leaving a very noir effect. Everything was softer. Bridget looked softer and even more inviting. She was leaning against the wall, waiting for him with a sexy smile and no visible signs of doubt or hesitations.

Did she reach for him first, or was it him who grabbed her? Did it matter? All he knew was that they ended up wrapped around each other in the shadowy hall, her back to the wall, one leg hooked around his thigh. Their mouths came together in a furious-paced kiss, twisting, and pushing. Her kisses hit him like a freight train every time. The idea that this time they didn't have to stop or worry about an audience. That they could just keep going...

His hands tugged her hips forward. She moaned into his mouth, rubbing against him until he thought he'd lose his mind. He was hungry for her. Starving. Her fingers grabbed at the waist of his jeans and he realized she was fumbling with his belt. Someone else was hungry, too. A low growl rose in his throat as the kiss grew even more frenzied.

Hands were flying now, unbuckling, unbuttoning and unzipping. She had flats on, so she was able to kick them, and her jeans, to the side. But he'd slipped into his winter boots before walking across the slushy parking lot, so his jeans—and briefs—fell to his ankles and stayed there. He didn't care. He'd stopped caring and thinking about anything other than burying himself in Bridget McKinnon the minute they'd come together in the hall.

It was as if those few minutes apart to secure the building had fanned the flames instead of cooling them. He'd give her the rest of tonight in the comfort of a warm, soft bed with sweet words and slow moves. But right now? He needed her. And since she was practically climbing him at the moment, she apparently felt the same way. Still, he wanted to be one hundred percent certain. As his fingers began sliding her panties down her thighs, he spoke against her mouth.

"You sure?"

"God, yes!"

He'd grabbed a condom from his pocket before his pants dropped. He quickly put it on, then cupped her bottom and lifted her just enough against the wall so that he could enter her. She was as ready for this as he was, and he slid in easily, letting out a loud groan as he did.

"You're perfect. Fuckin' perfect…" He nipped at her shoulder and started to move. She did her best to move with him, even as she was suspended in midair in his arms. He quickly lost all track of who was doing what. There was no up, down, floor, wall. Just the two of them connected in a way that made his heart feel like it was going to burst right out of his chest. No words. Just sounds and heavy breathing as he drove into her until stars appeared behind his closed eyelids.

"Bridget…oi, Bridget…"

Her fingernails dug into his shoulder blades through his shirt. They weren't two people anymore. They'd melded together as one, and they reached the climax with a tangled cry of triumph. Right there in the hallway of the Purple Shamrock. All the thoughts that left his brain a few minutes ago came flooding back now as he rested his head against her shoulder and waited for his pulse to steady.

He'd told her he didn't want a quick bang, then took her against a wall. Was he a jackass for doing it? She'd been as enthusiastic as him, but still. A wall. He cringed. He was forty, not some horny teenager. Bridget tapped the back of his head lightly with one finger. Her breathing was as ragged as his.

"What the hell are you thinking so hard about?"

"Tryin' to decide if I should be apologizing or…"

"Or doing a victory dance? I vote on the latter. Good Lord, Finn. That was amazing… Oh!" His body had taken one last shudder against her at the word amazing. "But I'm losing feeling in my legs, so if you could relax your…"

His hands were holding her body off the ground, clutching her very fine ass tightly. He muttered an apology and reluctantly let her legs slide down until she was standing on her own. Her knees nearly buckled, so he kept a light hold on her hips to steady her. The hem of her sweatshirt fell against his hands. His jeans were still around his ankles. Very smooth,

O'Hearn. He was quite the charmer, wasn't he? He grimaced.

"Not exactly the romantic interlude I'd intended, but things just…"

"Happened? Yeah, they did. And it was fun. At least it was for me." Her brows lowered in concern. "And I thought for you, too?"

He shook his head to clear all the pesky doubts away. "Definitely fun. Like…the most fun I've had in a very long time. Maybe ever." He gave her a quick kiss on the forehead. "I'm sorry for getting in my head so much. It just caught me off guard…this… here…" He glanced down at the pants at his ankles. "Like this. You deserve…"

"Whoa." She pressed two fingers against his mouth. "I was a very active participant in what happened. And where. And how. And Finn?" Her right eyebrow rose high, and there was a mischievous glimmer in her eyes. "I liked it. A whole hell of a lot." Her smile deepened. "Your mouth isn't the only thing magical about you."

He barked out a laugh, and his chest finally began to loosen. He'd spent so much time over the past two years doubting every decision he'd ever made that it had become a habit. But she was right. Not about the magical part, although that was nice to hear. But the hot sex they'd had was mutual in every way. And just because he'd had her against a wall with his pants around his ankles didn't mean he couldn't follow it up with candles and wine and an actual bed.

"Did you like it enough to repeat it?" He reached up to hold her fingers, kissing them at the same time. "In a more…horizontal position? With fewer articles of clothing? In an actual bed?"

She didn't answer right away, but it didn't feel like hesitation as much as consideration.

"Tomorrow is the Shamrock's biggest day of the year. A long, busy day that'll start early."

"Is that a no?" *Please don't be a no…*

She grinned.

"Not a no. Just a statement of fact." She moved to the side, pulling on her jeans and tucking her pink panties into a back pocket. That move was enough to arouse him all over again. "To make up for the lack of sleep, though, I may have to ask you to lower your standards and help with our tacky American celebration of St. Paddy's Day."

He bent over to grab his own jeans, buckling his belt with a wink in her direction. "I think we already started a tacky American celebration that St. Paddy would definitely not approve of. The moral ground has been lost. May as well keep it going, yeah?"

THE MORAL GROUND has been lost…

The words should make Bridget feel ashamed, at least a little. But they didn't. Instead, she felt a sense of…victory. Not for having loose morals—she knew Finn wasn't serious about that. They were two consenting adults. But there was a personal victory in letting go of her defenses and just going with the moment for once. She'd given up the role of The Responsible One, and damn, it felt good. Would there be regrets tomorrow? Maybe. Probably. But tomorrow was hours away, and the idea of spending those hours in a nice warm bed with Finn O'Hearn was too tempting to turn down without at least some consideration.

If she and Finn were a mistake, it had already been made. If they were going to regret it, why not make it a night worth the regrets?

But of all nights, the night before St. Patrick's Day. So much work to do tomorrow. It would be more practical to wait and think about this…

Finn cupped her face in his hands, planting a soft kiss on her lips. He pulled back, looking resigned.

"It's okay, love. No pressure. We don't have to do anything tonight. The memories alone will keep me…"

She traced her fingers through his black hair and went on tiptoe to kiss him. He groaned and gripped her tighter, taking control of the kiss. People teased her for being a control freak, but she gladly conceded to Finn. He took over her mouth and her breath and her heart. She was completely lost in him, ready to drop her jeans again right here in the cold back hall of the Purple Shamrock. Her back bumped the door. Finn reached behind her to take the handle, murmuring against her mouth.

"My place or yours?" he asked.

"We'll never make it up the stairs at this rate. Yours."

Finn chuckled and pushed the door open. The blast of cold air did nothing to cool off the fire burning between them. Neither did the laughter as they locked up the pub and hurried across the parking lot and into the house. They did it all while tangled up in each other, kissing every few seconds, stumbling on the icy front steps, fumbling with the keys, shedding their coats in the entryway and the rest of their clothes on the way to the bedroom in Finn's apartment.

They didn't slow down until they hit the mattress, laughing and out of breath. Finn propped himself up on one elbow and ran his hand down her side, sliding from her shoulder to her ribs, her waist and her hip without saying a word. The only light was from a lamp out in the living room, brushing through the doorway, soft and sensual. He stared at his own hand intently as it made its way gently down to her thigh, then slid between her legs. He traced up the thigh of her other leg, then back between them again. Her hips rocked up against him and he stopped, pressing his fingers against her.

"Uh-uh. We have all night, love. No rushing this time."

His fingers began to move, and she moaned his name as she lay back to let him have it his way. Because his way was delicious. She'd take control later…much, much later…

There was no doubt Finn knew his way around a woman. Between his fingers and his mouth, he'd had her crying out more than once before he reached for the nightstand and pulled out a box of condoms. She couldn't help laughing, but at the same time, she felt just a shadow of worry.

"That's a lot of condoms, Finn."

It was a joke. Sort of. Had the room just chilled, or was her busy brain trying to ruin everything?

Finn had gone still. He hesitated before holding up the box.

"Bridget, I bought this months ago." His voice was gentle but serious. "And it's still sealed. That one in my pocket is even older than these." He set the box on the bed and ran his fingers up her arm. "We've both been burned by cheaters. I'm not that kind of guy. I don't... I don't do one-night stands." He frowned. "And that's not what we're doing."

She covered his mouth with her hand. "Stop. I wasn't trying to slut-shame you, Finn. I had no right to say that. You're a grown man who had a whole life before we met. I've lived a life, too. It was just a little freak-out moment. I'm sorry."

He smiled against her fingers, his eyes shining with mischief again as he reached for the small blue box. "So you don't mind if I unseal this now?"

She snatched it away from him. "Even better, let me do it."

Finn sucked in a sharp breath when she slid the condom on, playfully running her fingers up and down. He was on his knees between her legs, and his head dropped back, eyes tightly closed until she released him. His gaze nearly set her on fire as he stretched out over her, teasing her until her back was arching to reach him. He dropped his head next to hers and whispered roughly in her ear.

"I'm going to need you t' spend more time touching me like that, love. But right now I need t' be in you…"

And then he was. The wall sex had been hot and fun, but this? This was so much better. They moved together, her legs wrapped around him, sheets twisted around their feet. He'd take her right to the edge, then bring her back again, slowing down until she was whimpering with desire. Then he rolled so she was on top, and that was…incredible. His hands reached up and tangled into her hair as she took control of the game. She was just about to achieve what she wanted when he gave a laugh and rolled again, pinning her to the mattress and holding her hands above her head. As if knowing she was about to lose her mind, he drove hard and fast, and they both went with a loud cry. He collapsed on her, face buried into the pillow. Their bodies pulsed a few more times, but all they did was groan and hold each other tighter. Bridget had one question on repeat inside her head.

What the ever-loving hell was that?

Before she could ask the question out loud, she realized Finn's breathing had suddenly slowed. His weight pressed down on her. He was asleep. Or unconscious, which was a serious possibility after… whatever that was. More than sex. More than love-making. More than anything she'd experienced. She was a little light-headed herself. Or maybe that was lack of oxygen, since he was crushing her. She pushed on his shoulder. He grunted, then slid to his side. His arms were tight around her, but at least she could breathe. She'd assumed he was sleeping, until he squeezed her and murmured against the back of her neck.

"You feel so good, love. Stay with me, yeah?"

She grinned. As if she had any choice with the way he was holding her. As if she'd want to move, even if she could. She patted his arm.

"I'm staying."

It seemed as if she'd just blinked, but the next time she opened her eyes, the alarm clock read three o'clock. In the morning. She stretched, and felt Finn's strong arms around her from behind, holding her firmly against him. He let out a breath against her neck.

"I was wondering when you were going t' wake up." His lips brushed her shoulder. "Not that I mind holding on to you, love." He gave her a quick squeeze. "But that snoring of yours…"

"I beg your pardon!" She turned to meet his laughing eyes. "I do not snore. I…I purr." Her snoring wasn't news to her. She'd been teased about it since she was a teen.

Finn chuckled. "Purr, eh? Let me think…" He

shook his head. "Nope. Not a purr, unless you're referring to an engine purring. Like…a big engine. Diesel, maybe…"

She swatted at him, but he easily blocked it, grabbing her arm lightly and holding it against her chest. She was trapped. And she didn't care. In fact, she moved back against him, making him hiss when her butt touched his growing hardness. He was clearly enjoying this playful exchange as much as she was.

"Sorry if I disturbed your beauty sleep, professor."

"You didna' disturb a thing, love. Everything you do is a delight to me."

"Wait until you hear me pass gas…"

He laughed, pretending to push her away, but not releasing her completely.

"Oh, that's lovely. How did we go from earth-shattering sex to talking about farts? You're a true romantic, Bridget McKinnon." He pushed her onto her back, grinning down at her in the darkness. The only reason she could see him at all was because of the lights from the pub parking lot shining through a slit in the curtains. His hair was practically on end, dark and shining. His eyes gleamed in the muted light, and his fingers traced across her stomach. It made her shiver. And then her stomach grumbled.

"And there she is again!" Finn laughed. "Any more noises this heavenly body of yours can make?"

Bridget covered her face with her hands. "I refuse to apologize for being hungry, but wow, that was embarrassing!"

Finn sat up so quickly that his absence sent a chill across her skin. "Come on," he said. "I'm a bit peaked myself. I'll make us some omelets."

"At three in the morning?" She sat up, starting to cover her breasts with the sheet, then realizing it was too late for modesty. Finn tossed her a T-shirt that was hanging from the back of the bedroom door. It was soft and used, and it smelled of Finn and sweat. Combined with the general odor of sex in the room… She'd make a fortune if she could bottle that heady combination. She tugged the shirt over her head and hopped out of bed to follow Finn, tugging on her panties along the way—the tee wasn't quite long enough for her to feel comfortable walking into a kitchen.

He was cracking eggs into a bowl, and humming to himself. It was a haunting melody, and she guessed it was Irish. Not Irish like "The Unicorn," but real Irish. The Irish of "all their wars are merry and all their songs are sad." Her grandmother used to repeat that Chesterton quote a lot, and Bridget never understood what it meant. But watching this bookish, dark-haired Irishman standing at the stove wearing nothing more than a pair of sweatpants hanging low on his hips… She started to get it. The Irish were deeper—and darker—than laughing leprechauns with their pots of gold. She slid onto one of the counter stools.

"You're really making breakfast?"

He glanced over his shoulder. "Aye, I said I would.

It's gonna be a long day, so maybe we should call it pre-breakfast." He flashed her a grin. "Happy St. Patrick's Day, Bridget."

"Happy St. Patrick's Day right back at you."

He tossed some sliced onions and mushrooms into a small pan, letting them cook up nice and tender. Meanwhile, he poured some egg into an omelet pan—the man had an omelet pan—and swirled it around as it cooked. He scooped half the mushroom mixture onto the egg, along with a pinch of shredded cheese, then folded it in half. He slid it onto a small plate for her and went to work on a second one for himself. The golden brown omelet on her plate was practically perfect, and she dove into it, letting out a moan with the first mouthful.

"Oh, wow. This is so good." She swallowed. "I didn't realize how hungry I was."

He raised one brow. "Your stomach seemed to know."

She laughed. "True. I was so busy tonight…last night…whatever. I don't think I actually ate anything. I just grabbed snacks from the bar. And then all of that…um…"

"Wild sex? Horny escapades in the hallway? Hot lovemaking in my bed?"

He slid his own omelet onto a plate, filled two mugs with coffee and joined her at the counter. She grinned.

"I was going to say physical activity, but yes, those all work, too." What a surprising night. Then again, she should have seen this coming. The chemistry between them had been off the charts. It was only a matter of time before they succumbed. Was it a mistake? She didn't realize she'd asked the question out loud until Finn answered.

"Only if we let it be."

"What?" She reached for her coffee, feeling a need to clear her head.

"You asked if tonight was a mistake. And I don't think it has to be. We're grown-ups who had a very grown-up evening that lasted until…" he gestured down to his plate with a grin "…until pre-breakfast. We had fun…at least I know I did. There's nothing saying we can't do it again, as long as we're clear where we stand." He finished his omelet, as cool as could be, as if they were discussing the odds of snow that day, then waved his fork in the air. "We agreed we were exploring chemistry. I think we've determined that the chemistry is quite real. So there's nothin' sayin' we can't continue. Like adults." With his brogue, the word came out as add-ults. Such a little thing, but she liked it. She liked him.

"You're suggesting we spend more nights together?" Her belly warmed at the thought, making her squirm on the stool.

His shoulder rose. "Everyone thinks we're doin' it anyhow. We'd have no reason to hide it."

There was something to be said for not hiding things. The fake engagement was killing her because she had to lie to people she loved. But this idea wouldn't require any lying at all. The fake engagement would be the perfect cover for a real affair. She closed her eyes tightly, suddenly dizzy from all the stories.

"This is getting so confusing."

Finn tugged her off the stool to stand between his legs, sliding his arms around her waist and holding her close. His forehead rested on hers, his eyes glowing like dark emeralds in the soft kitchen light.

"I'm sorry, love, for dragging you into the engagement mess. But if we can have a bit of fun out of it, is that a bad thing?"

She closed her eyes again. Something rankled inside of her.

"Is that what tonight was? A bit of fun?"

That was actually what they'd agreed to. No strings, exploring possibilities, etc. But standing here, having omelets together, with him touching her…it felt like something…more.

Finn's brows gathered, and he hesitated before answering.

"I…I guess that was a bad choice o' words, love." He pressed a light kiss on her lips. "I didna' mean to trivialize it. What went on between us was a lot more than…what I said. To be clear, I thought tonight was…incredible. I mean, girl, that was life-altering sex. You were…amazing." He kissed her again, and she let herself melt a little this time, which prompted him to deepen the kiss. Finally, he pulled back, regret etched on his face. "No, I need to finish this thought before you distract me again. I'll confess, I thought this would be a let's-see-where-this-chemistry-takes-us night and we'd get it out of our system."

Bridget stiffened, but he rushed on before she could protest. "I know, I know. That sounds bad, too, but admit it, you didn't think we'd be all...that... all that we were...what we felt..."

Finn had a point. She thought this would be a night of uncomplicated sex and that's it. She frowned. No, that wasn't true, either. She'd known deep in her heart that there would be nothing simple about making love with Finn. And the tangle of feelings wrapped around her heart right now proved she'd been right.

"I guess," she said softly, speaking her thoughts out loud, "we need to figure out what comes next."

The corner of his mouth lifted. "Next as in the next few hours? I have lots of ideas for that."

"Uh...no. I mean next as in once the sun comes up."

He stared at her for a moment, and she had to steel herself to keep from squirming under his earnest gaze. It felt as if he was examining her from the inside out.

"Bridget, I care for you. I'll still care for you when daylight comes. But you were right earlier when you said we both have damaged hearts. We both needed to take a step toward moving on, to trust someone enough to have...intimacy. Passion." He kissed her forehead. "Tonight was huge for both of us, but if you're lookin' for more...for love...I don't think I have it in me… I may never have it in me to do another relationship." She raised her brow, and he gave her that crooked grin she lov…liked so much. "Well, not a real relationship, anyway. My heart's not ready. May never be ready." He dropped his head and shook it back and forth. "God, I sound like some melancholy soap opera character from one of my mum's favorite shows." He sighed, then looked into her eyes. "What I'm sayin' is I want more of what we've had tonight, but you need to know I may never be able to give more than…this."

She could see the honesty in his face. He was putting it all on the table, and she appreciated that. She knew a little about his past, but apparently there was more to tell. A divorce that somehow forced him to lose his job and leave North Carolina. A drastic fall from grace that brought him from a prestigious university to a private college in Rendezvous Falls.

"Your divorce was that bad?"

His mouth got even tighter, his lips nearly vanishing. A muscle in his jaw twitched. But he didn't look away.

"She fell in love with my best friend."

Bridget didn't breathe for a moment. She'd been betrayed by Clark, but not like this. No wonder Finn was so adamantly relationship phobic. Her heart broke for him. Talking to him always made her feel better, so she offered the same chance to him.

"Tell me about it."

CHAPTER THIRTEEN

FINN GRIMACED. HIS divorce was the last thing he wanted to talk about with Bridget standing warm and soft in the circle of his arms. But they'd already lain naked together, and were talking about doing it on some sort of continuing basis, so she had a right to ask some personal questions. Not talking about important things was one of the reasons his marriage had failed.

"I lost my wife, my best friend and my job in the course of just a few weeks." He tried to keep the edge from his voice, but the bitterness was still there. "So yeah, it was bad."

"How did that happen?" Bridget settled back against his arms, and he finally realized she was standing while he sat.

"Come on." He led her to the sofa. She curled up under his arm, her head on his shoulder. He tugged the throw from the back of the sofa and covered her legs with it—as much to avoid the distraction of her long, curving calves as to keep her warm. Once they were both settled, he took a deep breath and continued.

"It was the classic story, I guess. Boy meets girl. Boy falls in love. They get married. Girl falls in love with boy's best friend and coworker." Bridget took a sharp breath, but his hand kept her head on his shoulder. He needed to get through this. "Boy's former best friend says something stupid at college commencement. Boy punches former friend in the face while on the podium in front of thousands. Boy loses his job as well as his girl. End of story."

She pulled her head away from the hand that had been cradling it and stared at him, wide-eyed.

"You punched him? Good for you."

"You can find video of it online, I'm sure. But I feel no pride in it. The school had a zero tolerance for violence, of course, so I lost a job I loved." He paused. "I lost everything I loved."

"I'm so sorry, Finn. How did you find out about their affair?"

He described how he'd been in denial for months. The signs were all there. Dori suddenly started taking all these evening classes and weekend trips "with the girls." Finn was busy with a major paper he was writing, so he figured it was good that she was being independent. At least they weren't fighting anymore.

At the same time, Vince, a teacher in the university's school of medicine, became more evasive and distant with Finn. Made excuses to cancel their weekly tennis games and early coffee meetings before classes. Like a fool, Finn had been worried about his friend, pressing him to open up and "talk out" whatever was bothering him. It was an offer Vince had always turned down, of course, even though they'd shared so much in their years of friendship. As that final winter dragged on, Finn ended up feeling isolated, abandoned by those closest to him, with no idea why. For a man who didn't mind being alone, he was suddenly very lonely.

"I didn't put two and two together until the end of the final semester, at an alumni reception. I'm sure it had happened a dozen other times, but I didn't see it until that night, when Dori and Vince stood together." It was the worst night of his life. Worse than the divorce. Worse than the commencement ceremony. It was the moment he realized everything he thought he knew was a lie.

"I'd gone to the bar for drinks, and when I came back, there was just…something in how they were standing in the corner. The way they were talking so low, the look in their eyes, the way their hands brushed together. I stood there in the doorway, clutching three drinks in my hands, and realized I was staring at two people who were in love with each other."

His chest tightened, reliving the shock and pain of that moment. "I think it would have better to catch them in bed or something, so I could tell myself it was 'just sex' or a slip-up that might be fixable, but…they were in love. With apparently no guilt at all. I'd known Vince for eight years. Dori and I had been married for six. And they'd both just…left me behind without a thought."

That was the biggest betrayal of all. Not that they'd fallen in love with each other, but that they'd even given themselves the opportunity to fall in love without giving him the slightest clue that they were about to destroy his life.

"Of course," he said, "losing my job was on me. I threw the punch. I'd confronted Dori that week and she'd confessed everything. She'd packed her bags two days before the commencement ceremony and moved right in with Vince. Just like that. I was… reeling…trying to grasp what was happening." It was a miracle he was able to function at all. "Then Vince gave me some sort of smirking, superior grin, or at least that's how I took it. I don't know. Up until then, I hadn't hit the anger phase of my reaction. I'd been in denial and shock. But sitting on the dais with him so soon after… The rage just came out of no-where, and I…I completely lost it." He ran his fingers through his hair. "It's the first time I'd ever punched anyone, and I put every ounce of my anger into the swing. Broke his nose. But there was no satisfaction in it. I think I was really more angry with my-self than them, for not seeing what was right there in front of me. Angry that I could trust two people who would…"

"Whoa, easy there, big guy." Bridget's voice was low and smooth as she rubbed her hand on his chest. Her hand was right above his racing heart. He real-ized his whole body was tight and angry. Her fingers on his bare chest started to work their magic, though, and he drew in a steadying breath. She looked up at him with shining eyes. "I'm sorry to make you relive it. You don't have to say anything else…"

His hand cupped her head against his shoulder again, but her fingers continued to stroke his skin with an even rhythm.

"Not much more to say. I lost everything that day. Some of the kids posted the video of it online and started calling me 'slugger.' Students do that shit to haze professors, and we usually ignore it. History departments tend to be very staid places, and no one wanted to hire Slugger. I gave myself a personal sabbatical and went on a research trip to Rome. Sitting in the Vatican's library for a few months gave me the solitude I needed. But if I wanted to keep my work visa in the US, I had to come back and get a job."

"You didn't want to go back to Ireland?"

"I love my homeland, but I've lived in the States for over ten years now."

"So how did you end up at little Brady College in Rendezvous Falls?"

"Well, like I said, my reputation was a bit too tarnished for the larger schools." He gave her a sardonic grin. "Fisticuffs at commencement and all the scandal involved…I was a risk they weren't willing to take." He leaned back against the cushions. "But Howard Greer was willing to give me a chance. With conditions."

She huffed a laugh against his chest. "Like getting engaged?"

"Yes, like feeling cornered enough to create a fake engagement. He wants me to prove my commitment. And I get that. He wants to get that new history building done while the endowment money is there so he can create a prestigious program before he retires. He's probably hoping to have his name on it—his legacy. He wants me to anchor it all, but he also knows that eventually the bigger schools will come calling me again. Time heals all wounds and all that." He'd already had inquiries from some West Coast universities, where his downfall hadn't been as big a story on the grapevine.

"Are you going to leave?"

Something in Bridget's voice made him pause. There was a weight to the way she'd asked the question, as if she was personally invested in the answer. After just one night—and not even a complete night at that. He looked at the kitchen clock. It wasn't quite four o'clock. He kissed the top of her head and tried to deflect the question.

"I'm not packing my bags yet."

"Yet?" She pulled back and glared at him. "You mean, you might? You're thinking about it?"

"Well, I…"

She slugged him in the shoulder. "Then what the hell are we doing lying to everyone for this engagement thing? Why do you care about what Greer thinks if he's right, and you're leaving anyway?"

He shook his head sharply. "I can't even think about going anywhere until I get my green card, and that takes time. And I don't mind having some stability in my life after all that's happened. And just a reminder—the whole fake engagement story was not part of my plan. That's the opposite of stability, but I need to hold on to this job. I need to prove I can do that, even if only to myself." He straightened and pushed back into the corner of the sofa to stare at her. She was gorgeous with her red hair mussed and wild from sex, falling around her ivory, freckled face and those wide, dark eyes. Being with her was the opposite of stability, too. But he needed her in ways he couldn't begin to define.

"Bridg, I can't predict the future any more than you can. All I can say is that right now, in this moment, Rendezvous Falls is where I need to be. It's where I got a second chance to stay in the States." He couldn't resist reaching out to cup her cheek in his palm. "It's where I ended up engaged to a feisty redhead who rocked my world tonight." She smiled at that. "It's where I want to make love to her again." He kissed her. "And again." Another kiss. She was practically lying on top of him now. "And again."

Their bodies were like matches and gasoline. In no time at all, they were both naked and breathless on the sofa. He was rocking up against her, and she straddled him, ready to take him in, before she let out a frustrated groan.

"Condom…"

"Ah, shit…"

She made him so crazy he'd almost forgotten protection. It was stupid. Her touch made him stupid. He arched his back again, feeling the heat between her legs and wanting to be there. Right. Now. She raised up and settled over him, pausing until he looked at her face. He was literally twitching with need. Frantic. But her expression made him stop.

"What?"

Her smile was mischievous. "I've been on the pill for years, for…female stuff. I tested myself after that jerk in California, and…I mean…I'm good, you know? Health-wise." Her cheeks went rosy. "If you want to…"

Oh, God, he really wanted to. But they were already playing with fire here.

"I'm good, too, love. But the condoms are in the next room, and there's no need to risk a real baby in the middle of our fake engagement."

Her lower lip jutted out in a pout before her eyes lit up. "This moment is too good to be ruined by moving. But there's something we can do that won't require condoms." She slid back, settling herself between his legs and sliding to kneel on the floor. Oh, yeah. His head fell back and he let her take charge. He moaned her name, then called it out loudly. By the time he came he was practically speaking in tongues, yelling half words and cries of triumph and release. His body twitched and jerked for what seemed like ten minutes after she'd finished. As the bursting stars faded from behind his eyelids, he reached down and pulled her up to lie on his chest.

"Fu-u-u-c-k." His breathing was so rapid he was having a hard time forming words. "What the everloving hell was that?" He gave her a squeeze. "Don't answer. Don't say anything. Just…wow. You took me to heaven and back, love."

She burrowed into his arms. "Glad I was able to satisfy you."

"Satisfy? You witch, you turned me inside out, then put me back together again. I have never…"

He'd never made love like that. Ever. But what did that mean? What did Bridget mean to him? To his life? He felt a rush of emotion, and realized it was panic. Was he on the rebound here? Was he falling for the first woman to rock his world since his divorce? Could he trust any of the feelings he thought he had for Bridget? Or was this all a lie like the first time?

"Hey, where'd you go?" Bridget's voice was soft, but concerned, as it brushed past his ear. "I can feel you trying to overthink this. Relax. You were right. We can have some fun without getting too invested in this. We're two grown-ups who make each other…" he let out a hiss as her hand slid down to grasp him againh "…who make each other feel really good. And that's enough for now."

She was right, of course. On both counts. She made him feel really good. And they were grown-ups who could handle a consensual sexual affair. Especially when the whole town assumed they were, anyway. How difficult could it be?

THE MOST CHALLENGING St. Patrick's parties at the Purple Shamrock were the ones that happened on St. Patrick's Day, like this year. The fact that Bridget was operating on just a few hours of sleep made it that much worse. She winced as a group of revelers let out a whoop from the far corner of the pub.

Kelly caught her, her brow arching. "If I didn't know better, I'd say you were suffering from a hangover, cuz."

She was. A sex hangover. Too much of a good thing was still too much. Her mouth twitched. It was also a really good thing. Last night had been full of really good things. Her eyes darted toward the back hallway, where Finn had...

"Are you okay?" Kelly tried to put her hand on Bridget's forehead, laughing as she did it. "You are out of it tonight, girl."

She pushed Kelly toward the bar. "I just didn't get a lot of sleep, and now I've got twenty thousand things on my mind. Go take care of our customers while I broil more mini Reubens."

They'd been serving corned beef and cabbage all afternoon, but the dinner hour was sliding by. Now it would just be drinks and lots of free appetizers—included in the cover charge—to help folks soak up the booze. She'd made a deal with local driving services to provide everyone a safe ride home. If a group had a designated driver, that person wore a bright green bracelet and was not served alcohol. Instead they had free soda and iced teas to choose from. Bridget shuddered at the memory of her dad slapping his pals on the back as they staggered out to their cars twenty years ago. How they'd never been sued for some tragedy was a miracle, and she'd always vowed she'd do things differently. No one left the Purple Shamrock these days with car keys if they were too drunk to drive.

The musicians from Buffalo had played one set during the dinner hour, and were setting up again to play throughout the evening. The upbeat tempo of the Irish and folk tunes had people tapping their toes and smiling. It was a grand party, and she was glad she'd given Nana what she wanted.

Mike and Kelly waited on tables. Timothy was bouncing between the kitchen and the dining room, wherever he was needed. And Luke was tending bar, with help from Finn. The day had been too busy for them to talk much, and they'd agreed over their second breakfast that they'd try to behave as they had been lately in public. No sense getting others invested in this if it wasn't going any farther than a few nights together. But she already knew she wanted more than a few nights. He caught her looking, and gave her a playful wink before turning to a customer.

Nana was sitting on the far side of the bar, around toward the back where things weren't quite as crowded. Mary was with her, big as a house and looking like she was ready to deliver that baby any minute. Her hand was rubbing back and forth across her swollen belly, and her eyes narrowed as if in pain a few times as Bridget watched. Nana didn't seem to notice, laughing at something her friend Vickie was saying. Bridget watched Mary for another moment. Maybe it was just normal discomfort—it's not like Bridget had any idea what pregnancy felt like. It had never been the "right time" for a family with her and Clark, which was probably just as well. But now she was in her thirties and for the first time, that invisible clock was beginning to tick.

Last night Finn said he didn't want any surprise babies, but did he want babies some day? And was that really any of her business? They were keeping things casual. Day by day. Very mature of them. But after they talked in the middle of the night, they'd gone back to his bed and made love slow and sweet, over and over. It was the kind of lovemaking that didn't feel...casual. Another hearty Irish cheer went up from a nearby table, making her jump. She had to focus on getting through tonight before she examined her feelings for Finn. Or for babies. She was just turning away when she saw Mary's shoulders rise up and her eyes close tightly. Uh-oh.

Bridget caught Mike and told him to take over in the kitchen, ignoring the surprise on his face. That was generally her fiercely guarded domain, and Mike had very little experience in there. But Jimmy and Marta were back there, and Mike was a fast learner. At least she hoped he was. She nearly ran right into Luke Rutledge when she took a shortcut under the bar to get to the other side to help Mary.

"Hey, Boss! What are you..." He saw her expression and his smile faded. "What's up?"

"Call Mary's husband. Simon's home with the kids, but their neighbor is on call for when Mary goes into labor."

"But Mary's right th..." He started to point, and

fell silent when he saw Mary's ghost-white face and the tears gathering in her eyes. Luke's tone was all business now. "Got it. Call Simon. Get him over here. Who's got the kitchen?"

"Mike's helping Jimmy, for now. They'll need help, but the bar…"

A warm familiar voice spoke behind her.

"I'll handle the bar."

She spun and found herself in Finn's arms. She panicked for a moment, because they were in public and they'd agreed to keep things quiet. But then she remembered that everyone thought they were engaged anyway. Which meant Finn could hold her and kiss her whenever he wanted. And wasn't that going to be fun?

Amusement lit his eyes. "I'll take care of things here, yeah? And you can go with Mary." She didn't move, enjoying the feeling of being in his arms. He tipped his head in Mary's direction. "Now, Bridget. Before she has the babe on the bar."

Oh, right. Mary. Nana had noticed Mary's distress by now, and there was a flurry of activity as everyone rushed to help. Bridget was headed that way when she looked over her shoulder at Finn and mouthed a quick thank you. He tipped an imaginary hat in her direction and turned to the beer taps.

Mary didn't have the baby in the pub, but she very nearly gave birth to Gavin Patrick Trask in the back seat of her husband's SUV as he raced toward Geneva. Bridget sat next to her the whole way, and was pretty sure Mary broke a few bones in her hand during contractions. But her cousin managed somehow to hang on until they reached the emergency room. There was no time to get her up to Maternity—she had the baby right there in the ER behind a curtain, screaming curse words at her poor husband the whole time. The whole ward laughed, then cheered at the sound of the infant's cries.

Nana had wanted to come with them, but Bridget insisted that Kelly get her home. Her immunity was compromised and, odd as it seemed, a hospital—especially an emergency room—was one of the worst places for her to be hanging out. Bridget called her as soon as Mary and the baby were settled in a room. She could tell her grandmother was miffed about being left behind.

"Nana, it was bad enough you were at the pub tonight with all those people," Bridget said, keeping her voice low in the hospital corridor. "But coming here, where you know everyone's sick with something? Come on." She was so tired. She glanced at her watch and groaned. The pub had closed an hour ago. "Besides, you didn't need to be out at this hour. You shouldn't even be up at this hour. You'd better be calling from bed."

"Stop lecturing me, girlie. I'm on the sofa, if you must know, but I'm in my nightie and robe. And I've made myself a nice nest of pillows and blankets here, so I'm fine." Her voice softened a bit. "You must be tired, too."

She huffed out a soft laugh. "Not as tired as Mary is." She glanced into the room, where Simon and

Mary were admiring their new son. "Now I just need to figure out how to get home, since I rode her with Simon."

"Don't worry about that," Nana said. "I sent you a ride."

Bridget's brows lowered. "You sent me a ride? What do you mean? One of the Lyft drivers?"

"I think she's referrin' to me, love."

She turned with a smile at the sound of Finn's brogue. He splayed his hands.

"She called and complained at the lack of news she was gettin' from here, and sent me to check on things." He stepped closer. "And to get you home safely."

Bridget said a quick goodbye to her grandmother and slid the phone into her back pocket.

"But who'll keep me safe from you?"

He slid his arms around her with a smile.

"If all goes as planned, no one."

He kissed her. It was sweet and affectionate at first. But as usual with them, it quickly built to sizzling.

"Okay, you two." Mary called out softly from her room. "Keep that up and you'll end up with one of these little bundles before your wedding day."

Bridget pulled back, blushing fiercely.

Finn laughed, then looked at the nurse headed their way and mouthed an apology to her. He and Bridget stepped into the room, and Finn admired the copper-haired baby sleeping in Mary's arms.

"I've heard—" he gave Mary a pointed look "—that

there were rumors that was going to happen anyway. That Bridget and I were having what you Yanks call a shotgun wedding."

Mary blushed furiously. "I didn't spread any rumors. I just asked your fiancée a reasonable question at the time. And now I'll ask you one. Do you want the pitter-patter of little feet around the house one day?"

Simon chuckled. "Pitter-patter? More like a thundering herd these days."

Finn looked back to Bridget, who was trying very hard to look nonchalant about the whole conversation. The corner of his mouth lifted into a wry smile.

"I wouldna' mind a bairn or two someday."

A very specific spot in Bridget's belly started doing somersaults, and she blew out a soft breath. What would it be like to have miniature Finns barreling around the house, black curls bouncing?

Mary stared at Bridget. "Why do you look so surprised?" She gestured between the two of them. "You got engaged without talking about a family? And here I thought you were the big planner."

Bridget stammered, and Finn came to the rescue, dropping his arm around her shoulder. "She's only surprised because I mentioned multiples. I don't think I've told her yet that I believe in a traditional Irish Catholic family with three, four, maybe five or six children." A light squeeze told her he was teasing, thank God. She batted her lashes at him.

"Why stop at six? Let's go for nine and have our own baseball team."

Mary's mouth dropped as Finn replied. "I don't like odd numbers. Make it ten."

She gave him a little hip bump and grinned. "By the time we have ten babies, you'll be in a nursing home, you old man."

"I won't!" he protested. But he started to count in his head. "Well, maybe by the time the youngest starts primary school." He nodded and tapped her nose with his finger. "Unless we start right now."

Simon and Mary laughed, but Finn and Bridget stared at each other in silence. She was pressed tight against his side, and the hand that had just tapped her nose was now settled lightly on her neck. All the talk about babies and how they were made had taken both of them back to last night in their minds.

"Oh, damn, I don't think he was kidding, Mary." Simon chuckled. "They might start here and now." He pretended to shield the baby's face with his hand. "Think of the children!"

The joke was enough to break them out of their trance. They shared a quiet laugh and said their good-nights to the tired and happy parents. As they headed to Finn's car, Bridget realized just how tired she was. She'd had very little sleep in the past thirty-six hours, and it caught up with her in a hurry. She barely remembered sliding into the car before sleep took her over.

CHAPTER FOURTEEN

BRIDGET WAS SNORING before Finn got out of the hospital parking lot. He should probably feel guilty for her exhaustion. Their very…active…night the evening before was certainly to blame. But as hard as he might try, guilt refused to come. Because guilt meant regret, and he had no regrets about making love to Bridget McKinnon.

He'd made a second breakfast when they crawled out of bed, bleary-eyed but satisfied, at eight o'clock. She'd been determined to head straight to the pub and start getting ready for their St. Pat's festivities, but he'd convinced her she needed some sustenance to recover from all that activity. He'd grilled up some corned beef hash and poached four eggs to drop on top of it. She ate like a woman who hadn't seen food in a week, and then she headed up to her place to shower and change. She'd stopped on the way back down to suggest they avoid too many PDAs during the party.

"We've maintained our dignity in public so far, and I'd like to be consistent." She'd winked at him, and she'd never know how close he'd come to pulling her back into his place for another session in bed. "We don't know how this is going to play out, so let's just…be cool."

He'd agreed, promising to keep a respectful distance at the party. He knew how he wanted things to "play out," but she had enough on her mind that day to get into that conversation. A conversation about sleeping arrangements—his place or hers—and perhaps more talk about her intriguing offer to skip condoms the next time around.

She was still asleep when he got to the house and parked his car behind hers. Mike told him the pub was always closed the day after St. Patrick's Day, so the family could rest and recover. He touched Bridget's shoulder, but she just mumbled something unintelligible, pushing his hand away. This was going to be interesting. He was thankful for those hours at the college gym as he opened the passenger door and lifted her into his arms, kicking the door shut behind them. Bridget slid her arms around his neck and murmured something before falling asleep again with her head on his shoulder. He managed to get inside without dropping her and stared at the wide staircase. Yeah, that wasn't happening.

He carried her into his place and laid her on the bed. If he thought carrying her in was a challenge, undressing her without her help was even more interesting. He left her in her underwear—going any further felt creepy with her asleep. Then he joined her, pulling her in close as he tugged the covers over them. Having her in his arms felt so…right. As if his arms had been made just for this. He buried his nose into her hair and inhaled. She smelled of the pub's kitchen and the hospital's halls, balanced by her light, floral perfume. She smelled like everything he'd ever wanted. He rested his head next to hers and fell into the deepest, most restful sleep he'd had in years.

Finn woke to the smell of pancakes and coffee. Soft morning sunlight came through the bedroom curtains. He could hear Bridget moving around the kitchen, humming to herself. What would it be like to wake up every morning like this? He stretched and smiled to himself. It would be pretty damn nice. He stopped. He'd thought the same thing about someone else once, too. He swung out of bed, cursing himself. Dori had no place in his thoughts right now. It wasn't the same. Bridget called his name from the kitchen, and pushed his doubts away.

They slept at her place for the rest of that week. Her home was larger and sunnier than his. Comfortably furnished and filled with vibrant colors that suited her. It was interesting that so many in town thought of Bridget as being tense, or more accurately, terse. Testy, even. But he'd come to see that she was just…intense. Intensely focused on the responsibilities that filled her days. On the people she cared about, like Maura. When it was her with him, though, she relaxed. She laughed. She slept in his arms. She rocked his world in bed. In the shower. On the sofa. Against the kitchen counter…

It was still casual, of course. They told each other that several times a day. Totally casual. And so easy. Everyone already thought they were engaged, so they never had to worry about "slipping up" in public. But most of their time was spent alone with each other, and that was just fine with him. Once in a while he had a memory of Dori tap at his memory, but he pushed it aside. He wasn't going to make the same mistake twice. This wasn't that. This was…casual.

They'd been together for ten fun, sexy, casual days when he surprised her with this trip to Syracuse. She didn't know where or why they were going, and that annoyed her to no end. She'd spent the whole ride up the Thruway with her arms folded, grilling him, but he didn't give in. He just kept changing the subject to the weather or asking about the pub. It wasn't until he was parking the car downtown that he gave in to her pestering.

"This is a market research trip, love." He took her arm as they left the parking garage. "Checking out the competition in a way."

She laughed. "Syracuse is not my competition, Finn. No one's driving from here to Rendezvous Falls for a pint."

"Maybe not. But Luke told me that people from Syracuse do come to Rendezvous Falls for festivals and wine tours and whatnot. So why not look at what they expect from an Irish bar?"

They'd stopped at the corner, and she looked up in surprise, her mouth falling open. Even Finn thought it felt like he'd stepped through a portal to a Galway sidewalk outside a genuine pub. The gold lettering above the window read Kitty Hoynes Pub.

"I've heard of this place," Bridget said, "but I don't really get why we're here."

He put his arm around her shoulders and led her to the door. "First, I really do want you to see a traditional-style Irish restaurant for inspiration. Second, I wanted to see a genuine Irish place." He held the door open as she went in. "And third, it was time you and I had a date outside of Rendezvous Falls, where no one knows us."

She looked at the beautiful wooden bar that extended through two adjoining rooms, then back at him as she thought about what he'd said. "Why where no one knows us?"

"Back home, everyone sees us as an engaged couple…" He held up his hand. "Yes, I know that's my fault. But it's hard to just be us there. And I like us."

Her dark eyes shone. "I like us, too."

They took a table toward the back of the bar, near the small stage. Bridget analyzed the menu, and for a moment he thought she was going to order every appetizer they had. The owner—a genuine Irishman like Finn—stopped by their table during dinner and laughed as Bridget grilled him about the menu. But he was gracious and not only answered her questions, but brought the head chef out to meet her. While the two chefs talked, Finn and the owner shared stories of home and talked about some of their favorite athletic teams there. By the time the entertainment started, Bridget had tapped pages of notes into her phone.

The waitress brought them two Irish coffees, and she slid the phone back inside her bag.

"I'm sorry. I haven't been a very good date, have I?"

He shook his head with a smile. He'd enjoyed watching her learn and question things. Her excitement was contagious. "'Tis fine, love. The date was only one reason we came here, and there's still plenty of time."

She scooted her chair closer to him, so they were both facing the stage. The place was hopping, packed with college students and couples who were singing along with the songs enthusiastically. Bridget had a second Irish coffee, but he regretfully passed on another, knowing he had a long drive home. She was snuggled next to him, and they were holding hands and singing. Bridget knew more of the Irish rebel songs than he thought she would. Maura had taught her Irish grandkids well.

It was early morning by the time they got home. Funny how he kept thinking of it as that…home. They kissed their way up the staircase, and Finn made a mental note to make sure they made love on that staircase someday. But not tonight. Tonight, Bridget was laughing and singing between kisses, and he wanted her in bed. Warm and soft and…his. Warm and soft and…home. Where he belonged.

Not forever, of course, but for now. They made

slow, sweet, sexy love to each other. She fell asleep after, and he sat on the edge of the bed and watched her, with her red hair spread across the pillow. Not forever, he told himself. He kept telling himself that. He didn't know if he'd ever have another forever in him. If he'd ever trust anyone with his whole heart again. But he couldn't fool himself, either. He was falling for Bridget, and falling hard.

If this wasn't going to be forever, then it was going to hurt like hell when it ended.

BRIDGET CARRIED TWO pieces of framed artwork out to the dining area, where Finn was waiting with a hammer in his hand. Ever since their trip to the Irish restaurant in Syracuse two weeks ago, she'd been combing through online catalogs and making plans. She handed him the first print, which was a peaceful Irish landscape complete with thatched cottage. He held it out and nodded in approval.

"Just like home." He grinned at her. "I feel like I created a monster by taking you to that place."

"I kept thinking I wanted to change the Shamrock, but everyone expects it to be Irish." She looked around the freshly painted dining room. The walls used to be dark green, but now they were a soft yellow—the color of straw thatch. The room was not only lighter, but also warmer and more inviting. "I never thought about leaning into its Irishness until you came along." She went on tiptoe and kissed him.

"I never thought about a lot of things until you came along."

It was a big confession, but he didn't seem fazed. He held the print off to the side and returned the kiss. "Glad to help, Bridg. It's going to look brilliant."

They hung the paintings she'd ordered, one over each booth. Pretty soon the new lights would be installed, with Celtic swirls in stained glass panels. There would be stained glass on the windows as well, each with a different Celtic design. Customers were already commenting on the fresh look of the place. Yes, it had cost some money, but the St. Patrick's party she'd had to abandon when Mary went into labor turned out to be a huge success, so she had some cash on hand. And she'd been frugal with her purchases, like her grandmother taught her to do. If she could get the permits secured for the patio and have that done by summer, this pub might just start earning her a decent living. Enough to buy out her cousins, even.

"Where do you want this one?" Finn asked.

"Over that last booth in the back, where Nana likes to sit. I let her pick this print."

He put the hanger on the wall and hung the picture. He turned back to her.

"How's Maura? I haven't seen her this week."

Bridget smiled, and it felt good to combine a smile with conversations about Nana. "She's doing better. And…" She stepped into his open arms. "I talked

to her this morning, and the doctor said the tumor
is shrinking."

"Oh, babe, that's amazing! I'm so glad for her.
And you." She burrowed into his hug, craving the
warmth and security of it. Craving him. Then she
remembered what else her grandmother said.

"But we do have a little problem."

He pulled his head back to look down at her.
"With Maura? What is it?"

She gripped his upper arm, where her favorite
dragon tattoo was hiding under his shirt, right above
the Celtic band on his bicep. Her fingers couldn't
help tracing the outline she'd memorized.

"I think she suspects something."

"About her cancer?"

She smacked his arm. "No! About us. She's starting to ask some very pointed questions about how
we met and when I knew I was in love and…" She
stopped, realizing what she'd just said. But once
again, he didn't seem to pick up on it. Finn may
be a professor and researcher, but he didn't pick up
on subtle relationship clues very well. Or maybe
Finn was firmly committed to staying casual. She'd
stopped saying it so much, but he mentioned it almost daily. "Anyway, it feels like she has doubts
about us. And now she's invited us to a McKinnon
family dinner."

Finn frowned. "I've been to dinners at Maura's."

"No, I'm talking a full McKinnon family dinner.

Everyone. And it can be intense. Especially if she's trying to trip us up somehow."

"Why would she do that? She's seen us kissing and dancing and holding hands. It's not like we're suffering in each other's company these days." He gave her a playful wink.

That was no lie. Bridget was downright craving Finn's company. No matter how close she was, she wanted to be closer. Even now, as she stood in the circle of his arms, she wanted to press closer up against him. She couldn't get enough of him. Because she'd fallen in love. She swallowed hard, trying not to show her affection in her eyes. He'd been adamant that he wasn't ready for a serious relationship. His ex-wife had hurt him badly, and Bridget understood. But her heart didn't.

"Hey, there are the lovebirds!" Kareema walked into the pub and came to a dead stop, looking around the redecorated space. "Wow! This looks great, guys. What a difference!"

Finn released Bridget and turned to greet Kareema. She'd joined them at Bridget's apartment for dinner last week, along with Evie and Mark Hudson. It had been a night of food, drinks and laughter over a wild game of Cards Against Humanity. All night, she'd watched Finn getting to know her friends, and her friends falling in love with him, just as she had. He'd said he wasn't a party animal, but once he'd gotten to know everyone, he'd let down his guard and showed his sly humor and competitive side.

"I'm just the guy with the hammer," he said to Kareema. "She's the one with all the great ideas."

"I've known how clever that fiancée of yours is for a long time, Finn. Once you guys are married, she'll be showing you all of her craftiness, trust me." She handed a small bag to Bridget. "Here's that anti-cancer shirt you wanted me to pick up for your grandmother. I had to hunt to find one with the least amount of pink on it, but I think this one will do. The shirt is blue, with mostly yellow print. It says 'Great Boobs are Worth Fighting For.'" Kareema smirked. "Can't argue that."

"Thanks, Kar. She saw them at that shop in Geneva a month ago but was so sick she never said anything to me until last week. This will make her day."

"Anything for Maura," Kareema answered. She patted Finn on the shoulder. "See you later, Indiana." He rolled his eyes and laughed. They'd given him the nickname last week. He said he hated it, but Bridget thought he was kidding himself. He was liking the friends they were making. She watched him talking with Kareema and felt a pinch on her heart. When they ended this fake engagement—as Finn kept assuring her he'd do once he got tenure—it would be more than her who ended up hurt. It would hurt their friends, too.

He walked back to her after Kareema left. "What's wrong, love? You look sad." He swept her into his arms and swung her around, startling a laugh out of her. "There will be no sadness today, woman. Let's get back to the house and get ready for this scary family dinner. And stop worrying so much. I'm a very good actor."

And that was the problem. He was a good actor. And she wasn't. She was falling in love. And she had a very strong feeling that he wasn't.

He set her back on her feet with a big smile.

"We'll be fine, babe."

CHAPTER FIFTEEN

ONCE AGAIN THE McKinnon home was bursting with people. All of Maura's children and most of her grandchildren had come home for the baptism party for Mary and Simon's new son, so every bedroom was filled, along with a few rooms at the Taggart Inn. Maura knew she was one of the reasons everyone had come home. People were worried. People wanted to see her, just in case. It sounded ghoulish, but it was practical, and she understood.

Some days, she wondered how long she'd be around. Or how long she wanted to be, on the days when she ached all over and threw up if she even thought about food.

But today was a good day. She was starting to have more of those. Her next treatment wasn't for a few days yet, and she was starting to get her strength back from the last one. Not that she was ready to go run a marathon or anything, but she felt pretty good for a bald old woman with cancer. In fact, that's exactly what she told Father Joe Brennan when he asked, making him laugh out loud.

"Well, Maura, my dear, you look pretty good for

a bald old woman with cancer, too. And your sense of humor is intact, which is a blessing." He gestured at the T-shirt she was wearing, and pulled up a chair next to her favorite resting spot downstairs—her beat-up old recliner lined with pillows and quilts. "And now you have a new wee grand babe to love, and a wedding to look forward to."

She spotted Bridget and Finn across the room. They were standing close. His arm was on her shoulders. But there was worry in Bridget's eyes whenever she glanced up at him. No one else would pick up on it, but Maura knew this girl better than she knew herself.

"Yes, Joe, you're right. But that engagement was so quick. Do you really think...?"

Joe laughed softly. "Maura, I know love when I see it, and those two have it. Sometimes it really does happen just that fast."

"What's happening fast?" Vickie and Cecile walked up to them. "Who are you...?" Cecile followed their gaze. "Ooh, those two. Yeah, that was interesting. I didn't see those two together at all at the start, but boy, ever since St. Patrick's Day, they've been hot and heavy, haven't they?"

Maura nodded, unconvinced.

"Maybe. But there's something. I just can't put my finger on it. It's like they're not quite on the same page."

Cecile pulled up a chair. "Do you want us to do some sleuthing? The book club's read enough spy stories that we could be spies ourselves. What do you suspect?"

Vickie rolled her eyes. "We aren't spies any more than we're matchmakers." But she looked from Maura across the room to Bridget and back. "But if you want us to see what's really going on with those two, I'm sure we could try." She frowned. "I'll start with Rick. He knows Finn best, and he's definitely been acting weird ever since the engagement became public. He didn't even show up today, and I think it's because he's avoiding us."

Maura listened as Vickie went on about Rick. Across the room, Bridget beamed up at Finn. As much as Maura liked the smooth-talking Irishman, she wasn't about to let him hurt her granddaughter in any way.

FINN RODE HIS bike to work the next morning, soaking up the sunshine and smiling at the memory of how Bridget had woken him that morning, burrowing under the sheets and…um…surprising him out of a sound sleep. And he didn't mind one little bit. He'd returned the favor, losing himself in the woman who'd so quickly become as much a part of him as his arm or leg. It was impossible to look into the future and not see her in it.

He waved at a few students as he entered the campus and found the bike rack, but his smile faded slightly. They'd fallen so fast for each other. Was Bridget a rebound? It didn't feel that way, but how would he know the difference? He couldn't help re-membering that he'd been in love before, and had been convinced that he and Dori were forever-and-ever-amen. Until they weren't. He'd misjudged her. He'd misjudged his own ability to know what was happening in his own house. In his marriage. In his friendships.

It wasn't the same with Bridget, though. They'd been so open with each other. And when they were together, the whole world just felt…right. Aligned. Balanced. Proper. He liked her. He respected her. And who was he kidding? He loved her. He was in love with Bridget McKinnon, and every time he thought about it, he felt both a warm thrill and a shiver of fear. A shadow of doubt that wouldn't leave him alone. It wasn't her fault. This was all on him. The doubts would go away eventually. If he ignored them long enough.

"Nice helmet, Finnie." Rick's teasing voice broke through his thoughts. "Did you get that in the kid's department at Wally World?" His friend folded his arms across his chest and nodded at the bicy-cle. "Since when did you start pedaling your ass all over town?"

"Oi, give me a break. It wouldn't hurt you to get a little more exercise, old man."

"And squish my family jewels on that little seat?" Rick shuddered. "I don't think so." He fell into step alongside Finn and they headed toward the annex where their offices were. "You've got a heck of a smile on your face these days. I take it this 'fake' relationship…" Rick made air quotes with his fingers "…is turning more real than anticipated? And can I say, I really hope so, because it would let me off the hook for keeping your secret safe from my best friends. If the lie becomes reality, there's no secret to keep."

Finn shrugged. "It's definitely more than anticipated. I'm just not sure how real it is." He halted, surprised at his own words. It was the first time he'd spoken his fear out loud.

"I've seen the eyes that girl gives you, and it looks about as real as can be." Rick stepped ahead and opened the door for Finn. "Is this about what happened in Durham? Let me give you some advice." He clapped Finn's shoulder as they entered the building. "Never hold new relationships up to old ones. There are too many variables to make a fair comparison, and hindsight is never accurate. It'll lead to nothin' but trouble, my friend."

He thought about that advice for the rest of the day. It was impossible for Finn to just forget what happened to his marriage, but it wasn't fair to Bridget to hold her up to that disaster as some kind of mirror. She wasn't Dori.

The students in his afternoon class had the typical April restlessness. It was a combination of anxiety over finals and excitement about graduation for the seniors, or looking forward to summer break for the rest. He barely managed to hang on to their attention as he discussed Brian Boru's legacy in Ireland. Probably the only thing that saved him was venturing into a discussion of Boru's three wives and some of their entanglements with other Irish kings. One of the students declared it sounded like Real Housewives of Munster, and the attention of the other kids perked up after that.

He was still smiling about it when he got home. That smile deepened when he saw Bridget walking around the pub to the small section of parking lot and snowy lawn behind the building. Last night they'd made love until almost dawn. They talked about dreams they had and dreams that had been dashed. They talked about the value or worthlessness of various social media platforms, and he flat-out refused to open an Insta account as the "Irish Professor," despite her claims that his looks would automatically build a following.

"You said Greer wanted to pimp you out for the new history building. Becoming an influencer online would give him the attention he's looking for!" She'd laughed as she said it, strolling naked from the kitchen to her bed with a plate of cheese, meat and crackers. He'd snatched the plate from her hand and tossed it on the nightstand, pulling her into bed with him and ending the debate by kissing every inch of her body. Slowly. Deeply. Worshipfully.

He watched her now, talking to Michael, her arms sweeping out toward the lake below as she tried to make her point. She was arguing for that outdoor patio again. The woman was always fighting for something. Always pushing to do more. Pushing the people around her. Pushing herself. Finn used to be like that. Motivated. Competitive.

Dori and Vince had broken that part of him. He thought it was gone for good. But Bridget was doing something to him. She was pulling him along with her, and giving him little glimmers of hope. Like... long-term hope. For the future. For them. Which made no sense. There was no them except at night between the sheets, and occasionally pretending in public to keep up the game of being engaged.

He got out of the car and slammed the door more firmly than he'd intended. He needed to remember that—that this was temporary. For show. Except the nights, of course. That was brilliantly real. Frighteningly real for him. Because he couldn't afford to let himself hope again. He was bad at relationships, and if things got any more real, he'd have to seriously examine what they were doing and how clear his judgment was. He turned toward the house. Distancing himself now would probably be the smartest move. His foot hit the top step.

And he reversed course and started across the parking lot. They had time before he had to worry about that. And he couldn't stay away from her. Not yet, anyway.

She flashed him a bright smile when he walked up to her and Mike. It was a smile that shot straight to his heart. He'd survived the family dinner she'd been so worried about, and seemed to have the Mc-Kinnon stamp of approval. Would they really have to stop? Would he be able to?

"Hey, Professor!" She gave him a quick kiss, as if it was the most natural thing in the world. His arm wrapped around her waist and he tugged her closer, speaking against her mouth.

"Hey there, bar wench."

Bridget laughed and pinched his arm.

"Oi, such violence!" He rubbed his arm and stepped back, tugging her ponytail as he did.

Mike cleared his throat, gesturing between them. "I hate to interrupt whatever this is that I'll never be able to unsee, but we have some business decisions to make."

"I know...sorry." Bridget winked at Finn before turning to her cousin. "I know it's a lot of money, but if we can get the bank loan, I think we have to do it, right?"

Mike grimaced, staring at the ground and rubbing the back of his neck. "Do you really need another payment to make? You've got the house mortgage on top of promising to buy us out. And now you want to add another loan?"

"But this won't be that much. The patio should pay for itself if we can get it built by the Fourth of July weekend. That's the first big festival of the summer, and we can pack this place with tourists and locals by advertising the view of the fireworks both nights."

Finn followed her gesture toward the back of the

lot. She had a point—the pub was high enough above the town to have a clear line of sight to the college and the lakeshore below. He'd heard about the Americana Festival, with parades and fireworks on both July Third and July Fourth, set off from barges out on the water. He imagined a patio set up out here would put them at nearly eye level with the fireworks, which would be incredible.

Mike took in the view too, then shrugged.

"At least you'll have two incomes now."

"What?" Bridget's forehead wrinkled in confusion.

Mike pointed at Finn. "You'll have your husband to help. With the two incomes, you should be able to swing everything." He grinned. "I hope you told your fiancé about the debt he's taking on with you."

Bridget's cheeks went bright pink, and Finn rushed to answer, reaching out to take her hand as he did. His little fighter.

"Don't worry about the money, Mike. I've already told Bridget I'd be interested in buying out the family shares in the Shamrock if that helps." He squeezed her fingers to keep her from protesting his blatant lie. Mike's eyes went wide.

"It would help me, that's for sure. What are you, Irish royalty or something?"

"There's no such thing as Irish royalty." Finn couldn't help himself from clarifying Irish history. "Not anymore, at least. But I've done okay with the teaching gig."

Bridget's head was shaking back and forth, sending that red ponytail swinging.

"I am not taking your money."

Mike laughed. "He's going to be your husband, Bridg."

"He's not…"

Finn pulled her in for a quick kiss to silence her, doing his best to ignore the quick stab of hurt that she was that quick to deny him. He held on to her and whispered in her ear.

"Helping is the least I can do. We'll find something that works, okay?"

She didn't relax in his arms, but she nodded against him.

Mike threw up his hands and walked away. "You two can figure your shit out without me. I'll try to beat the guy down on the price of doing this patio thing."

Finn didn't let her go until some of the tension left her. She sniffed and looked up at him.

"I'm sorry, I didn't mean to scare you by blurting that out."

"I don't care about that." He brushed a loose strand of hair from her face. "I only care about you."

And it was more true than he'd realized. Not only was she the best lover he'd ever had, she was funny and strong and loyal and…he was falling in love with her. For real.

Her expression was troubled. "Finn, I know this is all fake…"

"Hey, what you and I have between us is as real as it gets."

"Then do me a favor. Don't try to pay me off."

"What? That's not…"

"First you offered to let me keep a ring if you'd bought one. Now you want to give me money for the pub? It makes me feel…"

He cupped her face in his hands, feeling like an idiot.

"I never meant to make you feel like I was…compensating you. You put yourself on the line for me, and I'm just trying to show you that I appreciate it."

"Before you leave, you mean?"

"I'm not leaving."

"You're leaving me. The semester's almost over. You'll get your tenure and your security and we'll be…"

"Isn't that what we agreed?"

She hesitated, then nodded without looking him in the eye. "We have an agreement. But what does that have to do with what we have…between us?"

He pulled her into his arms and kissed the top of her head. What did she want to hear?

"We promised one day at a time, love. We don't have to make a decision today."

"But someday we will."

He didn't answer her. Because he truly had no idea what was going to happen.

CHAPTER SIXTEEN

KAREEMA TOSSED HER large leather bag on the floor near the bar and slid onto a stool with a dramatic sigh.

"Bad day?" Bridget grabbed a tall glass and reached for a cola from the bar cooler.

"Oh, no, girl. I need more than fizzy sugar today."

Bridget stopped and looked at her, brows rising.

"It's not even four o'clock. On a Tuesday."

"I don't care if it's ten o'clock in the morning. Give me a glass of wine. Stat."

"O-kay." She did as ordered, filling two glasses with the pinot noir Luke Rutledge had delivered from Falls Legend Winery that morning. "What happened?"

Kareema rolled her eyes and emptied half her wine in one swallow. "It's one thing to deal with the teen attitudes and the practical jokes and their complete inability to refile books properly. But sex? In my library? No, ma'am." She waved her finger in the air. "No. Ma'am."

Bridget's laughter bubbled up. "You caught students trying to have sex in the library? During school? Wow, I..."

"Oh no, baby. Not students." Kareema dropped her head back, staring at the ceiling and groaning loudly. "I will never unsee what I've seen! How can I unsee it?"

"Wait. If it wasn't students…"

No. It couldn't be.

"That's right. Not students. Teachers. Teachers, Bridget!"

Bridget leaned forward. "Who?"

Kareema shook her head. "As much as I'd love to spill, I can't. I promised them I wouldn't. But my eyes, girl. My eyes."

"Were they, like…doing it?" She couldn't imagine how they could hide that. "Or was it just…?"

Kareema's glass hit the bar firmly. "There is no 'just' about walking around a corner with an armful of books and seeing a chipper little blonde English teacher on her knees giving a BJ to a Spanish teacher in the back of the stacks. I mean, for real. What am I supposed to do with that?"

Bridget coughed, trying to hold back her laughter. "What did you do?"

Kareema's shoulders started to shake. "Well, the first thing I did was wonder why I can't get any action in my own damn library. Then I imagined some kid walking over, although they were smart enough to pick the aisle with nothing but math and science textbooks—not the sort of books students seek out on their own." She started to laugh. "I cleared my throat and tossed my armful of books on a shelf very loudly. He zipped up his pants so fast I'm surprised he didn't zip his little member clean off. And she jumped to her feet and started to cry. She cried, Bridget."

"Oh, my God. Did you report them?"

Her friend leveled a look at her.

"Did I mention she cried? And I thought he was gonna throw up. His face turned green, for real." She finished her wine. "I shushed them both, and read them the riot act in the lowest decibel possible. Turns out they're married…"

"Uh-oh…"

"…to each other."

"No way!" Bridget laughed. "They're married and they tried to pull that where they both work?"

"Oh, it gets better. Turns out today is his birthday, and this is something he'd fantasized about, so wifey decided to make his dreams come true. In my library. I told them to get the hell out and never come back unless they came alone. Jesus, give me strength." She shook her head again. "Okay, now I'll take that cola."

Bridget obliged, still giggling. "You definitely win the prize for Most Interesting Workday, Kareema."

"Are you saying no one's ever been caught in this bar trying to get it on?"

Her face warmed as she thought of the night before St. Patrick's Day. The night Finn made love to her against the wall of the back hallway.

"Oh, that's a story right there in those eyes of yours. Who was it? Where?" Kareema's mouth fell open, as round as her eyes were becoming. "Oh hot

damn. It was you, wasn't it? With that hot Irish fiancé of yours? In here? What the hell! Am I the only
woman in town not getting any in public places these
days?" She pouted. "I need to find me an adventur-
ous lover." Then she leaned forward, dropping her
voice dramatically. "How was it?"

At least this was one thing she didn't have to lie
about.

"Um…it was…awesome."

Kareema sat back on the bar stool.

"Damn, you and this guy are for real, aren't you?"

She wasn't sure what to say to that. Her feelings
for Finn were getting more real every day, but she
still wasn't sure what would happen next. What he
was feeling. She looked at her childhood friend and
blurted out the truth once more.

"I think I love him."

"Think? You're getting married, so I hope you
love him."

"I mean really love him, Kar. Like…life-changing,
can't-live-without-him love. It's…it's scary to feel so
much. To want him in my life forever. I never thought
that kind of love would happen for me, you know?"

Her friend reached out and took her hand. "I'm
so happy for you. I'm also jealous, but most of all
I'm really happy for you." She squeezed her fingers.
"You deserve this, Bridg. You're always so busy taking care of everyone else that you don't think about
what you need or want. But you deserve this. I see
real joy in your eyes, and it's joy that has nothing to

do with your family or this stupid bar. It's in your heart, and you need to hang on to that, honey."

Their conversation was interrupted when some early bird diners came in—including some of Nana's book club cronies. The old folks had been spending a lot of time here lately. She didn't object to having more business, but she couldn't help feeling like they were here to watch her. Helen Russo and Rick Thomas came in first, and were followed a few minutes later by Lena and Cecile. Sure enough, they chose a booth facing the side of the bar where she and Kareema were talking. Kelly took them menus, but they all made a point to wave to Bridget.

Kareema stood and grabbed her coat. "I gotta run. Thanks for listening to my Very Bad Day story. And remember what I just told you." She pointed at Bridget's chest. "Hang on to that deep love you're feeling for Hotty McIrish. That stuff's precious. Not everyone's lucky enough to find it."

Bridget couldn't help wondering if it would still be considered lucky if that kind of love ended up being one-sided.

Finn heard the door open behind him, but figured it was one of his students. They'd had quite the debate about the Book of Kells and how priceless relics like that had been buried all over Ireland to protect them from the British "reformers." Someone probably wanted to make a point about Elizabeth I or something.

"Hello, Finn."

He froze. No, that wasn't accurate. His internal organs turned to ice. Arctic dust able to be blown away in the slightest breeze. He closed his eyes, willing this to be a bad dream. Some sort of daytime nightmare that would go away if he wished hard enough. But his ex-wife spoke again, calmly and clearly and very real.

"You won't even look at me?"

He turned on his heel, his fingers curling into fists before he met Dori's eyes. Seeing her again was like a razor cut—a quick, sharp slice across his heart with a delayed burn of pain. She looked the same… maybe a bit softer somehow. Her short blond hair was layered and styled to perfection as always, but the sharp edges of her face and figure had softened. She'd always been so tightly put together, with bright red lips, artfully shadowed cheekbones and clothes that clung to her slender body.

But her lips were blush pink now. Her clothing was more subdued as well. Casual wool slacks and a lightweight sweater under a jacket. Classy, but relaxed. Finn tried to remember if he'd ever thought of Dori as relaxed before. Was this what happy looked like on her? He'd admired her edginess as a strength, but had it been bitterness all along? Had he ever made her happy? She was still waiting for him to say something. His internal argument spilled out in his angry tone.

"Why are you here, Dori?"

She flinched, then raised her chin. "Wow. Okay. I'm trying to sell some medical equipment to the hospital in Geneva, and since I was so close, I thought I'd stop by and…" Her head dropped, breaking eye contact. "Check in on you, I guess. I wanted to see if you're okay."

His eyes narrowed. What was she up to? He nodded toward the door. "Come in and close the door. I have half an hour before my next class." She did as he asked, then sat in one of the chairs opposite his desk. She glanced at the second chair as if suggesting he sit there, but he walked behind the desk and took his seat there. Distance felt like a real good idea right now. "And yes, I'm okay. Considering. Any other questions?" He knew this was more than just checking in.

Dori smoothed her jacket before finally looking up again.

"Finn, I'm sorry for what happened. I know I've said that already, but I want you to know I…I mean it. I know…Vince and I know…that what we did hurt you." She swallowed hard. "We've been concerned. We care about you…"

Finn snorted. "Stop, okay? Just stop. You're obviously here to make yourself feel better, not me. If you cared about me, you wouldn't have screwed my best friend." He shuffled some papers on his desk, trying to look as unruffled as possible. The last thing he wanted was Dori and Vince laughing over how they'd destroyed him. Maybe they never did that, but whenever he thought of them together, that's what he pictured. After all, the joke had always been on him. "So why don't you head off home to North Carolina and live the life you chose. Or are you cheating on him, too?"

Her body went rigid, her back not even touching the chair.

"I'm not cheating on Vince. We love each..." She bit her lip, so he finished the sentence for her.

"You love each other? Are you sure? After all, you took a vow to love me, remember?" His shoulders sagged. "Seriously, Dori, you need to go. This is pointless. For the love of God, leave me in peace."

Her blue eyes went soft and shiny. It looked like actual regret, but he never knew with her.

"I hate that we've come to this, Finn." She leaned forward, placing her hands on his desk. He withdrew automatically, even though she couldn't reach him. Her lips pressed together in a thin straight line. "Vince and I never intended for this to happen..."

He welcomed the icy sensation that returned to his chest. Anger was a lot easier to deal with than wondering how sincere she might be.

"You never intended, eh?" He leaned forward and she sat back. They were playing a tense game of seesaw right now. "Then what happened, Dor? Did you accidentally end up naked in his bed while married to me? Did he accidentally stick it where it didn't belong? Did he forget he'd been my friend and mentor for years? Did either one of you think of me at all?" He waved his hand in disgust. "You know what? I don't care. Get out."

There was a beat of silence as they both settled back.

"I'm pregnant."

He barked out a laugh to cover the stab of pain he felt. They'd talked of starting a family, but Dori always said the timing wasn't right. Apparently he was what wasn't right.

"That's great, Dor. Just fuckin' great."

"I wanted to tell you myself, Finn. I didn't want you to hear it through some gossip grapevine. I thought you deserved that much."

"I deserved a lot of things. Too bad neither you or your new husband thought so."

"And again...wow." Dori stood, staring down at him, her brows gathered together in anger. "What we did to you was shitty, Finn. I get that. I'm sorry I fell out of love with you. I'm sorry I didn't say so when it happened, which was long before Vince and I started anything. Just because I apologized doesn't mean I came here expecting your forgiveness." She pulled her purse over her shoulder. "But you need to do something with all this anger. Talk to someone, Finn, before it consumes you. Our divorce was almost two years ago. Sooner or later, you need to move on."

He leaned back in his chair, working hard to look bored. Trying to ignore the voice in his head whispering that she might be right.

"Oh, I've moved on, don't you worry. In fact, I'm engaged to a lovely lass here in Rendezvous Falls." He gestured toward the door. "So go start your new family with a clean conscience, Dori."

Her jaw dropped. "You're...engaged?"

"Yes, and don't ask about her, because it's not your

concern. You and I are exes, Dori, with nothing tying us together." He finally stood, but stayed behind the desk. "You don't ever need to show up here again." She started to speak, but he raised a hand to stop her. "If you care about me half as much as you claim to, then stay out of my life, Dori."

She stared at him for a moment, then nodded and turned to go. She was just opening the door when he spoke again. They'd been married for eight years. He hated what she and Vince had done to his life—and his heart—but he couldn't make himself hate her. His voice softened.

"Congratulations on the pregnancy, Dor. Have a good life. Really. But don't send me any baby announcements or Christmas cards, okay?"

Dori gave him a quick solemn look over her shoulder, nodding before she walked out of his life one last time.

Finn sat down so hard the chair rolled back a foot or more. Jesus. Just when he thought he'd stuffed all his feelings deep inside, there they were, simmering on the surface like a deadly oil slick. He really knew how to pick 'em, didn't he? A beloved wife who lied and cheated. A trusted friend who stabbed him in the back. They'd blown his life to smithereens, and now they were building their own little idyll, baby and all.

He didn't wish them ill—he wasn't that kind of guy. But damn, it hurt.

CHAPTER SEVENTEEN

"WAIT A MINUTE…" Bridget held up her hand with a laugh. "Zayne Rutledge, did you just say you have a website? You? The ultimate hermit is online?"

The dark-haired man across from her couldn't hide his slow smile. Luke's brother was one of the most painfully shy people she'd ever met, but lately he'd been showing up at the Shamrock every month or so. It was always at quiet times, when the place had pretty much cleared out. That was astonishing regularity for a man who once vowed to burn the place to the ground in a drunken rage years ago. He'd only been nineteen or so at the time, and was moving down the path his father had laid out with his example—a drunk looking for good times, and if he couldn't find good times, a fistfight would do. He'd been an absolute terror in high school, but somehow he and Bridget had formed a friendship that had survived his determination to destroy his life.

A terrible car wreck a few years after graduation had left him with a permanent limp and an even bigger chip on his shoulder. His best friend had been driving that night, and had died in the fiery one-car crash. It had been whispered back then that Zayne had been driving, but the police had witnesses who confirmed the other guy was behind the wheel. Still, the whispers persisted, driving Zayne to withdraw even further from society. For a while, he'd lived in his parents' old trailer up on the hill. His father had died in prison, and his mother died not long after that, probably worn out from trying to keep her fragile family together. But last year he'd purchased a run-down old house out on Manford Road.

"So tell me, how do you take orders when you can't get to a house that might be in Omaha?"

Zayne lifted a shoulder. "It's up to the clients to get me good measurements. I sketch it out. They sign off on it. I build it to match their specs." He sipped his ginger ale. "Most of my clients are builders or general contractors, and they usually know what they're doing. Either way, I get paid. And I'm getting more than enough to stay busy these days."

"Listen to you." Bridget leaned on the bar with a grin. "Talking about clients and specs and making a steady income. Your life has taken quite the turn, hasn't it?"

Four or five years ago, Zayne had picked up a job helping Bill Garfield refinish the old trim work inside one of the Painted Ladies of Rendezvous Falls—the Walleston Mansion on the shores of Seneca Lake. Bill had to be almost eighty, but he was a master craftsman in high demand with all of the old homes in town. He'd become an expert on Victorian houses. And he'd given Zayne Rutledge, with one of the worst reputations in town, a chance. Zayne was supposed to just follow Bill around and clean up after him and hand him tools.

But something shocking happened. Zayne found something in the outside world that he actually liked. Not only that, but he was good at it. He had the patience to refinish and repair delicate gingerbread fretwork in the old houses and make it look brand-new again. Bill gave him more and more responsibility, and by the time Bill was ready to retire, Zayne was ready to step up and take his place. He bought Bill's shop, and rumor had it he'd been quietly buying more business properties around town. Old Man Garfield still helped now and then. And now he had a website. It was an absolute wonder.

"Has life changed since high school? Uh...definitely. That's the whole point to life, isn't it? Growing up. Working. Giving back." He raised one brow at her look of surprise. "Yeah, yeah, I know. I'm the guy who threatened to clock your dad if he didn't let me run a bigger tab at this place, as if I didn't already owe him a hundred bucks for booze." He shook his head. "I was an idiot back then. I'm probably still an idiot, but I'm an idiot with a website as of this morning." He finished his soda and slid the glass over to her. "And what about you? You've changed, too. You're running the place you couldn't wait to get away from in high school. And you're..." He gestured toward her. "Smiling. Didn't see a lot of that back in the day. My brother says some Irish guy is keeping you warm at night."

Her cheeks flushed. "Yeah, that's what's making the difference. Some Irish guy." She meant to be sarcastic, but the truth was, that Irish guy really had made a difference in her world. Things were brighter. Lighter. Easier. Sexier. She was starting a future with Finn. She was becoming convinced it was a real one, not the fake story that had brought them together.

Zayne chuckled. "Whoa. All I have to do is mention him and you're all dreamy-eyed and distracted. Is this guy the one?"

Yes. But she wasn't going to admit that to Zayne Rutledge before she said it to Finn. She laughed off the question.

"Puh-leez. It's not like I was some dime-store-novel heroine looking to be swept off my feet." She wiped down the bar, then lifted the hinged section and stepped out to face Zayne. "But I am having fun."

"Good for you, Bridg. You deserve a little fun." He plunked a few bills on the bar to cover his lunch and drink. "I gotta go. Iris Taggart wants me to refinish that ebony staircase at the inn, and we have to figure out how much she's gonna pay me. That woman is tighter than bark on a tree when it comes to money."

"Yes, but she'll also send you home with a bag of Piper's blueberry biscuits and refer you to ten other people in town." She knew it was the last thing a guy like Zayne Rutledge wanted, but she couldn't help herself—she threw her arms around his neck and hugged him. After a moment of surprise, his arms folded around her, too. "I'm so proud of you, Zayne. Maybe you and I are just late bloomers. It's taken us a while to find our paths, but we figured it out."

He gave her a quick squeeze and stepped back with a grin. And was that a hint of red on his cheeks? "Thanks, Bridget. We're both growing up, I guess." He put his hand on her cheek for just a second. It was surprisingly intimate, in a friendly way. "That Irish dude is pretty lucky."

She finished cleaning off all the tables and headed back to the kitchen to get ready for the dinner crowd. That's when she saw Finn sitting on the other side of the bar. He'd apparently helped himself to a drink, because there was an empty whisky glass in front of him. She grinned, surprised and pleased to find him there. But the smile was not returned, and there were shadows in his eyes.

"Finn? What's wrong?"

His mouth twisted into a facial version of a shrug. "Not a thing, Bridget. Not a damn thing. Just admiring how history likes to repeat itself."

"What?" Had she missed something? "Did I do something, or is this about school, or…?"

"Did you do something? Nothing unexpected, I guess. Got any more of this stuff?" He held up his glass.

Bridget put her hand on her hip and gave him her most no-nonsense look.

"I may not have mentioned this before, but I am not a fan of passive-aggressive behavior. Stop talking in circles."

"Who, me?" He feigned shock, earning a darker glare. "I'm just that 'Irish dude' you're 'having fun with.'"

It took her a second to catch up. He'd been there for her conversation with Zayne. Or at least part of it. "Wait…is this about Zayne? Oh, please. We've been friends since high school. Instead of eavesdropping and making assumptions, you should have come over and introduced yourself."

Was he being serious? Was he jealous? Offended?

"Actually, I'd planned to do exactly that, but it seemed awkward with you in his arms."

Okay. Jealous. And clearly ticked off.

"Finn, we're friends, and he'd just told me some great news. Zayne hasn't had an easy life, and he's finally turning it around. I hugged him because I was happy for him." She paused for effect. "For my good friend."

The lines of tension around his eyes eased, but he was still unhappy. As if he wanted to believe her, but didn't. Now she was the one getting ticked off.

"Just to be clear, there is absolutely nothing wrong with me hugging a friend, male or female. I'm getting this vibe that you're expecting an apology, and that ain't happening. I mean, I'm sorry if you got offended, but now that I've explained what happened, you should be over it."

He raised his right brow high. Usually she thought it was hot, but right now it felt like she was about to get a lecture.

"First, you're supposed to be my fiancé, so PDAs should only be with me. Second, we're sleeping together. You may call it 'just fun' with your friend, but it damn well means something to me." He seemed to deflate in front of her all of a sudden, as if that was more of a confession than he'd intended. The fact that they were sleeping together meant something to her, too. The fact that she was falling in love with him meant even more. He jammed his fingers through his hair. "I'm so bad at this. I don't know how to read people anymore…"

She wasn't sure if he was talking to her or to himself. They'd discussed his broken marriage several times, but maybe it had done even more damage than she'd suspected. Deeper damage. She reached out and put her hand on his forearm, which was tight and hard.

"I get it, Finn. Someone broke your trust, and now you're second-guessing yourself. But you know me. I gave you my word we were going to be monogamous through all of this." She stepped behind the bar and refilled his glass. "In fact, I'm the one who demanded it. So I'm not going to be the one to go flirt with someone else. Or worse. And I think you know that if you'll really think about it logically."

His laughter was dry and humorless. "That's the problem, Bridget. I can't think logically around you. And speaking of my lovely ex, did I tell you she was here this week?" Bridget stepped back. What did that mean? Was he still in contact with Dori? He was staring at the floor now, his face hard. "She showed up at my office yesterday to 'check on me' and update me on her happy new life with my former best friend." The words were spoken in a light tone, but there was a dangerous edge to them. This was a new, darker Finn than she'd seen before. His jaw was rigid, his fingers tight on the glass as he drained it.

He'd been quiet last night when she'd crawled between the sheets after midnight, but she'd figured he was tired. Or thinking about his paper. Or the alumni cocktail party coming up that weekend. The one he'd invited her to, explaining how critical it was that she be there as his partner while they schmoozed with potential donors to complete the history building. It was hard to keep track of what was real or fake anymore. Did he need her there at his side as his lover and friend, or as his fake fiancée to save his job?

But he had woken up last night, and they'd talked briefly about their days before he pushed her back on the pillows and made fast, hard love with her. They'd both fallen asleep after, but still… There'd been plenty of opportunity then, or this morning over coffee, for him to tell her something as important as the arrival of his ex-freaking-wife.

He let out a long, heavy sigh. "We only have a few weeks left o' this fake engagement, and then y' can go off to hug whoever you want without worrying about me."

Bridget wasn't sure what offended her the most—his casual reference to their relationship ending as if it meant nothing, or his inference that he'd ever hold control over who she was friends with if it were real. The first was too complicated to digest in a matter of seconds, so she went with the second.

"Just to be perfectly clear, even in a fake engagement—or a real one, for that matter—I will never be worrying about what my partner thinks of my friends and how I act around them. You're being a royal Irish ass right now, and I don't like it."

His eyes went wide in surprise, then narrowed again. "I just walked in to find my partner laughing about me being a bit o' fun on the side, and hugging another man. I've a right to be pissed, Bridget."

"And I explained that you saw two old friends celebrating good news. It's up to you to decide to believe me or not. I won't defend something that wasn't wrong in the first place." She stepped back, her chest tightening.

This moment suddenly felt...big. If Finn couldn't trust her, she wasn't sure how they'd move forward. If he was going to punish her for the misdeeds of his ex, how would she ever be on solid ground with him? As much as she loved him, how could he ever love her if he never saw her? She'd been in one relationship where she hadn't been valued enough. Had she just stepped into another?

Finn went still. She had a feeling he'd just real-

ized the importance of this conversation, too. It was
more than a disagreement. It was potentially a fun-
damental roadblock to their future. His hand slid to
the back of his neck and he rubbed it, staring off into
space in silence.

"Finn, why didn't you tell me about your ex-wife's
visit? It seems like kind of a big deal, and it's obviously rattled you." She had a feeling that visit had
everything to do with this argument. "We could have
talked about it instead of letting it fester and bubble
up as a silly fit of jealousy."

The lines around his thinning mouth deepened,
and his jaw worked back and forth as if he was bat-
tling himself. Maybe she shouldn't have called it—or
him—silly right now. But she also wasn't going to
let any man, even the one she loved, make her feel
guilty just because a troublesome piece of his past
had shown up.

FINN TRIED TO hold on to his temper. He counted to
ten, then twenty, then thirty in his head. He pulled
in air through his nose and blew it out through his
mouth, although his lips were barely parted. The
emotions swirling around inside of him were mixed
up in each other, and he knew Bridget didn't deserve
all of them. But…silly fit of jealousy?

He was a grown damn man who'd been cuckolded by his wife and his best friend. He was right
to be cautious. Suspicious, even. One burned, twice
shy and all that. It was smart. Considering the way
he'd been wrecked in the past, a defense mechanism

wasn't a bad thing. He refused to think otherwise, regardless of the way his conscience was trying to remind him he was falling in love with Bridget. He wasn't proud of the way he was suspicious of his own feelings for her, but who could blame him?

"I think we'd best end this conversation, Bridget, before one of us says something they can't take back. Like calling the other silly."

The flash of guilt on her face told him she knew she'd gone too far.

"This is obviously not silly to you, Finn, and I'm sorry. But…"

"We're just goin' in circles here, Bridg. You don't get it, and I'm not in the mood to explain it to you. Let's just…step back, okay? Give each other some space. You weren't wrong when you told your friend we were having fun. We were." She flinched inwardly at his use of the past tense. "We agreed we had an end date, and it's right around the corner. Maybe it's time to…"

He couldn't even remember what he'd started to say. He was getting lost in the hurt in her eyes as she moved from behind the bar to come around and face him. He pressed forward. "We need to slow this down. I don't know if I'm ready to be in…" He caught himself before he used the L-word. "I'm clearly not ready for…more. I don't want to use you. And I won't let myself be used."

She bristled. "Excuse me?"

He held up both hands and took a few steps back. If he hadn't, he'd have pulled her into his arms and kissed away her anger and damaged pride. But it wouldn't help either of them to try to kiss this away.

"I'm not saying you and I are…over. But… we need to take a break. I need time to think this through. I can't afford another mistake."

He knew it was the wrong word as soon as he said it. It hung in the air between them, sizzling and dangerous. She pulled her shoulders back and her eyes narrowed to slits.

"So I'm a mistake now? I'm using you? I see…" Sarcasm dripped from her voice. "I'm the mistake you crawled into bed with and had wild sex with last night. I realize now it was angry sex that had nothing to do with me. But yeah, I'm the mistake. I'm the user in this relationship. Sure."

It hadn't been angry sex. It had been urgent, yes, but only because she'd set him on fire with just a touch when she crawled into bed. He'd had a shit day and she'd made it better just by being there. He opened his mouth to tell her that, but it was too late.

"You know what? Screw you, Finn O'Hearn." She waved her hand in disgust and turned away. "Or should I say I won't be screwing you? Take your so-called break and figure your shit out. Let me know when you're ready to be a grownup." She stalked away, every step angrier than the one before it.

He had a sinking feeling the only mistake here today was his.

CHAPTER EIGHTEEN

BRIDGET SAT ON the edge of the bed, staring at the cocktail dress hanging on her closet door. She and Nana had found it in a Geneva secondhand boutique last week, and Nana insisted she had to buy it for Greer's big alumni event as a surprise for Finn. Well, he'd be surprised, alright. If she could ever summon up the courage to go.

The dark green satin dress had an empire waist and was cut to hug her body. The bodice was beaded, but not in a sparkly, New-Year's-Eve way. The light lines of green beading swirled across the satin, in almost the same color, with just the tiniest number of gold beads as accent. Understated enough for a bunch of college professors and foundation donors, but cut just low enough—and in the right color, of course—to catch Finn's eye. But that was back when she thought Finn loved her.

The cocktail party was tonight. They'd barely spoken a word since their argument Wednesday. A muttered greeting in the hall downstairs, without making eye contact. An "excuse me" when she'd gone to the basement to do laundry and caught Finn there.

The morning after their argument, he'd quietly told her that he didn't expect her to carry on their charade publicly any longer. He said he'd make up an excuse for Greer as to why she wouldn't be at the party. Or perhaps just tell the man the truth. Finn could lose the job he'd worked so hard for. Which meant he'd leave Rendezvous Falls. And Bridget wasn't ready for that to happen. Sure, it would be easier not to see him all the time if they couldn't patch things up, but it would also be permanent.

A quiet knock on her front door made Bridget jump. Was it Finn? She did her best to smooth her hair back and straighten her wrinkled T-shirt, wishing she'd taken time to slap some lipstick on or something. She opened the door as casually as possible, hoping she looked cool and composed.

"Nana? What are you doing here?"

"Well, that's a fine greeting. Good morning to you, too." Nana gave her a sweeping glance, and Bridget knew the woman hadn't missed a rumpled detail. "Are you going to invite me in?"

"Of course. Sorry." She stepped aside. Nana walked in, taking in the unusually disheveled look of the place. Nana had a lighter spring to her step these days. She was still thin and pale, but she'd just had her last chemo session and the doctor was hopeful that she wouldn't need a full mastectomy. Her grandmother was a lot more hopeful now. They all were…at least when it came to Nana's health. Bridget was feeling a lot less hope for herself.

"Reminds me of when your father was alive. He wasn't much for neatness, either. This isn't you, girl. What's going on?"

All the time she was speaking, her grandmother was walking around the apartment, straightening things on tables, taking in the dirty dishes in the sink and the empty bottles of Guinness on the counter. Maybe Bridget had let things go too far. Nana stopped at the bedroom door, spying the green dress. She turned with a bright smile.

"Oh, that's this weekend, isn't it? I wish I could see Finn's eyes when he spies you in that little number. What shoes are you going to wear..." She looked over her shoulder as if suddenly realizing the conversation was one-sided. "Bridget?"

Should she tell her grandmother everything? As much as she wanted to get Nana's wise advice, confessing to a two-month lie seemed cruel. Or maybe she was just a coward. She was too worn out to know the difference anymore.

"Finn and I had a little disagreement. No big deal."

Funny how lies continued to come so easily.

Nana looked around the apartment. "This looks like it may not have been so little. You've been off your game all week, honey. What happened?"

God, she was tired of coming up with half truths to tell everyone. It had been easier when she thought they were falling in love for real. But now the fake engagement was mocking her, making her second-guess every word she said to the people she cared about.

"It turns out we both have a jealous side, Nana."

And massive insecurities and trust issues and fears.

Nana sat on the sofa and patted the cushion for Bridget to join her. There was no point in resisting. Her grandmother took her hand in hers, and it was all Bridget could do to keep from crying at the tender gesture. She'd already cried too much, but the tears were welling up again. She blinked them away as Nana spoke.

"Bridget, you've never had a jealous bone in your body. You just like to be in charge, and you panic when you're not." The words were said gently, but hit Bridget hard.

"That's not true…"

"Girl, you've wanted to be in charge since you arrived in Rendezvous Falls twenty-some years ago. Since you were a little girl, you've tried to control our disorganized family, you've tried to control the pub—even before your father passed." Nana slowly shook her head. "You like things done a certain way. Your way. That's not always bad, mind you, because you're a bright, competent woman. But it can come across as something different. But jealousy? I don't believe it."

Was she right? Was Bridget upset because Finn had taken her control away? Hell, he'd taken more than that. He'd taken the ground right out from under her feet the other day. And yes, he'd left her feeling completely unmoored and with no sense of control at all. No plan. No solution. Just an emptiness and an ache in her heart that wouldn't go away. She had a feeling it might just be there forever.

"His ex-wife came to town." That's what had started all this. The woman who broke him in the first place came back to see what more damage she could inflict.

"I know." Nana raised her stenciled brow at Bridget's look of surprise. Her hair hadn't started coming back yet. "Oh, honey, don't let my chemo brain fool you. I may forget what you said five minutes ago, but I know what's going on in this family and in this town." She lifted a shoulder. "And she stayed at the Taggart Inn."

That explained it. Iris Taggart and the book club brigade had been busy again. Bridget rolled her eyes, and Nana chuckled.

"I know you're not jealous of his ex. She's the one who broke his heart, and Finn's a smart man. He's not going back to her. Besides, she's married. And pregnant."

Bridget couldn't breathe for a moment.

"Pregnant?" He'd never said a word. "Is it…?"

Nana sat straight as a rod, pulling her hand from Bridget's. "His? You're not seriously asking that, are you?" She reached out and gave her a light smack on the back of the head. "I said you were a smart woman, but I may have overestimated you. Of course it's not his. I'm surprised he didn't tell you that himself, though."

So Finn's friend had not only stolen Finn's wife, he'd stolen the future Finn had wanted. No wonder he was so mad at the world.

"To be honest, I didn't give him much opportunity." The argument had broken out fast and hot. "Like I said…jealous."

"Not jealous. Scared. You can't control his past, and that's what freaking you out."

It was so much more than that, but Bridget couldn't get into it all without giving up the engagement lie, and she needed to talk to Finn first. Figure out how they were going to handle it. What their stories were going to be. She might be hurt and angry, but she still didn't want him losing his job or his chance at permanent residency here.

"Maybe you're right. Maybe I'm being silly. It's all been so…"

"Fast?"

She gave a short laugh. From the moment she'd met Finn, things in her life had started happening at breakneck speed.

"Yes. Fast." She frowned. "And out of control. Do you really think that's the problem? That I want to control Finn?"

"Whoa. Slow down, honey." Nana held up a hand and chuckled. "I'm not putting any blame on you. First—because I don't know what happened. Second—because in a relationship, everything takes two. Even the problems. You said you both had jealousy issues. What's Finn's?"

"He saw me with Zayne Rutledge and...he didn't like it. He grilled me on why we'd hugged and..."

"You hugged Zayne Rutledge? Why?"

Bridget threw her hands in the air. "You sound just like Finn! Zayne's business is doing well, and that guy needs good news a lot more than most people. We've been friends since high school, and I was happy, so I hugged him."

Nana considered that for a moment. "That's a logical explanation, but I'm guessing Finn didn't think so?"

Now it was Bridget's turn to hesitate. Had she actually said all of that to Finn before things went off the rails?

"I'm taking your silence as a no." Nana patted her hand. "Why not?"

"I didn't like being questioned about it. I mean, I've been on my own all my life, and..."

"Hang on. What do you mean you've been on your own? Isn't your last name McKinnon? Don't you have half a dozen cousins in this town? Not to mention a grandmother?"

"Well...yeah...but that's not the kind of thing I was talking about."

"And didn't you date that Clark fellow in California for years?"

"I may as well have been on my own in that relationship, Nana. I was just a glorified housekeeper-slash-business-manager for him."

"But you thought you were a lot more than that, didn't you?"

She swallowed hard.

"Yes." Her voice fell. "I thought I was a lot more, but I wasn't."

"So now you're Miss Independent."

"Yes."

"And yet you're engaged." Nana pointed to the antique diamond ring sparkling on Bridget's hand. "And you never thought about this before that? You and Finn never figured out how to compromise on things? What did you think, that putting on that ring would automatically make everything perfect?"

Bridget winced, remembering Piper Montgomery's words from a few weeks ago. Perfect is over-rated.

"We need to work on our communication, I guess. The argument was all over the place. First he was mad, then I was mad, then we were both mad, and after a while I wasn't even sure what we were mad about!"

Her grandmother laughed. "Welcome to love, girlie. I've got a news flash for you—relationships are hard work. The more it's worth keeping, the more work it will take. And once you and Finn are married, you're not going to be able to retreat to separate apartments and sulk for days." Nana looked around their cluttered surroundings. "You can't walk away in a huff just because your feelings got hurt. You've got to stand and fight through it."

"But I'm not the one who walked away." Or was she? She wasn't sure now that she thought about it. "I'm so confused."

"Of course you are. It's your first big fight." Nana patted her hand. "And it won't be your last, and half the time you won't even remember who or what started it. You're a McKinnon. You're going to blow off steam once in a while, and it sounds like Finn's cut from the same cloth. So now you have to decide. Go after him." Nana paused. "Or don't. With every big argument you have—and it sounds like you might have a few—you'll need to make that choice. It's easy to pull the hermit routine and ignore the hard stuff." She took Bridget's hand again. "But you've never taken the easy way out once in your life, honey. If Finn was wrong, tell him so. If you were wrong, apologize. Then talk it out. That's what grown-ups do. They deal with things and move forward." She glanced toward the bedroom door and the green dress hanging there. "I'm thinking that dress might at least help to get him listening."

Nana had a point. Finn couldn't ignore her if she showed up at the party tonight. And afterward they could talk things out. She started to relax. It was a solid plan. And a plan meant she had something to manage. Which meant Nana was right about her.

She was a control freak.

"WHERE'S THAT FIANCÉE of yours, O'Hearn?" Logan Taggart appeared at the table next to Finn. He'd been doing his best to fade into the woodwork in the corner of the college library. It had been transformed for the cocktail party, with café tables draped in white linen and lace. The tables were scattered around the stacks. Floral center pieces with tall, narrow candles graced the tables and pretty much every flat surface in the room. The librarians had probably had a fit about it, but Greer was the boss, after all, so he tended to get what he wanted. Must be nice, Finn thought uncharitably. He took another sip of whiskey. It was his second glass. Third, if he counted the shot he'd had at home.

"Bridget doesn't feel well. What brings you here?"

Inventing an illness was the easiest and least offensive excuse he could come up with when he'd arrived. It grated on him to keep fabricating things, but this didn't seem the time or place to say they were through. It was even more grating that he didn't know if they were through. They'd argued. A rambling argument where they both seemed to be dancing around whatever was upsetting them. Looking back, he wasn't even sure who was more angry, him or Bridget. But maybe the argument was for the best. They'd always planned to fake break up anyway. Hopefully Greer wouldn't hold it against him if it happened before he got his tenure—and visa—secured. He tried to catch up with Logan's answer.

"…Iris came down with a cold, so she asked Piper

and me to represent the Taggart Inn at this shindig. Not my style, but the inn is packed with out-of-towners for graduation and this alumni gathering, so it's good business. The college is a big part of our revenue."

Finn nodded absently, his mind back to tallying all the messes he'd made since arriving in Rendezvous Falls. Jumping at the first rental he found because of Greer's pressure, then letting the same man pressure him into stumbling into a fake engagement. At the time, he thought it was foolish, but harmless. The ache in his chest was telling him something very different now. Logan was still talking.

"...so I told her we'd have to build a bigger fence to hold that damn dog we got at Christmas, because she just won't stop growing. And Piper said, 'Fine, go build it,' so now I have to build a stockade fence on top of building the patio she wants out back." Logan emptied his beer, looking around at the growing crowd of suits and silk dresses. "Which is what I should be working on instead of being here. Luke said his brother might be able to help with rebuilding the old gazebo out there. Apparently, my fiancée has pronounced this the summer of a perfect backyard." He winked at Finn. "But you know all about bossy fiancées, right? Bridget must be a handful."

Finn frowned. "Bridget's a business owner, and she knows what she wants and how to get it. That doesn't make her a handful. It makes her an independent woman."

Logan straightened. "Hey, I'm sorry. I didn't mean it like that. Bridget's on the business owners association board now, and Piper she's one of the best assets they have. I was making a bad joke—Bridget has a reputation for being a bit of a control freak, and my Piper can be the same way. Everything's a negotiation, but we've found our rhythm with those conversations."

"How?" Finn blurted out. "How did you figure that out?"

The other man gave him a slow smile. "Practice. Lots and lots of practice. We've been together since before Christmas, so we've had time to figure out how to talk things out, and how to trust that we have each other's—or the kids'—best interests in mind." He hesitated, tipping his head to the side in thought. "Trust is probably the biggest piece. Getting all butt-hurt about something makes us defensive and dug-in, and that's when things get twisted around. Once we realize we both want the same thing and just have different ideas how to get there, then the negotiating part is a lot less intense." His smile deepened. "And speaking of the master negotiator, here she is."

Piper Montgomery was petite, with golden-blond hair and a bright, wholesome smile. But when she settled into Logan's embrace, that smile showed a hint of devilishness, and Finn noticed her hand pinched Logan's ass, making her man chuckle as he kissed the top of her head. They were relaxed and comfortable together. Partners. Something he and

Bridget had found in moments, but couldn't seem to maintain.

Trust is probably the biggest piece...

It was a simple enough concept. A decent guy would trust the woman he loved. But Finn wasn't there yet. Oh, he was in love, alright. But even that wasn't enough to let go of the doubting voice that wouldn't stop telling him to be careful, be cautious. To remember that love had tricked him once before. It wasn't fair to Bridget, but he didn't know if he'd ever get past it. A waiter—actually a student pressed into service at the event—walked by with a tray of drinks. Finn snagged one and drained it, earning raised eyebrows from both of his tablemates.

Logan turned to Piper. "Hmm. I think someone's pulling up the castle gates, babe, and it's not Bridget."

"What the hell does that mean?" Finn didn't like being the butt of some private joke, no matter how much he liked Logan and Piper.

Piper's mouth had formed a soft O, but his tone made her stand taller. She might look like cookies and milk, but he had a feeling she was more like polished steel.

"It means he thinks you're protecting your heart by building a fortress around it and closing the gate, like I did once. I pushed Logan away rather than deal with my own issues." She grew somber. "It's a good thing he was willing to fight for us, or I could have ruined everything."

Logan watched Finn set the empty glass on the table and shook his head. "I don't know what's going on with you and Bridget right now. Whatever it is, the bottom of a glass isn't going to help." He paused. "I thought you said she was sick tonight?"

"I did. She is."

"Well, she seems to have recovered. She's charming the pants off of Howard Greer as we speak."

Finn's head snapped up. There she was, red hair falling in loose waves around her shoulders over a dark green dress that sparkled just a little as she laughed at something Greer had said.

She was the woman he loved. And the woman he might never be able to trust with his heart, through no damn fault of hers. He'd been an absolute shit to her this week. He'd told her they needed to stop being together. And she'd still shown up. For him.

He didn't deserve her.

And Bridget deserved far better than him.

CHAPTER NINETEEN

HOWARD GREER HAD trapped Bridget at the entrance to the library-turned-cocktail-lounge. Apparently Finn had used a headache as her excuse for not attending, and Greer was now giving her a long list of migraine cures. If she told him she'd never had a migraine in her life, he'd know Finn lied. So she smiled and nodded.

"My sister uses over-the-counter stuff, but my niece has to use prescription meds, and even then she often misses a few days of work every month, poor thing…"

"You know, I thought it was a migraine coming on. That's why I told Finn I didn't think I could make it." She spotted him in the far corner, talking to Logan Taggart. She had no idea what he'd think of her arrival. "But it turns out it was just allergies. You know—change of seasons and all that. The sinus medicine and a hot pack worked so quickly that I decided to surprise him."

Greer nodded with a grin. "I keep telling that man how lucky he is to have a gal like you, Bridget. A successful businesswoman. A lovely lady, especially in Irish green…" He waggled his eyebrows as his gaze ran down her dress. "And you're loyal to the man. Giving yourself in marriage and all. He'll go far with a woman like you at his side. Maybe he'll even have my job someday."

The college president was older than her grandmother, and clearly nowhere near as progressive.

"Just to be clear, Dr. Greer, I'm not giving myself into anything or to anyone. I'm not a prize at the county fair."

His eyes went wide. "Of course not." He cleared his throat loudly. "I'm sorry. Sometimes my language time-travels back to the '50s when I have a drink or two. What I was trying to say is that it's tough to find yourself in a relationship when you've been on your own for a long while." His voice trailed off and he seemed lost in thought for a moment. "It takes some…compromising. But you two seem to have worked that out."

If only that were true.

"We're doing our best."

"Oh, I'm sure you are. There's nothing quite as lovely as young love, my dear."

She gave him a bright smile. "It's not always lovely, Dr. Greer. Sometimes it's positively messy."

They both laughed, and she took her chance to move away. "And now I need to go surprise the man before the party's over."

"Go ahead. But I'll catch up with you in a bit to introduce you to some alumni. Finn was a risk, but I think he's going to be a great asset to the school, and to the new history building. And now he's marrying the owner of the Purple Shamrock, a place most of the people in this room have frequented." He had the good grace to look embarrassed. "It sounds crass, I know, but we need this funding, and you two love-birds might just be able to charm some of these folks into opening their wallets."

"What's good for the school is good for the town. And for the Shamrock." She patted his arm. "Finn and I will do whatever we can." *Now please let me escape.*

"What are we doing, exactly?" Finn appeared at her side, touching her back lightly with his fingers. The contact sent a shiver up her spine. Was he doing it for show? God, she couldn't wait to get past this stupid act they were putting on for everyone so she'd stop questioning every move he made.

"Ah, O'Hearn! Look who made it to the party after all. I was just telling Bridget I may enlist you to help do some fundraising tonight. You know, shake some hands, use that damn accent of yours to charm everyone out of a few thousand…" A tall, silver-haired man walked up to them, and Greer's voice went into booming, happy overdrive. "Hey, Jeff! I'm so glad you made it. Have you seen the model of the new history building we're proposing? Let me show you…"

And they were gone, leaving Finn and Bridget standing alone. He promptly removed his hand from her back, triggering a rush of tears pressing behind her eyes. It was just for show. He lowered his head so no one else would hear.

"What are you doing, Bridg? Why are you here?"

"You invited me, remember?" She tried to keep her voice light, but it cracked just a little. His blunt question made a direct hit on her heart. "You said this was important, and I told you I'd be here for you." She gave him a pointed look. "I keep my promises, Finn."

His face blanched. Message received. She wasn't Dori. She'd never hurt him.

"And I told you I'd make excuses for your absence."

She turned to face him and put her hand on her hip.

"Do you want me to leave?"

He took a sharp breath, and his eyes seemed to really focus on her for the first time. His shoulders fell.

"I never want you to leave, love."

Ooh… Hope leaped upward inside of her. She reached for his hand, but instead of seeing love shining in his eyes, she saw nothing but shadows of doubt and regret. His tone made his words sound as if he hated to admit how much he wanted her. Nana told her to fight, but Finn's demons wouldn't leave him alone, and she didn't know how to fight that.

"Finn…" Before she could continue, a couple walked up to Finn.

"Are you Professor O'Hearn?" When Finn nodded, the woman rushed on. "Oh, my son D'Shawn took your class on Celtic history, and he loved it! And this is a boy far more interested in who's playing the Lakers than who vanquished the Irish."

Finn gave her a charming smile. More charming than the one he'd given Bridget.

"No one ever truly vanquished the Irish, ma'am."

They all chuckled, and the woman continued. "That's what he told me. He loved how you compared the historical facts to all the computer games and series he loves about Vikings and dragons and castles." She sobered. "I minored in history myself, and I never managed to get him talking about that stuff. If this is the direction the new history school here is going to take, we are happy to contribute." She extended her hand. "I'm Dr. Vanessa Bridges, and this my husband, William. He's on the alumni board."

Mr. Bridges shook Finn's hand. "Professor, the alumni association wants this capital drive to be a success, and we've already told Dr. Greer that we'll get the drive started with a hefty donation…"

The conversation went on, and Bridget took the opportunity to watch Finn in action. More people walked up, and soon he was charming a small crowd of potential donors. If he managed to get the capital drive off to a strong start tonight, Greer wouldn't care if Finn was engaged or not. She had a sinking feeling that their fake engagement was the only thing still holding them together.

Greer himself walked up just then, his voice booming and pulling in the group's attention.

"Well, it looks as if you've all discovered the newest addition to our history department." Greer put his hand on Bridget's shoulder. "And he's engaged to Rendezvous Falls royalty—Bridget McKinnon here is the owner of the Purple Shamrock. I'm sure many of our alumni members have shared a few nights at that place, right?"

There was a burst of laughter as they turned to look at her. Rendezvous Falls royalty? Really? Ugh. She barely managed to keep from rolling her eyes, and only because people seemed to be waiting for her to say something. A few people laughed. There were some oohs and ahhs. Finn was silent and unsmiling. Greer nudged her and she jumped.

"Oh...yes...The Purple Shamrock is all mine... well, my family's..."

A woman spoke up from the back of the group. "Does that mean Professor O'Hearn will be a part-owner when you get married?"

Yes, of course. Their eyes met. But that's not what his eyes said. They were thoroughly shuttered now. Withdrawn. Blank. Cold. Bridget raised her chin and slid her arm around his waist with a bright smile. She wasn't going to let him scare her off. She was going to fight for him.

"Of course he will! But right now, he owes me a dance, so if you'll excuse us..."

There was a soft, sultry song playing. He couldn't refuse her without making a scene, so he followed in silence. His arms folded around her when they got to a small open area by the travel books that was supposed to be a dance floor. But there was a distance there she couldn't break through, even when she was pressed up against him.

"Finn, we'll get past this." She gave him a gentle pinch. His mouth quirked up in one corner, and he finally looked down at her. "But not if we don't talk. Come on, babe. Talk to me."

The almost-smile vanished, but he raised his hand to cup her cheek.

"You're so lovely."

"I'm glad you think so, but why do you look so sad when you say it?"

His brows lowered and he gave his head a quick shake.

"Not here. Come on…" He led her off the floor and toward the doors leading outdoors. There were two guys out on the steps smoking, but they were far enough away that she and Finn had privacy when he leaned on the stone wall framing the stairs and pulled her close.

"Bridget, we have to stop. I can't do this anymore."

Her heart stuttered to a halt, then restarted, irregular and panicked.

"You mean the engagement? Your job is probably secure now that funding is coming in for the new building, but that just means we're free to explore…"

"We started on a lie, Bridget, and I won't continue on one."

"I don't know what you mean."

"It's my fault. I made you think I could do this.

That I could fall in love again." His head fell back and he stared up at the sky. "Shit, I thought I could do that. But I can't."

She waited for more of an explanation, but none came. The two smokers went back inside. An older couple left the reception and nodded as they went down the steps. A cardinal tweeted in high chirps from the apple tree fifty feet away. Normal, everyday stuff happening at the moment she knew her world was teetering at the brink.

"You're saying you don't love me?"

He huffed out a dry laugh.

"That's the problem. I do love you." She started to smile, feeling hope, seeing a future with this man. But his next words sent it crashing down. "But I loved Dori too, and she shattered me. I thought I'd put the pieces back together, but Dori's little visit proves I haven't. I may never be whole again." He looked straight into her eyes, his own dark with heavy emotion. "I don't know if I'll ever be able to trust again. And I don't mean trust you, I mean trust myself. My judgment. My choices."

"Look, if we love each other, we can make this work." She leaned in. "And Finn, I love you."

Finn shook his head as if he didn't want to hear those words from her. Not exactly the response she'd dreamed of. "If anyone knows for a fact that love isn't a cure-all, it's me. It's not some magical key that unlocks paradise. That's the stuff of myths, not facts." He took her hands in his. "It wouldn't be fair to you to keep you in a relationship where you won't have my whole heart. You deserve better than that, Bridget." She was stunned into silence, staring at his still-moving mouth. "You have to understand that I'm doing this for you."

She sucked in a sharp breath through narrowed lips, then hissed it back out at him.

"Bullshit!" She yanked her hands away and stepped back. "It's bad enough you're trying to dump me, Finn, but don't you dare blame this on me."

His face paled. That cardinal continued to chirp, and it was getting on her nerves. Finn reached out, but she staggered back so he couldn't possibly reach her. She was in the center of the cement stairs now, breathing heavily. He stayed near the stone wall, watching her warily.

"I'm not blaming anything on you, love."

Her voice rose. "Don't call me that. Don't you dare call me that. You don't even know what the word means."

"Exactly!" He threw his hands high in frustration. "That's what I'm trying to tell you. I don't know what it means. I don't even know if it's a real thing. Why would you want to love a guy who might not ever be able to love you the way you deserve? You're smarter than that, lo…Bridget."

Her hurt settled in her abdomen now in a ball of fury. She braced her feet wide and pointed at him. "Who are you to determine what I want? What I deserve? What I'd be willing to accept?" The anger was burning hot now. She slapped her hand on her chest. "I get to decide those things. Is this why you've avoided me all week? Ever since your ex showed up and fucked with your head again?"

The answer came to her so quick and bright it was like being hit by lightning. Her breath quickened and her knees went weak.

"Oh, my God. You're not doing this for me at all. Not even close." He opened his mouth to object but she talked right over him. "You're a coward, Finn O'Hearn. And a liar."

"Bridg…"

"No! Don't speak." She waved her hand in his direction. "You lied to me just now when you said you're trying to protect me. You lied when you said you were afraid you weren't good enough for me. You don't care about me at all in this. You're only concerned with protecting yourself." She took a small step toward him, then stopped, afraid if she got any closer she'd pummel him with her fists. "Oh, sure, you're in love with me, but you're afraid it won't work out. You're afraid you'll make a mistake. You're afraid we might get mad at each other. That I might walk away. That this might not be real love after all." Her anger faded as sorrow surged. "And you think the only way to protect yourself is to walk away from loving me. Just in case."

His mouth was in a thin, hard line, but his eyes showed she'd hit the truth, so she kept going. "You think the woman who has pretended to be your fiancée for months now doesn't care enough about you. I've lied to half the town and all my family for you, but you're still afraid I'm not the real deal. I showed up tonight…in heels…to help save your job." Her arm waved widely toward the top of the steps. "I get it—you got hurt. Bad. But never loving again is not the way to handle it. Hurting me is not the way to handle it."

He finally managed to speak quickly enough to interrupt her tirade.

"That's what I'm trying to prevent. I don't want to hurt you…"

"You've already hurt me, Finn." A sob caught in her throat, but she managed to hold it in. "You know I love you but you're telling me we're done. And telling me it's for my sake, when you've just ripped my heart right out of my chest. Don't be expecting a thank you note from me anytime soon, because this big 'favor' you just did hurts more than anything else in my life, and that's sayin' something." She blinked, but not fast enough to catch the tears welling in her eyes. "You've got about five seconds to make this right and take that back. Take a chance, damn it."

He looked into her eyes briefly, but his gaze fell to the steps before he spoke in a low, tortured voice. "This may hurt you, and I'm sorry for that, but it's still better than…" His words trailed off as if he'd forgotten what he was going to say.

"Better than hurting yourself?" He winced at her suggestion, but he didn't argue. A cold calm settled over her. "Fine. I guess I know where I stand, don't I? Consider our fake engagement and our sleeping arrangement—because it clearly hasn't been a relationship—over and done. I'd throw my ring in your face, but it belongs to my grandmother. Can't wait to break her heart by telling her the truth about us. But there's a lot of that going around." She scowled. "Broken hearts, that is. There sure as hell hasn't been much truth."

MAURA THOUGHT VICKIE was about to go across the table at Rick Thomas. Judging from the way Lena reached for Vickie's arm, and the way Cecile shifted away from Rick, she wasn't the only one concerned. He'd finally come clean about Finn and Bridget's scheme to fool the town with their fake engagement story. But only after Bridget had finally come clean to Maura a few days ago, crying and begging forgiveness for lying to her.

"You knew?" Vickie glared at him. "And you didn't tell us? You didn't tell me? I can't believe it." She yanked her arm away from Lena and slumped back in her chair. "I thought we were friends, Rick."

They were sitting on the front porch of the Taggart Inn. It was one of those early June mornings that spoke more of summer than spring. The trees were leafing out in bright green, and hydrangeas were in bloom in a riot of pastel colors at the base of the porch.

Iris Taggart waved at her future granddaughter-in-law, Piper Montgomery, to bring them more tea. She obliged with a warm smile, her blond hair pulled into a ponytail and a bright yellow apron tied at her waist.

"How are you all doing this morning? Are you plotting more matchmaking? Or maybe a love rescue?" She looked at Maura as she poured more hot water in her teacup. "I heard about Bridget and Finn. I hope they can work things out."

Vickie was still glaring at Rick. "We're more likely to be plotting a murder at the moment."

Piper's eyes went wide. "O-kay then. If anyone could get away with murder, it's this bunch. I don't want to be a material witness, so off I go." She waved and left them alone. The table was silent before Maura finally spoke up.

"Look, I get why you're angry, Vickie, but that's not really helpful right now. Murder Rick on your own time. The good news is he finally told us the truth about Finn and Bridget. Good heavens, they started this whole thing to fool all of us, and they almost did." Except Maura had always been skeptical of the insta-love story. She'd thought maybe Finn needed a green card wedding. But Rick had explained that while it was a green card thing, it was more about saving Finn's job.

"Then the fake relationship became a real one. Bridget fell in love, even though she didn't want to. And I'm convinced Finn loves her back."

"I agree," Iris said. "Finn stayed at the inn for a while and he's good people. He wouldn't have done anything that would harm Bridget."

Vickie shrugged. "And yet, he did. He broke up with her weeks ago. Both the real and fake relationships are over."

Maura thought about that. "They're only over if someone doesn't do something. I sent Bridget to that college reception to fight for him, and Finn pushed her away, so it's going to be up to him now. We need to figure out a way to get through to Finn."

"Will Bridget give him another chance after all this time has passed, though?" Lena asked. "She put it on the line for him and he rejected her. I know Bridget well enough to know she's not one to let someone hurt her more than once."

That was a good question. Bridget had been practically glowing with rage since Finn rejected her. But in the quiet moments, when she thought no one was watching, Bridget's eyes looked shattered.

Maura shook her head. "They were juggling so many lies and secrets and baggage that it's no wonder it all came crashing down."

"Which means…" Cecile looked around the table with a conspiratorial grin. "That they're starting with a clean slate now. No more secrets, which is a much better place to start from, don't you think?"

Vickie looked back to Rick. "Gee, I don't know. What do you think, Rick? Is it better to not keep secrets?"

He stared up at the pale blue ceiling of the wide porch with a groan. "What do you want me to say, Vick? The man asked me to keep his secret. He could have been deported…or something. I don't really get how it all works, but he could have lost his visa and had to leave the whole damn country! That's kind of a big deal, so when he asked me to promise not to say a word, I agreed." He narrowed his eyes at Vickie.

"I've kept a few of your secrets, too, you old crone. You thought I was a hero back then."

"That was different."

"Was it, though?"

Maura raised her hand. "Okay, we're getting off track. We need to fix things with Finn and Bridget."

Cecile agreed. "We may not have hooked them up, but I'm sure we can get them back together. I mean, we are matchmakers, right? They're a match. So let's make it happen."

Lena looked between Vickie and Rick. "Isn't Finn staying with you, Rick?" He nodded. "Well, then, it seems to me you're the one to come up with a plan. You and Vickie." Vickie started to object, but Lena waved her off. "Get over yourself. This is about two young people who need help figuring out they belong together. Come up with a plan, and we'll put it in motion."

Rick looked like he wanted to be anywhere but there at the moment, but he heaved a loud sigh and looked over at Vickie. "You're the one with all the acting chops, Miss Diva. Come up with a way to force them together."

Vickie pulled a small notebook from her purse with a wicked smile. "I'm on it. And you're the literature professor, so write a story that will work. And make it a good one."

The group started to buzz with ideas. Maura watched and listened, praying this would work. Praying it wasn't too late.

CHAPTER TWENTY

"I DON'T MIND having a roomie, but this black mood of yours is a real buzzkill, O'Hearn." Rick Thomas set the containers of Chinese takeout on the table next to where Finn was glaring at his laptop. "Let's see if some crab rangoon and sesame chicken can cheer you up."

Finn sat back and sighed. "Sorry, man. I know I've been foul since I got here." He took a pint box and opened it, grabbing a crab rangoon and munching it down like a starving man. When was the last time he ate? Yesterday, maybe? "My head just won't stop spinning in circles and it's feckin' exhausting."

Rick grabbed plates and silverware and joined Finn at the dining room table, which was pulling double duty as Finn's office for now. Rick's house was one of the smaller—and older—Victorian homes in Rendezvous Falls. It wasn't far off Main Street, and now that summer was almost here, there was a steady stream of tourists going by on the weekends. The dining room had a bay window facing the street, so Finn could see a cluster of people out there now, pointing and taking photos of the yellow house with its green, orange and dark red trim work.

It had a rounded tower on one corner with a cone-shaped roof on it, like an ice cream cone had been dropped there. The rainbow flag was hung on one side of the steps, with the American flag on the other. Rick didn't talk about it much, but he'd served in the navy after high school and had gone to college on a military scholarship. The older man scooped some egg foo yong on his plate and covered it with an alarming amount of salty gravy.

"It's been a month, Finn. You need to figure your shit out."

"I told you I found a house. I'll be out of here as soon as I sign the lease."

The beige 1960s ranch was further from town than he'd like, but it was cheap and available and par-tially furnished. And being more removed from the town meant fewer chances of running into Bridget or her family. He was persona non grata with most of them, and he missed the McKinnons. But nowhere near as much as he missed her.

Rick waved his hand, chewing quickly so he could speak. "I'm not talking about that. I don't care how long you stay here. And forget that dumpy house you looked at. It's practically in the next town, and it's… boring. It's like you're trying to punish yourself…" He grabbed a pot sticker from another container. "Are you punishing yourself, Finn?"

"I don't need a shrink for a landlord, Rick. I need my own place."

"You had a place. With Bridget McKinnon. From what I've heard, it's still available."

"She won't get much action on the apartment until August when students come back."

"I wasn't talking about the apartment, dumbass. I'm talking about the place you still have in the woman's heart. It's not too late."

Oh, how he wished that were true. But he'd already hurt her badly, and would only do it again.

There was a knock on the door as they started cleaning up. Sometimes tourists would be bold enough to knock and ask to see the interior of the private home. Finn thought it was a ballsy move to request access into a stranger's house, but Rick would occasionally allow them to step into the ornate little foyer with its sparkling chandelier and large oil painting above the console table. The painting was from 1905, and showed the town as viewed from Seneca Lake, including some of the original college buildings. The painting was mentioned in the walking tour brochures handed out by the historical society. It was by a locally famous artist of the period, and had been a gift from a man Rick dated for years. Finn got the idea that guy was the One Who Got Away.

Finn closed up the takeout boxes and put them in the fridge as Rick went to get the door. He heard low conversation in the other room, and figured some lucky tourists had been invited in. That was a good reason to stay in the kitchen. Or maybe head up to his room via the back staircase. Before he could decide, Rick stepped in and gestured for him to follow.

Curious, Finn tossed a towel on the sink and went into the dining room.

The table was now occupied by several of Rick's book club friends. Finn met most of them at the engagement party at Maura's house. Vickie. Cecile. Helen Russo from the winery. That night seemed like a lifetime ago. Kneeling in front of Bridget and sliding that ring on her finger. The kiss that rocked his world. The beginning of their fake engagement and very real love affair.

He gave himself a mental shake and plastered on a smile.

"Oh, I didn't know there was a book club meeting today. I'll just get of your hair…" He turned toward the foyer and came to an abrupt halt.

Maura McKinnon stood in the archway leading into the dining room. He hadn't seen her in over a month, and she looked…good. She had color in her cheeks and an energetic light in her eyes. Her head was covered with a scarf—green, of course—and she gave Finn a warm smile. Why wasn't she glaring at him? He'd dumped her granddaughter. Broken off both the real and fake relationship.

The whole McKinnon clan had been cool, at best, since the day Bridget called him a selfish coward and walked out of his life. Mary sent him a cryptic text uninviting him from Katie's birthday party. He ran into Mike a few times in town, and Mike would just shake his head at him and walk away. Kelly was the most vocal. She'd seen him the day he moved his stuff out of Bridget's house and walked across the parking lot to rip him a new one, right there in front of Rick and Luke Rutledge.

She'd called him three kinds of an asshole for hurting her cousin, and banned him from the Shamrock. As if his heart could ever take walking in there again. Seeing Bridget. Remembering the night they made love against the wall in the back hallway. Kelly had nothing to worry about—the Shamrock was filled with nothing but pain for him.

Yet here stood Maura. Smiling. He blinked a few times and stared at her without saying a word, unsure how to react. Why had Rick brought him in here? Was this some intervention or...

Oh, shit. That's exactly what this was. Bridget told him about this book club and its fondness for meddling in other people's business. Finn glared at Rick, who looked a little guilty and a lot amused. Damn it. That boring ranch house outside of town was looking really good right about now.

"Seriously?" Finn ground his words through clenched teeth. "You're siccing the love brigade on me?"

Cecile, the rounded blonde with a bright smile and a perpetually pink wardrobe, burst out laughing, nudging the tall black woman at her side. Lena had half a dozen earrings in one ear, and at least that many rings on her fingers and bangles on her wrist. Cecile clapped her hands in delight.

"The Love Brigade! Oh, my God, that's fabulous! Can we get T-shirts made? Come up with a logo for us, Lena. I think we finally have a name for our book club."

Lena was pursing her lips, trying not to laugh, but she finally shook her head with a chuckle. "It is pretty catchy."

Rick started grumbling behind Finn. "I knew this was a bad idea. I never should have let you biddies talk me into this."

Vickie Something—Finn couldn't recall her last name—sat up straight and angry. Finn remembered her now. She'd been with Greer at the Shamrock the night this whole mess got started. Great. She shook her finger in Rick's direction. "Don't play innocent for your friend, Rick Thomas. You're the one who said the only place we were guaranteed to find him was here. Now will someone please get Maura a chair?"

Finn turned to Maura, feeling like an idiot. "I'm sorry, Maura." He pulled out a chair for her. "Have a seat. And honestly, I don't blame you for wanting to let me have it, so go ahead." She sat, wearing an odd, secretive smile. He rushed to fill in the silence when she still didn't speak. "Tell me what a bastard I am. I deserve it. I hurt your girl, and I'll stand here and take whatever you want to throw at me."

Cecile piped up. "Oh, did you hear that, Maura? He's giving us permission to throw things. Would this candlestick do?" She lifted one of Rick's heavy brass candlesticks from the center of the table, but Rick quickly grabbed it away from her.

"No one's doing any throwing in this house, you

dingbat. The house and garden tour is coming up next month and I don't want to be patching holes in the walls."

Vickie rolled her eyes at Cecile. "Maura didn't come here to throw things." She turned her gaze back to Finn, with very little warmth. "As tempting as it might be for some of us. You played us all for fools, Finn O'Hearn. Lying to Howard and carrying on this elaborate ruse just to keep your job. Dragging Bridget into it. You both have apologies to make for all the lies you told."

Finn glared at Rick. They knew about the engagement. Rick held up both hands and backed away.

"I didn't tell them! I mean…not until Maura already knew something was going on. Seriously, you try lying to that woman." He gestured toward Maura. "And trust me, I'm in the doghouse for not letting them know before they figured it out for themselves."

Vickie huffed out a grumbling sigh. "You're going to be groveling a long time before I forgive you for lying to me. I can't believe you kept it a sec… Oh, never mind." She waved her hand. "We'll deal with you later. Today is for Maura, and so far we haven't let her speak a word."

The fact that this ambush was Maura's idea didn't bode well for Finn. She was the one he'd hurt the most. Besides Bridget, of course. He closed his eyes tight, then took a seat next to her, turning his chair to face her.

"Let me explain…"

She shook her head and spoke at last.

"Bridget explained everything to me. I knew there was something off with the story right from the start." She paused. "But I let it go when I saw it might become the truth. You started to fall in love for real after the St. Paddy's party."

A flood of memories washed over him. Making love in the hall. Going back to his bed for the rest of the night. And the next night. And all the nights after that. The laughter. The sex. The love. He couldn't imagine ever not loving Bridget. But it was too late now.

"Maura, I'm sorry. I screwed up my life, which is a particular talent of mine. But this time I screwed up someone else's life, too, and I hurt your family with all the lies. That's on me, not Bridget." He stared at the floor, focusing on the frayed edge of the dark red antique rug against the highly polished hardwood floor. "And yes, I fell in love with her. Don't you see? It's because I love her that I had to break things off…"

Snickers and outright laughter broke out around the table. He looked up in surprise. Even Maura was chuckling at him.

"I know you probably think that's true, but it's a load of horse shit, Finn."

He couldn't help his sad smile.

"That's pretty much what Bridget said at the time."

Maura nodded. "I raised a smart girl." She winked at him. "Look, we're laughing because we've seen this before. This idea that breaking someone's heart is somehow the brave and noble thing to do. Come on. You're a smart man. Smart enough to know you aren't doing this for Bridget's sake, no matter how many times you tell yourself that story."

He sat back and closed his eyes. Why couldn't anyone understand? "No offense, Maura, but it's the truth. I'm terrified of hurting her if we…"

"A-ha!" She held up a finger and pointed it right at his face. "There's a bit of truth at last. You're terrified. You're so wrapped up in 'what-ifs' that you won't let yourself take a chance. The only one you're protecting here is you. The only one you're punishing here is you. You love that woman, and she loves you." Her voice hardened. "So do something about it."

"Damn it, Maura, I've already broken it off! Do you really think Bridget is going to just shrug that off and take me back? She was furious, and I don't think that's changed."

"She was hurt, Finn." It was Helen who spoke up. "Hurt and rage can look alike, but they're not. Hurt can be healed." She hesitated. "I understand what you're doing. Whether it's Bridget or yourself you're trying to protect, you're refusing to let love into your life. And that's always a mistake. Losing my Tony a few years back nearly destroyed me. I almost lost the winery because I was in so much pain that I stopped functioning. We were supposed to have so many more years left to enjoy together, and he was gone in the blink of an eye. But I wouldn't trade my time with him for the world." She waved her arm around the table. "And I'm not the only widow sitting here. Lena lost her husband when their children were babies. Lena, would you give up your time together to protect yourself from the pain?"

Lena scoffed. "Hell, no. My years with Marcus were the best years of my life."

"See?" Helen looked back to Finn. "Love brings risks. And plenty of opportunities for pain. And anger. Lord knows, Tony and I had more than one big blow-out through the years." Heads nodded. "Tears were shed. Hearts were hurt. But to refuse to even try when you have a chance for a love like that? Oh, honey, you're both making a big mistake here."

Cecile fluffed her bright blond hair and cleared her throat loudly. She was a colorful one, with powder-blue eye shadow and sparkly eyelashes in the middle of the afternoon. But her smile was warm and sincere.

"My Charlie and I are still happily and thankfully together, and our marriage is blissfully happy." Vickie rolled her eyes, but Cecile just shrugged. "It's true! But what I'm trying to say is that it isn't all sunshine and roses. We almost split up about twelve years ago." There were a few gasps. "Seriously! As we got older, things got more…challenging… intimacy-wise. We both thought the other had lost interest. We doubted each other and we were hurt and angry. Right in the middle of our biggest argument ever, we realized we were just heaping assumptions and fear on each other with no actual conversation. Once we talked it out…" She blushed slightly, but

Finn had no idea why until she continued. "…and got more creative with our sex life…"

"Okay," Lena said. "Moving right along…"

Cecile rushed to speak over her. "My point is that talking and trusting and saying you're sorry can go a long way. And getting creative, of course."

Finn had no idea where this conversation was going, or why.

"Ladies…" He glanced up at his current landlord. "And gentleman, I appreciate whatever it is you're trying to do here, but Bridget and I are over." Those words felt heavy on his heart. "We built our relationship on a lie."

"So rebuild it." Maura's words were soft and low, but opened a spot in Finn's heart he thought was permanently sealed off. The spot where hope lived.

"Rebuild?" Was that possible?

"You're pretty determined that what you had was bad," Maura continued. "Tainted by the fake engagement story. Your job stress. Your divorce. My illness and its effect on Bridget. Your breakup." She reached out and put her hand over Finn's. "If you're really convinced all of that makes things impossible to repair, then don't repair it. Start fresh. Leave all the baggage behind. Tell her you love her—or better yet, show her you love her. And begin your own story together. A real one."

He sat in silence, considering Maura's suggestion. He and Bridget had started under a heavy load of stress. They helped each other, but maybe they gave too much? No, not too much. Love was never too much. But neither of them had let go of their fear to look ahead with clear eyes. No, that wasn't true, either. He was the only one still hobbled by his past, by his fears. Bridget had moved beyond hers. She'd been willing to take the chance with him. And he'd pushed her away.

The fog lifted. Bridget had been hurt in the past. Taken for granted. And she'd risen above it and handed her heart to Finn. His head dropped into his hands. He was such a stupid, chickenshit asshole.

There were chuckles around the room, and Maura was laughing out loud.

"Well, I wasn't going to use those exact words, but yes."

He realized he'd stated his confession out loud. His face heated, and Rick clapped his hand on Finn's shoulder.

"Sometimes the truth hurts. But you know what they say—the first step to recovery is admitting you have a problem."

"Yeah? Then what's the second step? Because I have no clue what to do."

Cecile raised her glass of wine. "Don't you worry, Finn O'Hearn. That's what the Love Brigade is here for!"

BRIDGET DIDN'T REALIZE how much effort she was putting into scrubbing the top of the skillet surface until Kelly spoke up from in front of the sink.

"Are you trying to clean that thing or kill it?"

She stopped, blowing a loose strand of hair from her face.

"Are you talking to me?"

Kelly laughed. "Yeah, DeNiro, I'm talkin' to you. Your knuckles will start bleeding pretty soon if you don't ease up a little." She walked over and set her hand on Bridget's shoulder. "Look—you're leaving slivers of steel wool all over. You're killing the scrub pad, for sure."

She was right. But Bridget wasn't ready to concede that yet. "It needs a good scrubbing once in a while. I'll wipe it down and oil the surface before I cook anything on here. I know how to take care of my kitchen, Kell."

"Life is about more than kitchens, cuz. When's the last time you got out of this place and had some fun?"

Not since Finn dumped me.

"It's been a while, but it's fine. Business is picking up…"

Thanks to Finn's suggestions.

"And I can't take a break until the patio is done."

Because if I step off this property I might run into him somewhere.

"We need it open by the Fourth of July. It'll be the perfect place to watch the fireworks over the lake."

Kelly frowned. "I thought the contractor told you he couldn't do it by then?"

That was just one of many things that had gone wrong lately. It took forever to get the permits from the county and town. By the time they got the final go-ahead, Pete Helmsworth had taken on another hardscaping job in Watkins Glen. He was the only guy around with the talent to take on the slate patio she'd envisioned, with a big fire pit and stone benches all around the perimeter. The teak tables and chairs, built to withstand the weather, were scheduled to arrive that week, but there was no place to put them. The yard behind the Shamrock had been bulldozed level, but that was the extent of it. After three days of rain, it was a muddy mess out there. And the Fourth was only ten days away.

"You're right. It's hopeless." She sighed. "I'll have to take out a loan to cover the expenses. Assuming I even qualify for one…"

"Whoa!" Kelly folded her arms and stared. "Stop the pity train right there. I never said anything was hopeless."

"My whole life is hopeless at the moment." She scrunched her face up. "Yikes, that did sound pathetic, didn't it? Sorry. I'm just tired and frustrated."

"And lonely?" Kelly's words echoed Bridget's thoughts, but she didn't want to go there.

"Don't. My heart can't take talking about Finn anymore. It's over."

Kelly shrugged and headed back to this sink. "It doesn't have to be."

"He broke up with me. Ended our fake romance and the real one." She returned to scrubbing the grill. "I'm not begging."

"No one said you had to beg, but you could go after what you want."

"I don't want a man more concerned with protecting his own heart than protecting mine."

"But he thought he was protecting you. I mean, the guy's an idiot, but aren't they all? Is that really unforgivable?"

"He hasn't even asked for forgiveness, Kelly."

He'd quietly moved out of the apartment one evening while she was at the pub. She'd seen Luke's truck over there. It was Luke who told her Finn was living with Rick Thomas until he found a place.

Kelly turned again. "He hasn't reached out at all?"

He'd left a voice mail. Sent a text or two saying they should talk.

"Not with any kind of urgency."

"Have you reached out to him?"

"No, I haven't. I've said all I need to say." She kept scrubbing, and sure enough, scraped her knuckles on the grill. "Ow. Please, Kelly. Give it a rest. I need to move on. He doesn't want me."

Finn always complained about his lousy judgment in relationships, but Bridget wasn't much better. First Clark didn't love her enough to fight for her, and now Finn had left her rather than put any work into their relationship. She was apparently very discardable.

The kitchen door swung open behind her. She was surprised to see her grandmother standing there.

"Nana! Is everything okay? Did I forget an appointment?"

"Can't a woman stop by the family business just to say hi?" Nana grinned. The smile warmed Bridget's heart. Ever since the doctors told them that the tumor responded so well to the chemo that they'd only be doing a lumpectomy, Nana's smiles had been a lot more frequent. Her chemo was done. The doctor said she'd probably be on medication for the next few years as a precaution, but things looked good. The nightmare was receding from all their lives.

She hugged the woman who'd raised her. "You can stop by any time at all, and you know it. Do you want to sit? There's a stool there by the counter..."

"Stop fussing over me. You know I don't like it." But she did take a seat. "I'm here to ask a favor of you."

"Name it." Bridget leaned against the counter. "I'll grant pretty much any wish you make..." She thought of her conversation with her grandmother last week, and the one she just had with Kelly, and decided to add one condition. "...as long as it has nothing to do with Finn. You all need to stop trying to put us back together."

Nana straightened, looking offended. "Did I say anything about Finn?"

"You haven't said anything at all yet, but I only have that one condition on the favor. What would you like me to do?"

"I want to go to Boston to see your Great Aunt Irene. My sister sent me an email and asked me to visit."

"O-kay...and you want me to...?"

"Well, to drive me there, of course."

"Me? I have the Shamrock to run. Why not

Mike…" She spied her cousin slipping toward the back door and pointed at her. "Or Kelly?"

Kelly threw her hands up. "Not me! I'm taking summer classes, remember? Busy busy busy."

Bridget narrowed her eyes. "Not too busy to ask for a night off to go to Rochester with your friends last weekend."

Before the argument could escalate, Nana made her decision clear. "I don't want Mike or Kelly or Mary or Timothy. I want you." She picked at some invisible piece of lint on her capris, not meeting Bridget's eyes. "I think you and I deserve a girl's weekend, and you need to get out of Rendezvous Falls for a few days."

Bridget started to object, but Nana waved her off. "I promised this wasn't about Finn, but it is about you hiding in this building and your house for weeks now. It's not healthy, and getting away for a few days will help. We'll do a little shopping and maybe take that dinner cruise on the harbor. We can do it mid-week, so the Shamrock will be fine without you."

Kelly raised her hand. "Can I be in charge?"

Nana chuckled. "Didn't you just say you were busy busy busy?"

"But this would be real-world work experience for extra credit in my business class. Come on, let me be the boss. Temporarily, of course."

"Boston?" Bridget's voice trailed off. It wasn't the worst idea, now that she thought about it. A road trip away from Rendezvous Falls and all things Finn. It was almost funny that Nana thought she was spending all her time at the bar and home to avoid thinking of Finn. His memory was everywhere here. Hell, she had to force herself to go down the back hallway to lock up at night. The thought of him pressing her to the wall and… She blew out a quick breath. Going down that road would bring nothing but more hurt. Maybe getting out of here was just what she needed.

"Okay, Nana. As long as we don't go on a weekend. It's not like I have any construction to oversee." She gave the back window some side-eye. "The patio isn't going to happen anytime soon."

"I don't know why we need that patio, anyway." Nana stood. "I'll call Irene and tell her we'll be there Tuesday. We can come back Thursday?"

"Uh…yeah. Thursday's good. It'll give me time to figure out a plan for the Independence Day party. I guess it'll have to be indoors like last year, and people will have to go out to the parking lot to watch the fireworks."

Her grandmother gave her an odd Cheshire cat grin, like she was keeping a secret and was downright gleeful over it. "You never know what'll happen, honey."

"What does that…?" But Nana was gone, moving faster than Bridget had given her credit for, leaving nothing but a swinging door.

Why did this innocent trip to Boston feel like some sort of trap?

CHAPTER TWENTY-ONE

FINN ACCEPTED A beer from Luke and joined him on the circular stone bench surrounding the fire pit on the new patio. It had been a hellish three days, but they'd made it happen. The Purple Shamrock had a beer garden.

Logan Taggart had worked out the design details with the original contractor and had everything they needed delivered within an hour of Bridget leaving for Boston with her grandmother. Logan had done some building through the years, and turned out to be a bit of a wizard at laying stonework. Luke's brother, Zayne, had helped Luke with the framework and roof of the new outdoor bar. Mark Hudson, husband of Evie, the owner of the Spot Diner in town, had painted a mural on the back wall of the pub of an Irish landscape, complete with castle ruins and a frame of shamrocks.

Several McKinnons had helped, too. Mike had lugged wheelbarrows full of stone for Logan and Zayne. Patrick and Kelly had kept the bar and restaurant open for business. Mary brought lunch and… supervised. She was the only holdout on this idea.

Not the beer garden, but the idea of Finn trying to win Bridget back. He'd caught her glaring at him more than once as they'd worked late into the evenings trying to finish. Like right now, as she came out of the pub with a plate of scones.

She walked over and held the plate out to Finn and Luke, raising an eyebrow at the beers in their hand.

"Maybe I should have brought pretzels instead of scones."

Luke had already grabbed one, and crumbs flew when he tried to answer, his words slurring around the scone.

"Don't be silly. Your scones go with everything, Mary. Including beer."

Finn took a scone. "Thanks, Mary." He motioned around them. "What do you think?"

Her face softened as she took in the beer garden, fenced in on one side to hide the parking lot, but open to the lake view below. The sun was low in the sky behind them, muting the summer glow of Seneca Lake. They'd just finished setting up the tables and stools Bridget had ordered, and Kelly was dashing around, setting weighted glass globes with candles in them as centerpieces.

"I think…" She looked back to him. "I think you really know how to make a grand gesture, Finn. But what makes you think all of this is enough to win my cousin back after you broke her heart? She could still kick you to the curb, you know. She's stubborn like that."

Luke laughed, sending another cloud of scone crumbs flying. "Jesus, Mary. Thanks for being such a ray of sunshine. A lot of people have busted their asses to get this done. I don't know if my back will ever recover from handling all this stone. How about a little appreciation?"

Mary's mouth dropped open. She clearly hadn't expected Luke to light into her. Neither had Finn.

And Luke wasn't done. "This man's whole heart is resting on Bridget's reaction to this, so maybe give him a break."

Finn clapped his hand on Luke's back.

"It's okay, Luke. Mary's right. This could all blow up in my face. But just to set the record straight, I don't expect her to forgive me because we built the beer garden. This..." He looked around and shrugged. "This is just to get her attention. She won't take my calls. She won't answer texts. She's made it clear she wants nothing to do with me. I have to get her to stand still long enough to listen to me. That's all I'm hoping for at this point. For her to listen while I tell her what a complete ass I am and how sorry I am and how much I love her. This pile of rocks..." Luke protested that, but Finn kept going. "This may not make her love me. But Mary, I'll do whatever it takes to earn her love again. This is just a start. I won't give up."

Mary studied him thoughtfully, accepting the glass of orange juice Kelly handed her. "You gave up once."

"No." He shook his head emphatically. "I screwed up, but I didn't give up. I panicked. I doubted myself, but I never doubted her..." He stared at the lake. "Well, I did doubt her, but it had nothing to do with her. I let my past get tangled up..." He ran his fingers through his hair. "Shit. I know I hurt her, Mary, and I'm sorry. I promise you I'll never do it again if she'll take me back."

She nodded slowly. "Okay. I'll hold you to that promise, Finn. And you don't want to cross this Irishwoman right now. I'm running on too little sleep and a whole lot of momma bear hormones these days." She glanced at her watch. "You'll know what's going to happen in a few hours. Bridget texted me that she and Nana will be back around nine."

She set the plate of scones on the bench, patting Finn's shoulder as she straightened. "For the record, I'm rooting for you."

That was good to know, but the only person who mattered right now was on a highway, coming home to a surprise gesture she might...or might not...be happy about.

"Nana, I'm happy to drop you off at your house. We're going right by..."

"I told you, I want to go to the pub. Mike said he'd pick me up there. That way you can get to your place and get some sleep. You've been driving for hours." Nana adjusted herself in the seat, sliding the seat belt away from the tender area where her port used to be. "You must be exhausted."

She was a little tired. Boston was a six-hour drive, and she'd done it all. Not that Nana hadn't offered. But Bridget knew she was worn out, especially on the way home. The visit with Nana's sister had been… different. Irene was a character and a half—flamboyant and loud in contrast to Nana's quiet strength. She had a brownstone in the city, and it was filled with colorful art, most of it done by Irene and her friends. Never married, she'd traveled the world for years, teaching wherever she could pick up a job, sometimes doing stage acting or lounge singing on the side, always up for an adventure.

Irene filled their visit with museums and restaurants and probably more walking than Nana was ready for, but she'd never let her sister know that. She'd been a trooper, and Bridget had done her best to make sure Nana sat at every opportunity. The trip had been good for both of them, though. Nana sat up late with her sister and talked about old times and family doings. Bridget had a change of scenery to jog her out of her sorrow over Finn. Nana had been right, she'd buried herself in work to keep from dealing with things.

Finn said he might never trust her with his heart. As angry as she'd been, the truth was she'd never be satisfied with just a piece of him. She wanted all of him. Or nothing. She'd ended up with nothing, and she was going to have to find a way to deal with that.

They probably did need to have a talk, since he'd managed to keep his job at the school and would be staying in Rendezvous Falls.

Vickie Pendergast had filled Nana and Bridget in on the story last week. Finn told Howard Greer the whole story about their fake engagement and why he'd done it—to secure his position at the school. Greer had lectured Finn for over an hour, but in the end, admitted it was partly his fault for pressuring Finn to prove he was serious about staying in Rendezvous Falls when Finn was already so anxious about his visa. The fundraising for the new history building was off to a strong start, and Greer credited Finn for a lot of that. In the end, he'd told Finn he was on a tenure track if he stayed, and would no longer have to jump through hoops to prove himself.

Bridget was happy for Finn. He could finally relax and start building a future. It just wouldn't include her, even though they'd be sharing the same small town. They'd need to figure out a way to navigate that. They were two mature adults, so it couldn't be that difficult, right? The sun had sunk behind the vineyard-covered hills by the time she pulled into the Shamrock. She got out of the car and stretched with a low groan.

So much to do before next week's Independence Day party. But it would have to wait. She was too tired to do anything tonight other than checking in with Kelly and heading to the house and her bed. Nana waited while Bridget took her small bag from the trunk and they walked inside. It was quiet, but it was a summer Thursday night. It was always slower when the college wasn't in session. That's one of the reasons she'd wanted the beer garden... She stopped that thought in its tracks. Maybe next year.

Mike was at the bar with Kelly. Mary and her husband were there, too. The baby was in his carrier, and Mary was rocking him on the bar as she picked at a basket of onion rings. Their other two kids were running around the tables and jumping off the edge of the stage.

Patrick came out of the kitchen and waved in greeting.

"There you are! This is turning into a regular family reunion tonight."

Bridget looked at everyone and frowned. "Why are you all here?"

Mary rolled her eyes. "Thanks for the warm welcome, cuz. Just a coincidence, really. We stopped for dinner, Mike's here to meet Nana, and these two..." She waved her hand at Patrick and Kelly. "They work here, in case you've forgotten."

Bridget couldn't help thinking there was more to this coincidence.

Nana took a seat next to Mary, then turned back to Bridget. "Oh, shoot, I almost forgot! Can I borrow that pink cardigan of yours? You know, the sparkly one with the three-quarter sleeves? I want to wear it to the breast cancer support group luncheon this weekend. We're talking about having a walkathon this fall to raise money for research."

"Uh...sure, Nana." She'd always thought her grandmother hated pink. "I'll drop it off tomorrow..."

"Oh, honey. Could you just run over and get it now? I want to make sure it'll work with the top I want to wear under it." Nana sat back with a smile that brooked no disagreement. "I'll wait here for you."

Bridget sighed. When Nana decided she wanted something, she wanted it right then. No sense in arguing.

"Okay. I'll be right back." It was dark, with just a narrow swath of purple on the western hills where the sun had set. The parking lot lights were flickering on as she stepped outside. She decided to leave her car where it was. She could always move it after she gave Nana the sweater. She couldn't figure out the request for anything pink, but maybe Nana just wanted to fit in with the other ladies.

She stopped abruptly halfway across the lot. What was that glow from behind the pub? Was that... smoke? She broke into a run, pulling her phone from her pocket as she did. She was just about to tap in the final "1" on 9-1-1 when she got to the gateway to what had been a barren, muddy expanse a few short days ago. Not anymore.

Flagstones had been laid over the large area. The tables and stools were set up, with candles flickering softly. A low stone wall in the center surrounded a fire pit, which was where the smoke was coming from. A fire blazed in the center. It was surrounded by a water-filled moat, where the flames danced in reflection. The outer ring of stone doubled as seating. There was a bar in the corner, next to the back wall of the pub, where…was that a mural? It was a scene of the Irish countryside, and Bridget's open mouth curved into a smile. It was all exactly as she'd imagined it. It was perfect.

But how…?

The strings of light bulbs overhead came on, making her blink and jump at the same time. The lights made it easier to see the small stage area in the other corner, and a little wooden dance floor in front of it. That's where Finn O'Hearn stood, hands in his pockets, head lowered, looking at her through heavy brows. He looked intentionally casual, but she had the feeling he was ready to bolt.

The shock of the patio had rendered her speechless, but she walked toward him, stopping near the fire pit.

"What…? How…?" She looked around, seeing more details with each glance. "I don't understand what's happening." Her eyes narrowed. "Or what you're doing here."

His head moved up and down slowly, his jaw working back and forth. He shifted his weight. He was nervous. He should be.

"What's happening is that you have a lot of people who love you and we came together this week to give you something you wanted. A beer garden."

Her lungs screamed for air, but she couldn't breathe. She stopped breathing at the word "we." He'd counted himself among the people who loved her, and it...hurt in a sweet, scary way. There had to have been some planning for all of this to come together.

"Nana was in on this," she said. "The trip to Boston was set up to get me out of town."

His mouth twitched, then he nodded. "She'd already planned the trip, but Mike was going t' drive her. And yes, in case you're wondering, she set this in motion. Along with her book club buddies."

Finn was standing there, looking bashful and scared and a little amused. He was talking to her as if he'd never ripped them apart. She hated that his presence gave her the tiniest flicker of hope. Her voice was colder than she'd intended.

"And how did you get involved?"

He didn't flinch. He was staying steely calm, as if he'd expected her anger. That made sense—he had to know she wouldn't want him here. But there was a tiny-but-insistent voice in the back of her mind calling her a liar. A tiny part of her heart thrilled to be in this space with him, even if they were ten feet apart.

"Your grandmother helped me see the...uh...error o' my ways." He raised his head to look her straight in the eyes. Her knees went weak and she had to hold the back of a nearby stool to steady herself. She'd never seen him looking so vulnerable. So earnest. He cleared his throat and took a small step toward her.

"I was an arse before. You were right to call me out for bein' a coward, love. I...I really did think I was keeping you safe from me hurting you, but I was keeping myself safe, too." He took another step. "I was so afraid of being wrong about us, about you...that I'd get my heart torn up again...but..." He stopped, his hands rising, then falling to his side. "I love you, Bridget McKinnon. And that love isn't going away. I don't want it to. I want us to..." He moved closer. She told herself to retreat, but her feet refused to move. "We started out all wrong, with all the lies and stories and hiding and..." A flame lit in his gaze, scorching her with its heat. "And it was a hell of a good time."

A laugh bubbled up in her throat. He wasn't wrong. They'd had a lot of fun together. They'd shared their histories. They'd shared their bodies. They'd shared their hearts. Until he rejected her. The laughter slid away.

"Finn, we had good times, but I could never stop wondering if it was..."

"An act?"

She nodded, chewing on her lower lip. She looked up at him. "I just realized I got mad at you for doubting, but the truth is...I had my doubts, too. The whole fake engagement thing..."

He was right in front of her now. "There is nothing fake about how I feel about you, Bridget McKinnon. I love you." He reached out and took her hands in his, sending a tremor of desire racing through her. "I want us to start all over. Start clean. No more lies. No more acting. No more worrying about what's happened in the past."

"Start over?" Was she grasping at straws here? Or did he mean what she thought he meant?

"You want us…"

"I want us to build this relationship from the ground up, Bridg." He chuckled, glancing around. "I've gotten my hands dirty for three days getting ready for this, and I'm not afraid to get them dirty again. We'll go slow…build a foundation…a real one this time. And when I ask you to marry me this time around, it will be one hundred percent real. As solid as this rock wall…"

She let her laughter loose this time. "Enough with the building analogies, Finn. I get it." She searched his face for any shadow of doubt. "Are you sure? The last time…it hurt. A lot."

He cupped her face in his hands, and she leaned forward, clutching his shirt. She'd missed his touch so damned much. His breath was warm on her face, but not as warm as the rumble in his voice.

"I swear by all that's holy, by St. Patrick himself, that I will never hurt you again, love. I'm not saying I won't screw up once in a while, but I don't ever want to cause you pain." He touched his lips to hers. "Don't you see? Hurting you hurts me. Our hearts are one heart, Bridget. You're as much a part of me as the air I breathe, and I swear that touching you like this…it's the first real breath I've taken in weeks. You're my…my life. My everything. I love you…"

"Finn?" She arched her brow at him, sliding her hands up his back under his shirt.

"Yeah?" His nose brushed hers.

"Shut up and kiss me."

He chuckled, sliding his arms around her and pulling her tight.

"Yes, ma'am."

The kiss went on for a long time. She had no idea how long, but…long enough for her family to file out onto the patio and surround them by the time she pulled her head back. They hooted and hollered and yelled suggestions for what might come next. She and Finn just laughed and kissed again, earning more applause.

As he trailed more kisses down her neck, he whispered against her skin.

"Your family is crazy."

She turned her head and winked.

"If my heart is your heart, my family is yours, too."

He groaned, but she saw the laughter in his eyes.

"That's a package deal I can handle. As long as I have you, I can handle them. Hell, as long as I have you, I can handle anything."

They kissed again, and she heard champagne being opened. The first night on the patio. The first night of their lives together.

For real, this time.

EPILOGUE

September

"I THINK YOUR mother is determined to force me into buying an entirely new wardrobe with all her cooking." Bridget looked out over the dark gray Atlantic Ocean and grinned back at Finn. "We'll have to do one of these hikes every day just to work off the breakfasts alone. And that trifle your sister made for dessert last night. I swear I've never eaten so much food!"

His dark hair ruffled in the wind, matching the motion of the waves far below them. They were headed up the Cliff Walk path above the small town of Kilkee on the western coast of Ireland. Low, steely clouds scuttled across the sky, threatening the one thing she'd learned was a constant in Ireland—more rain. But the sky directly overhead was blue, and the sunlight turned the foam on the waves snow white against the dark water.

He followed her gaze to where the waves crashed against the rocky cliff.

"I tried t' warn ya." His accent had thickened over

the past five days with his family in his homeland. "The O'Hearns are big on hospitality. And here that means food."

He wasn't kidding. Two days ago they'd taken the "family tour" throughout the countryside of counties Kildare and Laois, which, for some reason, was pronounced Leash. Bridget had given up guessing pronunciations here. All the traffic signs had English and Irish versions of words, and the Irish words looked nothing like the English ones. She may as well have tried learning to speak Vulcan.

They'd spent Tuesday driving from cottage to farm to homes where the front door opened right onto narrow streets in tiny towns. She'd met a dozen or more of Finn's aunts, uncles, cousins, cousins-twice-removed, and friends that were considered relatives. Everyone welcomed them with food and drink.

First up was Bridie O'Hearn. Bridie was a wizened old woman living alone on a small farm at the end of a narrow lane. At first glance, it didn't look as though she had two pence to rub together, but she'd served shots of whiskey as soon as they walked in, then served a feast for lunch. Soup, roast pork, potatoes, homemade bread and a cake for dessert that had to be ten inches tall.

There had been more food at the farm they went to next, along with a sip of poteen, the Irish version of moonshine. Bridget's lips had burned for an hour afterward. Then scones with butter at the next place, with Guinness. And the last stop on the way back to Sallins, near Dublin, was when Bridget had tried to refuse any more. She thought she'd burst if she ate or drank anything else, but the hostess kept pulling out bottles of booze and soda, determined to find something that Bridget would accept. That's when she realized she was offending the woman by refusing.

Finn caught up to her as they neared the top of the walk, sliding his arm around her waist. She leaned into him, soaking up his warmth, since the sun had decided to duck behind the clouds again and the wind was fierce. She looked up with a grin.

"I don't think I ever thanked you for saving me at your aunt's house the other night. I gave up and chose brandy because I figured it would be a smaller portion, but then she handed me that soup bowl of a glass…"

"And I came to the rescue by splittin' 'twith you." He nodded. "Aunt Mary is old school—never let a guest leave t'irsty or hungry."

She laughed, reaching up to capture a lock of hair that whipped her in the face. "She never has to worry about that. Holy cow, the wind is intense up here!"

"So's the view. Turn around, love."

She did, and took in a sharp breath. They were a hundred and fifty feet above the pounding surf. A sharp cliff dropped to the foaming water crashing against it. The contrast of dark rock and white foam was a work of nature's finest art. The tarmac walking path was a safe distance away from the edge, but Finn was leading her closer to the edge.

"Okay. This is close enough, thanks." She dug in her heels. "What is it about the Irish that they don't put safety rails anywhere?"

Finn snorted. "I think we've always figured if a person is foolish enough to fall off a cliff, that's on them. Why ruin the view for everyone else with some nasty fence?"

"Well, it is quite a view, Finn. It's incredible, and I've never even heard of Kilkee before."

A harsh gust of wind sent fine mist up from the crashing waves below, and Finn pulled her closer. She gladly wrapped her arms around his waist as he answered.

"Oi, everyone knows the great Cliffs of Moher, but you saw yesterday how crowded that can be." They knew they were in trouble when they saw four tour buses parked at the information center. The cliffs were hundreds of feet higher than this one, but there were people everywhere. Finn had seemed disappointed when she didn't want to stay there longer, but he couldn't argue that the crowds were annoying. Today they were alone, other than an older couple they'd passed sitting on a park bench halfway down the path, and a lonely golfer braving the wind at the neighboring course.

"I got the feeling you wanted to stay there longer yesterday," she replied. "Is that a favorite spot of yours?"

An odd smile played at his lips, as if he was doing his best to squelch it and was having a tough time at it.

"All o' Ireland is proud of the Cliffs of Moher, but I actually prefer these smaller spots. But you had to see at least some of the tourist traps here. If not, you'd just be sittin' at Mum's kitchen sampling everyt'ing."

She rubbed her waist with her hand. "No! I mean, that sounds awesome, but my God, I can't eat any more than I already have. But I do need to pry a few more recipes from her and your sister. That trifle last night…" She sighed. "That whole meal felt like a celebration dinner or something."

He laughed. "It was a celebration. Of you. Being here." He kissed her forehead. "They adore you, you know."

"Yeah, I know. That's why they keep throwing dinners for me. But last night was different…" Now that she'd said it out loud, she realized it was true. Last night had been strange. They'd driven home to find the dining table covered with an exquisite lace tablecloth she suspected only saw use on Easter and Christmas. Candles flickered in a candelabra, reflecting off the Waterford crystal at the place settings. She pulled back to look at him. "And what was up with all the whispering in the kitchen? Your sister seemed pissed at you."

His jaw worked back and forth, and he finally started to laugh.

"You caught that, eh? Come 'ere, love." He led

her to a stone bench set back a little ways from the cliff's edge. He sat, then tugged her down into his lap. She squealed in surprise, but he just shook his head to silence her. "Sit still, or I'll be embarrassing me-self with a tent pole in my pants." She settled in and wrapped her arms around his neck. She loved him so much, and told him so. His emerald eyes went dark with emotion.

"I love you, too, Bridg. That's what last night was all about. You see, something was supposed to happen at the Cliffs of Moher yesterday, but there so many feckin' people crawling around…" He shook his head, closing his eyes with a chagrined smile. "I had plans, Bridget. As usual, you upended them."

The sun burst out from behind a cloud, bathing them in a bright, warm glow that seemed to extend in a small circle around the top of the cliff. Finn looked up, squinting, then lifted one shoulder as his eyes met hers again.

"I guess this is how it was supposed to happen all along, then. Just us on a cliff o'er the sea, sittin' in the rare Irish sun." He shifted her in his lap as he reached into his pocket and fished out something small and square. A box. A jeweler's box. It was dark green, and she saw the words Dublin, Ireland in gold lettering under a logo she didn't recognize.

"Finn…" She breathed his name, trying to slow her racing heart. Was this really happening?

"I'd intended to drop to my knee outside O'Brien's Tower yesterday, but there were those busloads of kids and tourists crawlin' all over it. Then you said you were ready to go, and…" His smile deepened. "I was in serious trouble with me ma and sis last night after I'd texted them to say it didn't happen. But I'm not waitin' any longer. And I'm not kneeling on this feckin' rock, either." He shifted again, so they were face-to-face, her arms resting on his shoulders. He held up the box, and flipped it open.

"Bridget McKinnon, of the wild McKinnon clan in Rendezvous Falls, will you accept the love of a poor Irish professor with a questionable clan of his own?" His teasing smile softened, his eyes serious now. "Will you marry me, Bridget?"

She looked down at the intricate gold band of Celtic knots and a small, yet perfect, diamond in a low setting that would be practical in the kitchen. Finn's lips brushed her cheek, his words barely a whisper. "It's Maura's diamond, love. We agreed it wasn't a good idea to use her ring a second time, but she insisted I use the stone to have a new one made. So it's still your Nana's diamond. And you still haven't said yes…"

The sun made a rainbow of colors flare up in the diamond, matching the flame flaring in her heart. Tears blurred her vision and clogged her throat, but she nodded emphatically, swallowing hard.

"Yes, Finn. Yes, of course I'll marry you. And your family."

He barked out a loud laugh.

"Oi, we both come as a package deal, don't we? The best package ever."

He kissed her, gently at first, then with increasing fervor. It wasn't until he started tipping her back that she remembered the ring was still in the open box in her hand. She pushed against him with her free hand, and he must have realized why, because he sat her up quickly. They both stared at the box, where the ring was sparkling safely.

"Let's get this on my finger," she suggested with a laugh, "before it rolls off the cliff."

He looked down at the frothing surf and shook his head. "I've heard rumors of lads jumping off these cliffs at high tide, but even for you, love…no." He slid the ring securely onto her finger, and they both admired it in silence for a moment.

"I love you, Finn." She kissed his cheek, which had been brushing against hers. "But I really hope your family isn't planning another banquet-sized meal tonight."

He chuckled, holding her hand in his and turning it so the sun glinted off the diamond. "After I promised on my soul that I'd definitely ask you today, we agreed to dine out tonight. We'll meet them all in Cashel. There's a lovely restaurant in a converted church there."

"You know I loved seeing the Rock of Cashel that first day."

"Now you'll see it at night with the lights on it. It's pretty spectacular. The restaurant is right at the base of the hill." Finn kissed her again. "And there's a very nice hotel nearby."

"A hotel room? All to ourselves?" She groaned with relief and anticipation.

Mum and Dad O'Hearn hadn't put Finn and Bridget in separate rooms, but they had put them in the bedroom directly above their own. The old house was fully updated, but there was no insulation between the two floors, meaning their every move was broadcast below. They'd had to be very creative since their arrival. The shower made an excellent lovemaking spot. And his parents did leave the house occasionally.

Whenever that happened, she and Finn would dash upstairs to muss the bedsheets, then straighten them again as soon as they were finished. But no matter what they did, they were always aware and listening for someone to arrive home or knock on the bathroom door.

"A real hotel room. All to ourselves. Sally will drive Mum and Dad home after dinner, and you and I can stroll to the hotel and…maybe watch the telly for a while. There's a good show that…"

She turned and straddled his lap, her knees on the bench on either side of his hips. She held his head in her hands with a laugh.

"No telly. No nothing, other than getting naked and staying that way for hours and hours."

His eyes shone with both heat and amusement.

"Let's work that into our wedding vows, shall we?

I, Finn O'Hearn, vow to get naked with you for hours and hours, day after day, until death do us part."

She hesitated. "Will we get married here or…?"

His arms slid around her waist until her chest was pressed against his, their faces just inches apart.

"We'll be married in Rendezvous Falls during the holiday break. My family will come t' meet your family, and I'm sure chaos will ensue." A gust of piercing wind ruffed his hair and sent hers blowing across her face. "But we won't care, because I'll whisk you away after the wedding to spend a long honeymoon far from all o' them." He shuddered at another gust of wind. "Preferably on a warm beach somewhere. Alone."

"You know what? That sounds like a perfect plan." She stared into his eyes, feeling a warm flood of love washing over her. How lucky was she, to be loved by a man like this?

"In fact…" She pressed her lips to his as the Atlantic roared against the rocky cliffs below. "It sounds like a perfect life."

* * * * *

"I'm sorry. That must be hard." Meredith looked at him
for a long moment, as though she wanted to ask questions
about the situation, but then her face softened and she
smiled. "And yes, I suppose Sophie can call you Cam,
since you prefer it. And we're neighbors, after all."

"Do you want a lemonade or something?" he asked,
because he'd had company manners drilled into him
since he was practically an infant.

"No, thank you. It looks like it's going to rain soon, so
I need to have Sophie put away any books or dog toys she
took out and then get them inside."

"Maybe another time," he said, and even as the words
left his mouth, he had no idea where they came from. He

wasn't here to make friends, no matter how pretty they were. He had work to do and a cottage to declutter and prepare for market.

And the look she gave him made it clear she was as surprised by the comment as he was. She frowned a little before giving him a friendly but distant smile. "Maybe. I apologize again for Oscar's intrusion. And for Sophie's, I guess. I'll talk to her about respecting boundaries, but it's harder without a fence, I think."

He laughed. "You seem very determined to put up a fence between us."

The smile faded. "Fences help everybody remember where they're supposed to be. And you know what they say. Good fences make good neighbors."

Cam wasn't sure if that message was as directed at him as she'd made it sound, but he'd do well to take it to heart. As she crossed the invisible boundary into her own yard, he turned around and went back inside, leaving Elinor to enjoy the last few minutes of sun before the rain hit.

Don't miss
More than Neighbors *by Shannon Stacey,*
available June 2020 wherever
Harlequin Special Edition books and ebooks are sold.

Harlequin.com

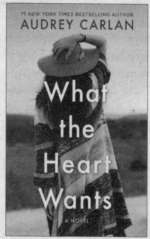